ONE SHILLING.

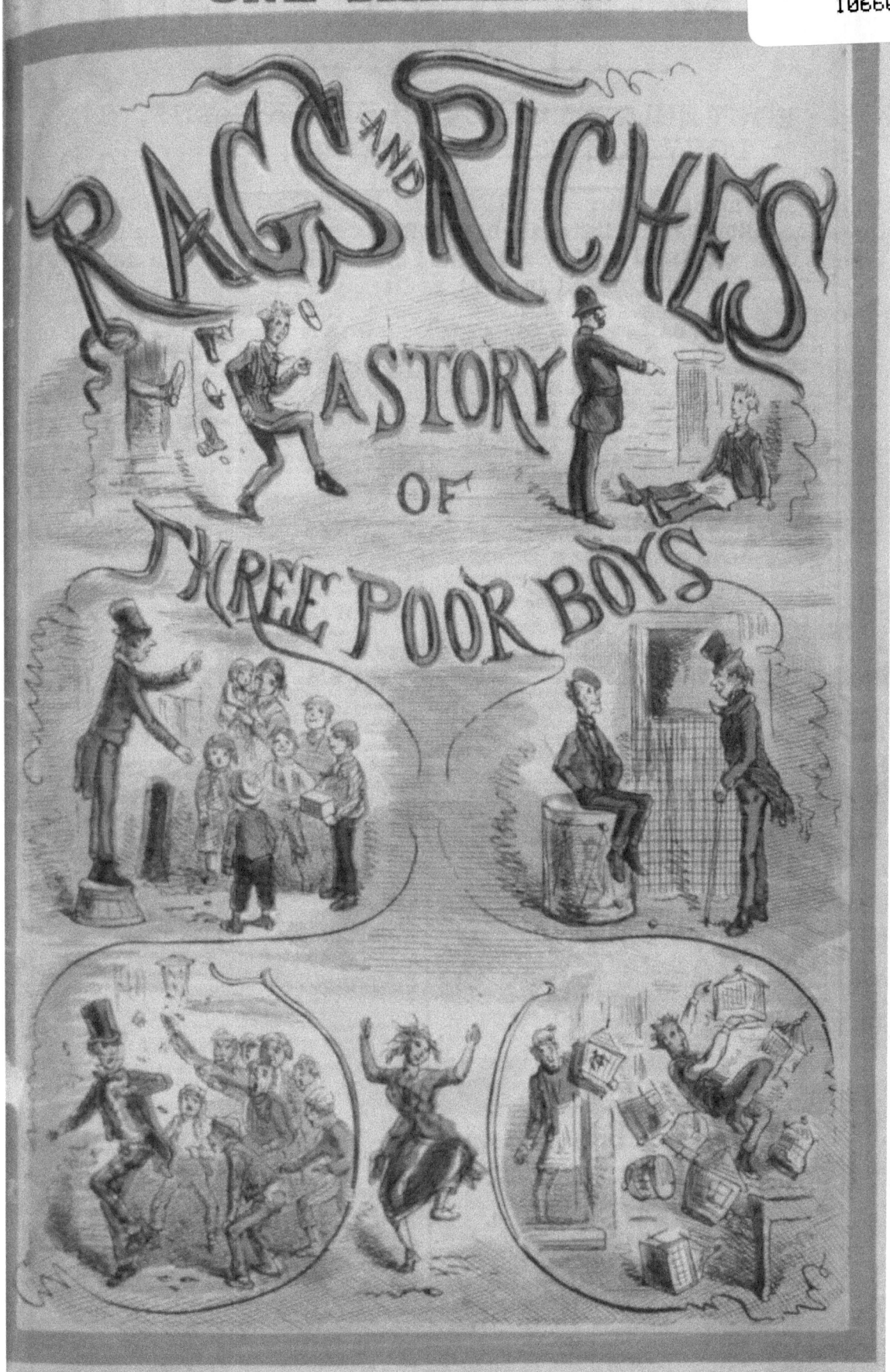

RAGS AND RICHES

A STORY OF THREE POOR BOYS

LONDON : HOGARTH HOUSE, BOUVERIE STREET, FLEET STREET, E.C.

RAGS AND RICHES

A STORY OF THREE POOR BOYS

RAGS AND RICHES;

A Story of Three Poor Boys.

By E. H. BURRAGE, Author of "Spangles and Gold," "For Honour," etc., etc.

CHAPTER I.

MAKING FRIENDS.

THE stream of life is flowing towards the centre of the city; men on foot, in cabs, crowding the omnibuses inside and out, some lightly scanning the morning's paper to obtain a brief knowledge of the day's news; others smoking a cigar or sucking a short pipe with an eagerness which shows that the time for the enjoyment of the narcotic weed is (for that morning at least) drawing to a close; and some sitting thoughtfully, with bent brows and calculating eyes, seeking out short cuts in the road of life to lead them sooner than their neighbours to the goal of Gold.

There are a few men working slowly the other way; and many idlers and loungers, for the most part, are standing still, listlessly watching the panorama of life—men who have long given up all thought of floating pleasantly with the stream which passes by—men who have lost all interest in the race for wealth, and as a straw driven by the tide into some nook, the home of a restless eddy, whirls round and round, they stand aside and see others floating gaily by.

These city loungers are poor; poverty has put such a brand upon them that they must carry it to their grave. The jaded, colourless face; the trembling hands; the bleared eyes; the hopelessly seedy clothing—from the pinched, coarse hat, once black but now a seedy brown, to the boots, trodden out of all shape, and beyond the power of the most determined cobbler to repair—will never leave them until they fade out from their little circle at the public-house, and go away and die, Heaven alone knows where.

There are noises in the air—the noise of wheels and horses, the snorting of the engines on the Ludgate Viaduct, the murmuring of thousands of voices; but, above all, above the sounds of wheels, horses, engines, and men, rises the shrill voice of a boy—

"Box o' lights, sir?"

There is not much in that cry, and thousands pass it daily by unheeded; not so one man, who halts before a youngster with a small box suspended from his neck by a piece of cord.

The boy is apparently about twelve years of age; hatless and bootless, with his slender body covered by the relics of a discarded coat and trousers, held together by sundry ingenious contrivances composed of cord and pins.

The gentleman—for gentleman he is, although his coat is threadbare and his gloves giving way at the finger ends—looks not at the meagre attire of the boy, but at his bright, upturned face, really a handsome one, and putting a hand upon his curly head, says—

"How's trade, my lad?"

It was a strange question, and one which might have raised a laugh at the expense of the boy, if some opulent merchant had been standing by, but the lad answered seriously—

"Very bad, sir. I only sold two boxes yesterday—it was wet, sir."

"Ah, it was wet," repeats the gentleman, dreamily, "and a wet day is very bad for you."

"It is, sir," rejoins the boy; "if we gets them wet, they are no use."

"Just so," the gentleman replied, with the same abstracted air. He appeared to be revolving something in his mind, and as he stood by the corner of Bride Lane, with the boy standing patiently before him, the two formed an excellent study for an artist.

"What is your name?" the gentleman suddenly asked.

"Tom, sir."

"Tom what?"

"Only Tom, sir," returned the boy, opening his eyes.

"What are your friends?" asked the gentleman, quickly, with a sudden accession of interest.

"Haven't any, sir."

"No father?"

"No, sir."

"Mother?"

"Never heard of her, sir."

"Where do you live, Tom?"

Tom gave a knowing look around at the street, and replied evasively—

"You will allers find me in here, sir, from nine in the morning until twelve at night."

"That's not answering my question. Where do you live? where do you have your meals? and where do you sleep?"

Tom quietly scratched his head for a few moments, and appeared to be meditating a bolt; but something in the gentleman's face appeared to give him courage, and he replied to the query, Irish fashion, with another question—

"Is you a mendicity, sir?"

"A—a what?" said the gentleman, with a puzzled look; "what is that?"

"Chaps as chivy us, and takes us up afore the beaks, sir."

"Oh, I see—mendicity officers. Oh, dear me, nothing of the sort. So you have no friends, Tom, and you won't tell me where you live?"

"I don't live anywhere reg'lar," replied Tom. "It's just where I can, and it just happens who's on the beat."

Again the gentleman looked puzzled, and Tom, interpreting the expression of his face, proceeded to explain—

"You see, sir, some p'licemen is kind—others isn't. P 42 has you off the doorstep in no time; and there ain't no chance o' more than ten minutes' snooze at a time. He's on here now, so I goes up to the Garden, where M 74, who is wery kind-hearted, never looks into the baskets, so we has our snooze as nice as can be."

"Now here is a lesson for me," murmured the gentleman to himself. "He is grateful for being allowed to sleep in the streets, while I—but there, the lesson is learnt, let me profit by it."

"Tom," he added aloud, "how would you like to have a change of life?"

It was Tom's turn to be puzzled, and he looked so.

The gentleman continued—

"By a change of life, I mean to be removed from the misery of the streets, to have a comfortable home to live in, a bed to sleep in, and to have no dread of the footstep of P 42. How would you like that?"

"Very much, sir."

"Then, Heaven willing," said the gentleman," clapping him lightly on the shoulder, "you shall have it. Look out for me every morning during the next fortnight. If I turn up, you will leave this life for ever; if I do not appear in that time, forget that I ever came near you."

He turned away, and was hurrying off without making a purchase from poor Tom,

when he suddenly remembered his omission, and turned back.

"Never mind the lights," he said, tossing sixpence into the box. "I never use them."

The next moment he was lost in the stream of life going city-wards, and Tom turned into Bride Lane, the quietude of that salubrious retreat being conducive to the mental occupation of thinking over this strange meeting.

Tom was so abstracted in his mind that he left the sixpence lying among his wares, and suddenly cannoned against a youth travelling in an opposite direction.

This youth was about the same age as Tom, but rather taller, and, owing to his long, shambling legs, looking taller than he really was.

He wore no cap or jacket, but he had a tolerably good waistcoat, covering his narrow chest, with trousers, boots, and a small leather apron.

He glared at Tom for a moment, his red head glistening in the morning's sunlight, as if he wished to annihilate him with a look, but finding Tom invulnerable in this respect, he demanded—

"Where are you shovin' to?"

"You ran against me," rejoined Tom.

"Don't you tell me that," returned the other. "*Me* run agin you? It's agin the laws o' society and natur'. *Me* run agin a boy without boots? It's like your darned imperence to say so. Do you know who I am?"

"I've seen you before," said Tom.

"I should think you have," cried the other, triumphantly. "There ain't many hereabouts as don't know me. Everybody knows Inky Work-it-out."

"What a queer name," said Tom, with a grin; "Inky Work-it-out."

"It's the name I goes by," said the other, who seemed to have grown suddenly communicative. "Really, I ain't got no name. 'Cos why? Nobody knows who I am; but you see, youngster, it comes this way. Do you know old Work-it-out?"

"The cobbler?"

"No, the shoemaker," said Inky, scornfully, "I don't work for no cobbler. I'd sooner p'ison myself, for I am of nobble blood. Well, old Work-it-out, which his real name is Harris, but he allers is puttin' up scores at the pubs, and has to work 'em out, and so gets a name, you see; old Work-it-out bein' a single man, lives alone, a-pinin', as it were, for somebody to love him and for to love."

"Oh!" said Tom, apparently not much interested in the story.

"That's so," continued Inky; "now jest sit down on the halley steps, and I'll tell ye' the story of my nobble birth."

Tom smiled, and sat down as requested. Inky, covering his knees with his leather apron, and clasping his hands, continued—

"While old Work-it-out was a-pinin' for somethin' for to love, a-sittin' in his shop arter dark and in the dark, for he'd burnt all his candles and forgot to work 'em out, and so couldn't get no more, a knock comes at the door.

"It was a reg'lar buster, and made him jump off his stool like winkin', for he 'spected to have the man in from the Helephand pub for a old score which the old man wouldn't work out at no price, so, although he jumped orf the stool, he stood still and listened."

Inky's face now showed signs of intense emotion in the form of perspiration, and Tom, interested at last, put down his box so that he might give his utmost attention to the narrator.

"Arter the busting knock," continued Inky, "there wasn't another, so old Work-it-out, thinking it was only a printer's boy hevin' a lark, and they are allers a-thumping at his door and shutters, sets down ag'in, and feels about in the dark for a screw of bacca, he dropped just afore.

"He'd jest got his 'and on it," said Inky, "I've heard him say it a hundred times, when he dropt it agen. 'Cos why? He heard a little voice a-crying at the door."

Here Inky, like a skilled story-teller, paused to give interest to what was to follow. Tom, with open mouth and eyes, was fully prepared to swallow all.

"He walks to the door," said Inky, "and arter listenin', throws it open, 'specting to see he didn't know what, unless it was some woman with a child. But there wasn't no woman, no nothing, but a small hinterestin' infant, about three months old, and that was me."

"Was it?" exclaimed Tom.

"It was," replied Inky; "there I laid on the doorstep, wrapped up in gorging raiment, lookin' bootiful—I've heard Work-it-out say I was a picter.

"He takes me in and sends for the perlice, but they wouldn't come, a-cause he'd often sent for 'em afore, when he'd got the deriddledum trimmings on, and only two months fore had tried to stab the hinspector with a awl, which he worked out by making a new pair o' boots with soles that came off in a lump, while the 'spector was on duty in a street fight.

"So the perlice wouldn't come," continued Inky, "and Work-it-out didn't know nobody else to send for, so he kep' me an' brought me up by hand."

"And gave you the name Inky," suggested Tom.

"He did—arter I'd got into a liking for the business, which I had a shy at as soon as I could toddle, inking the soles and inking myself up to the werry eyes, and so he gin me the name of Inky."

"Can you read?" asked Tom.

"Rayther," answered Inky, proudly. "I've been to a heavening school every day for two years."

"Would they have me?" asked Tom, anxiously.

"Not in them togs," replied Inky, "unless you've got a 'stificate of nobble birth, like myself."

"But you don't know you were nobly born—how should you?"

"It can't be totherwise," returned Inky. "'Tain't poor people as hev their young 'uns stolen. 'Cos why? Who wants 'em? But it's the hairs to nobble estates as get bolted orf with, and whosomever lives to see the day—I shall be found out by my wenerable father. What's your name, young 'un?"

"Tom."

"Well, Tom, whensomever that day comes remember this—pride of birth shan't keep me from bein' a friend to you—*you* shan't want for nothin', and if yer behaves yerself, you shall sometimes sit down at the same table."

"Thank you," said Tom, gratefully.

"I means to have two footmen behind my chair," pursued Inky, "and I'll hev 'em fat'uns—a-cause they looks well; and I'll allus have a 'ole houseful o' wisiters, and a man to blow a trumpet when the dinner's ready, and a brass band to blow up all the time we are eatin'."

"Won't that be jolly fine," exclaimed Tom, breathlessly.

"I'll do more than that," continued the high-born Inky; "every other day I'll give a feast—a regular buster, to the poor. I'll roast 'ole bullocks and 'ole sheep, and everybody shall dance round 'em for an hour afore they sit down to dinner."

"I never heard of such things," interposed Tom.

"But I'll do 'em, every one of 'em," rejoined Inky, carried entirely away by enthusiasm; "I'll have the lot performed when I've found my r'yal father and come into my property—and remember this, Tom, I'll stick to you, for I like you."

"Thank you, Inky."

"We'll have prime times, Tom; and you can bring your father and mother, and—"

"I never had any," said Tom.

"You hadn't?"

"No."

"Where was you born, then?"

"I don't know."

"Who found you?"

"I found myself," said Tom, "one morning in Covent Garden, being moved on by the police."

"Now here's a stordinary go," cried Inky, turning white with excitement. "We may both be nobbly born, and our muturel fathers be a weepin' and a wailin' in their lordly halls, with our mothers in contineral hystericks in the front parlour."

"I don't think I could have had a royal father," said Tom, with a doubtful shake of his head.

"You ain't so likely as me," said Inky, "acause you were never wrapped in gorging raiment, and nobody don't seem to keep you, to collar the reward like old Work-it-out hev done for me—but you may be nobbly born for all that, and I adwise you to look arter a nobble father, as I'm continerally doin'."

While Inky was speaking, the adventure of the morning returned to Tom's brain, and amidst an impressive silence on the part of his listener, he related the substance of his meeting with the gentleman, his promises, and the coin subsequently bestowed. Inky did not think much of the concluding performance.

"You ain't the son of a nobble," he said; "but it may turn out as you is a offspring of a halderman, or some such common chap. A real nobble would hev chucked a handful of gold inter yer box, an' swaggered orf with a cigar in his mouth. What sort o' gent was he?"

"Very handsome and sunbrowned."

"How old?"

"I don't know; 'bout thirty, p'raps."

"Dressed well?"

"I think so."

"Had he a gold chain, a diamond pin, and patent boots?"

"No!"

"Then he's only a common chap arter all; but don't lose him, for he's better than nothing. Hallo! there's the clock striking ten. Shan't I catch it from old Work-it-out. I say, young 'un?"

"Yes!"

"How is you fed?"

"Very bad," replied Tom.

"So am I—for one nobbly born," returned Inky; "old Work-it-out keeps up my witality principally with strap ile."

"Is it nice?" asked Tom.

Inky winked intensely, rolled his tongue in his cheek, and pointing over his left shoulder, turned away.

"Where can I see you to-night?" he asked, looking over his shoulder.

"Here," said Tom.

"Be here 'bout six, without your box, and I'll give you a treat. You haven't got no boots anywhere, have you?"

"No: never had," replied Tom, sadly.

"Then I'll bring you an old pair o' mine," said Inky. "One of the soles is gone, but the uppers looks well when they're dubbined. I'll bring my mate, Sam Smarty, with me—there goes the quarter—oh! shan't I catch it from old Work-it-out."

And Inky, with a final nod of encouragement, tore himself away.

CHAPTER II.
INKY AND HIS MASTER.

SCEPTRE COURT, Fleet Street, at the time of our story, was a strange place, and is a strange place still. It was a long, narrow passage with a gamut of inhabitants running from the high tone of extreme respectability to the lowest note in the scale of life.

Flanking the entrance were the two establishments of two thriving tradesmen, with offices above their shops, letting to respectability at enormous rentals; this was the shell of the court—the whitening which hid the festering sepulchre, the varnish hiding the varied graduations of misery and decay beyond.

Two steps down the court stood a small beer-shop, its dingy front standing like a barrier to all strangers who sought to enter there, and opposite this place for the degradation of the public was a small shop with a dingy front also, and the smallest of small rooms in the rear, and there lived Mr. Benjamin Harris, boot and shoe maker, otherwise, old Work-it-out, a lean, wizard-like old man, much given to idleness and the beer-shop over the way, but passionately devoted to the more pretentious establishment, just in the main street, where spirituous liquors could be obtained.

Old Work-it-out fully deserved his name, he worked out everything—beer, bread, and meat, even washing, when he had any done, and even his rent. He did but little else in the retirement of the court, he was shut out from the world, living in his peculiar way, as hundreds live, almost entirely unknown. He was not popular in the court, for although he had brought up the deserted Inky "by hand," he rarely showed any love for children. On the contrary, he waged war with the court's progeny, and the court's progeny waged war with him.

They threw cabbage leaves and every variety of refuse through his open door, surreptitiously broke his windows, blocked up his keyhole, squirted water over him as he sat upon his bench working out some score, sang offensive personal ditties, with still more offensive choruses, under his very nose, and did their best to make the cantankerous old man a pariah and an outcast among the people.

He, in return, laid wait for them in various ways, and assaulted those he could catch grievously with a supple strap, originally intended for the sole use and benefit of the nobly-born Inky; he pulled their ears and tweaked their noses, and, in his cups, defied their parents, who, for the most part, knew their children were quite a match for him, and let the old man alone.

Once this strange warfare took a serious turn. Work-it-out, enraged beyond control by a youth, the eldest scion of an Irish family living half-way up the court, who had the audacity to walk straight into the shop and bonnet the old man as he sat at work (Work-it-out always affected a tall hat), sprang up and pursued the delinquent, not only to the door of his house, but into the very sanctum of his parents, a small front parlour, where a family of eight ate, drank, and slept.

Two minutes afterwards Work-it-out was thrown into the court like a limp rag, with every particle of breath pummelled out of his body, and his clothing, none of the best or strongest, torn to smithereens.

From that hour he invaded the enemy's country no more, but contented himself with fighting on his own ground, or skirmishing upon the borders of the court, where even, unto the hour of our story, the warfare waged fast and furious.

It may be imagined that the highly-born Inky came in for a share of the fights, and a very large share to boot.

His goings forth were one continuous series of "bolts," and his returnings as stealthy as those of the midnight burglar in search of prey.

He was seldom without a black eye, bestowed upon him by one or the other of the youthful enemies of old Work-it-out— scratches and bruises he received almost daily, in fact, he lived the life of a dog, and was the youthful Ishmaelite of Sceptre Court.

The houses beyond the beer-shop and the abode of Work-it-out graduated, as we have said, in respectability, the nearest being occupied by hard-working people, and the furthermost by a number of persons not entirely unknown to the police, with a strong body of the labouring Irish between.

Isolated from all the world, yet in the midst of it, Sceptre Court stood alone. Every Saturday night a wild carnival was held there, with the beer-shop for the head-quarters of the revellers, and the busy throng of people passing within a few feet of it, by the entrance of the court, knew nothing of the rough and tumble joviality going on.

Personal allusions were made, and settled by fisticuffs or the impartial arbitration of neighbours, without the interference of the police; and although that body of able-bodied men knew as well as the court itself what was going on, every man in blue played the part of the Pharisee, and "passed by on the other side."

Saturday night was a dreadful time for Work-it-out and Inky, but they bore up bravely, and lived on through the storms of abuse, sarcasm, scratches, blows, and bruises. Work-it-out dealt punishment where he could, and Inky received blows from the elder juveniles, "and took it out" of the youngsters whenever an opportunity offered; and thus stood Sceptre Court at the time of this most veracious story.

One little ray of sun, scarcely thicker than a man's arm, struggling through the court, and glancing through the cobbler's windows, fell upon the old man's head, as he hammered lustily at a pair of boots, the soling of which was intended to settle for certain "little go's" of cold gin at the gorgeous palace round the corner. The old man was much in earnest, for his lips were parched, and his throat was dry, and every house closed against him for the time. Money he had not— Work-it-out had seldom a penny—so, as certain things must be, when a nameless gentleman of sombre hue or necessity drives, the old cobbler manfully pursued his work, without looking up, until the clear-toned bell of St. Bride's announced the hour of ten.

Then he laid down his hammer and listened and bending over, flattened his face against the window to obtain a side view of the entrance of the court.

"They ain't a layin' wait for him," he muttered; "then what's keepin' the warmint? He's getting sleepy, I think—when he shows up I'll rouse him a bit."

He took from a nail a broad, supple strap, well oiled, and well cared for, which he stroked gently, after the fashion of a sportsman with a favourite gun, and laying it on his bench, contemplated it with an air of deep satisfaction.

"You are a beauty," he murmured, "there's no gammon about you—once you lands, they knows it well. It was a nappy thought when I named you Stinger—for sting you does, and no mistake—Inky knows you well."

A sudden disturbance at the entrance of the court aroused him from his reverie, and darting to the door, he beheld his servitor in the grasp of four small boys, one of whom was hanging by Inky's back hair, two holding his arms, and the fourth dabbing a huge green paint brush into his face.

The simultaneous appearance of Work-it-out with his strap, and the painter, who had been decorating a shop front at the corner, and suddenly missed his brush, scattered the enemy, and Inky, sputtering fearfully, with one eye completely obliterated for the time being, was dragged into the cobbler's place of refuge.

"Wipe your face," said Work-it-out, "and be sharp about it."

Inky, sputtering and sniffing, rubbed his face with a coarse piece of canvas, a process which resulted in making him like a green monkey suffering from a bilious attack. Work-it-out watched him with a wrinkled face, lightly dangling the strap in his right hand in a portentous manner.

"Now," said the cobbler, when the cleaning process was over, "where have you been?"

"To Carter's Alley," replied Inky, with his one useful eye upon the strap.

"I know that," said Work-it-out, "for I sent you there; but where else?"

"Nowhere."

"Don't tell me lies."

"It ain't no lies," persisted Inky, "one nobbly born never tells no lies."

"Nobly born," rejoined the old man with a sneer upon his wrinkled face, "what do you know about bein' born? you weren't born—you was found."

"I know I was," returned Inky, "on this doorstep—in gorging raiment."

"You're a fool—gorging raiment, indeed," said Work-it-out; "you was wrapped up in a dirty yaller hankerchief."

"I warn't."

"You was."

"I warn't. You says so acause you popped the gorging raiment. Sam Smarty says so, and he knows."

Muttering something the reverse of a benediction upon the head of Sam Smarty, Work-it-out fell upon his *protégé*, and gave him such a dose of Stinger that he shivered again, but no cry escaped him.

"You can't make me holler," he said, as he sat down with difficulty upon his little stool in a corner. "Nobbly-born chaps never hollers, if you tears 'em piecemeal and powders their bones."

"Don't talk bosh to me," said Work-it-out, taking up his hammer and setting himself to work, "but nail a pair o' top pieces on to the heel o' them boots, and give 'em a coat o' dubbing."

Inky raised from the boards a pair of very rude boots, and surveyed them with a look of deep disgust. He turned them over and over, and finally placed them again upon the floor.

"What's your game now?" demanded Work-it-out, looking up, and extending his hand towards his favourite weapon.

"I ain't agoin' to touch them boots."

"Why not, you fool?"

"Acause they're Barking Bailey's."

"Well, what of that?"

"He's a sneaking bailiff, as robs the poor of their furniter."

"He does his dooty, like another man."

"He's a cold-blooded villain—the minion of the law."

"Take up them boots."

"Shan't."

"Take 'em up."

Inky folded his arms, and smiled contemptuously.

"Cut me up into piecemeal and I doesn't do it," he said.

The cobbler, now fairly aroused, gave Inky another staggering dose of Stinger, but, as before, elicited not a sound or any acknowledgment of pain.

"Still I hollers not," said Inky, "and I doesn't do the boots."

"You raging idiot," growled old Work-it-out; "I wish my arm was stronger. I'd give a pair o' soles for three of rum just now. Then I'd bring you to your wits."

"You couldn't," said Inky; "the nobbly-born never yield."

"Nobby-born!" sneered the cobbler; "what do you think you are?"

"The son of r'yalty, or a dook."

"Bah!"

"I may be only the offspring of a lord," said Inky, "or a hadmiral; but the hadmiral's the lowest, and I doesn't go no lower than that for nobody."

"Why don't you stick to your work?" demanded Work-it-out.

"So I would," rejoined Inky, "if it wor fit for nobble blood. What do you stick in this 'ole for, where I'm parsoncuted night and day, and my nobble blood drawn from my nose in pints."

"Go on with your work," growled Work-it-out.

"Shan't," returned Inky. "It's all very well for you. *You* don't mind being chivied and pelted, for you are wulgar born, and what little you does feel, when you gets a hextra buster, you drowns in liquor, but the proud parian blood never gets buffy, but suffers a martindom with the stockingism of a Nindian chif. Why don't you move, and get rid of this wulgar court?"

"Where should I move to?" demanded Work-it-out.

"To the West-end," returned Inky, "among the airistocrats. There would be some pleasure in soling and heeling of a dook's boots, or puttin' a neat patch into a barrowknight's. But low and wulgar boots I can't abear, and I casts 'em off for ever."

So saying, Inky rose to the climax of his rebellion, and, again raising the offending boots of the bailiff, cast them from the shop into the outer air of the court.

It is a well-known fact that there is a limit to human endurance, and there was especially a limit to Work-it-out's.

Rising from his bench like a giant in his wrath, he, with Stinger in hand, fell upon Inky, and Inky, determined upon resistance, boldly closed with him.

At close quarters Stinger was comparatively harmless, so, avoiding his usual weapon, Work-it-out, with open hands, smote his adopted son hip and thigh.

Inky, undaunted, manfully rained a shower of blows upon the ribs of his master, declaiming meanwhile against the audacity of one so vulgar attacking one so highly born.

To the credit of the lad, be it said, he never once used his feet. The grim faith he had in the greatness of his birth forbade that he should use such a questionable mode of defence as his feet when he encountered his enraged master.

Work-it-out, fully aroused, was a man without sense or reason—he was simply a man beside himself. The defiance of Inky, and his subsequent determination not to touch the boots of a bailiff, roused his ire, and his final resistance did what was required to drive the old cobbler into an uncontrollable state of fury.

The struggle which followed upset all the arrangements of the shop. Patterns, lasts, leather, and boots in every stage of progress towards completion or repair, were mingled, in hopeless confusion ; both the benches of Inky and his master were upset, also the nail-box, containing a great variety of " brads," and, as a wind-up to the entertainment, the " nobbly born " was thrust into the court like a shot from a gun.

Work-it-out's fury did not end here, for with the consistency of his nature, he immediately hurled after his adopted son every article he could lay his hands upon.

Odd boots, lasts, measures, and the various tools of his trade, rained upon the head of the devoted Inky, who, although summarily ejected from the home of his youth, manfully stood his ground, as became one of the upper classes, and a scion of the blue-blooded race.

"Go it, old 'un'," he shouted, " 'tain't me as is goin' to pick 'em up. There goes young Smiffers with a top boot, and you've broke a winder at the Blue Griffin ; don't be afeared, you can't hurt me."

Whether these words of Inky's had any effect upon Work-it-out, we are unable to say, but certain it is that he suddenly desisted in his maniacal performances, and busied himself with the recovery of his property, Inky looking on with the calm, contemptuous air of a superior being.

"Don't leave nothin' about," he advised " there goes Paddy's measure a-floatin' in th gutter, and sarve you right. Ah! you ma look at that odd boot, young Smiffer's go t'other, and when you gits it again I wishe you joy. This is a performance of a wulgar born old cobbler ; I'm ashamed on yer, an I casts yer off. You hev made a precion himage of yerself."

To all this Work-it-out made no reply, bu collecting all he could of the various article he had discharged from his shop, he retired and closing the door with a bang, was lost to the public eye.

Then it was that Inky became consciou of the presence of his acquaintance, Tom who was standing near, his blue eyes fillec with wonderment at the scene, and the ghastly appearance of Inky's face, where the green paint lingered fondly still.

"What do you think of this, young 'un ?' said Inky.

"Have you quarrelled ?" asked Tom—almost a superfluous question it would seem, but Inky did not think so.

"It's a little tiff," he replied, " sech as we've had afore ; the nateral anticism of the wulgar and nobbly born. But Work-it-out is bound to give in, as he can't get on without a boy, and he can't git no boy to live with him in this court but me."

" How's that ? "

" This court," explains Inky, " is the worst in Fleet Street, and that's saying a lump ; the life of a s'perior sort o' chap here is werry fer from a joke ; it's chivy, chivy, every hour of his precious life, as soon as he shows his nose among these precious himps ; but here they comes agin, and if yer don't mind I'll jist take a cool walk in the hopen street."

A body of the youthful inhabitants, displaying at this moment a tendency to turn upon Inky, that youth and his friend Tom prudently beat a retreat—once in the public street they were safe, and then they parted ; Inky renewing his promise to meet Tom in the evening, and appointing St. Bride's Church as a place of meeting.

" I'll bring the boots, never fear," he said, " and Sam Smarty with me. You'll like Sam, for of all the coves—but there, wait till you see him ; so good-bye for the present, Tom."

Tom nodded, and threading his way among the crowd, his shrill voice was soon heard above the din—" Box o' lights, sir—here you are, sir—box o' lights ! "

CHAPTER III.

AN EVENING AT THE CRYSTAL HALL.

SAM SMARTY—the bosom friend of Inky Work-it-out—was a true specimen of a large body of youths to be seen about Fleet Street and the Strand, any hour of the day and night.

Sam was a portion of that great civiliser, the press; it was Sam's hand which guided the virgin sheets to the hungry machine, and Sam's eyes saw them thrown from the drum, with news to shake the world or to delight the multitude. Sam knew the latest intelligence long before the main body of the nobles in the land; hours ere the public were allowed to touch the important broadsheets, they had passed before Sam's eyes; stock-jobbers slumbered in their beds, innocent of the few lines which Sam saw repeated by thousands, which would crumble their fortunes on the morrow; news from foreign lands was known to him before the ambassadors from those places; in fact, Sam fed a machine at a mighty printer's, and was, in plain terms, a "printer's devil."

He was naturally a defiant youth; his shirt-sleeves rolled tightly over the muscles of his arms spoke volumes; they were turned up winter and summer, in the sanctity of the printer's room or in public, and no man or boy living had ever seen Sam, except at very rare intervals, in even the semblance of a coat.

He worked for Messrs. Kidem and Blowhard, the great printers, and he was the leader of their tribe of imps, who made the precincts of Gough Square hideous during the dinner hour.

Who organised a system of prosecution against a dealer of old clothes, and drove him to other climes?—Sam. Who deluded innocent boys, strangers to the neighbourhood, to have a ride upon a printer's truck, and then bound them there, Mazeppa fashion, and made their faces hideous with printer's ink of various colours, and finally chased them into main thoroughfares, where policemen, aggravated by long hours of duty, fell upon them like the wolf in the fold?—Sam.

Who came out strong on the Lord Mayors' days, and with mock helmet and truncheon paraded the streets at the head of a band of rebels in defiance of heavy-booted officials, to the alarm of weak-minded women who had front places in the crowd?—Sam.

Who was it that grew jubilant when the men in armour came, and made affectionate inquiries after the mace-bearer's health, and boldly walked between the ranks of enfeebled watermen bearing overpowering banners?—Sam.

In fact, who was the leading imp of that neighbourhood of imps?—Why, Sam Smarty, the friend of Inky Work-it-out.

Sam was a careless youth, a brigand of the courts, a youthful outlaw in the very heart of civilization, the bane of the quietly disposed, and the policeman's curse.

The most active of the officials had watched, waited, and pursued him in vain; he was as active as a cat, and as slippery as an eel, and no man could lay a hand upon him. So, with defiance on his brow, he walked amidst the stream of life and feared no man.

This was the youth with whom Inky proposed to meet Tom, and the two turned up punctually at six o'clock, it being Saturday, and an off night for the able assistant of Messrs. Kidem and Blowhard.

Sam was cleaned up a bit for the occasio and he came with a jacket, but he carried on his arm, with his cap in one of the pockets, as one would carry robes of state when there is no decided necessity for their use.

Inky kept his word about the boots, and produced them from under his apron as soon as the trio met.

Judged from a trade point of view, these boots had many imperfections; the soles had gone the way of all flesh, and the uppers had sundry openings in them not designed by the original maker; but Tom was grateful, and he cordially thanked his humble friend.

Sitting down on the church steps, he made arrangements to put them on, Sam watching the proceeding with the phlegmatic coolness of his race.

"Not that boot," he said, "that's for the right foot; t'other's the left. Now there you is, a real swell. How do you like 'em?"

"They seem very heavy," returned Tom, hobbling about, "and loose."

"Lace 'em tighter about the ankles, Inky," said Sam; "that's it; now they're better. They'll come easier by-and-by."

"I hope so," said Tom, making a grimace.

"I say, youngster," rejoined Sam, after a moment's survey of his new chum, "how long have you been in this line?"

"What line—boots?"

"No; box o' lights, rags, starvation, and so on."

"As long as I can recollect," replied Tom; "all my life."

"Dashed if I should have thought it," said Sam; "would you, Inky?"

Inky replied "that he thought there was something superior to the general run about Tom—about up to a Halderman of the Corporation, or a husher of the Old Bailey, and that was why he took a fancy to him; but he didn't think he was of nobble blood."

Sam expressed his opinion that "nobble blood" was the greatest swindle out, and proceeded to question Tom upon his past life.

"It's no use asking me," replied the boy. "I've been nothing but a box o' lights ever since I fust found myself a running about in Covent Garden. I don't know no more."

"Then I won't ax you for more," said Sam ; "but if you don't turn out something in Inky's like, may the next Lord Mayor frighten me with his coach. Now, Inky, what's the programmy ?"

"I've got a shilling," said Inky, "which I made by finishin' off a pair o' boots when the old willian was a drinkin' hisself blind round the corner, and I propose a wisit to the Crystal Hall."

"That's your sort," rejoined Sam ; "you know the Crystal Hall, young 'un ?"

"Never heard of it," said Tom.

"Here's a state of ignorance!" cried Sam, turning to Inky with a pitying smile. "Not know the Crystal Hall—and this is a land of hedication, with men allus a taking up the cause of the people ? Come on—I'm disgusted. You stand treat to-night, Inky, for I've been fined two shillings for ramming Toffy's head into a pound of ink. I've owed that to Toffy for a long time, and he's got it at last. Toffy's a sneak."

Sam, burning with a sense of Toffy's delinquencies, was going off at a great pace, when Tom, after hobbling a little while in the rear, called a halt.

"No hurry," said Sam, "we've an hour to spare—but I was riled, and no mistake. Keep 'em on, you'll get used to 'em, and walk your own pace and we'll keep with you."

There was need for a reduction of the pace, unless Tom either removed his boots or lagged behind ; but as he had no intention of doing the former, being rather proud of this addition to his dress, he was grateful to his friends for accommodating their pace to his.

The trio struck through the bye street by the back of St. Bride's and over Blackfriars Bridge—the old one with its feeble stone arches, already giving way before the pressure of time—Inky on the way explaining to Tom how he had returned to the establishment of the indignant Work-it-out without any serious result.

"We is old friends," he said, "and a few hasty words don't spile the friendship of years—so when I went in, old Work-it-out looks up and ses, ' So you've come back ? ' ' Yes,' I ses, ' I'm back ; ' and then I sets down, and lays on the hink and dubbin like anythink—but I wouldn't touch Barker Bailey's wulgar boots—and no mortial, not if even he was a hinkspector, or a supperintending of the perlice, could er made me."

The Crystal Hall has a gorgeous sound, but the Crystal Hall was not a gorgeous place. It lay in the very heart of Bermondsey, and to the major portion of London was entirely unknown.

It was nothing better than a shanty erected upon a piece of waste ground behind a public-house—the rude narrow walls first covered with a coat of whitewash, and coarsely garnished with a few cheap ornamental devices.

It was a place much patronised by the youths who were aware of its existence, for the price was low, and the performance of a high melodramatic order. There the bold baron, with his bag of gold, and the defiant peasant, were indeed at home ; there vice was always punished, and virtue always triumphant, as we know it is in every-day life ; there rightful heirs are never wronged, and the summary mode of settling a disputed claim prevented even the thought of a possible Tichborne case.

As a place of entertainment, it deserved the appellation of a "miserable hole," bestowed upon it by virtuous gentlemen with five hundred a year and a comfortable home; but it was not the "hot-bed of vice" they were anxious to make it appear.

It is true that hundreds of lads assembled together, with many a black sheep among the flock ; but the majority came, paid their penny, saw what was to be seen, and went home none the worse than they had been the day before.

The performance had nothing against it but its inferiority. It lacked the elements of the ballet, and other more questionable pieces of the more fashionable theatres, where the burlesques ride rampant over true genius; but being a Crystal Hall, with the price of admission one penny, and thus brought within the pale of the poor and needy, it must of necessity be "pernicious" in the eyes of our lords and gentlemen, who go nightly to see Schneider and other public celebrities of a very unquestionable reputation.

The Crystal Hall had no glare of gas outside ; no blazing stars or magnificent transparencies ; nothing beyond a coloured lamp, with the words "Crystal Hall" upon it; which, without the words, would have shone with advantage by a doctor's door.

There was a little crowd of juveniles in the street as our trio of friends came up, for the door was not yet open, and there was a deal of shouting and whistling to shock the ears of the peaceful and pure-minded, and occasionally words were used which would have been out of place in a drawing-room ; but nothing else that gentility or virtue in black need have shrunk from.

"There'll be a rush," said Sam, "and if we stand on this side there's no chance. Stand here, Tom, and when the door opens, make straight for the middle of it."

"Got the money ready, Inky ?"

Inky nodded, with three penny pieces

between his teeth, which was a difficult matter.

"Put your hands on my shoulder," continued Sam, "and keep with us, Tom, or you'll know of it. Inky goes first with the money."

Tom, all excitement at the prospect of an evening's entertainment, took up the position required, and the next moment there was the noise of bolts being drawn—the door flew open, and the tide of boys surged through the opening.

For a moment Tom felt that he must be separated from his friends; but recovering from the first pressure of the crowd, he clung to Sam's shoulder, and that youth, experienced in the ways of the Crystal Hall, calmly worked his way round, until they reached the pay place, where Inky dashed down his coppers and pointed out his friends.

In a moment they were past a burly man who guarded the narrow opening by the money-taker's box, and tearing along a narrow passage as if for their lives.

Another door was passed, and then the glories of the Crystal Hall burst upon our hero.

It was a very low place, but to Tom, whose whole life, as long as he could remember, had been passed in the cold streets, it was a haven of bliss.

Pizarro, when the riches of Peru burst upon him—Columbus when he sighted the shores of America—felt no more genuine emotion than this homeless, friendless lad when he first entered the Crystal Hall.

Sam and Inky, accustomed to this form of dissipation, were inclined to ignore the painted shields upon the wall, and the chandelier pendant from the ceiling, from which it may be assumed the shanty took its title—but Tom was all rapture, and the delight in his heart found a vent in his glistening eyes.

"Ain't it prime?" asked Sam, who had marked the happy look of Tom.

"It is," was all Tom could say.

"But it's nothin' to the old Drury," said Sam, with a rakish air; "wait till I've had a good week, and I'll give you a treat to the upper gallery, that's a sight for you—this is nothing to it. Ordare!"

This cry, springing suddenly from the lips of Sam, startled Tom, but it was speedily accounted for by the musical sounds arising from a violin and cornopean—each performer doing his utmost to spoil the melody of his neighbour.

The air was brief, but ere it was completed the Crystal Hall was crowded, and the surging mass of juvenility slowly settled into their places to enjoy the entertainment.

A variety of cries resounded throughout the room—inquiries of "what had become of Jack?" and "where was Jenny?" mingled with invitations to distant friends "to come over, for they'd room there." But all this rapidly subsided as a man in a yellow wig and painted nose came forward to sing a comic song.

Sam and Inky hailed him as an old friend, encouraging him with the cry of, "Go it, Dobley!" but Tom could only stare with might and main, for in that bewigged and painted man, he recognized through wig and paint the gentleman who had addressed him that morning by Bride Lane.

CHAPTER IV.

DOBLEY, THE COMIC SINGER—A FRACAS AT THE CRYSTAL HALL.

TOM, albeit not of a very romantic nature, had certainly entertained a higher opinion of the gentleman who had promised to be his friend than was warranted by his appearance upon the stage of the Crystal Hall.

Gorgeous as that place of entertainment appeared in the eyes of this poor lad, he had a vague, half-defined idea, that one would not look there for the aristocracy, or even the higher middle classes; and the budding hope that this man would prove a serviceable friend, which he had nursed throughout the day, faded out.

He felt the disappointment so keenly that he lost at once the glow of pleasure which had been burning in his bosom; the crystal chandelier looked mean and shabby, the gaily-coloured devices grew dull, and the two instruments, playing the preliminary air of a song, grated harshly on his ears.

"Go on, Dobley!"

It was only Sam Smarty giving encouragement to the performer, but Tom felt angry with his chum, as if he had committed some sacrilege, or outraged some tender association of his life.

"Now then, time's up," "Go it, Dobley," and a score of other cries rang through the room. Tom felt that something was wrong, and raising his eyes, he saw that the performer was staring straight at him, aghast, and apparently dumfounded.

"Play up." "What's the matter?" "Now then, don't keep us here a month," and so on, again shouted the impatient audience, but the singer did not appear to heed them.

Then the noises increased, and the yells uprose fast and furious; and when Tom's friend of the morning turned on his heel and disappeared behind the dingy curtains, the uproar was deafening.

Sam Smarty, who seemed to draw entertainment from every source, sprang upon the seat, and forthwith obliged the audience with a species of stationary dance, known as the double shuffle, uttering at times shrill whistles of encouragement to the other rioters.

This continued for some minutes, the limited orchestra, well knowing the disposition of the audience, hastily grasping their instruments, and retiring.

A few moments later, a stout, burly man appeared upon the stage, and removing a shabby white hat, with a black band round it, from his bullet head, motioned to the audience to be silent.

Curiosity obtained for him what he required, and the seething mass of angered juvenility gradually settled down.

"Laries an' genelmen," began the proprietor of the white hat, rocking slightly to and fro—as men do when under the influence of exciseable liquors—"laries an' genelmen."

"You've said that afore," interposed a voice.

"And I'll say it again," returned the speaker. "I'm proprietor of this hall, an' I'll do as I like in it. Laries an'—"

A universal yell of execration drowned the other word, but the proprietor, ignoring this display of indignation, stood firmly waiting for it to subside. After a little delay, the audience again became quiet.

"Now you've stopped," said the proprietor, "I'll tell you what's the matter. Sit down there, will you?"

Inky, whose interest in the disturbance had prompted him to stand upon the seat, was the party addressed. He replied with a scornful look, and the following impressive words :—

"None of the nobbly born ever sit down when talked to by a man in a white hat—sit down yourself."

"D—vo, Inky!" said Sam, immediately interested in the prospect of a row ; "don't give in to him."

"Not I !" returned Inky, standing on tiptoe. "Who stole the donkey?"

A deep flush overspread the proprietor's face, as a shout of approval followed this query ; but he passed the insult, and Inky's obstinate resistance, merely remarking that he should keep an eye upon him—and certainly, from that moment to the time he left the stage, his indignant glances were directed persistently at the "nobbly born."

"I come forrard," pursued the proprietor, "to inform you that Mr. Dobley is taken suddenly ill."

"He ain't," roared Inky.

"And can't perform to-night," added the proprietor ; "but the renowned Marley will appear in his place."

"Dobley !—Dobley !" shouted Inky and Sam together. "We won't have Marley."

Such cries are always infectious, and this one in particular was readily taken up in all parts of the room. "Dobley !—Dobley !— no Marley."

"If you don't have Marley, you'll have nothing," roared the proprietor.

He was a man with stentorian lungs, and his voice was heard above the din. The insult went through the hearts of the youthful audience ; it was a defiance which could not be borne by lads of spirit.

An orange, well aimed, pioneered the way for a multitude of missiles, and the enraged burly proprietor, having made a frantic effort to stand his ground, was obliged to beat a retreat.

Then the demons of discord and mischief broke loose. Boys hitherto pacific and inclined to support the side of order, went with the stream ; even Tom, excited by the shouts of those around him, lent a hand to the work of demolition. The love of destruction, latent in most breasts, burst forth furiously.

The seats were ripped up, the patches of coloured paper torn from the wooden walls, the chandelier reduced to a complete wreck, and all because a certain Dobley would not sing ; but it is doubtful if one of the youthful outlaws thought of the cause of all this, any more than the mob which tore down the railings of Hyde Park, when in full swing with their questionable work, thought of politics in any shape or form.

The riot increased ; in vain the proprietor, supported by the two members of the orchestra, reappeared and implored them to desist —in vain he threatened them with all the pains and penalties of the criminal code—he was laughed at, hooted, and held in contempt.

Then he charged madly into their midst, and smote some half score of the rebels heavily ; but multitudes prevail, and the multitude in this case, being armed with portions of the broken seats, was speedily victorious, and not only compelled the owner of the Crystal Hall to beat a retreat, but retained possession of his white hat, and made merry therewith.

The Crystal Hall was not a licensed place of entertainment, and therefore its owner was not entitled to the protection of the law ; nevertheless, he prevailed upon a member of the force to show himself, hoping to awe the youthful rioters. That member of the force came, saw, and prudently beating a retreat, remarked—

"That it would take 'arf the force to stop 'em now, and they had better 'ave it out."

And have it out they did. Every seat

"THE WUST, AND MOST INFORTENIT OF ORPHANS," SAID INKY.

being broken up, the room afforded a clear space for further proceedings, which at length assumed a very dangerous character. The boys, in a body, began to rush from one side to the other, shouting with delight as the Crystal Hall shook under the attack, and treating the whole affair as a capital piece of fun.

We have stated that the Crystal Hall was a mere shanty—a rude building erected on a waste piece of ground, and, of course, run up as cheaply as possible. This being the fact, it was not able to stand the succession of rude shocks which were given to it by some hundreds of boys rushing simultaneously from one side to the other.

It creaked, and groaned, and shook, and gave out other warnings; but boys are proverbially reckless, and all turned a deaf ear, until one end of the wooden walls gave way before an extra powerful rush, and fell into the outer air.

The collapse of the building was almost instantaneous, the other outer walls bent inwards, and the roof came down with a crash.

In an instant the scene was changed. All lights were out, and although more than half the boys had managed to blunder out when the wall fell, a great number lay beneath the *débris*.

All the mirth was over; in lieu of shouts and laughter, cries and groans rent the air, and shrieks for help arose from beneath the ruins.

The houses around were very thickly populated, and hundreds of people, alarmed by the crash, were speedily on the spot.

Lanterns, shovels, and picks were produced as if by magic, and amidst the warm encouragement of the mass, a number of labourers set to work.

Among those who escaped were Inky and Sam Smarty, who, as soon as the first shock was over, found themselves side by side.

The first question from Sam was—

"Where's Tom?"

"Don't know," returned Inky; "I lost sight on him afore the last rush."

"Was he before or behind?"

"I saw him work his way back a bit, as if he'd had enough of it; and I thought he looked a little frightened."

"Tom ain't the chap to funk—just work your way about a bit, and see if he's in the crowd. I'll stop here for you."

Inky worked his way through the crowd after the fashion equally familiar to boys and eels, while Sam remained, still keeping a sharp look out, and shouting, "Tom! Tom!" at the top of his voice.

In a few minutes Inky came back with a gloomy face.

"He isn't there," he said; "p'r'aps—he's gone home."

"He may be gone home," muttered Sam, "but it's under the roof—dead, p'r'aps. I say, Inky."

"What is it?"

"I shall never forgive myself if that poor little chap is killed, he seemed so innercent and good like—diff'rent to you and me."

"He was diff'rent," rejoined Inky; "he could patter better, and if he was in rags, he looked better nor both of us."

"If he's dead," said Sam, after a pause, "I'll drown myself—there, I will!"

A shout came from the foremost of the crowd, and many pressed forward to the front, eager to see what was the matter. The first victim of the disaster was being raised from the ruins by strong, but gentle hands.

It was poor Tom, insensible, and looking terribly ghastly in the glare of the lanterns.

"Stand back a little, my friends," said a firm voice, and a quietly-dressed man stooped over the prostrate boy, and made a brief examination of the injuries he had received.

"Not dead," he said, "and only one limb broken; give me a hand with him. The hospital is not far away. Now stand back, you boys, you cannot do any good."

The boys, Inky and Sam, involuntarily obeyed the command, and Tom was borne tenderly by, the crowd parting to give him a passage. Inky and Sam remained staring at each other in the utmost bewilderment.

"That's Tom," said Inky.

"I see it is."

"But who was that with him?"

"It looked like Dobley."

"It *was* Dobley; and not much like him when he's singing; why, he's quite a harystocrat."

"He looked quite nobby."

"I can't make it out," said Inky, scratching his head, "for he sartainly looked every hinch a gent, and somehow, he seemed to know Tom, too. P'r'aps it's his father—his nobbly-born father."

"Your hed is allers a runnin' agin nobble fathers, Inky."

"And so it will, until I finds my own; but I hope I shan't find him a comic singer—not as comic singers is all cadgers, but I couldn't stand a comic father. He ought to be bold and brave—a pouncin' on everybody, and makin' the servants jump in their boots whenever he spoke—that's the father for me; but a comic chap I couldn't abear. I'd rather live all my precious life with old Work-it-out!"

"You might do worse," rejoined Sam, philosophically; "poor Tom!"

"Hadn't we better follow 'im to the 'orspital?"

"They wouldn't let us in, but we'll look round by-and-by, as we go home, and ax 'ow he is."

They waited for an hour, and by that time the whole of the roof, being of comparatively light materials, was removed, and the injured and wounded, some twenty in number, removed to the hospital.

The rest had escaped with a few bruises of no importance, and fortunately none were killed outright.

"I'm glad of that," said Sam, when this fact was announced, "for it allers touches my 'art to hear of young 'uns dyin'. Old 'uns don't signify so much, they've had their spin."

"It's 'orrible to hear of young 'uns dyin', even if they is cadgers," returned Inky; "but when they is nobbly born, it falls on society like a thunderin' bolt!"

CHAPTER V.

INKY MAKES AN IMPORTANT DISCOVERY.

On their way home the boys called at the hospital. They found a crowd outside, and a beadle-like personage on the steps warning the people off. To him Sam addressed himself—

"I say, old man," he said, with an exasperating familiarity, "how's my mate getting on?"

The porter elevated his nose, and looked scornfully over the head of Sam and far away.

"You'd better answer me," continued Sam, in a tone of mild warning, "or I'll have you up afore the Board o' Works."

"Be off!" cried the beadle, raising his staff.

"How's my mate?" persisted Sam; "Tom, the little curly-headed chap with the broken leg?"

"Why don't you answer the boy, you bloated will'in?" demanded a beery plasterer in front of the crowd; "where's his rights and privileges as a Briton—where's his haberas corpus, if a chap like you is allowed to turn his nose up at the people?"

"Have you anybody here?" demanded the porter.

"No; but I may have, and who knows but as I may come myself? The world's a wale of tears, and men like me ain't arf paid. Tell the boy 'ow his mate is, or I'll chuck my trowel at you."

"Good again," assented a man, likewise beery, with two full-sized cabbages under his arm; "if it warn't for the likes o' him, we shouldn't be starved and driven like beasts o' the field; tell the boy how his mate is—sweet words don't cost you nothin'."

These two supporters of Sam found favour in the eyes of the crowd, and the liveried porter foreseeing a storm if he was obstinate, thought discretion the better part of valour, and addressed himself to Sam—

"The boy in question," he said, "is going on favourably."

"Thanky," said Sam, and bowing low, he came down the steps with Inky, arm-in-arm.

"As if he couldn't say that afore," remarked the man with the cabbages to the crowd, "but it's like 'em—the more you overpays 'em, the worse they is."

"You don't overpay me," said the porter, scornfully.

"Who does then?" demanded the other; "who is up airly and late, a toilin' and a sweatin', so that the likes o' you may roll in the fat of the land? Who is down-trodden by a bloated obligarchy to keep you in your midnight deborsheries and revels? Come on," he added, dashing down his cabbages, "if you are a man, and knows how to take a licking!"

The plasterer encouraged this idea, and spat upon his hands, as a preliminary to impending pugilistic proceedings; but the porter prudently withdrew, and left the crowd to remain or disperse at will.

Sam and Inky went towards their homes, and the two men who had supported them came walking by arm-in-arm, to "have another drain," the proprietor of the cabbages apparently oblivious that his property had been purloined by a one-eyed man in a slop and corduroys.

"We mustn't forget the young 'un," said Sam at parting, "but look up whenever we can, just for the sake of old days, you know."

Sam forgot that their acquaintance was of one day only, but the events had been of such a serious nature that he seemed to have known the boy for a week at least.

"I shall run over to-morrow," said Inky, "for it's Sunday, and I've all the day to myself."

They parted; and Inky went home to Sceptre Court, where he found a body of merry youths awaiting his return or any other prospect of fun which might turn up. This lawless body compelled Inky, to use a sea-phrase, to "lay off and on," until the coast was apparently clear. Then he made a bold attempt to reach the residence of Mr. Harris, alias Work-it-out.

But the enemy had only retired to an ambuscade in the shadow of a house in the court, and as soon as Inky had knocked at his master's door they fell upon him tooth and nail.

Two held him fast while a third smote him on the nose; but fortunately for Inky, his master was at home, and promptly opening the door, the poor boy fell into the shop.

To grasp Stinger was the work of a moment, but the assailants were quicker, being on their feet and off in a twinkling; but Work-it-out hated disappointment, so he gave Inky a dose for being rather later than usual, and commanding him to go to bed at once, he went out for his "night-cap" round the corner. Muttering anathemas upon the head of his tyrannical employer, Inky coiled himself under the counter, and was soon fast asleep, and dreaming that the whole court had suddenly collapsed, and all but himself buried beneath the ruins.

The morrow was Sunday, a day of rest for Work-it-out and his *protégé*, and a comparative day of peace in the court. The great example set by the world at large had a little effect upon that band of outlaws, inasmuch that the most degraded indulged in a wash, and made an effort to smarten up a bit.

Work-it-out invariably stayed at home, indulging in the perusal of *Reynolds's Newspaper* of the previous week, borrowed from the beer-shop opposite.

This highly commendable paper was the great literary weekly treat of Inky and his master, the cobbler revelling in the radical opinions there promulgated, and Inky devouring all the police reports, murders, suicides, and other light and refreshing paragraphs.

On this particular Sunday, Inky, having disposed of his breakfast, cut the paper in two portions as usual, giving his master the outer pages containing the outpourings of rabid republicanism, and reserving the weekly misdemeanours for his own perusal.

Inky's tendencies were of course aristocratic, and therefore he had no sympathy with the political tone of the paper; but Work-it-out, who looked upon the upper classes as a band of monsters and ruffians, was in the habit of reading aloud the most inflammatory passages of the leading articles, to the inexpressible wrath and contempt of his assistant.

Inky, as a rule, bore this infliction with tolerable meekness and patience, for if he disputed the soundness of the argument, or the veracity of the assertion, Work-it-out generally confiscated the other part of the paper for the remainder of the day.

On this particular morning Inky sat upon his stool in the corner working his way slowly through the paragraphs, getting tripped up by every word of more than two syllables, when a most astounding piece of news met his eye, and fairly took his breath away.

Work-it-out, who had been chuckling over a volley of abuse showered upon the "bloated nobility," turned down the paper, and was about to read the most pointed passages aloud, when he caught sight of Inky's face.

"What's the matter with you now?" he growled; "you look as if you was froze."

Inky opened his mouth and worked his jaws like a fish out of its natural element, but not a word came forth.

"If you make faces at me," snarled the old man, "I'll break a rool and give you a Sunday dose of Stinger."

"I'm not making faces," gasped Inky, "but oh!—at last—at last."

"P'r'aps you'll tell me what's the matter with you?" asked Work-it-out; "is it wind —or spasms?"

"No, it ain't."

"Then what is it? Dash it, if you don't out with it, I'll break every bone in your body. I wish I'd strangled you when I fust found you in that yaller handkercher."

"It would ha'e been the worst day's work in your life," cried Inky, rising triumphantly, and waving the paper like a banner; "old man, rej'ice with me this day."

"Of all the exasperatin' imps," muttered Work-it-out, "you are the most exasperatingist. What do you mean, you door-step brat—you red-headed son of nobody!"

"Old man," cried Inky, "beware—you will repent them words. Tremble in your boots, you old will'in—for *I'm found*."

"Found!"

"Yes—old man, and no more Stinger will I stand. Here's my father dyin' for want of his son—and I'm a goin' to ease the last moments of his wale of tears. Listen, and when I've done—ax my parding for havin' used Stinger on my nobble body."

Inky, with a face a-glow, looking like a harvest moon squeezed out of shape—turned the paper down to get conveniently at a corner paragraph, and read aloud:—

"It is strange that the heir to the magnificent Beauforth estates has never been found. The father of the missing child, the last marquis of the race, now in his eightieth year, lies at his mansion, 294, Belgrave Square, in a very precarious condition. At his death this vast amount of landed and funded property will revert to the crown. Here is an opportunity for the legislators of the country to do a noble deed. Why not divide the spoil of centuries among a starving people?"

The reading of this occupied Inky several minutes, and certain words were pronounced in his original style. We purposely omit his peculiarities to make it clear to our readers.

"There," cried Inky, dashing down the paper, "what do you think of that?"

Work-it-out glared at him like a goaded wild beast.

"What do I think of it?" he said; "what would any right-minded man, with the heart of a Briton beatin' in his buzzum, think of it? Divide it at once, I say, and let's all go cut for a day to Hepping Forest."

"Divide it!" screamed Inky, "divide *my* property, dashed if ever I heard of sich cheek. You'll get into trouble if you go on like this, old man."

"*His* property!" gasped the other, positively reeling under the force of the assertion. "He's daft—clean gone!" "What next," he demanded, turning suddenly upon Inky, "will you get inter that 'ollow 'ed of yourn?"

"Ain't it reason?" asked Inky; "here's a markis lost his son—and warn't *I* found? Do you think I'm a goin' to sit here while a lot of snivillin' old will'ins like you devours the funds of my parsimony. Not if I knows it. Stand out o' the way, and let me go to my longin' father."

"Put that paper down."

"Shan't."

Work-it-out made a dart at his adopted son, but Inky was too quick for him. Raising the latch, he darted into the court, and disappeared round the corner with the celerity of a sprite.

"I've raised a sarpent in my buzzum," muttered Work-it-out, "and he's turned, and stung me. Let me find another warmint on my door-step. It'll be werry hard lines for him, I'll swear."

Inky, with the precious broad sheet in his possession, made straight for the premises of Messrs. Kidem and Blowhard, the well-known printers of Shoe Lane, where he knew Sam Smarty was engaged in the performance of certain duties.

He had no difficulty in gaining admittance, and knowing the particular post of his chum, he made straight for the machine where Sam was standing with a few other ferocious youthful outlaws, waiting orders.

"What cheer, Inky?" demanded Sam, "you are as pale as a muffin. Is old Work-it-out defunct?"

"Blow Work-it-out!" returned Inky; "come here a moment, Sam."

They withdrew into the shadow of a corner, when Inky produced the paper, and re-read the paragraph.

There were many interruptions in the form of dabs of printer's ink and other missiles, for your printer's boy is a playful youth, and Inky was a stranger; but both he and Sam were absorbed in the wondrous intelligence, and ignored their proceedings.

"What do you think of it?" asked Inky, when he had finished.

"My hidear is this," returned Sam : "you cut and run for Belgrave Square at once, or there'll be a swarm of lost and found kids a droppin' on the dyin' Markis—and if you ain't sharp, he may bless the wrong cove, and leave him all his property."

"But hinstink," urged Inky, "that would show him which was the right party."

"Hinstink," returned Sam, "is gammon, specially with a markis; and why? A markis allers drinks heavy, and sits day and night with a gold goblet in his hand, a moppin' the ruby wine. 'Pore forth the Rhine wine, let it flow!' that's the song they sings, Inky, and my adwice is, don't lose a moment, or you'll be deprived of your property, and live and die with Work-it-out."

"I'm orf," gasped Inky, grasping his friend's hand, "and remember this—as soon as I comes into my property, I makes you a master printer."

"All serene," returned Sam; "but get away at once."

Inky departed forthwith at a smart trot, and Sam—the perfidious Sam—turning to a body of his co-mates, winked and said—

"Inky's gone to find his father, the Markis, down in Belgravia—the land of the nobs. Oh! won't it be a lark, and shouldn't I like to see Inky when he gets among the plush!"

And this was your friendship, Sam—fie—for shame!

Inky had no desire that the surprise should be too sudden, lest his noble father should be overcome; he therefore abandoned the idea of using the knocker, and decided upon ringing.

There were two bells, one on the right marked "Visitors"—another on the left marked "Servants."

Inky having laboriously deciphered these words, decided upon pulling the former.

"A long-lost son can't be a servant," he said; "he's a wisitor."

And Inky rang the visitors' bell.

Now the sound of the visitors' bell on such a day, and at such a time, was about equal in the ears of the men in plush, to the rumblings of an earthquake; and the two retainers of the Marquis of Beauforth especially appointed to door duty were staggered by the clanging which Inky's energy had made.

Both were in undress, and sitting before the kitchen fire, deep in the perusal of their Sunday paper—the *Observer*—both gentlemen being of a sporting turn of mind.

They stared at each other aghast, and for a moment neither could move.

"Was that the visitors' bell, Jeames?" asked one.

"It was, Tummas," replied the other; "it's your turn, you know; I answered last—yesterday, you know, at five o'clock."

"But who can it be?" asked Thomas. "It's like their impudence to disturb me on Sunday. Mary—my coat."

Mary, the housemaid, a devoted worshipper of Tummas's fine figure and resplendent calves, passed the gorgeous article of apparel, which the footman hastily donned, and rushed upstairs to make amends for the delay.

Drawing back the bolts, he gave the door a Belgravian swing, throwing it open wide with one tremendous jerk.

The sight which met the eyes of Tummas was overpowering.

A dirty-faced boy, in seedy clothes, and boots which would have been denied admission to the kitchen, standing on the spotless stone steps of number two hundred and ninety-four.

He had rung the visitors' bell, too! The double thought was too much for the man in plush, and, without waiting for Inky to explain his errand, he smote that hapless youth upon the ear, and sent him reeling to the pavement.

Then the door of the great mansion closed with a bang, and Tummas retired to the kitchen, glowing like a lobster in his wrath.

Inky's head, never of the strongest at the best of times, reeled beneath the assault, and he beheld the houses in the square wildly waltzing around him, turning upside down, and performing other feats which he had hitherto not dreamt of.

Added to this, a chorus of jangling music rang in his ears, which increased his confusion, and reduced him to a state of semi-idiocy.

In a few moments things took a better turn, and he revived a little. Then he became conscious of a watchful policeman standing by his side, and looking down upon him as if he had just discovered some wondrous unknown specimen of natural history.

"What's the move?" demanded the official.

"What move?" asked Inky, gingerly touching his still aching ear.

"Ain't there no better place than this for you to sit on?" inquired Y 96.

"'Tain't my fault," said Inky. "I don't want to sit here."

"Why do you do it, then?"

"Acause a man in calves gave me one under the ear."

"Where is he?"

"Gone in agin—number two-ninety-four!"

"Was you doin' a runaway?" demanded Y 96 sternly.

"I was not," replied Inky; "I on'y called upon the Markis o' Booforth with a bit of noos.'

"You callin' on him!" said Y 96; "come, that's a good 'un—what was your noos?"

"A cloo to his long-lost son—but afore I could out with it, Calves gave me the buster, and I sot down on the pavement a reg'lar oner."

Now Y 96 was a phlegmatic official, and was not much given to express surprise. The easy duty of a fashionable neighbourhood had left him with a temper unruffled, and although at first disposed to be indignant with Inky for daring to sit down upon a fashionable pavement, he had varied the monotony of the morning's duty, as we have seen, with a few light and easy questions of an affable nature; but this communication from the "nobbly born" upset his equanimity completely.

"You've got a clue," he said feverishly; "are you sure, boy?"

"I am sartain," answered Inky, with a proud smile; "and I've got the witnesses—I knows it, old Work-it-out knows it, and so does Sam Smarty—we're all ready to be sworn."

"Come this way," said Y 96—his hands trembling with excitement—"round this corner by the mews—it's quiet there; come and let us have a little quiet talk together."

"I'm on," said Inky affably; and they adjourned to the retirement of the mews together.

"Now, fust," said Y 96, with a confidential air, "let us be friendly and commoonicative."

"It's the wishes of my 'art," answered Inky.

"You knows of the reward?" asked the official, smiling.

"I've heerd on it," said Inky, smiling evasively.

"And therefore hopes to get it?" asked Y 96.

"No, I don't care much about it," replied Inky.

This piece of disinterestedness enchanted the official in blue, and he grasped Inky by the hand.

"My boy," he said with emotion, "we're friends from this moment."

"Don't be in a hurry," said Inky loftily.

"I'm not in a hurry, dear boy—but you says as you knows of the Markis's long-lost son?"

"I knows him well," replied Inky.

"And how long have you known him?"

"Some years."

"And you've never revealed it to nobody?"

"Never," said Inky, firmly.

"What a boy you are!" exclaimed Y 96, enthusiastically; "what a noble 'art you must possess."

"I'm nobble all over," returned Inky.

"You air—you air," assented the official; "anybody could see that with 'arf a eye—how about the Markis's son—where is he?"

Inky paused a moment, coughed slightly, struck a wonderful attitude, and exclaimed—

"Here's the nobble cove!"

If Tummas had cause for being staggered, and was staggered, what must have been the feelings of Y 96, as Inky thus proudly proclaimed himself?

He had suffered from boys before; apples and nuts had been hurled at his official head, personal reflections had been heaped upon him, tramps had defied him, and muscular navvies pommelled him, but this was the greatest outrage of all.

His surprise was great, but official phlegm came to the rescue, and he seized Inky by the collar.

"I've been gammoned afore," he said, carefully moistening the palm of his right hand—the hand at liberty; "but this is the greatest go I ever knowed—*you* the son of the Markis of Booforth—(smack)—*you* the heir to two million o' money—(smack)—*you* the chap as lived at home until he was twenty-one and runned away the day he came of age —(smack)—*you* the cove as they offers a thousand reward for—(smack)—why, dash your darned cheek!—take that—and that—and that—now cut, and let me catch you within a mile of my beat agin, and I runs you in."

Inky, barely recovered from the staggerer administered by Tummas, was driven back into a dazed state by the heavy open-handed blows administered by Y 96, and when that active and intelligent officer released him, he wandered away hopelessly confused, and did not recover until he found himself in Battersea Fields.

CHAPTER VII.
TOM AND HIS FRIEND.

IN the meantime, Tom lay sore stricken upon his couch in the hospital ward.

On either side of him lay a long file of the sick and wounded, struck down in the midst of the battle of life, some with scalds and burns, some suffering from fearful diseases, or others, like him, with broken bones and bruised limbs.

Tom's leg was set immediately after his arrival, and he bore the pain bravely, thereby making friends with the surgeon, which was a great advantage to a patient at such a place.

The nurses saw that the boy was a bit of a favourite, and bestowed upon him even more than their usual attention, so that, apart from the first great anguish, he had little to regret in being there.

To most people—those who have lived in happy homes—there would have been something horrible in that sick ward; but to Tom, whose wretched days had known no change, except in the matter of sunshine and rain, it was a haven of delight.

The ward, in his eyes, was a place fit for a king, the nurses women of high degree, the surgeon equal to a nobleman at least, and the bed—that couch with its soft pillows and cool, clean linen, hitherto unknown to him—was a marvellous piece of luxury.

The food, too—the, to him, rich, fragrant broths—were exceedingly toothsome, and the little patches of jelly, which he had seen often in confectioners' shops, and never dreamt that any mortal could be rich enough to buy, were delicious indeed.

The only drawback as regards himself was the physic, "cooling draughts," the nurse called them; they certainly were not palatable, and Tom made comical, wry faces when he swallowed them, but he hoped he should like them better by-and-by, and swallowed them gratefully, placing the cooling draughts among the other luxuries of this wonderful place.

But there were other things which he did not like—the groans and sometimes shrieks of those in pain. The ward generally was quiet, for each patient appeared to consider it his duty to suffer and be strong, but at times the agony they suppressed found a vent in a bitter cry, or a short prayer to Heaven for mercy, and then Tom's heart grew sad.

He did not suffer much himself after the first day, for skilful hands had set his limb, and young bones quickly heal, so he had the more time to think of the other sufferers who lay on each side and before him, each with his little card of treatment and diet nailed to the wall, above his head.

On the morning of the third day the surgeon brought him a paper, which he said a friend of Tom's had left at the door.

Tom, with tears in his eyes, said he could not read, so the surgeon read it aloud to him with a suppressed smile upon his face.

It was from Sam Smarty, and we give it verbatim.

CHEER, BOYS, CHEER!

don't be downy, Tom, for it might ha' bean wors—i know'd a chap as was cut up in a chaff mashine, and so they could not cure him, but they will cure you, and you will come out bright and spry—

Inky went last sunday to find his long-lost father, and came home so soar all over that he carn't sit down yit—he don't say nothing about it, but I guess he tumbled into the wrong shop, and got it hot—

keep up your pecker—

Rule brittaniar—

Sam Smarty—

"It's wery kind of him," said Tom, wiping a tear from his eye.

"Who is this Sam Smarty?" asked the surgeon.

Tom gave him a brief account of his short acquaintance with Sam.

"He seems to be a good-hearted little fellow," said the surgeon; "and the next time he calls he shall come in to see you."

Tom looked pleased, and throughout that day he dreamt of nothing else but the pleasure of seeing Sam Smarty, but it was not until Thursday morning that he saw him in person.

Sam came into the ward, under the care of the liveried official with whom he had a slight verbal encounter on the night of the accident.

The porter looked exceedingly lofty, and evidently felt that he had "come to something" in being usher to a dirty printer's devil.

Sam, on the other hand, was cool and affable, and when the porter pointed out Tom's bed, he thanked him, and apologised for having no coppers.

"It's Thursday," he remarked, with an agreeable smile, "and we literary chaps is allers broke about Toosday, as a rule; it's only the steady 'uns as has a copper on Wednesday, but that's the latest."

To this the porter deigned no reply, but retired with a sense of the indignity offered burning within him.

Sam went to Tom's side, and gave him a congratulatory shake of the hand.

"I've just seen the doctor chap," he said, "and he ses you'll be out in no time; a nice easy-going party he is, and I likes him much—the sort o' man I should be proud to call my friend."

"He's been werry good to me," said Tom.

"I 'spected that," rejoined Sam, taking a seat upon the side of the bed; "but don't say too much to him."

"About what?"

"Your life, you know, Tom; about bein' friendless and homeless, and havin' nothin' but the streets to look to for a parient."

"Ah! but I've told him all that," said Tom.

"You have!" replied Sam; "then you've put your foot in it! You're a lost cove!"

The face of Tom expressed the most violent alarm, and Sam hastened to explain, speaking in a very low tone—

"Your liberty's stopped," he said; "as soon as you can stand on your pins agen, he'll take you straight afore a beak—'Here's a 'ouseless chap,' he ses. 'What, another?' ses the beak. 'Yes, another,' ses the surgeon, 'and he's had his leg broke at a penny gaff.' 'That's wery bad,' ses the magistrate,

a shakin' his knowin' ole 'ed. 'but I can't punish him for that.' 'I don't want him punished,' ses the doctor, 'but put him in a Home, where he'll be away from the temptations of the streets.' Then the magistrate will ask you, what's your religion? and when you says you ain't got none, which you ain't, Tom, any more than you've got a satin wesket and top-boots, he'll order his clerk, in a 'perative woice, to write out a horder for a Home, and away you goes for five years, and once there," concluded Sam, impressively, "you is a lost cove!"

"What sort of place is a Home?" asked Tom, pale with terror at the direful prospect.

"Too reg'lar to be nice," replied Sam, "but they treats you pretty well; but, as I ses, too reg'lar. Herly rising—reg'lar meals, and no goin' out of the grounds. You sees nothing but the Home for years—as for a Lord Mayor's day, they would jest as soon give you a noppor'nity to dance the polka in the Queen's back parlour, as let you come anigh it. It's all Home, Home, and you sees nothing else."

"I don't think I should mind it, if there was nice broth and jellies, and a bed like this," said Tom.

"Don't you be led away—don't be derlooded," rejoined Sam; "wittles and beds soon wears off—the love of liberty don't—once shut up, you'll grow wicious. I knowed a boy once as went to a Home—he was a good 'arted chap afore he went—sold dailys—noosepapers, you know, in the streets. Well, they took him orf, and shut him up for a year—somehow he got out, and runned away. As soon as he got back to the city, he stole a loaf at a coffee-shop, and bein' found out by the proprietor, fought with him, among the crockery—viciously kicking over the piles o' cups and sarcers. He got a month for it, and now can't hold up his head afore his fellow man."

"He had no right to steal the loaf," urged Tom.

"Troo," replied Sam; "but he did it arter he left the Home; but I must away, old chap, as I goes on duty with the hevening paper—good bye, and keep up, as I sed in my 'pistle—keep up your pecker."

Sam then went on his way, and perhaps it is only proper for us to state, now the opportunity offers, that Sam's ideas respecting the Home for boys were somewhat erroneous. These institutions are very excellent things, and with the exception of one here and there, exceedingly well managed. Perhaps Sam's friend alighted on one badly conducted, and so became the corrupt being pathetically depicted by him.

On the following day Tom had another visitor.

He had fallen asleep towards the afternoon, into the happy sleep of approaching convalescence, and was dreaming of green fields, and running waters, which he had never seen, when the murmuring of voices at his bedside aroused him.

Opening his eyes, he beheld the man whom he had met in Fleet Street, and afterwards seen at the Crystal Hall, as Dobley, the comic singer, in conversation with the nurse.

"He's a going on as well as any one in the ward," the woman was saying, "and it's only a matter of time to cure him, I assure you, sir."

The stranger turned towards the boy, and saw that he was awake. Sitting down by his bedside, he took his hand, and asked him how he was. Tom said he was better.

"I have not been before to see you," said the visitor, "for I have been much engaged, but I have sent messages to enquire after you, and was glad to learn that you were going on well."

As he spoke, Tom felt instinctively that this man was far above the vulgar creature he had appeared to be at the Crystal Hall. His handsome face and well-knit frame carried to the most ordinary observer the conviction that he was no vulgar-born man.

While Tom was thinking of this, the stranger spoke of it—

"I suppose you were surprised, Tom," he said, "to see me at the Crystal Hall?"

"I was, sir."

"Ah! there are some people who would have been more astonished than you were," replied the stranger; "but thereby hangs a tale, of which more another day. All I have to say now, Tom, can be said in a very few words—as soon as you are well enough, I intend to remove you home."

"To a Home, sir?" asked Tom, remembering Sam's warning.

"Yes," replied the other, with a smile, "and to a very excellent home, too."

"Is it reg'lar, sir?"

"A regular home—I hope so."

"Not too reg'lar to be nice?"

"You are a strange lad," said the visitor; "tell me what you mean."

Tom hesitated.

Would it be right to lay bare before a stranger the candid views of Sam? Would it not probably lead the worthy Sam into trouble?

But it was possible to give Sam's view without naming Sam, and this, after a little thought, Tom did.

His visitor laughed a low, merry laugh, and laid his hand upon the boy's shoulder.

"The home," he said, "I shall take you to will be something very different to this; you will not be imprisoned, and you shall go into the streets every day, and, if you wish it, you shall see the Lord Mayor's show every year."

CHAPTER VIII.
INKY FINDS SOME NEW FRIENDS.

SOME years ago, when Islington was haunted by fewer omnibuses and had no tramways, two ladies lived in the retirement of the Liverpool Road.

We say retirement—and say it advisedly —for that broad and long thoroughfare, albeit abutting on and running parallel with the High Street and the Green, was then, nevertheless, a quiet, deserted, and almost unknown thoroughfare.

In the days we write of the vast Agricultural Hall was not built, horse shows were then unknown, no mighty wrestlers famed for muscular deeds battled the long Good Friday through, gigantic circus exhibitions had not been dreamt of, no Bands of Hope, some ten thousand juveniles strong, all sworn to live and die devoted to the pump, e'er mustered there—in fact, Islington was, in comparison with the present day, a haven of repose, a land of peace, and Liverpool Road was the quietest part of this place of rest.

In the cosiest part of the broad highway, studded by some trees with real green leaves, such as the country need not have been ashamed of, stood a quiet-looking, orderly house, with trimly-cut grass plat in front, and a well-swept gravelled walk.

The windows were neatly curtained, the doors and windows marvellously clean, and, suspended between the curtains of the lower room, were two canaries, which twittered and sang in harmonious rivalry throughout the summer day.

It was just such a place as a cosy old couple would have chosen to settle down in, and it was the house of a cosy couple, not man and wife, but a pair of old maids.

The Misses Pierson were two unworldly creatures, guileless as the babes in the wood, meek and gentle as lambs. They lived with little thought of the great world beyond, with its toil, suffering, and care, and passed their days content to know that all went smooth with them and those attached to their little home.

But they had known sorrow.

Long years before there had been three sisters—Laura, Fanny, and Bella—and three handsome girls people said they were—but now Bella was gone, had disappeared, and Laura and Fanny were sadly changed.

What became of their sister they never really knew; several letters arrived at intervals, but they bore neither date nor address, and all they learned was that Bella was alive.

This much she said, but never once declared that she was happy.

After a time these letters ceased, and the two sorrowing sisters bowed their necks to the yoke and left the world for ever.

They might have married at first, but they refused all offers, and leaving all friends, took the house in Liverpool Road, resolved to spend the remainder of their days in retirement.

As age came creeping on, there came with it a strange longing to leave behind them somebody who would hold their memory dear.

"Why not rear a child?" said Miss Fanny.

"What do we know of rearing?" rejoined Miss Laura, with a smile; "we are growing old and feeble—my eyesight is dim—no; if we choose at all, we must choose one beyond the first care of a woman."

"It must be a boy," said Miss Fanny. "I would not leave a girl alone and unprotected in the world."

"No," replied the sister, and then they both thought of the lost Bella, and tears rolled silently down their cheeks.

They often talked this matter over, of having been so far away from the world, and timid of coming into contact with it; but they took no steps towards the completion of their object, and probably they would have talked of it to the day of their death but for Jenny, their faithful servitor and housemaid.

She, with the licence allowed to an old servant, often joined in these discussions, and tendered her advice.

"There's hundreds of people," she said upon one occasion, "who would be glad to give you one or two, or even three of their children. I'm sure my sister, Mrs. Smarty, would be glad to get rid of some of hern."

"It must be an orphan," said Miss Fanny, to which Miss Laura assented, saying that—

"Children with parents have at least a protector in the world."

"Some parients," said Jenny, "ain't much of the protection in 'em, but contrairy opposite; but as you've made up your minds to a horphan, I'll look about me."

The next Sunday Jenny had leave of absence, and went alone to the city to see her sister, Mrs. Smarty, who was the mother of our interesting friend Sam.

Jenny arrived in time for dinner, and having saluted her nieces and nephews, nine in number, sat down and partook of the humble meal.

Jenny soon turned the conversation upon her home, and having bestowed the accustomed eulogies upon her mistresses, related the story of their longing, and asked her sister if she knew of an available orphan.

"It must be a horphan?" interposed Sam, dropping into the conversation with his usual airy grace.

"It must," replied Jenny, emphatically; "so don't think of it, Sam, for though you be my nevvy, and I loves you well, you are that rampageous that the whole of Liverpool Road, let alone our little place, wouldn't hold you."

"I likes my freedom," returned Sam, "and I worn't thinking of myself; but I know a horphan."

"Is he a printer's himp?" asked Jenny.

"Printers ain't got no himps," returned Sam, "we are all genelmen of the press. Where would you be without us? It's all werry well for the chaps as sets down and scribbles—spiles paper, I calls it—but what's the good o' that? we turns it out by millions; it is us who makes up the interlectural wittles for the multitood."

"I never did hear sech a boy," exclaimed Jenny, holding up her hands with horror.

"I know I'm a man of advanced opinions," continued Sam, clinching the impression he had made; "we knows a thing or two, we city chaps; we don't live in a 'ole-and-corner crib, dodgin' about wool-work and cleanin' canary cages; no, we is up and doin' with the lark, a pitchin' into our interlectural pursoots afore the like of you have got through your first batch of snorin'. Himps is we! what next I wonder! I blushes for you, Aunt Jenny, and I leaves you to finish that bit o' puddin' with a heasy conscience, if you can."

Sam, having finished this overpowering address, took his cap in his hand and went forth, chuckling over the idea of having prostrated his aunt with the power of his oratory.

"So they want a horphan," he said, as he walked meditatively down Shoe Lane; "well, I think Inky might have a go in. It can't hurt him to have a shy. He'd better go up airly; if Aunt Jenny saw him, she might take against him. I'll wisit my noble friend at once."

He crossed Fleet Street and passed up Sceptre Court, where a compound smell of dinners with a considerable dash of onions pervaded the air.

Sam was about to knock at Work-it-out's door, when the sound of contention within broke upon his ear.

"At it again," thought Sam; "the life they lives is almost as bad as a married one. Mornin', my friends," he said, affably, as he opened the door; "what's o'clock now!"

Inky was standing all flushed behind the counter, glaring at his master, who stood in the centre of the shop with Stinger in his hand.

Sam's question elicited no reply from Inky, so he turned to Work-it-out and repeated it.

"His wittles ain't good enough for him," answered the cobbler briefly.

"I should think not," roared Inky; "wot's a pig's foot to one of my parian birth? What's so aggrawatin' to a hungry chap as a pig's foot, all bone and skin?"

"Could I get anything else?" demanded Work-it-out; "ain't there a bit o' weal owed for now: and who's to pay it if you're allers runnin' about the streets in sarch of a nobble father?—you with a nobble father!" repeated the cobbler furiously; "it's my belief you never had one at all."

"Give me my gorging raiment and let me go," said Inky.

"I ain't got no gorging raiment," uttered Work-it-out.

"Then give me the ticket."

"What ticket?"

"The pawn-ticket—ha—don't come anigh me agin, old man, or I'll stab you with a hawl."

"Really," interposed Sam, with an agreeable smile, "this ain't the sort of thing, you know—wot's the good of it?—I thought you were better friends; Inky, come out with me for a minute while Mr. Harris compoges himself."

Inky, with one last contemptuous glance at the pig's foot lying in a broken plate, followed his friend out of the court and into Fleet Street.

"If there's one thing I likes to do better than another," said Sam, "it is to sarve a friend—Inky, I think I can put you in the line of fortune."

"I thought I was in it last Sunday," said Inky, gloomily; "but a buster from the cove in plush, and the bangers from the other chap——"

"Never mind that," interrupted Sam, "you made a mistake, that's sartain—but this is another thing altogether—listen to me, Inky."

In a few words the story was told, Sam concluding by offering a little piece of advice

"Don't lose no time," he said, "but run up airly to-morrow—just as they have had breakfast."

"Is a footman kep' there?" asked Inky.

"No, but I think there is a page-boy—at least there was, but you can lick him heasy."

"You're sure this ain't gammon, Sam?"

"Look here, Inky, I've got an orf mornin' to-morrow, and I'll go up with you—but I can't go into the house on account of Aunt Jenny—she's a bit afraid of me, and I wishes to spare her feelin's."

"I think I'll try it," said Inky; "'tain't like findin' a fortun, but a pig's foot for a Sunday dinner is the last door that broke the camel's back—it was a haged one, too, Sam, the werry hawl wouldn't go through it."

"Never mind, Inky, you've got over that."

"I want to get away from the court, Sam —it's worse than ever. Last night one of 'em—I think it were young Snivins, chucked a peck of winkle shells right over the old will'in and me as we sat at work; he was followed by another who throwed a large dob of putty at Work-it-out and set his nose a bleedin'. When Work-it-out rushed into the court they knocked his hat orf, and it ain't been seen since."

"A wi'lent lot," said Sam.

"A wicious lot, Sam."

"Heard anything of Tom?"

"No, Sam."

"I looked up yesterday for the second time," said Sam, "and met with a cordial reception from the big doctor chaps. The beadle was huffy but I soon put *him* down. Tom's pickin' up and will be out shortly— you'll stand by him if you get this horphan crib, won't you Inky?"

"I'll do the best I can," replied Inky, evasively.

"If yer don't," rejoined Sam, "I'll precious soon put a hole in yer drum; for if yer get the place, it's through my inflooence; and what a man sets up he can ginerally topple down—adoo, Inky, and remember, be airly at your post, for they don't want only one horphan."

CHAPTER IX.

A NEW HOME.—INKY COMES OUT.

THE two maiden ladies living in the Liverpool Road were finishing their frugal meal on the following morning, when Jenny entered.

"There's a boy wishes to speak to you, ladies."

"Has he come after the page's place?"

"I don't know, I am sure, ladies."

"Then show him in."

In a few minutes Inky, looking very demure and innocent, was ushered into the room. Jenny very dexterously swept the breakfast things into a heap and disappeared. The two ladies, looking very prim, drew up side by side, facing their highly-born visitor.

Time had played sad havoc with the ladies, and few who saw them then could have believed that they had once been beauties, courted, flattered, and almost worshipped by their admirers. Inky's private opinion was that "they were two 'orrible old wimin;" but he kept that to himself, and endeavoured to look as interesting as possible.

"What is it you want, boy?" asked Miss Laura.

"Is it the page's place?" added Miss Fanny.

"Oh, no, mum—leastways, ladies," replied

Inky, presently; "I wouldn't be a buttons at no price; I—I—I'm a horphan."

Here Inky put his knuckles to his eyes and squeezed out a tear. The ladies were touched.

"Poor boy, so you are an orphan," said Miss Laura.

"I—am," returned Inky, keeping up the watering business, finding it succeeded. "The wust and most unfortinet of horphans, robbed of my gorging raiment, and made to live with a old cobbler up a dirty court."

"What have you been robbed of?" asked Miss Fanny.

"Gorging raiment, mum."

"He means gorgeous raiment," whispered Miss Laura; "defective education."

"Oh, I see," assented Miss Fanny; then aloud to Inky, "Do you go to school—your education appears to have been neglected?"

"I ain't been edicated at all," snivelled Inky, "but kep' at work from daylight to dark, laid on to by Stinger till I'm that sore you couldn't touch a part of me without makin' me holler, and nothin' to live on but pigs' feet.

"What a peculiar diet!" exclaimed the ladies together.

"He's wus than that, ladies: he's a old will'in," replied Inky, thinking that Work-it-out was alluded to. "He robbed me of my gorging raiment, marked with a coorynet, as showed I wasn't born among common folks, and then when he's made the most of me by workin' the skin orf my bones, he turns me into the street."

"Who is this wretched man?" asked Miss Laura.

"His name is Harris, ali-as hold Work-it-out," returned Inky, "and he lives in sich a place that no ladies could go to him to ax questions, and if they did he wouldn't answer 'em. He's incoorable, that's what he is; no man as wasn't incoorable could lick a horphan as he's licked me."

"Go outside for a moment," said Miss Laura, "while I consult Miss Fanny; when I want you again I'll ring this small hand-bell."

Inky made a profound bow and retired, secretly chuckling over an anticipated success.

"Now, what do you think of this boy?" asked Miss Laura.

"His story is an extraordinary one, Laura."

"True; but it is plain that he has been ill-used and neglected in every possible way; did you observe his tears as he told his pitiful story?"

"I did; he evidently suffered great anguish."

"Suppose we give him a trial?"

"Without making any inquiries, dear?"

"What inquiries could we make, especially of this dissolute old man, who appears to live in a terrible place?"

"Still, we ought to know something of this boy ere we venture to introduce him to our home."

"So we ought, dear, and yet my heart bleeds for him. He shall come in again."

Miss Laura touched the bell, and Inky, with a resumption of his modest looks, entered.

"Boy," she began, "we have heard your sorrowful story, and should like to hear it confirmed. Have you any friends who could speak for you?"

"I ain't got a friend in the world, mum."

"Would not any of the neighbours say a word in your behalf?"

"Our neighbours is a bad lot, allus a drinkin' and fightin' it out from morning till night."

"What terrible conduct, my poor boy; still we must have somebody to support your story. Is there no one who will do it?"

"No, mum," returned Inky, reflectively, "unless it's Sam Smarty."

"Who is Sam Smarty?"

"He's a friend o' mine," replied Inky, "as hev stood by me when all the world turned cold and 'oller. Sam's at a printer's, Kidem and Blowhard; he 'olds a 'igh persition there, a sort o' young foreman, like."

"Smarty is the name of Jenny's married sister," whispered Miss Fanny.

"So it is, dear; this Sam Smarty must be her husband."

"Or son."

"Yes, or son. How old is this friend of yours, my poor boy?"

"He's goin' on easy for fourteen," replied Inky.

"It is her son. Touch the bell, dear, we had better have Jenny up."

Jenny quickly responded, with her arms whitened with flour, having been interrupted in the process of bread-making.

"Jenny, you have a married sister named Smarty?"

"I have, Miss Laura."

"Has she a son named Sam?"

"Which she has, Miss Laura, and although it may go against my grain to speak ill of anybody, I must say he is my nevvy, and a precious himp to boot."

"Is he a bad boy," asked Miss Laura, horrified.

"No, Goodness forbid!" replied Jenny, "for he is as honest as the sun, and wouldn't have a hand in anything wrong to save his life; but his ways, though playful, is aggrawating, and when it comes to four long streamers of coloured paper 'tached to your

INKY SEEKS WORK-IT-OUT, AND FALLS AMONG THE PHILISTINES.

back hair, with which I walked all the blessed way from his mother's house to the Hangel, and shouldn't have found it out then but for a feller who p'inted 'em out and picked my pocket at the same time, I am obliged for to speak, which a himp he is, and nothing else."

"Playfulness is not a crime, Jenny," said Miss Laura ; "you say your nephew is honest ? "

" I'd trust him with bags o' gold and pecks of diamonds."

" I'm glad to hear it. There is a friend of his—an orphan—who has called to throw himself upon our kindness."

"Is you at a printer's ? " demanded Jenny, turning sharply upon Inky.

"No, I isn't—I never had no chance of being anything but old Work-it-out's slave and a horphan," replied the sweet youth.

" I am glad to hear it," said Jenny ; " for one printer's himp in this house would make it a unbearable place in one hour and five minutes."

"Well, what do you say to this boy, Jenny ? "

" I says, do as the kindness of your heart teaches you, ladies."

"But suppose we ask your nephew about him ? "

"Sam wouldn't tell a lie," replied Jenny ; " and if he says well of him, you might give him a trial."

"Very good, Jenny. Take the poor boy into the kitchen and give him something to eat, while I consult with Miss Fanny. We will give our decision in half-an-hour."

It occupied rather more than that time to come to the decision, but Inky, meanwhile, was engaged in the consumption of a huge cold meat pie, something very different to the fare he usually had in Sceptre Court. When the bell rang, once more he went up, and presented himself to the ladies with an eye beaming with satisfaction.

"My poor boy," said Miss Laura, " we have decided to keep you here if the inquiry we shall make prove satisfactory, and we shall consider it our duty to bring you up in a manner becoming our adopted child. You will be well clothed, fed, and cared for, and I trust you will prove worthy of the trouble we shall bestow."

For a moment Inky was touched, and a ear rolled from his eye, but the egotistical opinion of his high birth which he entertained came to the fore again, and he accepted the position offered but as a step towards the high position he considered his due.

" I'll do my best, mum," he said, with a sniff.

"That is all we ask," said Miss Laura ; " at first we thought you applied to fill the vacant post of page—our last left us in consequence of his unhappy tendency to take things which he could not call his own."

" I'm honest, mum," said Inky, proudly.

" I've no doubt of it, I only named it in passing. This unfortunate boy was in the habit of pawning the spoons to frequent a dramatical place of entertainment ; he was arrested with eight oranges, Miss Fanny's penknife, and one shilling and fourpence in his trousers pocket, and showed such repentance that we declined to prosecute. I regret that his narrow escape had no effect upon him, for he passes here daily, and, fixing his head between the garden railings, makes the most hideous faces. What was that he said yesterday, Fanny dear ? "

" He said he was going to bring an action for inflammation of character—meaning defamation, of course."

" He is a bad boy," said Miss Laura, wiping a tear from her eye, " and I am very sorry for him. What is your name, my poor boy ? "

" I never had no name," replied our friend, " 'cept Inky."

" That is a very strange name."

" 'Taint a name at all," rejoined Work-it-out's protégé, with an injured air, " and he dursn't have given it to anybody but a orphan."

" We must find another for you, my poor boy ; what do you say to Isaac—Isaac Pierson."

" I likes the Pierson," said Inky, " but the Isaac has a flavour of Jews about it."

" Ingram, then ? "

" Ingram, I should be proud of, mum."

" Then Ingram be it. From this moment you are Ingram Pierson."

Jenny was at once despatched to the city, per omnibus, where she sought her lively nephew, to make inquiries respecting Inky.

Sam gave him a concise character.

" He's a horphan, and he's 'onest," he said; " I can't say no more."

With this recommendation Jenny returned to her employers, and the last thing required to make Inky happy was done.

" I'm in for it now," he thought ; " no more of the aggrawating court ; won't old Work-it-out wonder where I've gone to ! And, my eye ! ain't those two ladies soft 'uns ! I'll come out strong as soon as I've settled a bit."

This is not proper gratitude, Inky ; it is anything but a fitting recognition of the kindness of those two ladies, and verily you shall have your reward.

Later in the day Miss Laura despatched him to certain shops in Islington to purchase clothing more suitable than his present attire for his new home.

"Choose good things," she said, "such as young gentlemen might wear, and bid the tradesmen send them home with a bill, and I or Miss Fanny will pay."

"How much shall I spend, mum," asked Inky.

"Purchase whatever is required," was the reply; "the tradesmen and yourself will be the best judges of what is necessary."

Delighted beyond description, Inky departed, and devoted some time to the purchase of apparel calculated to astonish the public eye. Parcel after parcel was delivered at his new home, paid for, and deposited in a little bedroom especially designed for him, and in the evening when he returned, he was desired to dress forthwith, and show himself to his new friends.

It took him some time to do this, for most of the apparel was new to him; but at last he came down and presented himself to the gaze of the astonished ladies.

A thin, weazen-faced boy, in a tall hat with extra brim, a red plush waistcoat, long-tailed coat, high collar, and violent checked trousers, with straps; stout Wellington boots, green neck-tie, and yellow gloves.

"Dear me!" exclaimed Miss Laura, "I'm afraid somebody ought to have gone with you; these clothes will never do."

CHAPTER X.

THE MARQUIS AND HIS SON.

IN the sanctity of an aristocratic mansion in Belgrave Square sat a worn old man. Time, which should have dealt so gently with one whose way of life was so smooth, had furrowed his cheeks, thinned the once luxuriant hair, and attenuated his frame.

Once upon a time, when George the Third was king, that same old man had been famous at Harrow as the best athlete of the school; and afterwards, at Oxford, his prowess in various sports left stories behind him which had become part of the legendary lore of the ancient University.

A few years later the town rang with his wild deeds; but he slowly settled down, and was yet in the full strength of manhood when his first and only child was born.

The joy of having a son and heir was dashed by the sorrow of the loss of a wife whom he had loved with the hearty, open love of a true man and gentleman.

From that time he devoted his life to his boy; and, doating on him, gratified every whim. The result was inevitable.

If a man sows tares, what can he expect but tares to spring from the ground? If disobedience be nourished, how can he expect reverence and love?

The Marquis did not rule his own house-hold; the real head of it was his infant boy.

As the child grew older, he became more and more unruly; flatterers and parasites, of which he had no stint, combined to ruin him; the love of his father was ignored and forgotten, and he went his way whithersoever he wished with a calm contempt for the teachings and adjurations of his father, who loved him but too well.

A wicked career at school, and a mad time at Oxford, completed what the father had so unwisely begun—the young heir of the great house of Beauforth stood branded before the nation as an idle, graceless, hairbrained fool, who scattered wealth and riches, while the sons of cotton-spinners climbed o'er his head towards the pinnacle of fame.

When his twenty-first birthday arrived, the noble Marquis was ashamed to hold the usual revels to celebrate the majority of his son; but he sent for him, and for the last time adjured him to abandon his evil courses.

"My son," said the Marquis, "I implore you to remember the race from which you spring. The blood of the Beauforths has been poured out freely in the great battles of our land. Seven of our noblest fell during the wars of the Red and White Roses. Three fell victims to mad Cromwell's dictatorship. Five have made our name glorious as wise and upright statesmen. It has remained for you to drag down our house to the level of prize-fighters, jockeys, and the harpies of a reckless life."

The son was proud and reckless, and he replied—

"Most noble father of mine, thanks to your judicious training, and the adulations of consistent friends, I have in the very spring of life grown old in sin. Winter has grown upon me while the blossoms are on the tree. You taunt me with having lowered our noble name—I will bring it yet lower—I despise it, hate the luxury with which I am surrounded, for it has brought upon me the greatest curse which can fall upon man—satiety! Luxuries which others sigh and struggle for, my soul loathes; every cup of enjoyment I have drained to the dregs. Wealth, station, name, has no charm for me, and I leave you this day to drag the name of which you are so proud through the mire of a degraded life. Perhaps I may return to you purified by the ordeal; if not, I will die, as thousands perish every day, surrounded by the poverty of an oppressed people."

Mad as the scheme was, the heir of Beauforth kept his word. He left the home of his fathers, and for ten long years was unheard of.

Imploring advertisements were inserted in the papers, and large rewards offered in vain; and now the old man, broken by sorrow, sits in his solitary greatness and broods over the sad awakening from his early dream.

Where is his boy, the hope and heir of Beauforth? For ten long years he has been absent, and has made no sign. Is he alive or dead? Will he return to claim the title of the old house, or has his end rivalled that of the great duke, who died in a bye-street by the Strand, gaunt, wretched, and forgotten by the friends who shared his debaucheries, and feasted daily at his table?

These and a thousand other thoughts ran in the mind of the Marquis, as he sat there day by day. He must have sunk under it but for the hardy constitution which had made him so famous in his early days.

One eve, when the summer sun was sinking behind the western point of the square, the door-bell rang, and voices were heard in the hall.

The Marquis had long ceased to be curious, nothing disturbed him now, even the reports which he read daily in the papers, that he was fast sinking, he could have smiled at them, had he not long ceased to smile.

The voices below died away, and the next sound which broke the stillness was a light tapping at the library door.

"Come in," said the Marquis, and a quietly-dressed man entered.

The Marquis naturally expected to see one of his domestics, and he arose from his chair with the air of one surprised.

"Who are you, sir?"

The stranger bowed his head upon his breast, and said, in a low tone—

"Father, don't you know me?"

A bitter cry followed. The pent-up agony of ten long years was in that sound, and the proud old man held him in his arms.

"Talbot, my son, returned at last!"

For a moment they were locked in each other's arms, and then the father drew his boy towards the window.

"Changed," he said, "but still my son."

"Back at last," answered the other. "I have returned from my pilgrimage among the poor and degraded. I have sought to drag, not our name, for that I have hidden, but the blood of the Beauforths to the lowest depths, and failed. I have come back to claim my own."

"You have returned, Talbot," said the old Marquis, "and that is enough for me."

"But I come not back alone," returned the son. "In my madness I sought to drag a noble name through the mire. I longed to degrade the reputation of centuries. Let me atone!—with me I have brought one of the people, a homeless, friendless, wretched lad; one of the great mass of humanity born in poverty, and reared upon the shores of crime. I have taken him ere he has launched

upon that dark and awful sea, as an atonement to make amends for my miserable past. Let me elevate him; let me rear him in my own sphere, and show the proud around us that true hearts and noble blood exists yond the western part of this great place

"Who and what is he, my son?"

"A poor wretched lad, who never the shelter of a roof until an accident him to the hospital ward. Trust me, he prove worthy of his care; are not the bri diamonds dug from the dull cold earth, a think you, there are no human gems among the pitiful poor?"

"As you will, Talbot; but remember, this experiment has been tried, and failed."

"Wait until you see the rough gem I have found—poverty, dirt, and misery could not hide his brightness."

CHAPTER XI.
INKY'S PROGRESS.

MISS PIERSON was undoubtedly justified when she remarked that somebody ought to have gone with Inky to purchase his wardrobe, for the wild purchases made by that youth were enough to chill the very blood of those quiet elderly ladies.

"What the tailor could have been thinking of," said Miss Fanny.

"If you please, mum," rejoined Inky, with tears in his eyes, "he said as they was just the thing for a young gent as was enterin' inter life."

"The whole dress is preposterous."

"I am werry sorry," murmured Inky, rubbing his knuckles into his eyes, "but I never did do nothin' right—whersomever I goes I'm pitched into. Old Work-it-out was allers handling Stinger as if he was compelled by hact of Parliament, and now when I tries to do right and give pleasure to them as is so werry kind to me, I——"

"There, there," interposed the tender-hearted ladies in a breath, "don't give way; we only wish to see you dressed in a becoming manner."

"I thought this was just the thing," murmured Inky, who had a loving tenderness for his purchases, and resolved to stick to them if possible.

"You can wear them for the present," said Miss Fanny, "and in a day or two we may be able to decide what's to be done."

"Thanky, mum."

"You can take air and exercise in the back garden," said Laura; "but for the present don't leave the premises."

"I won't, mum."

So Inky was dismissed to the back garden, a very large piece of ground for a town house, with plenty of trees and a pleasant lawn.

There for a time perambulated Inky, musing on the past, present, and future.

"I guess by this time old Work-it-out's in a state of mind," he chuckled ; "he'll find it werry difficult to get on without me. Who'll carry the jobs home ? who'll fetch his beer and lickers ? who'll dubbin the boots and heel-ball the uppers 'alf as good as I've done ? No—the old willin will be worried and serve him right, for poppin' my gorging raiment, and keepin' the secret of my nobble birth."

"Talk o' gorging raiment," he said, after a pause, "here's a rig out to hide in a back garden with no hye to observe it. It's like the meanness o' them old wimming to keep me shut up here. Why should I be shut up here ?" he added, after a look round ; "the wall ain't high, and I can nip over and back like a shot, that is if t'other side is any place at all."

He cast an anxious eye at the house, the windows were all blank, neither the ladies nor Jenny were watching his movements. What was to hinder him having a surreptitious stroll for half an hour or so ?

Choosing the most secluded part of the grounds, he stepped upon a garden roller and looked over. On the other side was a narrow way, but evidently public, for it had been raining that morning, and the soil was trodden into mire by many passing footsteps.

"'Tain't the height," thought Inky ; "for I could nip over a higher wall than this, like a narleyquin. I'll wentur. If they finds me out I can't help it. Them ladies is the right sort to be gammoned heasy—so here goes."

Burning with a desire to exhibit himself before an admiring public, Inky forgot all caution, and, climbing to the top of the wall, dropped quietly into the lane.

"I can't go far," he thought, "just round about the neighbourhood a bit, and back sharp."

The lane led into a quiet square—a place even quieter than the Liverpool Road. There was one specimen of humanity in the area, and that was a grocer's boy with a basket, who was consulting his list of addresses, and softly whistling the air of a negro melody ; as Inky passed with a mighty swagger and a clatter of his heels to give due effect to his progress, the boy looked up, and beholding the strange specimen of humanity before him, reeled into the roadway.

"Hallo !" he cried, "the Emperor of Rooshia is out airly this morning."

"What do you say ?" demanded Inky, frowning upon him like a bandit chief.

"Your majesty has taken to airly risin'," returned the other, bowing profoundly, "a chap o' your standin' didn't ought to come out afore dark. How's the hempress ?"

Inky frowned more, but maintained his ground.

"When I sees a common chap like you," he said, "I despises him."

"You does," rejoined the boy, setting down his basket.

"I does," replied Inky, keeping an eye upon the other's movements.

"In that case" returned the grocer's assis tant, "there's only one way of settling the dis pute. If your majesty will put that cheap tile o' yourn down on a doorstep, I shall be most happy to give your royal highness a whop ping."

"I don't fight such boys," said Inky, turn ing awfully pale, "it's agin' my nobble nature."

"Then stand a bottle of ginger beer," said the other, sternly.

"There's no shop about here," said Inky, faintly.

"Tuppence is the price," persisted the other, "and you have your choice—the money, the ginger beer, or fight."

Inky was not exactly a coward, but the grocer's boy looked muscular, and the gor geous raiment would be sure to suffer in the contest, so with a sigh he pulled out the cop pers and handed over.

"When next you meet a provision mer chant," said the boy, "you be civil ; and if you wants the public to respect yer, put on a milder wesket."

Having administered this piece of advice, he raised his basket, and, whistling cheerily, went his way.

This was not a very good beginning, this was not the homage he expected, and Inky, turning faint-hearted, quickly sneaked back, and climbing the wall, dropped into the grounds again.

He had not been missed, but it was fortu nate that he returned so soon, for in a few minutes Jenny came into the garden to tell him that luncheon was ready.

He partook of it in the kitchen, Jenny plumping the things upon the table in a style which showed the mind of that estimable female to be very much disturbed, and more than once she turned an evil eye on Inky, who was gorging himself like an alderman.

At length the storm burst, and she turned suddenly upon the hapless youth.

"You're a beauty, ain't you ?" she said.

"What have I done now ?" demanded Inky, getting ready for a copious cry.

"Oh, you little humbug," said Jenny, viciously, "put down that knife, you'll make yourself ill."

"That's like you all," returned Inky, "dis pisen' a poor boy as hasn't got no father nor mother."

"I should pity such if you had any," said

Jenny, "a mother to see you dressed like that must despise her offspring."

"What have I done to you?"

"Bah, you little imp," exclaimed Jenny, "get away from the table and go up-stairs."

"To the ladies?" asked Inky.

"No," cried Jenny, in so loud a tone that Inky sprang back a couple of paces, "to your own room, and keep out of sight of us all, for the Lord's sake."

"I mur'n't talk to you," said Inky, growing suddenly rebellious, "and I shan't; who are you to order a orphan about?"

"Get up-stairs."

"I shan't. I shall go into the garden."

"You will do nothing of the sort," said Jenny; "a pretty figure to show to our neighbours."

"I shall go where I like," returned Inky.

It was a bold defiance, a challenge thrown down to Jenny, and she took it up like a woman of spirit.

Seizing Inky by the collar, she gave him an open-handed salute on one side of the head, which sent him reeling to the dresser, and a second on the other side, which sent him towards the door. Half stunned and bewildered, Inky had sufficient sense to see that he had taken his pigs to the wrong market, and so he hastened up-stairs to his own room, and locked the door.

Now Jenny had not taken all this upon herself without knowing the ground she walked upon. The fact was, the two Miss Piersons had a short time before expressed an opinion in her presence that they had made a great mistake in their adoption of Inky.

"I am afraid," said Miss Fanny, "that he is hopelessly vulgar, and what is to be done with him, goodness knows."

"We must keep him, I suppose," said Miss Laura, tearfully; "but he must not remain in the house. He shall be sent to school. Oh, Jenny," she added, turning to her faithful servant, "how could you recommend such a boy?"

"Me, mum," gasped Jenny, "me, mum?"

"You went after his character, you know," insinuated Miss Laura; "but there, Jenny, we will not reproach you. I am afraid we have got a bad bargain, and must make the best of it."

Jenny could only answer with a few tears, and leaving the presence of her mistress, she called Inky in to luncheon, and fell upon him as aforesaid.

Throughout that day the ladies held a long consultation as to what was to be done with their burden, finally deciding upon sending for the Reverend Mr. Marall, the

shepherd of a large flock which gathered around him every Sunday at his chapel in Canonbury.

On the morrow that gentleman came, and listened to the ladies' plaint, reserving an opinion thereon until he had an interview with the offending youth. Inky came into his presence sulky and rebellious, having spent a night in concocting schemes for the downfall of all those who oppressed him, from Work-it-out to the two ladies who had taken charge of him.

They thought it prudent to leave the young wolf alone with the pastor, and, therefore, when Inky entered the room, as directed by Jenny, he found the reverend gentleman alone.

"Good morning, boy," said the reverend gentleman, putting on his smile for pupils.

"Wot's up now?" demanded Inky, with a ferocious glare.

"Now, boy, be mild and temperate," urged the reverend gentleman. "The first duty of a human being is to learn self-control—the next, to live frugally and to dress modestly."

Inky took up the last part of the address very readily. It was evidently meant to be an attack on the red waistcoat.

"Ain't there any more on yer?" he demanded; "if the clothes don't suit yer buy me some better. Ain't it bad enough to be knocked off yer chair in the middle o' wittles by a Jenny woman, and to be called a himp, without havin' arf the parish in to howl agin a weskit."

"Gently, gently, my boy."

"Why didn't you bring somebody with you?" demanded the goaded Inky. "Ain't you got a brother—or a uncle? anybody's good enough to pitch into a orphan as have been robbed of his birthright and his mess of potash."

"I must beg of you," implored the Reverend Mr. Marall, "to listen to me."

"I shan't," returned Inky; "acause I know wot's coming. You are going to call me a wulgar cove. I sees the words on your lips. Well! so I ham; and wot would you be if you'd done nothing all your life but dubbin' Barker Bailey's boots and heel-ball the shoes of the wilest of the wile. You wouldn't look so smilin' and heasy-like if you had a mortial struggle with old Work-it-out afore hevery meal, and was put down to a tough pig's foot every Sunday. I should like to see you do it."

"My boy, we must all suffer and be strong," urged the visitor; "pray listen to me."

"I ain't strong," replied Inky, "and I won't suffer. It's werry hard for a chap to have a whole string of people brought here to bully him acause he bought a red wesket instead of a blue 'un."

"My dear boy, I am not here to bully you."

"Then what are you here for?" asked Inky, "to give me anything?"

"Yes," said the reverend gentleman, "to give you advice."

"Pooh!" exclaimed Inky.

"To give you the helping hand you so much need," pursued the reverend gentleman. "I will not reproach you—I will simply advise. Think, my boy, of the ladies who have been so kind to you."

"I does think of them," murmured Inky, getting the water-works ready.

"Think how deeply they must be concerned for your welfare."

"I does! I does!"

"And how you ought to strive to please them,"

"I'd do anything, sir—anything, sir, as long as the wittles is good."

"We will for the present waive your gastronomical allusion," said the reverend gentleman, with a gentle smile, "and dip into the future. Would you like to go to school?"

"I would, sir."

"And you would do your best to honour and obey your teachers?"

"I'd go ahead like winking, sir. I can read printin' now, sir."

"Come, we are getting on," said the visitor, and pursuing the same strain, he presently reduced Inky to a very desirable, tractable condition.

Before leaving, the reverend gentleman had an interview with the ladies, to whom he reported his success, with the intimation that he thought time and his good offices would make a worthy lad of the boy.

"His notions are crude," he said amiably, "and he uses words which one may call the offsprings of a humble life, but he expresses gratitude, and gratitude covereth a multitude of blemishes."

"It does," fervently rejoined the ladies.

"The day after to-morrow," said the reverend gentleman, "I will bring with me a friend of mine, who has for many years accustomed himself to the culture of the youthful mind; in fact, he keeps a school, and to him I shall leave the settlement of terms."

"We would rather you did it," said Miss Fanny, "we know so little of the world and its ways."

"Then I will settle them for you," said the visitor, with a very handsome commission beaming in his eye; "and although my friend is not very cheap, he does his duty thoroughly.

"We have plenty of money," said Miss Laura.

"You are among the blessed," assented the reverend gentleman; "will you see my friend when he calls?"

"We would rather not," returned Miss Laura, "gentlemen in our house are so—so —dear me, I hardly know how to express it —but if you can effect the removal of our charge without troubling us, we shall feel much obliged. Fanny and I will have a ride to Hampstead that morning, and return about two to dinner."

The result of the reverend gentleman's visit was, that the ladies were at peace, and Jenny, whose conscience pricked her for having insulted a friendless boy, took more kindly to Inky, and, as atonement, offered up a seed-cake, with which that youth made himself extremely ill by the extravagant consumption thereof.

CHAPTER XII.

A BOY MISSING.

THE intending visit of the schoolmaster was kept a secret from Master Ingram Pierson, otherwise Inky Work-it-out, and accepting the peace-offering of Jenny, as a promise of a life of luxury in the future, he went to bed with a light heart.

The next morning he breakfasted as usual, and having obtained permission to wander in the garden until the dinner hour, he immediately scaled the wall, and took a walk round the neighbourhood, causing considerable sensation, but bringing forth no adventure worth relating.

Early in the following day the two ladies departed in an open cab, leaving Inky to wander in the garden until the two gentlemen who were to take him in charge arrived. Jenny had instructions to pack his box quickly, while he roamed in the garden.

"With linen only," said Miss Fanny; "the rest of his attire will be provided by Mr. Marall or his friend."

They were shown into the parlour, and then Jenny went into the garden in search of the "nobbly-born," from whence her voice arose, as she called him aloud by name.

In the meantime the ladies were enjoying the fresh air of Hampstead, and wondered how the donkey boys could be so cruel to their beasts of burden, and commenting on the various people who passed by—admiring the healthy children and blooming nursemaids, or shuddering as a ragged tramp went slouching on his way.

It was a glorious morning, the sun shone brightly o'er the rugged waste, lending a charm to every furze-capped knoll, guilding the quivering leaves upon the trees, and tinting the many villas around with hues worthy of a fairy-land.

They were not far from the great city,

with its recking courts and crowded streets, full of ever-varying life ; they were not far from places where children were born and grew up men without ever seeing a green field; but, for aught that they could see or hear, the closely packed leviathan city might have been far away in the great desert of Sahara.

Hampstead, the paradise of cockneys, is full of beauty, nature in rough ornament has been prodigal of her gifts, and on that bright morning, too early for the tea-drinkers and kiss-in-the-ring parties from the wilds of Whitechapel and Soho, the ladies enjoyed the rural perfection of the scene.

A little after one o'clock they ordered the carriage to turn back, and, punctual almost to the moment, it drew up before their gate.

They descended, paid the man his fare, with a trifle for any refreshment he might need, and sauntered up the neatly-kept gravel walk.

The door opened, and Jenny, with a face full of consternation, stood before them.

" Oh ! Miss Laura—oh ! Miss Fanny !"

" Oh, Jenny ! what *is* the matter ? "

" That boy, ladies—that miserable boy."

" Is he ill ? "

" Oh, no ! ladies—leastways, I don't know."

" What can be the matter with the boy, then ? "

" Wanished," replied Jenny, in a sort of scream, as she sank in half-fainting condition against the door.

" Vanished !" repeated the ladies.

" Yes," replied Jenny, " wanished. I went into the garden for him, and missed him. Mr. Marall and his friend is there now, and we can't make out about him. Oh ! the dreadful state of mind I've been in, ladies. 1 gave him a little slap the other morning ; and oh, if he should have runned away on account of that I should never forgive myself —never."

" Let me pass, Jenny," said Miss Laura ; " I will see Mr. Marall at once."

It was a fact—Inky had indeed vanished.

How, our readers will be at no loss to guess; but why he was so long away demands a little, or rather a great deal, of explanation.

He had seen the ladies depart, and having ascertained from Jenny that they would be away for several hours, he resolved upon an expedition which he had entertained in his mind from the first hour of his settling in Liverpool Road.

" I'll go down and stagger the old willin," he thought. " I'll bring him down on his knees, and he shall ax my pardon for every dose of Stinger I've had. If he don't, I'll shut up his house and make a blankrupt of him."

Possessed of this amiable determination,

Inky left the quiet thoroughfares, and crossing by the Angel, went down the Goswell Road.

His journey to the city was as terrible as a wandering in a strange land : as perilous as a pass in the Himalayas during the retreat from Cabul.   Hordes of youthful jokers followed in his wake ; boys of a naturally serious turn of mind, bent upon errands for their employers, turned aside from the paths of duty to smite or hoot him ; children of tender years, inspired by the strange attire of the youth, uttered their first jokes, and lent their shrill voices to the youthful clamour in his rear.   Cabbage stumps, herrings' heads, bones, and other materials, hitherto lying rotting in the road, became utilized as missiles to " shy " at Inky's beaver.   Gratuitous criticisms upon his general appearance poured down like a torrent.   The very dogs, many of them homeless and living principally on fog and smoke, became joyous, and wagging their tails, barked an appreciation of the general fun.

Fortunately for Inky, he kept to the main thoroughfares, where a downright outrageous attack upon him was impossible ; had he turned aside into one quiet street or square he would have been lost—from beaver to boots he must have been wrecked.

On the whole, he kept calm through the trying scene, but occasionally, when goaded by an attack bolder than the rest, he charged among his tormentors, and upset a few of the weakest ; but this only inspired the foe, and they clung to him as persisently as ever band of juveniles clung to their favourite hero— Punch.

The most trying part of the journey was in the Farringdon-road, just by Coldbath Fields Home of Retirement for those who have not acted strictly in accordance with the laws of their country.   There a bold butcher's boy made a successful raid upon Inky's hat.

A swift blow sent it spinning in the air, and with a wild shriek of triumph, the persecuting band, like players at football, made a grand rush upon it.

Again kind Fortune intervened. A benevolent gentleman caught it ere a foot could reach it, returned it to Inky, and bade him get home as fast as he could.

Inky tearfully promised to obey, and speedily reached the street leading to Smithfield.   Then the juveniles turned back and went homeward rejoicing, knowing that with its crowded thoroughfares and vigilant police their victim was comparatively safe.

At the bottom of Holborn Hill Inky took stock of himself in a looking-glass at a ham and beef shop, and to his joy, found that he had suffered very little material harm. A white patch of chalk on his shoulder, and stains from cabbage stumps on his back and hat represented the principal damage, and were, after a few minutes' polishing with a handkerchief, removed.

"Now for Work-it-out," he muttered; "I'll bring the old man down this morning—down right on his bended knees to beg my parding."

Straight up Farringdon Street went Inky, turning into Fleet Street, where in the thick crowd he received nothing more unpleasant than a glance of amusement from the busy throng. At the corner of Shoe Lane he ran against Sam Smarty.

Fain would he have avoided his old friend, for Sam wore his paper cap, and was stained with evidence of his labours, but Sam was not to be denied, and taking Inky by the collar, swung him into the comparative quietude of that narrow thoroughfare.

"Well," he said, "don't you know me?"

"In course I does," replied Inky, with a sickly smile; "'taint likely I could forget you, Sam."

"Then why didn't you hear me?" said Sam, "instead o' runnin' on as if you was deep in debt and I was a bailey."

"I hardly noticed you, Sam, I was in sich a hurry."

"I've knowed the time when you wasn't in sich a hurry," was Sam's comment; "but now you are here let's have a look at you—my eye, wot a rig out."

"'Tain't bad," said Inky, smiling complacently.

"You look as if you was got up for the holidays," rejoined Sam; "but I don't like it."

"Why not?"

"'Tain't the thing—it's too loud—you looks like a flash Jew as had tried to turn Christian, and couldn't do it no how. How long will you be about here?"

"Almost all day," replied Inky, trying to end the interview.

"Then if I was you," said Sam impressively, "I wouldn't."

"What's agin it?" asked Inky.

"Everything—I leaves you to guess what would be the hend o' my mates gettin' hold of yer—I'm out on a errand, but by-and-by we shall all be out for dinner; don't you meet them. Well I suppose you are getting on tidy?"

"Bootiful."

"Plenty to eat and drink?"

"More than I can get over."

"Lots o' tin?"

"As much as ever I likes to ax for."

"Then remember old friends," said Sam, who had been artfully paving his way, "and hand over a bob."

"I haven't axed yet," returned Inky, "but I will when I goes back, and then I'll remember you."

"You had better," said Sam.

"I will—'strue's I'm living."

"Then I'm satisfied," said Sam; "and now what are you goin' to do for Tom?"

"What Tom?"

"Little box-o'-lights Tom—him as we took to the gaff and broke his arm."

"We didn't do it, Sam."

"We took him to the Christial Hall," said Sam sternly, "and there he got his arm broken—it's our dooty to stand by him—what are you goin' to do for him?"

"He's such a wulgar boy," murmured Inky.

"What did you say?"

"He's wulgar."

"Ah! so you've made up your mind to cut him."

"What can I do?" urged Inky. "It was only this mornin' as the ladies ses to me, 'Don't you bring any of your frens here, or so much as mention 'em, for we don't want nothing to do with 'em.'"

"They said that, did they? What did my Aunt Jenny say?" asked Sam.

"She corrobolated it."

"Indeed!" said Sam, folding his arms and looking thoughtfully at the pavement; "so poor little Tom is to be left in the lurch, is he?"

"I can't help him," said Inky.

"Say you won't help him, that's the best way to put it," returned Sam. "I'm sorry to find you turn out brummagen, Inky; not for Tom's sake, for he don't want any more help than you do—if so much—for he's taken up by a real gent—but I'm sorry to find you the wrong sort o' chap."

"Tom taken up by a real gent!" exclaimed Inky, absorbed in the intelligence.

"Yes, the son of a Markis—which I seed and knew at once, not as I'm goin' to tell you who he was or what he was. Tom's gone away from the orspital to a fine house among the big'uns up West—but he warnt too proud to know old friends."

"Wasn't he?" exclaimed Inky.

"No, he wasn't," exclaimed Sam; "for this mornin' there comes a big chap in plush and calves down to my house, and leaves a note. I opens it, and finds where Tom was gone to; and the note says he would be glad to see me as soon as I've the time to spare. He ain't well enough to come out yet."

"Tom can't write."

"I know that," replied Sam, sternly; "but the son of a Markis can, can't he?—and the son of a Markis wrote to me—to me, Sam Smarty—and ses he'll be very glad to see me."

"I think I'll call upon 'em," said Inky

"You called once," rejoined Sam, "and I advise you not to call again."

"Called when?"

"T'other week, when you got such a buster afore you could denounce yourself—when a open-hander sent you to the pavement."

"At No. 294, Belgrave Square?"

"That's the place."

"Then is Tom the son of a Markis?"

"No, he ain't; he's only a poor boy as have found a friend—and found wot he ought to. Inky, I blushes for you."

"I don't care for that," returned Inky.

"I blushes for you, Inky, and I'm astonished to see you here, 'specially when there's a reward out for you."

"A reward for me!" gasped Inky, opening wide his eyes.

"Yes; you know Liddle, the printer—drunken old chap, with a hand machine, in Gunpowder Alley—prints labels and so on?"

"I know him."

"Old Work-it-out heeled his boots—not afore they wanted it—and Liddle knocked him off a hundred bills. They got it up atween them, and it's a literary heffort which have shook up a lot of people, I can tell you. Would you like to see it? I've got one in my pocket."

"I should," returned Inky, frowning darkly.

"Then here it is," said Sam, drawing the paper forth, and handing it over.

Inky by slow degrees made out the following precious production:—

LOST A BOY.

AGED ABOUT THIRTENE YARES—

TALL, THIN, BENT IN ONE *leg and nearly squints, red hair and swares hes nobble born—wen larst sene was doing a arand to buy a pair of topeces with a lether apon on and a genral sneekin look.*

WHOSUMEVER WILL BRING HIM
TO MR. ARRIS OF SCIPTER COURT

shall pic out his own pare of soles and hav them put on while waitin.

"Well I'm dashed!" exclaimed Inky.

"I should think you was," returned Sam; "and so would any one be. Old Work-it-out must be wery serus."

"And so am I," said Inky, "as he shall find to his corse."

CHAPTER XIII.

INKY REAPS HIS REWARD.

"WHAT will you do?" asked Sam.

"Call on him at once," returned Inky, "and demand a explication."

"I should," advised Sam, with a dark look in his eye; "you are sure to catch him at home."

"Will you come with me, Sam?"

"No, the reward ain't offered for *me*, and I don't want to airn it, for my boots are good enough for the present."

"Well, I'll be off," said Inky, turning away.

Sam said something about it being the best thing he could do, which did not reach Inky's ear, and so they parted—Sam to work, Inky to Sceptre Court, to see his old master, and bring him down on his bended knees.

A more unfortunate time Inky could not have selected, for it chanced that, half an hour before, an itinerant band of negro minstrels had made the court gay, and left a body of wolfish juveniles hungering and thirsting for more amusement.

Blind to all but his hatred for his old master, Inky turned into the court, and at first was hailed as another class of comic singer—but not for long. In spite of gaudy dress, and manful swagger, they knew him, and surrounded their old enemy with yells that would have shaken the nerves of the most stoical Indian chief.

"Keep orf!" screamed Inky, who at once saw his deadly peril, "or it will be the worse for you."

"Oh, we'll keep orf," said the leader—young Smivins—sarcastically. "Jiminy, what a hat! let's have a peep at the lining."

In a moment it was turned inside out, battered, broken, and thrown upon the top of Work-it-out's little shanty.

Inky wept, implored, and fought; but, ruthless as the barbarians of Tartary, the youthful denizens of the court despoiled him. The coat being energetically seized by the tails, split up the middle—the waiscoat torn open, the buttons flying hither and thither—his pockets rifled, and the greater part of his outer clothing torn to shreds. In addition, he received a very promising black eye from Master Smivins, who seemed to be the most inveterate of Inky's foes.

And all this was done in high noon, with the sun shining somewhere about the city, and a policeman watching a flight of pigeons around St. Bride's Church. If such things are done in the green, what would be done in the dry?

"You'll all repent it," sobbed Inky; "I'll have all of you prisoned, if it takes the 'ole force to do it."

"What do you come here for, then?" demanded young Smivins, scornfully; "ain't it enough for us to look poor and ragged, but you must come up the court dressed like a peacock."

"There's such a lot agin me," sobbed Inky.

"We on'y acts accordin' to our feelin's," groaned young Smivins; "we didn't ax you to come here—you might have stopped away a long while afore we come to you."

"Did I ever do you any harm?" sniffled Inky.

"Did you ever do us any good?" asked young Smivins; "it's well known that you and Work-it-out sp'iled our tempers, and made us wicious. Go where you might, grown-up people, let alone boys, couldn't help dropping on you. Why did you stick your nobble birth under our noses?"

"Acause I'm nobbly born."

"It makes me ill when I thinks on it—nobbly born," said Smivins, completely overcome with disgust. "I feel as if I hadn't arf done with you."

"Give him one on the other eye," suggested a small boy, whose toilet consisted of a pair of trousers and one brace, with a fragment of shirt, worn apparently more for ornament than use.

"What did you come here for?" again demanded young Smivins, ignoring the suggestion.

"I came to see old Work-it-out."

"Did you? well, you can't—he's gone."

"Gone," exclaimed Inky.

"Shut up last night, and gone this morning. A chap bought all the stock sudden—there warn't much of it—and the place is cleaned out."

This was a fib, Master Smivins; but no matter.

Inky was too bewildered to reply, he could only stare at the shutters of the closed establishment.

CHAPTER XIV.
DEEPER AND DEEPER STILL.

The fact was that Work-it-out was inside; he had witnessed the disturbance, and not knowing the cause of it, failing to recognize his *protégé*, and knowing, by experience, that windows were never safe during a court disturbance, he had deftly put up his shutters and hidden himself inside.

"As he's gone," continued young Smivins, "you'd better go too, and the next time you shows up here don't come dressed up to Lord Mayor pitch, or it'll be the worse for you. If you want that hat of yourn, you can climb the spout."

"I couldn't wear it agen," said Inky, as he backed towards the entrance of the court, "it's only fit for a wagabond lot like you."

It was well for him that he was near the main thoroughfare, or they would have certainly sent him forth in the attire of Ancient Britons—that is, as much as nature gives as a birth-

right, and no more; as it was, the tails of his coat were seized, and, being a portion of a ready-made article, gave way promptly at the waist, leaving Inky with a short blue jacket split in two.

Once in the busy street and he had time to reflect. Sam had told him that towards Tom he had shown a shabby spirit; that was bad enough, but what was it to shabby attire? How could he face his kind friends in that crushed and forlorn condition.

Another thought troubled him; how was he to get home?

If his journey cityward had been one of peril, what would be his return?

How could he traverse the wilds of Clerkenwell and Islington and hope for peace?

How hide the dreadful work of the Philistines of Sceptre Court?

Once he thought of consulting a policeman, but he had a dread of the official proper, engendered in old days, when a top spun in Bride Court was larceny, and a game of knuckle-down in Bride Lane a capital offence; so he went on his lone way, the clock striking one as he turned into Farringdon Street and faced the north.

"I'll go another way home," he thought "I'll cut across Smiffell, up through Bunhill Row, past the Heagle; I knows my way, and kinder chaps may live there."

Alas! for his selection; who, knowing the route he had chosen, would not pity him?

Better have thrust his head into a hornets' nest; better have gone to Kaffir Land, and defied the all-potent medicine-men; better have sought a company of Thugs, rope in hand, than have gone by "Smiffell" and Bunhill Row.

Just before Inky arrived in the latter-named thoroughfare, there had been an alarm of fire at a factory near Old Street Road, but which had happily proved to be false, or a very small affair; but when Inky appeared, an engine, surrounded by the hosts of children from the Chequers, was in waiting.

People who rush out to see a fire are invariably disappointed unless they have a respectable "flare up;" and this feeling burns bright in the youthful heart, especially the hearts of the youthful Chequers.

Disappointed, they longed for prey, and Inky came.

He saw it when too late, and would have fled, but the ranks gathered close behind, and he could only go forward.

The youngsters were not vicious, they did not beat or maim him, they committed no assault and battery; but they hailed his coming with a glad song of triumph, and organized themselves to follow him whithersoever he might go.

Had Inky been simply in rags, his appearance would have caused no sensation; for alas! rags alone were too common there; but his rags were bright and clean, palpably the work of a foeman's hand, and not the work of time.

Inky had sinned grievously—for he had shown a meanness of spirit towards Tom which had alienated Sam from him; but if he sinned in his pride, he now suffered the bitterest mortification in his fall.

He could bear contumely tolerably well when clad in "gorging raiment," but to be hunted in rags was more than he could bear, and, leaning against the shop window of a bird-fancier, he wept bitterly.

The children, untouched by the tears, gathered closer round, until the bird-fancier, feeling rather sympathetic for Inky and nervous about his windows, went to the rescue.

"What's the matter, my lad?" he asked, touching the boy upon the shoulder; "who's been droppin' on you?"

"A 'ole gang of 'em," returned Inky; "they've stripped me."

"You seem to have been roughly handled," said the bird-fancier; "come inside my shop and rest a bit. Now, you born devils, what are you standing there for?"

"Yah! old Mopping Jimmy," cried one of the urchins; and the rest lifted up their voices in shrill chorus.

"Oh! you is lovely critturs," muttered the man. "Come in, my lad, and rest. They'll clear off in a little while—you only wants a street horgan to do it. I knows 'em; vicious and spiteful—every boy on 'em."

So Inky entered into the house of this humble Samaritan, and for a time was at peace.

The bird-fancier, though stigmatised as Mopping Jimmy, had a right to a better title, viz., Mr. James Podley; but the Podley was seldom used. To all friends and acquaintance he was "Jim" or "Jimmy," and scurrilous foes added the "Mopping."

Perhaps Mr. Podley did drink—his business was of the nature which required a deal of washing down; the smell of the place, with its countless birds and rabbits stowed away in every possible hole and corner, was, as the saying goes, enough to "knock you down." The cleaning work, too, was endless, and the spare moments of Mr. Podley were generally spent in far-off fields in company with his nets and a sympathetic friend or two.

Podley lived alone, but none of his neighbours really knew whether he had ever entered into matrimony. When asked a question on the subject, as sometimes it would happen, he generally became absorbed in the state of the atmosphere, and made some remark upon the prospect of good or bad weather.

He lived alone—did Podley, attended to his business, cooked, made his bed, and did his washing, so some said, whenever any washing was required.

The upper part of the house was let to various people, about five families in all, for your people of Bunhill Row lie close, and a side entrance in a little court kept the lodgers apart from business.

The general character of Mopping Jimmy, or, to be more respectful, Mr. James Podley, was that of a quiet, harmless man, who went his own way, and left other people to do the same.

As soon as he got Inky within the shelter of his house, he closed the shop door, and bade him take a seat upon a rabbit-hutch, which Inky, heated and worn out, immediately did.

"My lad," said the bird-fancier, "they have dropped on you heavy indeed."

"I was pulled and tore about to such a pitch," rejoined Inky, "that I thought they'd hev had my werry feet off."

"We've got a precious lot about here," said Podley.

Inky hastened to undeceive him.

"I got this in Siptre Court," he said, "in Fleet Street."

"In Siptre Coort, Fleet Street?" repeated Podley; "wot was you doing there?"

Here Inky's pride stepped in, and prompted him to lie.

"I was wisiting a poor man," he replied; "'im who I wanted to help."

"'Twas werry kind of you," said Podley; "an' how did you come to know him in sich a place? 'Spectable people don't, as a rule, know much about the courts."

Again the demon pride urged Inky on, and he lied again.

"Some years ago," he said, "I was stole as a child from my nobble parient—this ole man found me and took me back, for which I've been grateful ever since."

"I likes them sentyments," said Podley, approvingly. "You lives with your father and mother, in course."

"No; I lives with two aunts," returned Inky.

"Oh!" exclaimed Podley, who seemed to be troubled with a lingering doubt; "and where may your aunts live?"

"Liverpool Road."

"I knows it—big houses and very quiet-like."

"That's the crib."

"Well now, my lad," said Podley, "what will you take to drink?"

Inky did not mind if it was not too strong.

"You can put water to it," replied Podley; "as for my part, I takes it neat."

And Podley, to illustrate his meaning

INKY PAYS A VISIT.

tossed off a wineglass of colourless liquor, uncommonly like gin. He then mixed a small quantity with water for Inky, took another glass neat, seated himself, took a third to keep it company, then put the bottle away.

"If you don't mind, I'll see you home," he said. "In your condishing your life isn't safe. For, trooly of all the guys I ever seed, you are the most wonderfullest. They hev dropped on you, to be sure."

He looked at Inky as if he expected a refusal, but Inky was glad of the escort, and thanked him. The doubts of the bird-fancier were completely settled, and he arose with alacrity to lead the way.

"As for the shop," he said, "I can lock the front door. When they finds it closed, they generally goes away. Everything is safe. There's nothing worth stealing here 'cept the rats, and I should like to see any man but myself take 'em out of the cages."

He closed and locked the outer door, glancing quickly up and down the street. An organ was playing a jig by the church, and a multitude of children dancing around it. The rest of the road was comparatively clear.

"All right," said Podley, "come on."

With the bird-fancier by his side, Inky had little to fear; boys might chaff and grown-up people stare, but none dare lay a hand upon him. In less than half-an-hour the Liverpool Road was reached, and Inky pointed out the roof which had sheltered him.

Now that the danger was over, Inky would fain have ridded himself of his friend, but the bird-fancier was not to be denied.

"I'll jest step up and see your aunts," he said. "They might ax me what I'd like to take, and I am as dry as a fish."

Inky had no resource but to endure his companionship, and side by side they went up the neatly-gravelled walk. In a moment four wondering faces flashed at the front window, and the next moment the door opened, revealing Jenny literally boiling over with rage.

"Oh, you little willain!" she cried; "is this your gratitude for taking you from the gutter? Get away, and never let us see your face no more."

CHAPTER XV.
TOM'S NEW HOME—A VISIT FROM SAM SMARTY.

TOM lay dozing and dreaming in one of the big houses in Belgrave Square.

To him, who had lived so short a time and known so much of the turmoil of life, there was a strange hush upon the place, a ghostly stillness which he feared was the offspring of a dream.

Many times before, when, after a day of misery, hunted hither and thither, starved and beaten, he had crept into a basket in Covent Garden, to lay down and dream of some far-off, still country, where the ground was green and the sky blue, with babbling waters running at his feet, such as he had never seen in his waking dreams, and when the dull morning came, with its early life and bustle, he used to awake and cry because he could not dream on for ever.

Sometimes he had spoken to his little brethren in wretchedness, and asked them if they knew of this beautiful land; but none were certain of its whereabouts, some suggesting that it was Epping or Hampstead, which, in their imagination, lay so far away. Once a little fellow, with a pale face and large blue eyes, thought it might be heaven; but when he was asked by Tom what he knew of heaven, he could only say it was "the place where rich people and the parsons went to when they died." He knew nothing more.

Now the strange feelings of those dreams had returned without the green fields, blue sky, and running waters—in their place were costly cushions, gorgeous furniture, and handsome pictures; but the feeling was the same, and Tom hugged his dream in his breast, and prayed, as such an outcast lad could pray, that he might never wake.

Anon there came to him his strange friend, Lord Holbrook, the heir of Beauforth—he whom the Marquis had called by the name of Talbot. He might now have passed with safety through a houseful of his late associates, and none could have known him. Cheerfulness had resumed its sway, and restored to the hereditary nobleman once more his healthy looks.

Bending over the sick boy, he asked him how he was.

"Am I really awake, sir?" asked Tom.

"You are," was the smiling reply; "you must bear up, my boy. You will get used to this scene by-and-by."

"But all is so very beautiful," murmured Tom, "it is like what I used to think heaven must be—so quiet—so nice."

"Heaven is better than this poor place," answered Lord Holbrook, "and I will show you better things on earth—woods and fields —rivers and waterfalls, and a thousand other beauties of this glorious world. I have written to your friend.

"Sam Smarty, sir?"

"Yes; and he shall pay you a visit as soon as you are able to come down. Dr. Warren says you will be able to walk in a few days."

"I think I shall, sir; but it is so nice to lie here and think."

"You must not become a dreamer," said his lordship with a smile, "the world is made of men of action; idlers and dreamers are curses in the land. I want to make you a busy man in the world, and you must be up and doing."

Tom promised to do his best, but his manhood seemed to be as far away as eternity; he was so very young, and Time, when accompanied by Misery, crawls but slowly on its way.

In a few days Tom verified the doctor's opinion, and left his bed; clothing was provided for him, and a kind, motherly dame, in a dress which rustled musically in Tom's ears, helped him with his toilet, and when it was done, kissed him, and called him "pretty boy."

Then he looked into the glass, and could scarcely believe this figure before him was the wretched little bundle of humanity he had so often seen in the shop windows—ragged, shivering, and forlorn.

"A change, isn't it?" asked the dame with a kind smile.

Tom looked up with tears in his eyes—his heart was too full to reply.

He went downstairs to the library described by the housekeeper—where he found Lord Holbrook and the Marquis—the latter he now saw for the first time. The grand old man, looking like the ruins of an ancient castle, impressed him much, and, in response to the kind greeting he received, could only mutter a few words in reply.

The Marquis then questioned him about his past life, how he lived, with whom he associated, and their mode of living. The replies he gave produced a favourable effect.

"An honest lad," he heard the Marquis whisper; "Talbot, I approve of your project. See what you can make of this rough diamond."

Lord Holbrook said he had no doubt of the result, and Tom was dismissed to tea in the housekeeper's room, and a heap of books full of the most wonderful pictures he had ever seen.

Two days more of dreamy life, and then Sam Smarty came, dressed in his best, and was asked in by the very footman who had lain Inky low.

It required no very keen observer to notice that this overpowering domestic and Sam had performed a passage of arms on their way from the street-door, and any one might have known that Sam had come off victorious.

In fact, Tummas had admitted him on protest, and questioned him very much as to the object of his coming, although he had strict orders to admit the boy when he arrived.

"Boy," said Tummas, when this examination was concluded, "foller me."

"Calves," returned Sam, "lead on, and move yerself as if yer were goin' to airn a trifle, for once in your life."

"Are you speaking to me?" demanded Tummas, looking scornfully over his shoulder.

"I ham," exclaimed Sam, emphatically; "and if you wastes my time keepin' me here, I'll get you the sack. I've got inflooence with the Markis, so don't be a ass."

Tummas paused and pondered. Should he leave the boy to wander at will and find the Marquis himself; should he give him an open-hander, as he had done unto Inky, or should he ignore him and get out of his way as soon as possible?

"As soon as you've refreshed yourself with a nap," said Sam, "perhaps you'll go forward, or would you like the other calves up from the kitchen to help yer?"

"Hold your tongue, boy," said Tummas, magnificently.

"I never did see so neglectful a chap," pursued Sam. "If you gits the sack here, don't apply to me for a charackter."

"Insolence!"

"It's no use your tryin' to get over me," answered Sam; "and now if you don't show up smart, I'll go outside agin, and ring the bell until the Markis opens the door hisself."

Tummas could not stand against this, for Sam looked as if he would keep his word, and, bottling his wrath until a more fitting opportunity, the flunkey ushered him into the presence of the nobleman, announcing him in a tone of unmistakable scorn.

"Thomas," said Lord Holbrook, quietly, as he was about to retire.

"Yes, my lord."

"It is needless for you to discriminate between my visitors. Don't repeat your conduct, if you please. You understand me—leave the room."

This was the unkindest cut of all—outraged by a vulgar boy, and reprimanded before him! It was infamous. Tummas wondered why the walls of Belgrave Square did not collapse and bury the inhabitants in ruins.

He told his tale to James, and met with much sympathy from his brother plush, who thought "the Beauforts were degenerating, and if he heard much more of the same sort of thing, it would be his dooty to leave."

"We are a pair, Tummas," he said, "and can get our money anywhere."

In this reflection Thomas sought consolation; but ever and anon the figure of the offending Sam rose before him, and he ground his teeth with rage.

Upstairs all went well with Sam. In the presence of the nobleman his demeanour changed. He became respectful without being servile ; and although the splendid room could not fail to have an effect upon him, he kept his head clear.

First he was questioned about his acquaintance with Tom, and what he knew of him. Sam did not know much, but what he did know he made the best of, and expressed his opinion in a very fervent manner that Tom was one of the "right sort."

"Now, about yourself," said Lord Holbrook ; "of course I do not intend to adopt you, as I have Tom—but still I shall be glad to do something for you. The spirit you showed when you called upon this friendless lad at the hospital was a good one."

"I liked him, sir," returned Sam, "and that's why I went ; besides, I took him to the Crystial Hall "—Lord Holbrook shuddered— "and having been, as I may say, the cause of the accident, I was bound to see him through it."

"Quite right, my lad."

"As for adoptin' me, genclmen," continued Sam, "I ain't fit for it. A nobby life is quite out of my line—all I wants is work, and plenty on it, and fair play—and that's all."

"Still, you would like to improve your position in life," put in the Marquis.

"You see, sir—that is, my Lord Markis," replied Sam, "I should like a good many things, but I ain't fit for 'em—there's so much difference between me and Tom—poor as he was—as there is 'twixt a common chimley pot and a bit o' china."

The Marquis looked at his son, and they both smiled. Sam inspected the hearth-rug, and wondered how it would look in the little parlour at home.

"But about your education, Sam ? " said Lord Holbrook, "you might improve that."

"I goes to an evening school," returned Sam, "not one of the best, gentlemen—but 'tain't bad at the price, a penny a week."

"Suppose you were removed for a time from work, and put to a good day school ? "

"Couldn't think of it, gentlemen," returned Sam, shaking his head, "my money is wanted at home."

"But we could help your friends."

"I'd rather not, sir," answered Sam, flushing a little ; "such of us as can work ought to work—but there's my little brother Jack, he's doin' nothing but make mud pies—and George—both on 'em is very little, and if you does anything for them in the way of edication, we should be werry glad, and I will do anything at even' school—but I must work, for my money's wanted, gentlemen, and that's a fact."

Sam was so overcome by his unexpected powers of oratory that as he rose when he concluded, he looked like some distinguished gladiator staring and gasping after some mighty effort. Lord Holbrook looked pleased —Sam's sturdy independence touched him deeply.

"Well—well—Sam," he said, "you shall have your way—I will make arrangements for you to receive evening tuition, and your little brothers shall be cared for. In the meantime, you can call and see your friend whenever you please, until he goes away to school."

"Couldn't he meet me somewhere half way ? " asked Sam.

"Why ? "

"Well, you see, sir," said Sam, "I'm a little out of place in this part of the town, I don't feel comfortable like, and should be more at home with Tom—more in place, sir."

"Again you shall have your way," said Lord Holbrook, smiling. "Tom, take your friend to the housekeeper's room, and let him have some refreshment."

Then to Sam's utter consternation both the noblemen shook hands with him—Sam having wiped his hand, although it was clean enough, upon the leg of his trousers previous to the ceremony. When it was over, he with Tom adjourned to the housekeeper's room.

There the motherly old lady greeted him cordially, and asked Sam what he would like to partake of.

"Anything you have in the 'ouse, mam," replied Sam, affably, "don't send out for me."

Even Tom laughed at this. To him the Beauforth mansion contained all the produce of the earth. The housekeeper turned aside to hide her merriment.

She rang the bell, and the much injured Tummas, little suspecting the presence of the enemy, promptly appeared. The presence he stood in prevented an outburst, but darkly gleamed his eye, and nervously clenched his hands.

"Some cold beef and a little pastry," said the housekeeper, "and a bottle of the mild sherry."

"Has it come to this ? " Was Tummas to feed the hand that struck him. Was he to feed the youth who heaped contumely on his plush ——? It appeared so—and Tummas relieved, retired to seek the beef, regretting in his heart that the laws of his country prevented him from seasoning it with a little arsenic, for the especial benefit of his urbane foe.

When the luncheon appeared, the housekeeper saw that everything was right, and left the boys to themselves. This was kind, for it gave the lads what they required, a little freedom, and an opportunity to open their hearts to each other.

"My eye," exclaimed Sam, "wot a bit of beef; you will have to eat cold beef all the week. Sunday joint I suppose?"

"I have not seen it before," replied Tom. "We have so many things to eat that I cannot count 'em—and such nice jellies and tarts!"

"Don't talk too much about tarts," rejoined Sam, "until I've done with the beef. I never did taste such fat—it's marrer."

"A great change for me, Sam," said Tom, with tears in his eyes—the tears of joy.

"It's a buster," assented Sam. "Inky's got a good start, but I'm afraid he won't make much of it. I never did eat such fat and lean. I saw Inky t'other day—such a toff; got a tile on like the monnement, and a check and a 'arf about his legs, called a pair of trousers. It riled me to see him. I begin to think Inky is a duffer."

"What makes you think so?"

"Never mind, Tom, wot it is—it needn't disturb you. And so you gets this beef every day?"

"Or something better, Sam."

"I'm glad I ain't a goin' to live like this reg'lar," said Sam, halting with a piece of beef on the top of his fork; "for if I did, I werily believe I should bust—I feels like a porpus now. There! I drops the beef, and if you'll pass that tart with the hegg all over the top, I'll spile the look of him in a twinklin'."

Whatever portion of time was denoted by Sam we are unable to say, but certain it is that in a very few moments the egg-covered crust had gone the way of all flesh, and was lost to the world for ever. Sam then topped up with a couple of custards, and declared his meal was over.

"I'm afraid of the wine," he said, looking askance at the decanter, "but I think I'll take a little with water. I say, Tom, does they feed the chaps in plush this way?"

"I think so," said Tom.

"Then that's wot makes 'em so cheeky," commented Sam, "flunkies and lord mayors I can't abear."

Having expressed this opinion, Sam settled himself in an easy chair, and displayed a tendency to go to sleep, but the return of the housekeeper soon routed the drowsy god, and having taken leave of her and Tom, making an appointment with the latter to meet him on Saturday evening in the park, he went away.

To the last he continued to goad Tummas to a pitch of frenzy. That much-injured servitor was desired to see him to the door, Sam, on the way, advising him to "eat less wittles and do more work, and if he did there was a prospect of his growin' into a fine man some day."

"And look here," continued Sam, standing on the mat, and making an enormous display with one cotton glove—all he possessed of that article of attire—"look here, Tummas, if ever you do get the swop, and get hard up, don't be afraid to write to me at my orfice in the city. I ain't wenomous, and generally forgives a chap if he shows up civil, so p'raps I may be able to do a little for you."

Tummas made no reply, but closing the door quickly, went downstairs breathing like one just awakened from a hideous dream, and Sam, whistling cheerily, went gaily homeward.

CHAPTER XVI.
INKY THE OUTCAST.

INKY had no reply for the unexpected denouncement which fell from Jenny's lips. It came upon him like a thunderbolt.

Podley was the first to speak, and he addressed himself to Jenny with the air of a friendly mediator.

"Don't be angry with him, mum, he's been dropped on hevy by the vicious brutes as never could recognize a charitable act. 'Tain't his fault, mum."

"And who may you be?" demanded Jenny, turning upon Podley.

"My name, mum, is Jim Podley."

"Go away, feller."

"If you'll allow me a word, mum——"

"If you don't go and take that wretched boy with you, I'll call for a policeman."

Then came forth from the parlour the Reverend Mr. Marall, with a gentle smile upon his face, he put Jenny aside, and addressed himself to Podley—

"My good friend," he said, "take that boy away."

"Wot for?" demanded Podley, rather bewildered to find himself with a ready-made boy of thirteen thrown on his hands.

"We don't want him here," rejoined the reverend gentleman gently; "his coming was evidently a mistake from the first. You had better take him away quietly."

"Well, I'm dashed," exclaimed Mr. Podley, "what am I to do with him?"

"Anything you please; he is not required here. Jenny, go to your mistresses—they are nervous and agitated. They require your attendance."

Jenny, with a fierce, vicious look at the poor lad Inky, retreated into the parlour. Then the reverend gentleman emerged from the house, and stood upon the doorstep, serene and smiling.

"Now, wot I want is a explanation," said Podley, doggedly. "Who is this chap as I've brought with me?"

"I don't know," answered the reverend gentleman, serenely.

"No more do I."

"Then why are you with him ?"

"I found him in Bunhill Row—followed by a mob o' vicious young 'uns—and I took him in and arst him what he'd hev to drink. Didn't I, young 'un ?"

"You did," said Inky. "I took it with water."

"A likely story, truly," said Mr. Marall ; but likely or not, we have nothing to do ith it. Take the boy away."

"I never seed sich a game as this," said Mr. Podley, appealing to the front garden. "Here am I—Jim Podley—bird-fancier of Bunhill Row, as comes all out of my way to bring a lost kid home, and finds the kid shoved on me. I'm not goin' to stand it."

"If you attempt to leave this place without him," said the reverend gentleman, "I shall give you in custody."

"For what ?"

"Attempted extortion. You came to intimidate these two friendless ladies, but, fortunately, they are not entirely without supporters. I have a friend of mine—a very strong man—inside ; we have also weapons —fire-arms, and any attempt you may make to enter the house will be resisted with force."

"Now do look here," pleaded Mr. Podley ; "I'm innercent of any game, I swears to you. I brought the boy home because I thought he'd lost his way. I'm a poor man, and I know if I get taken up it'll go hard agin me, but I can't take the chap away."

"You must."

"He ain't no use to me."

"He is not wanted here."

"Don't be hard upon a poor man," pleaded Podley ; "I'm willin' to do anything square, but as for taking this chap 'ome I couldn't do it. Can't I oblige you another way ? If ever you wanted a few rats or sparrers for a match, I'd let you have 'em cheap. I've got a brindled bull-pup at home, worth five pounds, who killed forty-seven rats t'other night in four minutes, which Broken Billy says is the quickest time on record for a dawg of his age and weight. You can have him for a pound down, and I'll bring him 'ome anywhere this side o' Highgate. I'll do anything, but don't saddle me with a guy like "

I give you two minutes," said Mr. all, looking at his watch. "If not gone that time, I charge you. There is an icer coming down the road."

"But of all the games," again urged Podley, appealing to the grass plat, "such an unkimmin turn out—What have yer got to say for yerself ?" he added, turning ferociously upon Inky.

"I don't know," replied Inky, with tears in his eyes, "'cept that I'm a unforternet orphan."

"But I never did," cried Podley, "it's like a dream of the 'Mabrian Nights.' A kid chucked on to a bird-fancier—a man who lives alone in Bunhill Row. I can't do anything with him."

"The officer is approaching," said Mr Marall in a warning voice.

"How can you drop on a poor man like this ?" asked Mr. Podley, reproachfully. "What have I done to you? Did I ever sell you a hen lark—or a painted canary ? If sech is my offence, come down to the shop at once and have your pick. Are yer fond o' rabbits ? I've got a lop as won a prize— take it if you like."

"Officer !" said Mr. Marall, raising his voice.

The official was serenely contemplating the upper windows of a house where a buxom girl was cleaning the windows ; he, however, condescended to bring his eyes to earth and to Mr. Marall.

"Come this way, officer !"

"Never mind ! never mind !" said Podley, hastily, "I'm off. Come on, you little beggar ; I never did see such a game, never ! Come on."

And, seizing Inky by the collar of his dilapidated jacket, he hurried him from the garden.

It may seem strange that Mr. Podley was so easily daunted, but our readers must remember that Mr. Podley lived upon that strange boundary line of society running between the honest and criminal. Many men with whom he daily mixed were men whose characters were too well known to the police, and had he been ever so honestly disposed, he, as a bird-fancier, could not altogether deny himself to these gentlemen.

The ways of bird-dealing are strange, and we cannot expect too much refinement from men who follow that pursuit ; received at its best, it is a poor way of living, and every coin gained is hardly earned.

When such men as these are taken before "his Worship," they, as a rule, find scanty mercy ; they belong to a "bad lot," and it is necessary to "put them down."

Podley knew this, and although the charge of attempted extortion was utterly unfounded, he knew that appearances and the authorities would be against him, and he prudently beat a retreat.

Availing himself of the first turning, he got out of sight of the house, and then he turned upon Inky rather roughly, but not brutally.

"Here's a mess you've got me into," he said.

"I can't help it," returned Inky, industriously wiping his eyes with the corner of his jacket.

"What am I to do with you ?"

"I don't know."

"If I turn you loose, where will you go to ?"

"I ain't got nowhere to go to."

"Where do you come from ?—tell me the truth."

When Inky, with many sobs and tears, told his story from his earliest day with Work-it-out down to the time he met Podley in Bunhill Row.

"You told me lies this morning," said the bird-fancier, "and lies is bad ; don't tell no more. If you promise to be a good lad, I think I can do summat for you—can you clean birdcages ?"

"I—I—think so."

"Anyhow, you can try ; what you don't know I'll teach you—there's plenty for you to do, and in time, if you behave well, I may leave you my business. I've got neither wife nor chick in the world." Here the bird-fancier's voice became troubled with emotion. "And it don't matter much who has the shop when I'm gone—so we'll go home together, my lad."

And this is how Inky became assistant to the bird-fancier of Bunhill Row. There for the present we must leave him, and turn to our other friends.

On Saturday night Sam met his friend Tom in the park. Sam had smartened himself up wonderfully, and wore a small flower in his buttonhole to do honour to the occasion.

They took a seat upon the grass by the spring, and at once dived into their prospects. Tom told him that he was going to school, but not far away—only to Blackheath, where Sam was to come over and see him occasionally.

"I shall be very glad to see you," Tom said.

"And so shall I to see you," Sam answered ; "but I'm afraid I shan't suit some of the fellers you'll be with—I'm not the sort of stuff to take a polish—I *can't* do it ; now you begin to show the grindstone already—sich is hooman natur, as I read in a chap's writing the other day—some on us is di'monds and t'others millstones."

"I'm sure you're a di'mond, Sam," said Tom.

"I'm glad you think so," rejoined Sam : "but lor, what does it matter ? Have you heard of Inky ?"

"No, not a word."

"He's put his foot in it at Islington. He took a big man home with him who wanted to fight 'em all round, and both the ladies is in bed—sich is Aunt Jenny's story. She came to our house yesterday, and let me have

it for 'arf an hour—all about bad companions and evil ways, until I answered her with the language of the poets. Then she went off in a huff, and said she'd never come nigh us again. Mother cried a bit, but we shall see her next Sunday."

"It was very bad of Inky."

"I don't think he was so bad as she made out—anyhow, they've turned him orf ; I went round to Work-it-out's to see if he was there, but it seems that the old man is gone. He shut up his shop on the morning Inky went to the court, and it ain't been opened since. The coort would have it that he'd hung himself, and the door was broken open, but they found nothin' 'cept his tools and a chalk writing on the wall to say he'd cut the trade for ever. Here's a heap o' changes in a week or two."

"What has become of Inky ?"

"Who's to say ? I only hopes he won't go to the bad. He's a bit of a fool, but I know he ain't vicious yet, or I shouldn't hev had anything to do with him."

"If ever he is found, Sam, I should like to know. We must be a friend to him."

Sam said nothing, but he whistled softly, and threw a stone into the well by the spring. He was thinking of his last interview with Inky in Shoe Lane.

"After all," continued Tom, "he was the cause of my being taken away from the streets."

"There's some difference in you, Tom," said Sam, looking at his companion's dress.

"Such a poor boy as I was."

"Poor isn't the word—you were worse than poor. *I'm* poor—so is all my friends—we live in a poor house, in a poor alley—but we arn't ragged, starved, friendless, and 'omeless— and that's what you was if ever I seed anything of the sort."

"So I was, Sam."

"But there, Tom, old chap, I'll forget it. You are different now—you've got what you want, and a trifle over, and so have I. The little 'uns are goin' to school by day, and I'm to be taught by a first-rate chap in the evening. It's a fine thing for us—and when we are both growed up——"

"I'll never forget you, Sam."

"I know you won't," answered Sam, quietly ; "but at the same time I shan't expect to be allers with you—our ways must be different. If the Markis sticks to you—which he will, I'm sure—you'll be a flowery gent of the land ; but I shall be a master printer, which is all I ever hope to be, or want to be. But I say, Tom," he added, suddenly changing his air, "do you know Todd's printing place ?"

"No," replied Tom.

"It's up Wine Office Court—a big building. They prints the Daily Mellowchaff there. Well, we—that is, Kidem's lot, hev quarrelled with them, and we were to have fowt it out to-day, but I put it orf till Monday, as I wanted to keep the 'pintment with you. Will you come down and see it?"

"I'm afraid I can't," replied Tom, laughing.

"They meets in Gough Square," continued Sam, warming with his theme; "we musters in Shoe Lane, and don't I pity 'em when we comes together. We won't leave 'em much to brag about."

"Why do you fight?" asked Tom, simply.

"It's the constitootion of man," answered Sam. "I read it so t'other day in a big chap's book—the werry fust words in the werry fust page—so we are going to fight."

"Only with fists, of course."

"With fists and dabs of ink—but no sticks or stones. We know ourselves too well for that—we've too much respect for our country. We don't come any of your foreigners' hankey pankies—not we. Our motter is, a big field, a fair fight, and no faviour."

CHAPTER XVII.
PODLEY'S HOME.

THE establishment of Mr. James Podley, of Bunhill Row, was not overburdened with luxuries. His living and sleeping rooms were one; and his bed, lightly screened from any visitor, stood in the corner, with the foot towards the fire-place—a wooden, gaunt affair, with less linen upon it than most people would desire.

Around the rooms were cages and rabbit-hutches, but not so closely packed as those in the shop, for Podley had none but great favourites in his private apartment, the best vocalists and the most precious "lops"—prize winners at the various exhibitions, local and otherwise.

Until Inky came the remaining portion of the furniture of the room consisted of a table and a chair, but as the presence of a second party demanded something else for him to sit upon, Podley purchased a high stool—such as we see in lawyers' offices—for Inky's use, having some vague idea that all boys and children required a higher seat than grown-up mortals; and upon this Inky perched during meals, and looked down upon his master like one truly "nobbly born."

"I don't know where you are to sleep," said Podley, in the course of their first day together. "The cellar's too damp—I tried it once for the rabbits, and it gave 'em the cramps; besides, the sewer shows up a bit at times—and the rats might call."

"Anywhere will do for me," said Inky, remarkably humble.

"Well, it won't do to be too particular," replied the bird-fancier. "What do you say to the shelf at the top of the shop?"

"It's narrer," answered Inky, doubtfully, "and I might roll off."

"So you might. Then you must sleep on the top of the box with the game-cocks there. I'll run round to Simmons' and see if I can pick up a second-hand blanket for you cheap. If anybody comes, say I'll be back in a brace of shakes."

Inky promised to obey, but had no need to fulfil his errand, for Podley was back before a customer turned up, with a couple of stout blankets and a counterpane on his arm.

These, with a bundle of odd stuff for a pillow, and the top of the game-cocks' box for a base, made Inky's bed.

The next thing was apparel. Inky could not go about in his rags, so Podley—who appeared to have a little money about him—invested a few shillings in a second-hand corduroy suit, which fitted Inky like his skin, and gave him the appearance of a weazened polony.

Then all his requirements being supplied, the "nobbly born" settled down to his new life.

He found his master easy-going, especially when he had resorted to the cupboard, where he kept a bottle and a glass. At times during the day, and sometimes towards evening, Podley would grow maudlin, and confide the secrets of his trade to the watchful Inky.

"Painted sparrows," he told him one night, "is well nigh bust. People won't have 'em now. Lor! I've knowed the time when I've gone out with forty green sparrers, and called 'em love birds, and they've gone orf like Turks, among the city gents—but it was all found out. Birds will moult, do what you may—and lay the paint on as thick as yer like, the new feathers won't come up green."

"You can't do much to the rabbits," he would say; "for with them it is difficult to derlood, but I've made some skewrious lops in my time. Ah! my boy, this is a wonderful bisness."

Inky thought so too, but he rather liked it. It was better than laying on dubbin and heel-balling boots.

One night Podley took rather more than usual, owing probably to his having been out the greater part of the day in the rain, and was sitting in a meditative manner before the fire, when he suddenly turned to Inky, and said—

"So you is an orphan?"

"I ham," rejoined Inkey, "an unfortunit orphan."

"And never knowed your father?"

"No."

"Nor mother?"

"No."

"It's werry 'ard," said Podley, wiping a tear from his eye; "werry 'ard, and I feels for you."

"Was you a orphan?" asked Inky, after a pause.

"No," replied Podley. "My mother was nurse at St. Pancras Workhouse, and died in the performance of her dooty. My father —well, it don't matter about him."

"You knowed him then?" said Inky.

"I did," replied Podley, turning a leaden eye upon him, "and let people say what they will of him—he were a good man, and troo. They comed too sudden on him afore the meltin' pot was ready, and bein' a 'ole sack full of plate, the judge took a serus view on it, and gave him a lifer."

"Oh!" exclaimed Inky.

"Yes, a lifer!" rejoined Podley; "that was just as I got married—but why talk of that?—she's gone; my Mary Ann lef me for to roam."

"Where?" asked Inky.

"How should I know?" returned Podley. "She wrnt one Sunday morning when I was down at a sparrer match at Hornsey Wood. When I comed back she and my two prize lops were gone."

"Did she run away from here?"

"No, my lad, I lived in 'Ounsditch then— and arter all it was for the best; for when it tomes to four or five hand-over-head fights among the cages every day, it ain't good for the business, and you can't call it a life o' peace and happiness. But she were a woman —a lovely woman—twelve stun two the larse time she were weighed at Greenidge Fair."

Inky tried to look sympathetic, but in his heart he gloated, for here was Podley letting out his family secrets—secrets which might be of great service to Inky at some future time.

"But she's gone," continued Podley, after several minutes' silence, "and the bottle's empty—so you just get to bed, will you, and wake me when the cock crows, for I've got a meetin' on at Wood Green early in the morning."

Although Mr. Podley was very communicative in his drinking hours, he was a silent, close man in his sober moments, and he seldom said anything to Inky except what referred to the cleaning of the cages and the proper care of his live stock.

Inky often wondered whether his master was aware how glib his tongue was during his evening revels; but neither the face nor tongue of Mr. Podley furnished anything in the form of a reply, and Inky was too wise or cunning to open a subject which might create a breach between them.

This subject occupied a deal of Inky's waking thoughts, but there was another

which occupied a great deal more. He could not shake off the memory of his transient greatness.

Strange to say, he clung to the memory of the "gorging raiment" wherewith he had clothed himself; he mourned over its loss, and the brightest hope lying within his breast was that a day might come when he should be able to renew it in all its glory.

The trousers he had by him, also the front of the waistcoat, and these he treasured dearly, often spending the hours when Podley was absent in making ineffectual efforts to restore these articles of attire.

At length he made friends with a jobbing tailor, who lived in a court hard by, and giving a few coppers, the gift of Podley, down, and a promise to pay the rest as soon as possible, the two articles of raiment were decently mended and patched.

Still he was not happy; the hat and coat —he clung to them more than all the rest— were wanting. With a vague notion that the tailor might make them, Inky confided his wants to him, but the tailor shook his head.

"My lad," he said, "there's cloth to buy, and money must be found for it—and hats cost a heap o' coin; but if you wants to go anywhere for a Sunday, I don't know as I couldn't lend you one—I don't often go out myself."

Inky was overjoyed. He inspected the hat and coat, fortunately very much in the style of his old things, and begged the favour of a loan of them for next Sunday.

"I've got some fashernable friends up West," he said, "although people mayn't think it; I ain't so wulgar born as some may guess."

"I suppose you've got a futman in your family," said the tailor with a grunt.

"Nothing of that pattern," returned Inky contemptuously; "I'm a goin' to see the lord 'igh Markiss of Booforth—cousin to the Queen."

"Well, I'm dashed!" exclaimed the old tailor, pushing his spectacles up to his forehead, "are you gone clean daft, or what?"

"You lend me the things," said Inky, "and I'll show you if wot I say ain't true; send somebody with me, and see if I've told a fib."

"It's a skewrious tale," said the old man; "anyhow, you can have the togs."

"It's a good thought," mused Inky, as he walked homewards. "Yes! I'll go and see little Tom—and the Markis—if he's got 'arf a eye, he'll see that I'm out of my spear, and p'raps he'll adop' me. Won't I come out then?"

The consequence of this commendable determination was that on the Sunday morning following Lord Holbrook and Tom, sitting together, were informed by the ever-injured Tummas that a "boy was a waitin' at the door as wished to see his lordship," adding, that "he believed he was a friend of Master Talbot's"—the name by which Tom went, by desire of the Marquis.

Thinking it was Sam Smarty, his lordship desired him to be admitted at once; and Tummas, going below, indignantly desired Inky to walk up.

"I shall cut this service," said Tummas, in great disgust, when he reached the kitchen, "the werry hair is perfumed with wulgarity. Let us give notice to-morrow, Jeames."

Jeames, however, was more prudent; he looked up from his paper and said, "No life was a bed o' roses, and, after all, the service of the Markis was heasy, and they could put up with a snob or two."

An opinion in which Tummas was, after a little discussion, compelled to coincide.

When Inky entered the library he took off his hat and made a profound bow, worthy of the leader of a nigger troupe, then he held out his hand to Tom and afterwards to Lord Holbrook, who apparently did not see it.

"I hope I don't intrude," said Inky, when this ceremony was completed; "you bein' an old friend like, I thought I'd look in upon you in passing."

Tom smiled faintly—he was sorry to see Inky in such preposterous attire, and more sorry to observe his vulgar affectation of aristocratic ease.

Inky, on his part, was much impressed by all he saw around him; but he had schooled his mind as he came along to take things as they came, and be astonished at nothing. Finding that neither Tom nor Lord Holbrook gave any verbal reply to his questions, he proceeded—

"I should think you was werry comforble here, Tom—somethin' different to the streets and market-baskets, ain't it? Well, arter all, I'm glad I stood your friend, for I rescooed you from a life of poverty."

"Did you?" inquired his lordship.

"Why," returned Inky, with an agreeable smile, "it's all through me as you two was brought together. If he hadn't met me, he wouldn't hev known Sam, and he wouldn't hev gone to the Christiall Hall, which brought it all about, you know."

This was a most unfortunate speech, but Inky was not overburdened with tact, and thinking he had created a favourable impression, went on—

"I've thought a deal o' Tom, my lord 'igh Markis, and bein' nobbly born, stolen in my hinfancy by a wagrant cobbler, who kep' me all my life on strap 'ile and pigs' feet, which his name is Work-it-out, the old willin', he knows that my linen was marked with a corynet, and if he hadn't pawned it, I should have had it 'ere now to show you, my lord 'igh Markis, that I ought to be in a different spear, and one day I shall have my rights and my mess of potash."

"Was this an intimate friend of yours?" asked Lord Holbrook, aside to Tom.

"He introduced me to Sam Smarty," was all Tom could say.

"You know nothing more of him?"

"Nothing more."

"Did he visit you at the hospital?"

"No, sir."

"Did you invite him here?"

"No, sir."

Lord Holbrook arose and rang the bell, and Tummas came.

"Thomas, show this young gentleman out."

Inky arose. He saw in a moment that his mission had failed, and the ever-ready tears started into his eyes.

"Tom," he said, "will you desart me?"

"For the slight part you played in forwarding the interests of my friend here," said Lord Holbrook, "accept this."

He drew from his pocket a five-pound note, and passed it to the overwhelmed Inky.

"But, remember this," he added, "this settles the debt once and for all—you will come here no more. Thomas, the door."

Servants always take their cue from the master; and the consequence was that Inky was hustled out of the front door, and down the steps, with all speed; but he cared little for that, he was the possessor of five pounds —a fabulous sum, a mine of inexhaustible wealth to him.

Clutching the frail piece of paper firmly in his hand, he sped homeward, and reached the bird-fancier's shop just as its proprietor came in to tea.

"Hallo!" exclaimed Podley, "wot's this —more o' them precious toggery? Come, now, where did you get it from?"

An explanation was necessary, and Inky gave it, reserving to himself the fact of having received a five-pound note.

"So you've been to see the nobs," said Mr. Podley; "and what sort o' reception did they give you, and when are you to go again?"

Inky was obliged to confess that he had been desired to return no more.

"They're goin' out of town," he explained, "and when they come back they're goin' to remove, but they'll be sure to let me know where they are."

"My lad," said Podley, sternly, "a word in your ear. Pride is the cuss of nations, and it's the cuss of man. You draw off them togs and put them away for ever. These friends of yours, whoever they may be—your story, to say the best on it, is wague—these friends o' yours don't want you no more. It's pride as took you to see 'em. Let pride, if you insists on stickin' to it, keep you away."

"I think I ought to look 'em up some-times," murmured Inky.

"That's not what Posh Rottle thought—did you know Posh Rottle?"

"No, I didn't."

"Well, Posh Rottle was a low-bred 'un, a chap as did a bit o' horse chauntin' at Barnet Fair, and t'other things too noomerous to mentin', all on 'em ekvally shady; but Posh had a sister, a 'andsome girl, as sold flowers about the Bank, and there she met with Bruiser Bang, him as licked the Knobby Cob, and carried orf the light-weight belt.

"Bruiser Bang fell in love with the girl, married her, and took the Green Goat, at the back of the Haymarket, where he did a roarin' trade among the gents, who paid 'ansome sums to be knocked silly twice a week by the Bruiser and his men.

"Posh Rottle growed uncommon proud of this connection, and he was allus a-braggin' of his brother-in-law, Bruiser Bang, a-chuckin' him inter our teeth, as we may say, until it got a noosance, for we felt if he was too good for us why didn't he put up with the Bruiser, and stick there.

"Now, Inky, I knowed very well that the Bruiser didn't want to see him, and I axes him, sarcastic like, why he didn't live with his brother-in-law, or at least go and live with him for a month. Posh Rottle said he could if he liked; I said he couldn't; and then Posh gets his bile up, and says he was allus welcome at the Green Goat, and any of his friends, and if we choosed to go up one Saturday night we should be treated like princes.

"We nails him on his word; and bein' Saturday night, we proposes to go up at once. Posh drawed back, but we wouldn't have it, and we, Downy Daffer, Grey Thorn, and Bottle Jack, the knife-grinder, sticks to him, orjanises ourselves into a sort of body-guard, and makes straight away for the Green Goat.

"We got there about nine o'clock. The bar was full o' swells, some on 'em real, t'others draper chaps, tryin' to look the thing 'andsome. We has to elber our way through 'em—then Posh and his brother-in-law stands face to face.

"'Hallo, Bruiser,' ses Posh, holding out his hand, 'how goes it, my 'arty?'"

"Bruiser looks at him steady as an hawk about to pounch on a sparrer.

"'Who are you?' he ses

"'Posh Rottle,' ses the other, smilin' like a man sittin' on nettles.

"'Oh, indeed,' ses the Bruiser; 'you wait a minnit, my lad, and I'll attend to you.'

"In a few minutes all the nobs, real and flash, goes up-stairs, for they'd got a sparrin' match on that night, and we was left alone with the Bruiser. Then he comes round the counter.

"'These friends is yours?' he axes, pointing to us.

"We touches our hats perlitely, for, you see, the Bruiser was at the top of the tree. Then he opens the door, pauses, turns to Posh Rottle, who turns orful pale.

"'Look here,' he ses, catching hold on him by the collar, 'I married your sister, but I didn't marry her family. I don't want no skunks here—get out.'

"Lord, what a buster he did give him, to be sure, right in the wesket, which sent Posh clean across the street agin a whelk barrer—which he knocked over as neat as wax. When we seed this, we all follered in a hurry, jist in time to see Posh in a mortial fight with the whelk chap, which ended in both bein' locked up, and fined ten bob for being drunk and disorderly.

"Posh couldn't pay, so he does fourteen days at Coldbath Fields; and so I ses to you, beware 'o pride—it is a cuss—it was a cuss to Posh, and will be a cuss to you—so take orf them things, and let me never see them no more."

Whether Inky really took this touching story to heart, time alone will show; but certain it is, that from that time Inky's "gorgeous raiment" appeared no more at the bird-fancier's shop. What became of the five-pound note will be subject matter for a future chapter.

CHAPTER XVIII.

TOM'S PROGRESS—SAM SMARTY IN TROUBLE.

A FEW days after Sam's visit to Belgrave Square, Tom went away to school. It is not our intention to enter deeply into his life there, as our story will eventually deal with more important events of his life; we shall, therefore, limit our description of this portion of his career so far as is compatible with the sequence of our story.

Laurel House, Blackheath, contained about sixty pupils, sons of the upper middle classes, mainly under the guidance of a Mr. Morley, who was really a gentleman, and an excellent instructor of the young.

When Tom first appeared he naturally expected to be the victim of a deal of curiosity, especially as he could neither read nor write, and during the first few days he was pestered with all sorts of questions respecting his friends, where he had lived, why he was so ignorant, and so forth.

He answered truly—that he knew nothing of his friends, had never known them ; and that Lord Holbrook had taken him under his care—anything more he firmly refused to tell.

The fact of his noble guardianship stood him in good stead, and after a few days the pupils, old and young, let him alone, and he soon began to find very jolly associates among them.

Anxious to learn, and with good teachers, he progressed rapidly, picking up a tone of voice and manners with equal readiness from those around him.

It was a glorious time for the youngster, the world was all sunlight to him, sleeping or waking he was at rest, and the old life of misery and want was driven far back into the dim shades of the past.

Street life had made him active ; his limbs, though slender, were supple, and he soon became renowned among the boys for his prowess in climbing, running, and leaping.

One of the pupils, Harry Stanley, a lad of sixteen, became his especial friend and supporter, giving him good advice, helping him with his lessons, and initiating him into the mysteries of cricket and foot-ball.

All these things combined to create a marvellous change in Tom ; happiness gave him additional health, exercises lent him strength, and among the sixty pupils of Laurel House, not one more light-hearted than he could be found.

During all this, he did not forget Sam Smarty—the two boys, as soon as Tom could write a little, corresponded. Sam's letters were crude and quaint, but they were always directed in a dashing, flowing hand, the work of the evening tutor provided for him by Lord Holbrook—for Sam had too much sense to do aught that might bring disgrace or ridicule upon his friend.

The first letter Tom received related to the contest between the two printing establishments, which seemed to have been of a very obstinate nature. As these letters followed each other, a marked improvement was visible in both writing and spelling. We will give a few :—

No. 1.

"Cradle Coort, shoo lane.

"dear Tom,

"the First fite came of yesterday a drawed Battel owin' to the perlice—one of our men capterd And well whopped by the blu tyrant—the hootin and yellen was friteful—mr Potter the te deler is goin to indite the firm for a nosance—the firm doant care

for Potter and Jack Raley chucked a andfu of small stones all over his shop.

"truly yors,
"sam smarty."

No. 2.

"Cradle Coort, shoe lane.

"Dear Tom,

"I am getting on fizzin with my larnin—begin to spell like winkin—we had a trooce with the tother party, the Mellow. chaff men ; but they caught three of ours in the square and gave them too black eyes— all the wors for them when we meet agen Old Potter summoned Jack Raley's father for the stones, and could not prove it—he had to give Jack two shillins for lorse of time—we had sech a tuckout of black-jack and buls eyes—last night *somebody* bunged up Potter's keyhole, and he could not open his shop till an hour after usual time. I went in to buy a pennerth of figs, and he ordered me out, and chucked a bundel of firewood at me.

"truly yours,
"Sam Smarty."

No. 3.

"Cradle Court, Shoe Lane.

"Dear Tom,

"The final fight come off last Tuesday ; we licked, but me and three others got taken by the perlice, which we were fined for, and I got such a tanning when I got home as I hope never to hav agen. Old Potter was in the court before the magistrait, and gave us a bad character all round ; he said he lived the life of a dorg, and spent half his time rushing out after us—which wasn't true, because we only visited him during dinner-time ; also Mr. Grauly, the tailor, said we knocked his door-dummy over, and spiled a jacket worth ten shillings; and Todd, the fish-shop, said we stole his winkles—what a crammer ! but we were all fined, and pitched into for half an hour by his worship.

"Yours Truly,
"Sam Smarty."

No. 4.

"Cradle Court, Shoe Lane.

"Dear Tom,

"I have giving up fighting, and intend going in for the regular business. Larking is all very well, but it *does not pay.* You can see I am getting on famously ; and, mind you, I shall be a big man yot. I intend being the largest printer and publisher out, and if ever they offer me the Lord Mayor's chair, I *shall refuse* it—and that will be something to boast of. I shall be at Blackheath next Sunday, and shall be glad

INKY LOST HIS HOLD, AND CAME TO THE GROUND WITH A CRASH.

to meet you at the usual place—the Greenich Park Gates.

"your sincere friend,
"Sam Smarty."

Here our extracts from this correspondence cease. As for Sam's resolution to abandon fun in every way, we shall see how he keeps it.

Tom, of course, wrote interesting letters, giving sketches of his schoolmates, and their usual life at school ; and, as may be inferred from Sam's last epistle, the boys were in the habit of meeting occasionally, and very jolly their meetings were.

One day Lord Holbrook came to Laurel House to see how his *protégé* progressed. He arrived just as the boys danced into the playground, glad of a respite from those "everlasting books."

Tom saw him at once, and bounded to his side. His lordship looked at him steadily for a few minutes, as if to read what changes time and the school had made in him.

"Tom," he said, "this place agrees with you."

Tom smiled, and said he was very happy.

"Nice lot of fellows, I should say," rejoined Lord Holbrook. "Who is that strapping youngster, with a cricket-bat upon his shoulder ?"

"Harry Stanley," replied Tom eagerly ; "such a dear fellow—a regular brick. Shall I bring him over !"

"Do. I should like to know him."

Harry Stanley came, blushing slightly as he acknowledged his lordship's salute. A little conversation, satisfactory on both sides, ensued, and Harry was about to join some of his cricketing friends, when Lord Holbrook called him back.

"I suppose, Mr. Stanley," he said, "that it is often the custom for a new pupil to give an entertainment ?"

"Some of the fellows stand a spread," returned Harry ; "but it is only the richest can do it—there is such a jolly lot of us."

"But you know how these things are managed ?"

"I've had a hand in one or two," replied Harry, laughing.

"May I beg of you to execute a trifling commission for me ?" said Lord Holbrook, drawing out his portmonnaie. "Tom is a stranger to such things. Will a ten-pound note cover the expenses ?"

"Amply, sir," replied Harry: "more than enough.

"Well, do the best you can with it ; and when Tom comes home for his holidays, we shall be happy to see you with him for a few days—also any other friend who may be agreeable to you both."

In this way Lord Holbrook smoothed the path of the homeless lad he had adopted, and turned dismal night into a glorious, cloudless day.

CHAPTER XIX.
INKY AND HIS FIVE POUND NOTE.

UNDER certain circumstances, valuables are undoubtedly a burden.

If a rustic labourer were to win an elephant in a lottery, he would scarcely congratulate himself upon his good fortune. A banker's clerk presented with a mound of coal-ashes and dust, with the proviso that he should remove it from the spot in the course of three days, would scarcely thank the donor; and yet there are men who would leap into the air with joy at such a gift, and, knowing the proper channel, would turn the dark and dingy mass to bright, pure gold. A bachelor, with apartments in the house of a crusty spinster, when he is in arrears of rent, would certainly be embarrassed by the gift of a bloodhound from a man whom he could not refuse ; a policeman on duty presented with a bundle of summer cabbages ; a quiet city man with an untamed colt ; a blind man with a railway engine ; the beadle of the Burlington Arcade with a kangaroo and young—each and all would labour under a sense of embarrassment. But neither yokel, city man, policeman, or beadle, would suffer a tithe of what Inky did with his five-pound note.

He had no idea what to do with it. Whenever he had an hour to spare he strolled round the shops and watched the customers, to see if any of them changed a similar thing ; but the neighbourhood was poor, silver and copper were the usual medium of exchange ; gold occasionally, but never a note did he behold.

He asked Podley one night where five-pound notes were usually changed.

Podley answered, "At the Bank, in the city, just by the R'yal Exchange."

Inky went down the next night, but found it closed. On the following day he had a pair of canaries to deliver in the city, and stole half an hour to go to the Bank. Arrived there, the bustle, the beadle, and the imposing nature of the place, entirely upset his nerves. Clutching the piece of paper in his pocket, which was slowly but surely developing into the form of a curse, he retired.

"If I goes into a strange place," he said, "they'll think I stole it, and who's to say I didn't, if they gives me in charge ?"

There was a great deal of truth in this. Inky's sagacity was not far wrong ; most people would have thought he had stolen it, and none would have changed it ; so for another day he carried the bond of the old lady of Threadneedle Street crumpled in his pocket, until the wear and tear began to affect it.

Spreading it out one day on the counter, during the absence of Podley, he looked at the worn folds and sighed—

"It'll crumble away soon," he muttered, "if I doesn't get it changed; but I dursn't ax anybody. If I showed it to Podley, he'd nab it as like as not. Then what shall I do? I'll try old Mike, and if he can't, then I'll put it by until a nopportunity turns up."

The Mike alluded to kept a whelk-stall at the corner during the summer, which he changed for a potato-can in the winter. By the gossips round about he was reputed to be a miser, and enormously wealthy · but whenever Mike was chaffed about his riches, he answered neither Yea nor Nay, and left his querists none the wiser.

The probable truth is, that the poor old man had enough to do to gain a living, without a penny to spare; but it was his reputation which prompted Inky to apply to him to change the burdensome note.

We all know how wise in his generation he was, and his usual ability was strongly developed in this instance.

"I'll eat a couple o' pennorth," he said, "and then he must give me change."

But he had reckoned without his host. Long years of experience had taught Mike that "money down" was the only correct business principle—for him, at least; and when Inky ordered the whelks, and was about to make a rapid consumption thereof, he held forth a hand gnarled by the weather and checked him.

"Down with your browns," he said.

"Wot for?" demanded Inky.

"You knows what for," returned Mike; "the game don't go down with me. If you've got the money it's as well paid first as last."

"Have you got any change?" asked Inky, after a pause, during which Mike kept his hand upon the saucers.

"Yes, how much—a tanner?"

"No," returned Inky, looking cautiously around to see that nobody was listening. "No—it's a five-pound note."

"I thout so," said Mike, laying down a well-worn oyster knife; "one of the hold Joe Miller tricks. There's the change you want —cut it."

The change administered was a stinging blow on the side of the head, and Inky reeled half a dozen yards away from the stall.

"Wot do you mean by it?" demanded Inky, drawing near, "wot did you hit me for?"

"You get away," returned Mike, dexterously turning out whelks with a two-pronged fork; "you've got wot you want, so be off."

"It's a shame to hit a chap like me," blubbered Inky, getting up a copious supply of tears as two men halted near the stall; "I asked civilly for change, you brute."

"Why did you strike the boy?" asked one of the strangers.

"He ordered two pennerth o' whelks," replied Mike, "and then axes for change for a five-pound note. There's lots like him about here—makin' game of a poor old man."

One gentleman laughed, shrugged his shoulders, and passed on. The other sided with Mike, and advised a second dose of castigation.

"I knows 'em," he said, addressing Mike, "for I suffers from 'em. I ain't kep' a coffee stall for fourteen year for nothin'. The things I've had chucked in, you wouldn't b'lieve. T'other night, when I'd got the lid orf the pot for fresh water, one on 'em—just about that warmint's size—comes and puts 'arf a brick in it, and while I was fishing up the brick, another prigged a plum cake worth a shillin'. Knock 'em all over, I ses, whensomever or wheresomever you meets 'em, for they're allus up to something, and you can't go wrong."

Inky saw that he was on treacherous ground, and hastened away with the mental resolution to "take it out of Mike" upon some future occasion.

Having failed to change the note, Inky resolved to hide it; then the question arose —where?

The establishment of Mr. James Podley was limited to the back room, shop, and cellar; the back room was out of the question, the cellar was dark, damp, and infested by rats—therefore, the shop alone remained.

"I shall find a chink in the walls," he thought, "jest the place miser chaps used to hide their money in. I'll look to-morrow."

That night, absorbed in his thoughts, he sat upon the high stool facing his master. Podley did not appear to be in the best of humours; he had entered a favourite canary in a singing match, and at the important moment it had failed to pipe a note. Several times he cast sulky glances at his assistant, then he suddenly inquired—

"Wot's the matter with you?"

"With me?—nothing," replied Inky, startled.

"Have you got anything on yer mind?" pursued Podley; "you look as if you'd stolen something."

"Me stole a thing!" returned Inky, melting immediately, "wot hav I stole?"

"Nothin', as I knows on," rejoined his master; "and don't try it on here. You sell a sparrer or a bullfinch without handing me the c—t I'll skin you alive."

"I ain't sold a sparrer to-day," said the injured Inky.

"I don't know as you have, but you looks wrong about the mouth. Ain't you satisfied with your wittles?"

"I gets all I wants."

"Ain't the place good enough for you?"

"Yes, it is; I don't want better."

"That's all right," said Podley; "but you mind this: when at home, I wants to see you look cheerful—that's wot I want, and I'll have it. Don't come any of your nobble games over me. If I ain't good enough, go to your father."

"You know I ain't got no father," whined Inky.

"That's a good job—for your father," returned Podley, getting out his favourite bottle; "I does hate a wicious dispersition, or a chap in the sulks."

"I wasn't a-sulkin'—I was only thinkin'."

"Come off that stool and fill the kittle."

Inky obeyed with alacrity, and presently placed before his master a jorum of spirit and water, for although Mr. Podley preferred it neat in the day-time, he took it in the evening with hot water and sugar.

The first glass dispelled Podley's ill-humour, the second made him jovial, and the third made him maudlin.

"Never deceive me," he said, softly weeping, "never deceive me, my lad; for I took you from a life o' ruin, and brought you inter a 'spectable line o' business—so don't deceive your fren', Inky."

Inky vowed by all that was great and good he would not, and expressed his unalterable determination to study the interests of Mr. James Podley in preference to his own.

"I does all I can for the bisness," he said; "t'other day I got threepence for a tuppenny bullfinch."

"You did—you did; and werry smart it was of you, Inky."

"And then, if I sees people a-lookin' in the winder, I scratches the back o' the cages, and makes the birds hop about and chirp and look lively. I am sure I couldn't do more if the bisness was my own."

"The scratchin' o' the cages," said Podley, with wonderful gravity, "is a good hidear, and bein' your own, Inky, it shows the genus you've got in you. Parsevere, my lad, and you'll get on."

"I'll do my best; I allers does."

"I relies on you," returned Podley, and then he fell asleep.

On the morrow, shortly after breakfast, the bird-fancier went forth to keep an appointment, and Inky, left to himself, sought a place of concealment for his treasure. After a long and persevering search, he discovered a shelf high up the wall, just above the shelf which Podley had at one time proposed as a sleeping-place for his assistant. It was the very thing required, and Inky, mounting certain rabbit-hutches and breeding-cages, clutched the shelf, and prepared for the final lift.

Just then the door was darkened, and a voice inquired—

"What on airth are you doin' up there?"

Inky looked round, and beheld Mr. Podley surveying him with a look of astonishment.

Overcome by the unexpected sight, he lost his hold, and, in the midst of an avalanche or cages and hutches, came to the ground with a crash.

"Of all the himps—" growled Podley; "get up, and put em' straight. You've frightened a shillin' or two out of the birds. Hallo! what's this?—a five-pun' note? Now, master Inky, where did you get this from?"

CHAPTER XX.

A VISITOR AT BUNHILL ROW.

INKY clambered slowly to his feet, and stood before his master, abashed. He saw at once the inevitable interpretation which would be put upon his conduct.

"Speak, you young himp," said Podley, sternly; "where did you get this five-pun' note?"

"It was given to me by the Markis," replied Inky, measuring out his words as if they were drops of blood or gold.

"And you could keep such a thing from me," returned the bird-fancier, reproachfully: "me as have been quite as much as a father to you—more than yourn have been. Didn't I take you up when you hadn't a friend in the world?"

"You did," said Inky, blinking his eyes—the waterworks were in preparation.

"Who stood by you when even a reverend gent came out of the front door to announce you?"

"You, Mr. Podley—you acted werry kind."

"It's my nature," rejoined Podley; "I couldn't do otherwise, and this is what I gets for it."

"Oh, Mr. Podley," sobbed Inky, "I didn't know what to do with it."

"No," said the bird-fancier, "you didn't know what to do with it. You didn't want to keep every brass farden to yourself, did you, you precious cast-off of a smooth-faced reverend gent? Pick up them cages."

Sobbing most dolefully, partly through shame and partly in consequence of the discovery of his treasure, Inky restored the disturbed pets to their usual positions, and then proceeded to refill the water and seed glasses, which had been emptied by his untimely fall.

"I shall tell you what I'll do," said Podley, when this much had been completed: "I shall keep this slip of paper until I knows the trooth about it—and when I knows the trooth I shall stick to it still, for it is just the sum I wants for an apprentice, and as an apprentice you shall be bound to me."

This announcement brought forth Inky's tears afresh, and he sobbed, as Podley afterwards declared, "like a man and a boy piping for a wager."

"I ain't goin' to be bound to nobody," roared Inky. "I ain't a workhouse chap."

"You were precious nigh it," returned Podley. "Now put the shop straight, and come in to me."

In a few minutes Inky joined his master, and sat down in silent, sulky dignity by the fire. Podley, who had got out his favourite bottle and glass, eyed him several times as he sipped his grog, and at length he said—

"If you don't feel comfortable here, get out."

"Wot have I done now?" demanded Inky. "I don't think there ever was such a unfortunet boy ever born under the sun. If I laughs, 'tain't right—if I jist drops a tear, it's unmanly; and so 'tis whether I'm a-hollerin' or a-holdin' my peace, down I'm dropped on."

"My lad," said Podley, with drunken gravity, "I sees how it is—I've made too free with you. When master and man drinks out of the same glass, as you and I hev, there is sure to be a h'ist up. In futur we will keep our rerlative posishings. Go into the shop."

"Mayn't I go out for a walk?" asked Inky, slowly dismounting from his stool.

"You may not," replied Podley. "I see I must keep a tight hand over yer. Out yer goes, and sit on the rabbit-hutch—that's good enough for you, and move orf without leave if you durst."

If ever a boy was disposed to rebel against authority Inky was at that particular moment; but there was something in his master's eye which bade him beware. Mr. Podley showed for once that he was not a man to be always trifled with.

This stern resolution the bird-fancier kept; and the friendship which at first existed between him and his hopeful assistant was known no more.

He took his meals alone, and Inky feasted on the remnants; he drank in solitude, and Inky sat in sorrow in the shop. What became of the five-pound note Inky could never guess, for it was neither produced or alluded to by Mr. Podley until long after that eventful night.

This life soon had its due effect upon the truly unfortunate Inky. He became moody and distraught, sitting idly among the cages whenever his master was absent, neglecting alike the larks, bullfinches, rabbits, and other live stock of the establishment.

He did just sufficiently attend to them to escape severe censure, it was true; but Podley saw that the work was scamped; and the breach between him and the boy widened every day.

Inky soon began to entertain ideas of seeking a change of life, and he would have gone at once but for a resolve he had made not to depart without his five-pound note. As soon as its hiding-place could be found he resolved to lay violent hands upon it, and make good his retreat.

"He don't carry it about him, I know," thought Inky, as he sat one morning alone with the shop in charge, "and I don't think he's changed it. He's put away the note till he's done with his silver. Have he any other?" he added, with a darkening brow. "If he have, and I gets a-nigh it, away it goes."

The evil thoughts of Inky were interrupted by a voice apparently hoarse from cold. It had the twang of a woman's throat, although, alas! there was but little music in it.

"Hist! youngster, is your master in?"

It came from the door, where a woman's head was visible, thrust in with an air of curiosity. A woman's head, we say—the bonnet told that; but there was little else in the bleared and blotched countenance to distinguish whether it was woman, man, or brute.

"Hist! youngster, is your master in?" said the voice again; and a thin, quivering hand brushed aside the hair—or oakum, it might have been either—from the eyes, to enable her to see the boy more clearly.

"Mr. Podley ain't in," replied Inky, rising; "but I attends to the shop if you wants anything."

"I don't want anything," rejoined the woman, impatiently. "What should I want except a new body and soul? So he's not in. How is he getting on? Does his business thrive? Is he well off? Is he married again?"

As she poured out these questions in quick succession she passed the threshold, and stood revealed.

Inky was but a boy, and an ignorant one to boot, but the appearance of this wretched outcast called up an emotion within him such as he had never felt before. Her soiled, ragged, wretched dress consorted well with the matted hair. The bleared face looked like a picture that had once been passing fair but now trampled and torn, stained and scored by ruthless hands and feet. She was abominable to see. Horror and pity fought together in the boy's breast as he looked upon this degraded daughter of Eve who, from head to heel, from her crown of matted hair to her battered boots, was Ruin personified.

"Why don't you answer me?" she cried. "[s] he married again?"

"Who—who said he was married afore?" [s]immered Inky, not unmindful of the neces[sity] of keeping his master's secrets.

"Who says he wasn't. Does he?" asked [th]e woman sharply. "Does Jim Podley deny that he ever had a wife, eh? Answer me that."

"Oh, no!—I think not, mum," replied Inky, shrinking back from an angry gleam in her eye.

"He had better not," said the woman, with a grim smile, "or there'll be those who would come back from the other end of the world—would rise from their graves to give him the lie. He knows he had a wife, and he knows why she left him."

"I'm sure, mum, I don't want to know," said Inky.

"Why should you?" rejoined the woman; "it is no business of yours. A child can take a blow, and forget, but a true woman will not be beaten morn, noon, and night—sworn at like a dog, and housed and fed with less care than his accursed rabbits. Who are you, boy?"

She turned upon Inky with a frown as she propounded this question—but he was still keenly alive to his old desire of making a favourable impression, and he replied—

"I, mum, am a stolen kid."

"A what?" almost screamed the woman. "Did Jim steal you?"

"Oh, no, mum—he ain't of the stealin' sort. In my hinfancy, mum, I was born in Belgravia Square, and nussed in a lapse of luxury, ontil a old willin, gloatin' over my gorging raiment, laid wiolent hands on me, and carried me horf in the middle of the night. I ain't sartain where he took me to, mum, but some says as he laid up in Hepping Forest for a week to elood the pursoot. Arter that I wos brought up to heel-ball and dubbin, but I stuck out agin blacking Bailey's boots, and so we parted, and he's put another chap, named Tom, on my nobble father, who wos a box o' lights, and broke his leg at the Christial Hall."

"So you are only Jim's boy?" said the woman, who had listened but indifferently to this lucid story of Inky's birth, parentage, and fall in the world.

"Yes, mum."

"When will he be back?"

"It's rayther uncertain, mum, for he's gone up to the Green for some blue-rock pigeons for a match, and when he goes to the Green, he's allus a long time gone."

"I know—I know," the woman said; "he drinks with his mates, and is a good fellow —while his wife, when he had one—sat at home, alone, with dry bread for a meal. I'll come back directly, my boy; but don't say that I've been here."

She took her rags, dirt, and debauched face out of the shop, and Inky followed her to the door. He saw her go straight to the public-house, and boldly enter, like one familiar with that high-road to ruin.

"I wonder who she is," he thought. "Suppose it is—and yet—Podley said it was so many years ago; but it must be her. I lives among mystery. Wot with losin' my nobble parents and finding bird-fancier's wives, I'm like the chap in the book I read once. Let's see, wot was it called?—The Child of Fat— no, he was a lean 'un, I know, supple as a fawn, hairy as a cypher—no, zeepher, so he couldn't be a child of Fat, but he was a child o' somethin'—wot was it? It was somethin' which made him do things as he couldn't help; he shot his brother, p'isoned his mother, and hung his father, instead of other things, because he was a child of—of—Dastardly!— no, Destiny—that was it; and I'm a child o' Destiny, too, and a werry lively game it is for a kid, to be sure. I wish some other chap had it."

His meditations were interrupted by the return of the woman. She did not peep as before, but came boldly in.

"Is your master in?" she cried, fixing Inky with her eye, which had now an unnatural brightness.

"Not yet, mum."

"Let me see," rejoined the woman, walking straight to the parlour door, and throwing it open. One glance was sufficient, and she came back to the petrified Inky. "You have not deceived me—he is not here. So he lives alone?"

"No, mum; I'm with him."

"Strange," continued the woman, ignoring the interruption, "as such a cur should live. He struck me—beat me as he *dare not* beat a brute. I shall come again, boy—say not a word to him."

She was gone again, and Inky knew where to, without going to the door.

He felt a growing terror within him, and he wished for Podley's return; but half an hour passed, and his master was still absent; then he heard a wild cry outside, the shrill scream of a drunken harridan.

Alarmed, he scarcely knew why, he ran to the door, and there saw the woman who had been there, no longer stern, but full of the merriment which the demon drink gives rise to, dancing like a female dervish before the door.

There were some men, idlers, leaning

against the opposite house, who were laughing at the sight; but Inky felt as if he would fain have covered his face and shut out the sight, but he had no power; he could only stand and stare at the wretched object, brimful of the ghastly merriment, dancing, shouting, reeling, beneath the broad sunlit heaven.

Drawn by some irrisistible fascination, he went out upon the pathway to watch the mad woman, who twirled her arms, and danced wildly, like an uncouth fairy who had mistaken the time of revelry.

Suddenly she stopped, and cried aloud—

"Jim Podley!"

Then Inky saw his master sneak into the shop and endeavour to close the door; but the woman was too quick for him, and Inky followed close at her heels.

"What do you want here?" cried Podley, pale and ghastly.

"I am tired of wandering," returned the woman, with a reckless toss of her arms, "and I've come to live with you."

"Not with me," returned Podley—"if you drive me out of house and home."

"And that I'll do," was the fierce reply, "as sure as I am your lawful wife."

"You may ruin me, send me to the work'us," said Podley, trembling, "but you'll never live again with me. You've gone your own way for thirteen year—keep in it, and leave me in peace."

"I've gone my way thirteen years, Jim Podley," returned his wife, "and I'll go it still. It's my way here just now, and here I'll stay. Who'll stop me? You!—try it, and see what a house I'll bring about your ears. It's my way to come and go as I please, to do just what I think of at the moment, and you know it! Blows and bruises could not beat it out of me years ago, you know that; try and see if they will do it now."

"Inky," said Podley, turning to his assistant, and speaking like one in pain, "put up the shutters at once, for this 'ere business and I will part to-day.

———

CHAPTER XXI.

THE PROGRESS OF SAM SMARTY.

THE letters of Sam to his friend Tom must have prepared our readers for a change in the general appearance and demeanour in that able assistant to the famous printers, Messrs. Kidem and Blowhard.

That a change had taken place, we must admit, but it was not of a strictly revolutionary character. It is so hard for an Ethiopian to change his skin, or a leopard to get rid of his spots, and it must be freely confessed, that Sam Smarty, in spite of an acquired knowledge of the art of spelling and writing, was Sam Smarty still.

He was still the same merry outlaw; the chosen champion of the boys against the police; the terror of small traders who made themselves obnoxious. He still walked abroad, in his shirt sleeves, and a paper cap upon his head; he was inkstained. As of yore, he still loved a bit of fun; in short, Sam Smarty was still—a printer's devil.

And yet he was changed in many things; he was more serious when he was, as he termed it, "in the buzzum of his fam'ly." He gave up visiting gaffs, and sometimes he even went so far as to reprove his brother devils when their fun became more boisterous than was absolutely necessary for the purposes of mirth.

"It ain't fun," he said one day during the dinner hour, "to trip up blind men—not as any of you would do it—but I saw Billy Starks—yes! I saw you, my boy, upset a pile of apples on an old woman's stall; well, that was fun to you, but something different to her; apples cost money, and I saw tears in the poor old gal's eyes as the London pippings rolled down the gutter. Sech things, Billy, is all very well in a pantermine, because there's nothin' real, from the fairies to the bobby, who is allus in trouble, and it don't signify; but in real life it's downright cruelty, and we *men* of the press ought to know better."

"Why do you pick upon me?" asked Billy Starks.

"Because you are the wussest—I mean the worst," returned Sam; "it was you as put the sand into the old man's basket of Banbury cakes; and last Sunday I saw you painting a kitten with red ink. It isn't right, Billy, it's mean, and if you can't be funny without being cruel, don't be funny at all."

"Hear, hear," chorussed a band of young urchins listening, who were about as likely to profit by the lecture, as the kitten in question was to acquire the art of printing from the ornamentation it had received.

"I don't want to put myself up," said Sam, "or to yarn to you—*I'm* not a preacher, thank goodness; and nobody likes a bit of fun better than I do, but it must *be* fun, such things as we shouldn't be ashamed to talk about at home. If you've done a thing you are ashamed to talk about, then it had better never been done at all."

"I'll tell you what I proposes," broke in Bill Starks, "and that is, that we buy Sam a choker; here's my penny towards it. I'll sacrifice my arter dinner tart for it."

"I don't want a choker," returned Sam, quietly, "any more than you want cheek. I'm only giving an opinion about what I think is best for us."

"And who wants your 'pinion?" asked

Billy Starks; "you've growed uppish since Lord Molly Codlin purwided you with a private tootor, and sent your little brothers to a big school, where they wears werry small caps and yaller stockin's."

"I dare say you would be very glad of the same thing," said Sam.

"Not I," contemptuously rejoined Billy Starks; "I don't want no charity, and I don't go hanging to the skirts of the nobs; my father says, every true-born Briton ought to heave a brick at a swell, and they'd soon be put down."

"Your father, Billy, dare not set the example."

"He won't until there's a gineral rise, and hopes that will be when they gets such sniggerers as you to jine the Peace Society. When are you goin' to be sworn in to the Band of 'Ope?"

"Never mind that," said Sam; "you called me a sniggerer, didn't you!"

"I did."

"Then just come into the bit o' waste ground by the market, and I'll show you what a member of the Peace Society can do."

Billy Starks was not a coward, and he promptly acquiesced; but it was an evil day when he accepted the challenge, for Sam, in something under a quarter of an hour, so far operated upon his eyes as to make machine "minding" an arduous duty to Billy.

"That's the way we peace chaps act," said Sam, as he resumed his paper cap; "we dusts the t'other's cap, and make them peaceable."

Billy only dabbed his eyes and gory nose with a cotton pocket-handkerchief, but said nothing.

"Have you any more questions to ask?" inquired Sam, politely.

Again Billy Starks forebore to reply, but his half-closed optics spoke volumes.

It was evident that whatever queries he might have rambling in his mind were reserved for the present.

"But look here," said Sam, suddenly turning back, "what's the good of our keeping up a lot of quarrelling; we've had it out, and I've licked yer, Billy; never mind, when you get a chance you lick another chap. Yer can do it, for you're not a downright duffer. I'm sorry I shut your peepers up, but I'll do all I can to put you right. I've got sixpence, and I'll stand half-a-pound of raw beef to put you square."

Billy was not a bad fellow in the main, and he heartily closed with the offer.

The two, followed by a bevy of admiring friends, then adjourned to the nearest butcher's, where the flesh of oxen was obtained and carefully arranged round the contused optics.

There was much in this of the old British spirit, which prompts us to give a hand to a foe whom we have a few minutes before knocked down with "one" straight from the shoulder, and Sam met with his reward.

He became more popular than ever, even with the rival factions of Messrs. Todd, and other firms.

His name was, in a small way, as famous as that of the bold Robin Hood; it is true, the only sylvan glade he could call his own was Shoe Lane, but there he reigned paramount. When his voice was lifted up no dog dare bark.

His Aunt Jenny did not return on the Sunday he had named to Tom, for it took longer for her temper to cool; but she came a fortnight later, and finding her in a good humour, Sam ventured to pump her for the whole particulars of Inky's disgrace.

"What I want to know is this, aunty," he said, "did Inky really bring a blackguard chap to the house to kick up a bobbery?"

"A man—a low ruffing, came back with him," answered Jenny, evasively, "and the wretched boy was all in tatters, as if he had been fighting somewhere. So the Reverend Mr. Marall and his friend proposed that he should be sent about his business."

"I'll tell you why I want to know, Aunt Jenny," rejoined Sam; "the fact is I've taken against Inky for his meanness, but I likes everybody to have their doo. He got his rags through the lot in Sipter Court fallin' on him when he went to see old Work-it-out. Now if he went to see the old man through kindness, I should be sorry to hear that it was the cause of his gitting into trouble."

"And so should I," said Jenny.

"It isn't so much his bein' sent about his business," argued Sam, "for we are all liable to the sack; but most of us have got friends, but Inky hasn't, and wot's become of him is what troubles me."

"P'raps he's got a situation?" Jenny hinted.

"Bless your inercent heart," exclaimed Sam, "you don't know much o' the ways o' life. A sitivation! Where? and what? No, Aunt Jenny, he havn't got a sitivation, and he's running about starving, or he's turned thief, or he's been and gone and drounded—I mean drowned hisself."

"The Lord forbid!" cried Jenny, turning pale.

"Ay! aunty, you may well say that, for it ought to be on your conscience; and, mind you, it's not long odds about his ghost not showin' up sudden about twelve o'clock at night."

"I wouldn't have my dearies think of this for worlds," said Jenny, in the utmost terror, "their lives have been quiet enough for years—although it did take a long time to get over the sorrow about poor Miss Bella. Suppose this boy is—is—dead ? "

"Drowned," put in Sam.

"Drowned," repeated his aunt, growing paler each moment. "Suppose it was to get into a paper and they were to read it. I don't think they would ever smile again."

"It ain't the papers you need be afraid on," said Sam, "afraid *of*, I mean. I wish I could speak as well as I can write, but you can't alter all at once like a camelelion. Don't you be afraid of the papers," he continued with a complacent smile, "I've got some influence with the press, and if there's anything about Inky likely to crop up, I'll stop it."

"You havn't got no darned cheek, have you ?" put in Sam's father, a quiet-looking working man, who was smoking his pipe by the window.

"I've got enough to do credit to the family," answered his dutiful son.

"*You* stop the papers—what next ?" growled Smarty senior.

"Well, I don't want to boast," said Sam, "so I'll drop the subjec'. All I've got to say to Aunt Jenny is, that Inky was turned out unfairly, and if he's now lying on his back in a bye street starving to death, it isn't my fault, but it rests on one who ain't wery distantly related to this noble family."

Sam, of course, did not speak seriously when he hinted at the "nobbly" born lying on his back perishing for want of bread, but he thought it probable that his old chum might be getting very hard up, and a tinge of remorse, arising from the memory of their last meeting, prompted him to do what he considered to be a kind thing for Inky.

"P'raps they've took him up," thought Sam, "and sent him somewhere to school. Inky might be tempted to go wrong, and I should be sorry to see him afore his worshipful Lord Mayor."

As for Jenny, the words of her precious nephew made such an impression upon her that she went home wretched, and awoke the following morning with eyes swollen as if she had been weeping.

The two maiden ladies perceived these signs as well, and the first question brought out the doleful surmises of Sam Smarty, embellished with the fancy of Jenny's vigorous mind.

The train took fire. Both ladies shared in her consternation, and having but one male friend in the world, the Reverend Mr. Marall, they sent for him.

He came, listened to the story with a gentle smile, intended to have a consoling effect, and being asked for an opinion upon the matter, gave it thus :—

"Our little friend," meaning Inky, "was, I fear, not a promising boy. He bears a rebellious spirit, such as I feared would disturb the peace of this household. I therefore sent him forth with a man of Baal, whom I deemed to be an old associate. If I have made a mistake I am very sorry."

"But what is to be done ?" said M' Fanny, "the poor boy may be ill—dying.

"Send for him," said the reverend gen man, promptly.

"Where to ?"

"Ahem ! something must be thought of," said the reverend gentleman. "This requires much consideration ; will you leave it to me ?"

"Anything, everything," said both the ladies in a breath ; "do not spare expense."

"I will not," replied Mr. Marall, "and when I've found him, what then ?"

"We must provide him with a home—but not here. He must be educated, and bound to a trade."

"I will manage it all," said the reverend gentleman, and took his leave of the grateful ladies, who admired him more than ever.

He was so gentle, meek, and mild, so unworldly. Had no idea of loaves and fishes, this very reverend Mr. Marall—oh ! dear no, bless him.

Although unworldly, Mr. Marall had some knowledge of the ways of the world, and as it was necessary to find Inky, he went about it as any ordinarily keen mortal would. He consulted the police, and having bound himself to give a very respectable reward when the boy was found, he left behind a few ready and willing men to complete the job.

"When you have found him," he said, "say nothing—but come to me. I will then seek and restore the lost lamb to the fold."

The officer entrusted with the case said he would look up his reverence, and be as mum about his business as a drum without its skin.

He was as good as his word; in ten days he came to the reverend gentleman's house with news of the missing boy.

"He's down at Podley's, the bird-fancier, in Bunhill Row," he said, "and the sooner you takes him away from there the better."

"I will go at once," replied Mr. Marall, "and when I've brought the boy away you shall have your reward."

"But havn't I airned it now ?" grumbled the officer.

"You may for all I know, friend," returned the reverend gentleman, bestowing upon him the ghost of a wink, "but it will be as well to behold the boy prior to parting with the image and subscription of the Queen."

"Ah ! you're a downy lot, you meek and mild 'uns," said the officer. "I'll look round in the morning; you'll find the boy as right as a trivet."

We must now turn back for a few moments to the time when the renowned Jim Podley gave his assistant orders to put the shutters up.

He spoke in an undertone, but the words reached the ears of the woman whom ill-fate had made his wife.

"What's that?" she cried, sharply, "the shutters up—you keep 'em down, I say, you needn't close your place to beat me."

"Was I ever unkind to you, Mary?" asked Podley.

"I don't know—I forget," was the reply; "come in, man, and get me something to eat or drink, I don't care which."

"Don't leave me," whispered Podley to Inky, as he prepared to follow; his voice trembled with agitation, and his cheeks were ashen pale; "don't leave me, my lad, or she'll murder me."

"Where's my five-pun' note," demanded Inky, with his usual eye to the main chance.

"I'll tell you to-morrow, Inky," Jim replied.

"Now, are you coming?" cried his wife from the interior of the room.

The bird-fancier answered mildly that he was, and went, leaving Inky to ruminate on the game-cock box, over the strange turn in Mr. Podley's domestic affairs.

What passed the next hour he could not learn, for both Podley and his wife spoke in a low tone, but by-and-by there was the chink of glass, and their voices grew louder; mutual recriminations were exchanged, and many compliments, unfit for a boy's ears, passed between them.

There was one passage, however, which the boy especially remembered—it came from the woman.

"I left you," she cried, "without a penny, and you left me before. What mattered it to me whether I starved out or at home? You took me from a comfortable service, and promised to be a true man to me. Have you been so? Ah! 'twas an evil day when you took me from poor Miss Bella; and I must have been a wretch to have left her—alone in the world."

"Miss Bella was——" began Podley.

"Look here," almost screamed his wife, "you mind what you say, Jim Podley; she was as true a woman as ever lived—bless her sweet face and pure heart. There was another bit o' work from you men—a blight upon you!"

"Is it all my fault?" demanded Podley, striking the table with his clenched hand. "What of your mincings—your tempers?—wasn't I allus being nagged by you? Did I get a minute's peace? Wasn't it allus—

'Where have you been, Jim?' and 'What now, Jim?'—and who struck the first blow?"

"You took it up ready enough," was the scornful reply. "Pass that bottle here."

"You'll have no more in my house," returned Podley, who had grown quite valiant.

"Give me that bottle."

"Not I—leave it alone."

Then followed the sound of scrambling, and the utterance of suppressed passion; then came screams and blows, and Inky, alarmed, ran to the door to seek help.

He was met by a mild, placid gentleman, who came smiling up the steps, holding an umbrella before him in a very gingerly style, supposed to be typical of humility.

"Ha! my young friend," he exclaimed; "is it you? Dear me! what is that disturbance within?"

He was answered by the opening of the parlour door, and Podley holding his wife, screaming, tearing, and uttering the language of an infuriated woman, in his arms, dragging her towards the door.

"I'll chuck yer into the street ye came from," he hissed. "Keep that door open, Inky."

"My friend—my friend!" interposed the reverend gentleman, "this is unseemly—it becometh not a man to so far forget himself. Is this thy wife, daughter, or——?"

"Now, who may you be?" demanded Podley, halting. "Oh! I know you. You've done me a good turn afore, and I'll do you one now—out you goes."

He cast his wife violently away, seized the reverend gentleman by the throat, and locked in each other's arms, they rolled down the steps into the street.

CHAPTER XXII.

HAZELDEAN HALL.

IN the heart of beautiful, fruitful Surrey, stands Hazeldean Hall, one of the many country seats of the Beauforth family.

Surrounded by woods and fields for many a mile, not yet ploughed by the all-invading railway, it stands a record of the grand old times when every nook and cranny of the land teemed with romance, when knights and lords were really minor kings, and the "common people" were not unwilling slaves.

The old feudal days are past, but the Hall stands still, solemn and stately, surrounded by its satellites, the oaks, which have sighed in the summer and moaned in the winter, through half a score generations of men.

Once upon a time, kings had gone down in state to the Hall, it was large enough to entertain five hundred followers of the sovereignty, and in later times princes have not disdained to drop down quietly for a day's shooting or a run with the harriers; but the grandeur of old is gone, the Hazeldean Hall is nothing more than a quiet country residence for a nobleman.

But what was it to Tom when he was sent down there to spend his first vacation? It was Elysium—Paradise!—the massive trees forming glorious arcades, the sweeping undulations of the open grounds—the bubbling brooks and pools, stocked with respectable old tench and carp, bold in the security of long years without a solitary angler; the deer, the hares and rabbits, game—each and all had some new charm to him, and did their share towards the perfection of this, to him, unheard of, unthought of, land of beauty.

He was up betimes the first morning of his arrival, and out alone, brushing the dew-spangled grass with his feet—what a morning it was to him!

He seemed to drink the Spirit of Life, to imbibe elasticity, as he walked along; everything was so gloriously bright and green, as far above Blackheath as Blackheath was above the dark and dingy town which he now had learned to hate.

How he pitied Sam Smarty and all who were compelled to toil in its dingy air! and yet but a few short months ago, and he had broken one of the commandments, and envied Sam's worldly possessions, from his paper cap to his home in Cradle Court.

Crossing the park, he came upon a small river, and following its course, discovered a weir, with a wooden bridge of rustic simplicity crossing it.

He was standing on it looking at some curious wicker baskets fastened to the woodwork, and wondering of what use they could be, when a tall, broad-shouldered man, in a velveteen suit, came up and touched his hat. Yes!—touched his hat to the boy who had scarcely grown accustomed to boots upon his feet.

"Be ye Master Talbot, from the Hall?" he asked.

Tom signified that he was the young gentleman in question.

"Then I be told by my lord to look arter ye," said the man, "and show ye a bit aboot; in fact," he added, with a grin, "I be a sort o' outdoor wally like. My name be Dick Rowley—but I'm Dick to everybody, sir."

"Very good, Dick," replied our hero, who had picked up a certain free-and-easy air among his Blackheath associates, which sat well upon him, "and what do you propose doing?"

"Tain't for me to do that, sir," returned Dick, grinning hugely, "that be your look-out. My lord ses you're to do what ye please."

"But I don't know anything about the country," said Tom.

"Then I'll teach you," said Dick, readily, "and we'll begin with the heels."

Tom had an idea that Dick intended to give him a lesson in running, but he was soon undeceived by Dick's laying violent hands upon the wicker baskets, and hauling them ashore one by one.

"Now these," he said, dragging out a few slimy wrigglers, "is heels, you see, and warmints they is to hold, but if you catches 'em jist under the hear, where that fin is, you can hold 'em—like this—"

"I see," replied Tom, watching a frantic eel going through every possible contortion, but perfectly helpless in Dick's strong grasp.

"That be the way to hold 'em—now these chaps by young jack," he continued, pointing to a half-dozen vicious-looking young pike, "so we chucks 'em in again, and has 'em when they grows bigger—ha, ha!—we has 'em when they're big enough to eat, we does Them t'other things is fresh-water crabs—which the French gentlemen, when they comes down, do like, to be sure, but they is nasty eatin'—so back they goes."

In this way Dick emptied the various creels, edifying Tom with his country lore. After that Tom went down to his cottage, lying in the heart of a coppice, and covered in the most beautiful manner with ivy and honeysuckle, where the keeper's pretty, buxom young wife gave him some bread and milk.

"We beant got any youngsters yet," grinned Dick; and he plugged his mouth with a huge piece of bread, "for we were only married last Martelmas, but they'll come by-and-by."

"For shame, Dick," said his wife, bustling about; "you ought to know better than to talk afore the young gentleman that way."

"Where be the shame?" grinned Dick. "There beant no shame in truth, lass."

"Get your breakfast, Dick, and get out," was all the reply his wife vouchsafed him.

Dick roared again, as if he had uttered an excellent joke, and smiled at Tom, and Tom smiled in return, although, for the life of him, he could not see anything in it.

After this frugal breakfast, which Tom preferred to the most luxurious meal at the Hall, they went out snaring rabbits, and with this whiled away the happiest morning Tom had ever known.

At parting, Dick promised to meet him on the morrow, as he was engaged that afternoon, "looking arter some hens," he said, and Tom returned to the Hall where he dined with Lord Holbrook, and spent a dreamily happy evening.

A few days later Harry Stanley came down, and together, with the occasional services of Dick, they roamed over the entire estate, fishing, snaring rabbits, trapping weazels and stoats, and a score other occupations familiar to those who are country bred.

One morning they passed through the village—a single street, about a mile away from the park—and Dick, who was of the party, pulled up at the Spotted Dog for a " drop of beer."

" The weather's warm, and I likes a change from home-brewed now and then."

" I should like a bottle of ginger beer," said Harry Stanley ; " what say you, Tom ?"

" I'm thirsty enough to drink a dozen."

The ginger beer was bought, and Dick brought out his mug of beer and placed it on the bench.

" A public," he explained, " is allus sleepy like, and I can't sit in 'em."

The boys sat down beside him to rest, and were soon in the heart of a discussion about the various things they had seen and done that morning.

A shadow falling upon the table caused Dick to look up, and before them was a man who was evidently neither country born nor bred.

He was pinched, thin, with a general hungry look. His clothes, now threadbare and patched, mated well with the man.

" Well," said Dick, " what does you want here—on the tramp ?"

" Yes," returned the man, with a bitter frown, " I'm on the tramp—for the benefit of my feller-man. I'm on the tramp to save 'em from rooin. I'm on the tramp to get 'em to rise agin their suppressors "

" I ain't got no suppressors," said Dick, " and I'm werry well off."

" What does you call them ?" cried the man, pointing at Tom and his friend. "Ain't you under the heel of the bloated nobs—don't you tremble and bow down afore even spawn like them ?"

" If I does," replied Dick, " I'm not aware on it."

" No—your ignorance hath no limit," continued the stranger. " While all the rest of the country is up in arms, while all the work chaps are a-striking like a—a—winking, and crushin' the masters, who've crushed them too long afore—you are sleepin' and a-snorin' your lives away like pigs."

" You are a liar," returned Dick, quietly. " I were up at four this mornin', and had done a day's work afore you'd got rid of last night's boose."

" And this is my reward," said the stranger ; " this is what I get for givin' up a wallyble business to roam about the country, and degenerate my feller-man."

" Perhaps the business gave up you," put in Harry Stanley.

" Young feller," said the stranger, " you comes of a bad lot—the bone-crushin' olijarchy of a suppressed and down-trodding nation."

" I say, old man, you mind this," said Dick, rising ; " say what you like to me, but don't you insult these young gentlemen, or I'll take thee by the neck and give thee a souse in the horse-pond."

" Of course you would," cried the stranger, " or anything else. Go on, ye slaves ; lick the dust orf the feet as kicks you, grovel in the mire, bring up yer children to be slaves, and be humbly perlite to the beadles of the workus."

" We ain't got no beadle and no workus," said Dick.

" Then your poor must die in the ditches."

" They doesn't do nothin' o' the sort ; they leaves that to the likes o' you. So get away as quick as you please, and don't let me catch you hanging about here again."

" No, no," replied the stranger, tossing his arms after the approved manner of agitators, " I leaves you to your fate. I'll get back to the big city, where men hev got senses, and knows how to use 'em ; where every hour sees a fresh blow struck at the head of Tyranny, and one of the fetters—of slavery— knocked away."

With this flourish the pinched, spare advocate of man's rights struck his hat fiercely on the crown, gulped down a little sob, and departed.

" I've seen him before," said Tom, as soon as he was clean away.

" I've not," rejoined Harry Stanley, " and I don't know that I want to see him again."

" But his face and voice are so familiar," said Tom, pondering, " I am sure I know him well."

" Oh, bother him," exclaimed Harry. " Dick's ready ; let us go down to the warren, and see the rabbits feed. Come on. I'll run you to the corner."

CHAPTER XXIII.

A BREAK-UP AT PODLEY'S.

SAM had good cause for assuming that events of no common nature had taken place when the Reverend Marall went in search of the lost Inky.

The preliminary proceedings of Podley have been already described. He took the reverend gentleman by the throat, and the two rolled into the street.

Thus far all went well with the bird-fancier, but there the face of affairs was changed. Mr. Marall was a shepherd, but he was a lamb. His spirit, once aroused, he could fight, and fight tolerably well.

A PUBLIC BENEFACTOR COMES TO GRIEF.—"A RESCOO, A RESCOO, MEN OF HINGLEND," CRIED WORK-IT-OUT.

"Hands off, thou Amalekite," he cried, "lest I smite thee under the fifth rib."

"Pound away," returned Podley, himself setting the example.

The next moment Mr. Jim Podley received a well-directed blow in the lower part of his waistcoat, which sent him reeling into the street. His foe followed up quickly with two smart taps upon the face and another under the arm, all scientifically delivered.

"Brayvo—go it, choker," cried a beery dustman, and the cry was taken up by a score of other spectators, who, in the most impartial manner, proceeded to form a ring.

Podley was not defeated, and Mr. Marall was fairly roused, so amidst the encouragement of a delighted audience they closed again and fought like a couple of madmen.

It was give and take, but the balance of science was on the reverend gentleman's side. By means of a few skilful manœuvres he succeeded in getting Podley's head under his arm, or in chancery, as the professors of the "noble art" term it ; and while he pounded away at the bird-fancier, an enterprising lad bolted up a court with his umbrella and hat.

The shouts and cries rent the air, but above it arose the screams of a woman, who was endeavouring to break through the ring.

"Let me get at him," she cried. "I'll teach him to raise a finger against my Jim."

That was the voice of Mary Ann ; and when she had succeeded in working her way through, it was all up with the bird-fancier. The reverend gentleman was wiping from his face as fast as possible the signs of the fray. Triumph beamed in his eye, but the triumph was short-lived.

He was awakened from his joyous dream by a terrific open-handed slap in the face, followed by what seemed red-hot wires scoring his cheeks, but it was only the gentle Mary's nails, who, woman-like, was womanfully—if we may be allowed to use such a word—defending her husband.

"You brute," she cried, following up the first attack with increasing energies, "to attack my husband in that manner. I'll teach you to beat him like a dog. Take that."

"Off, thou fiend !" cried Mr. Marall, retreating hastily round the ring of spectators. Have you forgotten your sex ? Hold off, lest I be tempted to strike thee."

"You are wretch enough to strike anything —even a woman," she answered, giving him a vicious scratch from the bridge of his nose to the tip. "Oh, that I were a man—you should not go scot free."

In the meantime Jim Podley sat upon the ground with a couple of friends, one assiduously stanching the blood which ran from his nose, the other holding a pocket-

knife to a very promising black eye. Though defeated, he had enough consciousness left to recognize the valuable services of his helpmate, and tongue enough to give her a little encouragement.

"Don't spare him, Mary," he bawled. "He's nearly killed your Jim. Let him have it. There's a woman," he added, addressing his friends, "as a man ought to be proud on."

"That she are," rejoined the one with the knife ; "and she's now give the reverend gent another buster in the eye. Now she's got his choker off—now he's down."

It was true. The Reverend Mr. Marall, whose pugilistic acquirements had sufficed to prostrate Jim Podley, had fallen under the attack of his wife. That meritorious woman had succeeded in altering his interesting countenance to such an extent, that his absence from his flock for many weeks to come would be imperative.

Once on the ground, it would have fared still worse with him but for the spectators, who succeeded in dragging the infuriated woman away. and, guided by Inky, they carried her bodily into the private apartment of the bird-fancier.

The struggle over, the reverend gentleman began to cool. He first made inquiries for his hat and umbrella, and received from a hoarse-voiced boy the very unsatisfactory reply that " he wished he might get 'em," a reply which seemed to afford the general public food for unbounded merriment.

"'Tis all right, your honour," said a man who wore a rough fur cap ; "they're only borrowed for a few days. You come next Thursday week, about four in the arternoon, and you'll find them nicely brushed and cleaned."

"Is it possible," exclaimed Mr. Marall, "that during my struggle with those wretched people that a fellow-being can have been base enough to steal my hat and umbrella ?"

"Haven't I told yer," growled the proprietor of the fur cap, "that they are only borrowed ? If you think I'm a lyin' take off your coat and come on."

Mr. Marall declined this offer, for he said that if he proceeded after the fashion proposed he might eventually part with all his apparel.

"I am a man of peace," he said, "and seek only to live in harmony with my fellow-man. I would rest now if I could for a few hours, as I cannot return home until the eve."

The landlord of a beer-shop, who happened to be in the crowd, promptly took him in tow, and led him to his house, where a plentiful supply of water, towels, and a private room were provided.

There Mr. Marall laved his wounds and imbibed certain liquids calculated to restore the even temper of his pulse ; but neither liquids outside nor in could wipe away the record left by the nails of Mary Ann.

"What can I say or do ? " murmured the reverend gentleman, as he surveyed himself in a cracked chimney-glass. "I cannot preach for a month, at least. I dare not even show my face."

One thing he was, however, fully resolved on, that henceforth, he would have nought to do with Inky or his redemption from a low life. He might go his way and Mr. Marall could go his.

The general uproar in Bunhill Row subsided, the contests were o'er, and the general public had no particular interest in the affair ; but it was food for conversation for Jim Podley and his wife throughout the rest of the day.

She bathed his face and bound up his wounds. He, touched by this unexpected tenderness, called her "Mary, love," and other endearing epithets, long a stranger between them.

Nor did the reconciliation end here. The husband and wife, now apparently fully reconciled, resolved to make a night of it, and Inky was dispatched for a bottle of the colourless liquor in whose pellucid depths a lurking devil lies.

"This is not the night for any ill-feeling." said Podley, taking a seat at the end of the table, with a poultice carefully bandaged over his eye. "Inky, you shall jine us. Bring in a box for Mary, and sit on your old stool. But fust close the shop. We can do without any furder trade to-day."

Inky had the shutters up in a twinkling, for conviviality suited his noble soul ; and this strange trio passed, after their own fashion, a very pleasant evening. But this serenity was not destined to last.

The ocean might be calm for a while, but clouds were hanging about—dark, gloomy clouds, shadows of a past life which could neither be forgotten nor forgiven.

On the morrow the old wounds were re-opened, old taunts and recriminations given and replied to, alas ! in the old way.

Two horses pulling in opposite directions cannot run together in harmony ; man and wife, hopelessly at variance, never row together down the stream of life.

A fortnight of misery passed, fourteen days of such scenes as made Inky, much as he had seen of the dark side of life in the old court, oppressed with horror.

All things must end, and the end came to this.

One morning Podley, after a violent scene with his spouse, went out, thrusting Inky over seed bag as he passed as a gentle hint not speak to him, and came back no more that day. The woman, his wife, sat up far into the night, muttering vengeance as the church clock struck the successive hours, until Inky, coiled up on the top of the game-cock box, shivered like a jelly with terror.

The dread of a hundred terrible things passed through his mind. What if Podley came home the worse for drink ? Would he kill his wife or would she kill him ? Perhaps both might be murdered.

Inky shuddered, and drew the rug closer round him, as he thought of being left in the house with the dead bodies, but throughout that long night Podley did not appear, and Inky could not sleep.

After five the woman moved not, and the boy imagined that she was sleeping ; daylight peeped through the shutters, the cocks crowed and the birds chirped, while the rabbits moved restlessly about their hutches.

Glad of any change, Inky arose and opened the shop. As he rolled back the door, Podley's wife looked out.

"What are you doing ? " she asked.

"Taking down the shutters," replied Inky

"Daylight so soon," muttered the woman, "and Jim not here ? "

She spoke more to herself than to Inky, and without waiting for an answer went back to the room, softly closing the door behind her.

The shutters down, Inky swept out the shop, and then sat upon the doorstep, patiently awaiting the usual summons to breakfast, but the clock chimed and struck again and again, and still the strange, unhappy woman sat within and made no sign. The thoroughfare grew busy with life, men went to and fro bent upon business or pleasure, women started to the chandler's shop to make their meagre purchases, children came out to play, and the hour of ten was announced by the shrill-toned bell, and Inky remained breakfastless, the remorseless tooth of hunger gnawing at his empty stomach.

"I shall have to speak out in a minute," he thought. "Rows is bad enough to stand, but the want of wittles is wus. I wonder what she's doin'."

He was in a wondering frame of mind, and became absorbed in the movements of three men who emerged from the public house close by, wiping their mouths with the backs of their hands—pocket-handkerchiefs being scanty articles, and economically used, if at all, in Bunhill Row.

They were all stout, burly men, clad for the most part in velveteen, with an unmistakable air of " fancy " about them from top to toe.

They came straight towards the bird-fancier's, and halted only when the spare form of Inky barred the way.

"Mr. Podley ain't in," he said.

"I knows he ain't," rejoined the foremost, "but I'm comin' in to see his missus."

Inky gave way, and they entered, not with the doubtful steps of visitors who are doubtful of the welcome in store, but with the assured air of men who had every right to stand beneath the roof.

"Now then, Mrs. Podley," said the man who had previously spoken, opening the door of the back room, "you are a quick hand at movin', ain't you?"

Inky, who was walking behind, saw her rise and face the men with anger flashing from her eyes.

"What do you mean?" she asked.

"This, my dear," rejoined the man; "that Jim's sold off his house and stock, and I've bought 'em both."

"Oh! that's it," she said slowly, "but how am I to know whether it's true?"

"Here's the papers, all signed and sealed."

She only glanced at them, then sat down, and resting her head upon her hands, became wrapped for some minutes in meditation.

"Did he send any message to me?" she asked, at length looking up.

"He sent his best wishes, and hoped as how you would get along somehow. He also sent two suvrins, which are here. I ain't a good hand at speakin', but that's the best way I can put it."

"So he has done *that*," she said, rising, without casting a look upon the coins lying on the table. "A bad day's work for me, but a worse one for him. You hear me, don't you?"

"I hear you, missus."

"Tell him, when you meet him, that light as he makes o' me, I haven't done with him yet. Tell him that he *can't* hide from me, and if he goes to the other end of the world I'll find him out. Tell him, for all his cunning, that I've not done with him yet."

So saying, she went out, without touching the proffered money, and looking neither to the right nor the left, went straight out of the house and disappeared.

"I wouldn't be Jim," said the man, "not for anything—no, not for Gander's best pup—no, that I wouldn't. It will be a bad day for *him* when they meet again."

His mates assented, one remarking in a gruff undertone that, "Jim's gal seemed to be a cross-bred 'un, and one likely to play at knives and forks."

They then turned their attention to Inky, who had remained in a state of open-eyed, silent stupefaction, and he who appeared to be the master thus addressed him—

"You are Jim's boy ain't you?"

"I've helped him in his business," answered Inky, evasively.

"The same thing, my lad, and you needn't put too fine a p'int upon it. Jim's sent you ten shillings, which he says is nine and tenpence more than you are worth."

"I've been very useful to him," pleaded Inky, "and it's very hard I should drop inter this, as a noble chap stolen when he was a child of Fate—Destiny."

"So you're the child o' Destiny," said the man. "Where is he, and what's his line?'

"He ain't got no line, and 'tain't a man—it's—it's a thing which ain't wisible, but makes you do whatever it likes."

"Well, it seems curious, my lad, but it ain't no bizness o' mine. Take up your ten shillings, and tramp."

"Couldn't I stop with you?" asked Inky.

"I've got a boy," replied the man, "one of my own rearin', such as is worth his weight in gold; you two couldn't get on together; he'd eat you in a week, so pack up and morrice—bolt."

Inky, having a strong objection to the first-mentioned process, and seeing no prospect of a second engagement, put his spare apparel—the check trousers and waistcoat—into a piece of newspaper and prepared to depart.

"I've a word to say before I go," he said, pulling up at the door. "Mr. Podley is afeard of his wife, that I know, but he ought to be more afeard of *me*. He nabbed my five-pun note, the sole relic of my nobble father's nobble fortune. I shan't forget it, and when you sees him tell him to beweer of the child of Fate—Destiny—for let him go ahead revelling as he may, the hour of wengeance and my glorious triump must come."

"I ain't likely to see him as far as I know," replied the man, "but if I should I'll mention it. Now then, I expects my boy here every moment, and should he find you here he might make a clean bolt of you—so foot it, while you've got a chance."

Impressed by this solemn warning, Inky took one fond, longing look around the bird-fancier's shop, his eyes resting last on the game-cock box where he had so often courted repose, and, turning on his heel, went into Bunhill Row, with the wide, wide world once more before him.

CHAPTER XXIV.

A FRIEND OF THE OPPRESSED.

DEEPLY cogitating upon the wondrous phases of life, Sam Smarty pursued his way from the establishment of Messrs. Kidem and Blowhard, to the residence of Mr. Newbold Fizkin.

The errand Sam was upon suited his temperament to a hair; he was in search of copy, for Mr. Newbold Fizkin was contributor to a journal printed by Kidem and Blowhard, and a very lazy contributor to boot.

Sam's instructions were "to stop until he got it—if it was all night;" so Sam, knowing the disposition of the gentleman whom he was about to honour with a visit, made the necessary preparations for a long stay.

"Once in," he mused thoughtfully, "once in his house, I mustn't come out till I've got it. Let's see—I can do about twelve hours on a polony and bread—they can't refuse a man a drink of water."

He purchased his small requirements and stored them under his apron; and thus fortified, lost no time in reaching the abode of Mr. Newbold Fizkin.

A lover of the almost exploded Bohemianism, Mr. Fizkin lived in meagre, fusty apartments in Eagle Street, Pentonville, where he revelled, after a fashion, with a few congenial spirits, far into the small hours.

It is almost needless to say that Mr. Fizkin was in debt; he had read Goldsmith, and thought it the proper thing to be so; in fact, he had run the length of his tether, and being as we have already declared, an idle fellow, he would neither leave his present abode, nor settle with the band of small creditors who hammered daily at his door.

The consequence was, that he was in a state of siege, and when Sam rang the third bell from the bottom, Mr. Fizkin's own bell, he rang in vain.

Patient in the time of trial, Sam waited five minutes, and then rang again—then the sound of a sash being gently raised fell upon Sam's ear.

Looking up quickly, he beheld a head enveloped in a dingy smoking-cap, but he could not detect the features, as it was instantly withdrawn.

"It's no use coming that game," muttered Sam, giving the bell a third jerk, "I wants the copy, and I'll have it. Now, Mr. Fizkin, show up, or I'll set all the tinklers goin'."

Sam was spared this painful alternative, by the door being opened by a shock-headed girl, who was wiping her arms apparently fresh from the wash-tub.

"I want's Mr. Fizkin," said Sam.

"He ain't in," answered the girl, quickly.

"Then I'll come in and wait."

"You can't see him to-day, he ain't well."

"Ill or well," said Sam, "I must see him."

"He's very bad."

"No doubt—but he'll be better presently."

The girl tried to bar the way, but Sam was not to be denied, and he walked in.

"Now, Mr. Fizkin," he roared up the staircase, "where's that copy?"

"Who's there?" cried a voice from above.

"Me—Sam Smarty."

"Come up, you limb of the Evil One," rejoined the voice, "why couldn't you say so before?"

"I can't talk to people through brick walls," growled Sam, as he laboured up the dark staircase.

He knew his way pretty well, and opening Mr. Fizkin's door, entered.

That active and intelligent gentleman was lounging in a tattered arm-chair, facing another gentleman equally active and intelligent, who lounged upon an ottoman almost wrecked by many years of ill-usage.

"Now, Sam," said Mr. Fizkin, filling his pipe, "what do you want?"

"Copy," answered Sam.

"I posted it an hour ago."

"I'm to take it back, and I can't go without it," returned Sam, doggedly.

"I'll send it in an hour," said Mr. Fizkin, forgetting his previous assertion.

"I really wonder at you," said Sam, reproachfully; "had the machine waitin', and the whole routine of our establishment upset on account of your not sendin' in four columns. I wonder they stand it; when I'm master printer I shan't."

"You hear him, Twiddy?" said Mr. Fizkin, addressing his friend.

"I hear him," replied the other, "and see him too."

"Nice boy, ain't he?"

"Very. I hope there are no more in the family."

"Now, you would hardly think," pursued Mr. Fizkin, "that I have been more than a father to that boy. By his conduct this morning, one would think that I had been a foe—not a friend. And yet," he added, carefully wiping one eye, "I loved him dearly, and love him still."

"Base ingratitude!" murmured Twiddy, who appeared to be half asleep; "chuck him out of the window."

"You hear that?" said Fizkin, turning to Sam, "you hear the advice of a bosom friend, and a man of the world. He advocates the seizure of your youthful body by the strong arm of outraged Justice, and your being cast forth to the place from whence you came. Boy, what have you to say against the sentence of the learned Twiddy being carried out upon you?"

"Are you going to do the copy?" demanded Sam, sternly, waving his hand to imply that he dismissed Twiddy and his sentence as matters of no moment.

"Give him a roll of paper and let him go," murmured Twiddy.

"I'm not a goin' to waste any more time," said Sam. "I've got my dooty to do, and that's to sit on the stairs until you've done the copy, that's your dooty—do it."

He then retired to the shades and sat upon the head of the stairs. There he remained for half an hour, until summoned by Mr. Fizkin, who handed him a roll of paper carefully tied and sealed.

"Have you brought a cheque, Sam?"

"No, I ain't," replied Sam, unceremoniously breaking the seal, "and you don't expect a cheque for this, I hope. Mr. Fizkin, I blushes for you."

Sam then cast down upon the table a roll of plain paper, and retired once more to the staircase.

"He's too much for me," said Fizkin, with a sigh; "I suppose I must do it, Twiddy."

"I s'pose you must," murmured Mr. Twiddy.

"The sooner that boy gets the sack from Kidem and Blowhard's the better I shall like it," said Fizkin, sitting down to write; "he is the most pertinacious cuss that ever lived."

Then he began, and having broken the ice of laziness, scribbled away for a couple of hours without a halt, while Mr. Twiddy seconded the noise of his pen with a very unmusical snore.

Sam sat listening with a complacent smile, proud of having overcome the indolence of the Bohemian author, and at the end of the first hour partook of his polony and bread with much relish. In due time he was summoned, and Mr. Fizkin, lounging once more in his easy chair, pointed negligently to several sheets closely covered with writing.

"Roll them up," he said, "there is enough and to spare for your rapacious maw. Get thee gone, and let me get the fumes of the house of slavery out of the house."

"If I was a literary gent," rejoined Sam, anxious to bestow a piece of parting advice, "I'd have my work well forrard, and go down to Margate for a week, the sea hair would do you good—give your thoughts a polish."

"But you are not a literary gent," said Mr. Fizkin.

"Thank goodness I am *not!*" replied Sam, with great emphasis; "I wouldn't have the running of a harmless boy orf his legs about twice a week on my conscience for anything, 'specially when it brings that boy all the way from the city, without as much as purviding a sign of wittles for him."

"I have none for myself," returned Mr. Fizkin. "Twiddy, too, is stumpus, and I haven't even the usual sixpence for you."

"I'll put it down to next time," said Sam, easily; "but, lor'! what a difference it would make if you would only move yourself now and then! Did you ever try shower-baths?"

"Avaunt, thou demon," said Mr. Fizkin, feeling about for a foot-stool; "thou hast filled thy rapacious maw—why torturest thou me?"

"Adoo! Adoo!" returned Sam, tucking the copy carefully into his trousers pocket. "I takes my leave, genelmen."

Mr. Fizkin answered with a mutter curse, Twiddy with a snore, and Sam clatt downstairs into the street.

"Easier than I expected," he mused; "improvin'. A few more lectures from will make a man on him—*of* him. Dash I can't get hold o' that grammar-book."

His task performed, the mind of Sam was at peace, and although as good a lad as a printer could expect, he had his little failings, one of which was to loiter occasionally by the way.

Convinced that he would not be expected back at the office for two hours or more, he entered into the spirit of public affairs, beginning with a drunken man railing at the empty air, whom he advised "to go home and sleep it orf, for he didn't look pretty," a piece of advice which had so much effect upon the man, that he threw his hat at him.

"That's the way with 'em," said Sam, affably addressing a mild old gentleman who was surveying the drunkard with mingled pity and horror. "Yer may adwise, adwise, adwise, from mornin' till night, and they do nothing but chuck their tiles at yer. Hold up, old man."

The last remark was addressed to the party who had taken in an over supply of beer, who lurched forward at Sam, and fell upon his nose.

Sam left him there, and turned into Pentonville Hill, where a flock of sheep brought out his agricultural instincts, and he became a young drover instantly, yelling, whistling, and shrieking at the bewildered "muttons," whenever they diverged from the right track.

"Prime lot, these," he said, addressing the drover, during a pause.

"Prime or not," growled the man, "they are a cussed lot o' trouble. What do you know about 'em?"

"I lives a-nigh a butcher," returned Sam, "and my father once killed a cow with a horse and cart."

"Now you make a cut of it, will yer?" said the man, suddenly turning savage. "It's bad enough to hev to take these from the market to Paddington with ne'er a drop beer, without bein' cheeked by the likes you."

"Well, I'll say farewell," replied Sam; "but you'll be sorry for this afore long."

Finding the drover unsociable, Sam left him, and next forced his way through a group of people standing around a man who was selling some compound warranted to turn everything into silver or gold. Only staying to have the last penny in his pocket silvered and exhibited to the public as a specimen, Sam left the charlatan, and, meeting with a boy about his own age, who was carrying a tin bath over his head, at once lodged half a brick thereon with considerable force, to the infinite terror of the bearer of the burden, who thought that a house at least had fallen upon him.

"At it again!" cried Sam, peeping under. "Ha! would you be wicious?"

The boy had aimed a blow at him, and the two embraced, the struggle ending with the fall of the bath, and the two combatants rolling into it.

A policeman hard by interfered, and, dragging the two boys up, aimed a blow at Sam, whom he missed, and then smote the knight of the bath heavily.

"Hit him agen," urged Sam, from a safe distance, "and take away the b'iler. You know he stole it."

Without waiting to see what faith was placed in this assertion, Sam sauntered on, choosing the quiet ways, and conducting himself respectably for nearly five minutes, only during that time pitching the cap of a boy who was engaged in a solitary game of knuckle-down upon the top of a passing teacart.

The loser hastened after the cart, and Sam continued on his way until he overtook a seedy old man, carrying under his arm a three-legged stool.

"What a rum thing for a man to carry about!" muttered Sam. "Hev he stole it or what? The figger, too, seems familyar unto me. I knows the stoop, and the bend of the right leg, likewise that hackin' cough, and them shoes run down to heel."

He could have ascertained who it was by walking briskly to the front, and passing the wayfarer, but he preferred keeping his curiosity in suspense; surmising afforded him a little intellectual amusement, and lent a charm to his stroll, which was getting rather dull.

The old man kept on at a slouching pace until he reached the corner of a quiet street, when he put down his stool and mounted thereon.

Then Sam faced him.

There was no doubt about the person now, especially when he opened his mouth, and addressed a group of children in the style of itinerant orators.

"Friends and fellow-workmen," he said, "the time of the suppressor draweth nigh, the voice of the nation is lifted up, and men have awoke up out of a sleep. Already a bloated olijarchy trembleth in its painted halls, and the nobbles of the land are a shaking in their shoes. Fellow working men, be up and doin'."

"I thowt so," muttered Sam. "It is old Work-it-out."

CHAPTER XXV.

INKY'S WANDERINGS.

WITH ten shillings in his pocket, and the remnants of his "gorging raiment," Inky left the bird-fancier's, and began the world anew.

He would gladly have gone down to Sam for advice, but Inky was not entirely devoid of conscience, and that still small voice recalled to him his late conduct when he thought that he was growing rich, and above his more humble acquaintances of Fleet Street.

"He won't have anything to say to me," thought Inky, judging Sam's character by his own. "I was a great fool then—never mind, I shall know better next time."

Not until you have learned the lesson of adversity, most worthy Inky, and although you have found a low depth, there is a deeper still.

With his little bundle under his arm, and with no definite purpose in his head, he crossed Finsbury, and struck through the streets bearing down towards Shoreditch, ruminating upon the events of his life, and repeatedly regretting the loss of his five-pound note.

"If I could only hev changed it," he thought, "then I might have done something —started a tater can, perhaps. I've heard of fortunes being made in that line. Old Mike have made his money, and why shouldn't I?"

The thought of Mike brought on an appetite for whelks, and halting opposite the railway station, he changed the first shilling, and partook of four saucers of that mysterious and somewhat leathery fish, topping up with a few stewed prunes, and an oyster weighing about six ounces without its shell.

Much refreshed thereby, he strolled on towards the Hackney Road as far as Cambridge Gate, when, finding that he was getting too far into the country, he turned to the right towards Bethnal Green.

He was now in a maze of small streets, where the air was rife with the sounds of labour. From every door and window the noise of loom, hammer, or treadle came— weavers, basket-makers, box-makers, match makers, and a score of other trades, were crowded densely together, the very children in the street carrying packages to and fro, with all of childhood that should have been in their faces stamped out by the labour more fit for men.

"There seems to be plenty of work," thought Inky. "I'll have a try for it."

He entered a house where bundles of osiers and other things at the door showed it to be a basket-maker's. There was no shop window, and a man sat working in a room which had once been the parlour of the little house. At the other end of the room was a woman, with three children, mere infants, clustered at her knees. She was busy splitting the slender rods for her husband's work.

"What do you want?" asked the man, looking up for a moment, then busily resuming his work.

"Can yer give me anything to do?" asked Inky.

"No, I can't."

"I'm willin' to do anything," urged Inky, "and I don't want much pay."

"You've come to the wrong shop, my lad," said the man. "I've three sons out seeking work—times is bad with us. There's ten thousand people about here takin' parish relief."

"Then you think there ain't a chance about here?"

"Not a bit, my boy; we ain't got 'arf enough for friends and neighbours."

Inky bade him good morning, and turned away with a heavy heart. Too disheartened to try elsewhere, he wandered round and round the neighbourhood until nightfall, when, for the first time, he thought of the necessity of getting a bed.

Up to the present time he had never wanted a roof, however humble, to shelter him; but he now saw that the time might not be far distant when he would have nought but the streets to sleep in, and be glad of the very market baskets which he knew Tom used to inhabit during the dark hours of the night, and which he had often spoken of with the utmost contempt.

"If I should come down to it," he muttered, as a cold perspiration broke out upon him, what a go it will be! 'Tain't as if I'd been used to their company, and if I goes among 'em a stranger, they'll fall foul o' me like a lot o' young savages. Oh!" he groaned, "I know's 'em well."

He thrust his hands into his pockets, and rattled the money he possessed; this cheered him a bit. For the present, at least, he had the means of obtaining and paying for a place of rest, so he looked about for a suitable place, and easily found a house with a lamp bearing the inscription, "Cheap Beds."

It was not a very enticing-looking house, but Inky's time had not been cast entirely in pleasant places, and he was therefore not very fastidious.

The door stood partly open, and, pushing it aside, he entered. The passage was rather dark, and failing to perceive a mat riddled with holes, stumbled over it, and measured his length upon the floor.

"Who's there?" growled a voice.

"Only me, sir," answered Inky; "a poor boy as wants a night's lodging."

"Then why couldn't you—you come in quieter? Turn the handle of the door to the left."

Inky felt about for the handle, and after a few moments, filled up by the invisible gentleman with language not fit for ears polite, found it.

Acting as desired, Inky found himself in a small room, where a man was sitting on a cane-bottomed chair before a fire, smoking and drinking.

It was a warm night, and the heat of the fire in addition made the room so stifling that he staggered back.

"There ain't many as can stand it," said the man grimly; "but I've lived all my life at the 'quator, and without a fire I should shiver like the deuce. What's your name?"

"Inky Work-it-out."

"Can you patter flash?"

"What's that, sir?"

"All right, never mind. Town or country? Come nearer; oh! town, I see. Now, where do you come from, and what's your swag?"

"I ain't got no swag," said Inky, in an injured tone. "I'm a honest lad, without friends, nobbly born, and lorst by the nuss in my childhood. I was arterwards turned into a kid—child of Destiny, and chucked about by a bird-fancier, who's runned away from his wife, and left me to the parsecution of a chap in a fur cap and welweteen."

"Well, you ain't tongue-tied," said the man; "how much money have you got?"

"A shilling," replied Inky, who was too canny to declare the full amount of his wealth.

"Put it on the table, and I'll give you supper and bed for it; although I shall lose 'arf-a-crown at least by you."

Inky put the coin on the table, and asked if the supper was ready.

"No," replied the host, "but it'll be on the table at eleven sharp, when all the boys are sure to be in. The room's at the end of the passage; go there and wait.

It was barely nine o'clock, and Inky was very hungry, but he was afraid to complain, and went out to find the place where supper was eventually to appear.

He thought his host alluded to his own children—workers probably—when he spoke of the boys; and expected to find the supper room a similar place to the one he had left, but to his astonishment, it proved to be a very large hall, about thirty feet from end to and, and twenty wide, with two rows of tables, and forms to match.

This he could see by the light of a gas burner, half turned down. Having no instructions to the contrary, Inky put on the gas, and proceeded to take a more minute examination of the room.

There was much to puzzle him. The tables and forms were scored deep with initials and other forms of engraving; a gallows being, apparently, a very popular form of illustration.

The walls were illustrated also in a very profuse manner; some pretty fairly done, a mackerel and a mutton chop in coloured chalks especially so; but most of the artistic efforts were wanting in anything at all approaching talent, the execution and subject chosen being of the very coarsest description.

There was one person who appeared to employ the artists' time to a great degree, for at least fifty portraits of him in different attitudes were depicted on the walls, with underlines for the most part complimentary, but some of an undoubtable insulting character. His name appeared to be Ripper Gooch, although Ripper alone was the general appellation.

The following are some of the notices of this gentleman:—

"Ripper as a flying stationer" (hawker of street ballads); "Ripper Gooch in his Kingsman" (coloured neckerchief); "Ripper wopping the Knuller" (chimney-sweep); "Ripper arter a week on Cag-mag" (scraps of food—odds and ends)—here he was depicted as lean as a greyhound—and many more of the slangy style—all Greek to Inky, who puzzled his mind over the strange caligraphy for an hour or more, but could make nothing of it.

"I wonder what a flyin' stationer is?" he thought, "something in the hacrobat line? Kingsman, too—sounds like summat on a stage. I've got into the company of showmen—that's wot it is; lord! won't it be jolly? I think I'll go upon the road, and be a baring bold. Hullo! here comes somebody."

With a crash the door opened, and a body of boys, numbering a score at least, rushed laughing and shouting into the room.

CHAPTER XXVI.

INKY'S FRIEND.

THE new-comers lost no time in making themselves acquainted with Inky, for they rushed into his arms, as it were, as soon as they entered; one taking charge of his bundle, and the rest displaying a strong desire to inspect the contents of his pockets, but Inky resisted this stoutly, doubling himself up like a hedgehog, so as to foil their efforts, unless violence was adopted.

This, however, was not done, for after a slight struggle they left the boy alone, and turned their attention to the bundle.

"Oh, criminy," cried one, as he held up the dilapidated checks, "here's a Sunday soot—who's this as have honoured us with a visit? Is it the Dook of Lambeth, or the Fust Lord of Ammersmith?"

"Stow your red rag (tongue)," interposed another, sternly, "don't you see he's a freshman. I say, younker, you don't patter flash?"

Inky, who had borne his wrongs with ill-suppressed indignation, answered, "No."

"Then we'll talk clean lingo to you," rejoined the other. "Who are you, and wot's your name?"

"My name," returned Inky, after a moment's reflection, is "Inkybus Pierson."

"Werry good, Mr. Inkybust—and where did you hang out last?"

"What do yer mean?"

"Where do you live?" returned the other, impatiently, "who's your father? who's your mother? and how's your uncle?"

"I ain't got no relations," said Inky, "leastways I've got 'em, but I can't find 'em. They was stolen from me in my hinfancy."

"That's a rum story."

"It's troo, every word on't," rejoined Inky, with tears in his eyes, "and the old willin is now a livin' on my parsimony, with Tom, as was a box o' lights, and although Podley thinks he hav' got orf clear with my five-pun' note, he'll find it out, for the hour of triump for the Child of Destiny cometh on."

The boys listened with a wondering attention to Inky's somewhat confused story, and by their looks it was plain they could make nothing of it. He who had been questioning was puzzled more than all.

"I ain't 'cute at some things," he said, scratching his head, "but this beats all—I must leave it to Ripper Gooch to settle."

"Who is Ripper Gooch?" Inky could not help inquiring.

"The risin' man of his time," answered the other, "he's risen from the kinchin lay (robbing young children sent with money on errands) to be a prop nailer (one who snatches pins from gentleman's scarves); and Leary—that's the chap as keeps the ken here—says he'll be as great a rampsman (a thief who uses violence) as there ever was; he's king here, that's what he is, and when he comes, you mind your mouthings."

The air of these strangers, their slang and tone, roused even Inky's sluggish instinct, and he felt that an ill wind had blown him into a harbour where there was very little of real safety. He made up his mind to beat a retreat as soon as an opportunity offered.

Their queries ended for the time, Inky's strange companions drew apart, and apparently left him to do as he pleased ; one of them lighted a fire in the grate, and they all gathered around, conversing together in an undertone.

Inky gave them what he considered to be sufficient time for them to forget him, and then stole cautiously towards the door. One, two, three steps, and then a voice pulled him up sharp.

"Where are you going, stranger ? "

It came from the boy who had previously addressed him.

Inky hesitated, coughed, and replied with an unmistakable tremor in his voice—

"Only to—o—o—see wha—at sort of a night it is."

"Sit down," was the cool rejoinder, spoken in a tone of command ; "there'll be plenty here directly to let you know how the wind is."

The "nobbly born" smiled faintly and complied, he felt as helpless as a mouse in a trap.

The time rolled slowly on for nearly an hour, the boys still whispering to each other. Inky sitting motionless, with his hand in his pocket, tightly clasping the remnant of his worldly wealth.

"I won't give that up," he thought, "without a mortial struggle, if they are ten to one ; but it's very 'ard to be a child of Destiny."

He brooded deeply over his unhappy fate, until aroused by the entrance of more visitors, among whom were several men in stature and strength, although young in years, not more than nineteen, but full-blown specimens of the curse of large communities —the rough proper.

They required no certificate of character ; the thick-set frame, the bull neck and beetling brows, spoke plainly, and stamped them indelibly with the words "ruffian and rogue."

They, of course, bestowed an immediate attention upon Inky, whom they could have, metaphorically speaking of course, turned inside out in two minutes, but for the dread they had of the renowned Ripper Gooch, without whom, apparently, nothing out of the usual course could be done.

As the time rolled on, company increased by two's and three's until about thirty at least must have been assembled there, and Inky gathered from the few words he could pick up—no easy matter, for their language was plentifully bespattered with slang—that the great man alone was needed to complete the party.

He came at last, followed by Leary, the master of the house, who walked with one hand upon his shoulder, and leaning with the other upon a stick ; Mr. Leary was labouring under an aristocratic complaint, the gout.

Inky had been picturing Ripper Gooch in his mind as a burly ruffian of herculean frame, but he was doomed to disappointment. Mr. Gooch was a tall, slim young man, with features and manners which would have been tolerably good had they not been hopelessly flash.

In response to a general greeting he raised his hat, bowed in the style of the bucks of old, and sat down.

"Anything fresh to-night, Leary ? " he asked.

"Trapper's caught, and got a three months' summary," replied Leary.

"What for ? "

"Loiterin' on suspicion."

"Trapper's careless. Who's the freshman ? "

He pointed to Inky, who, impressed by the reverence paid to this reigning leader of petty rogues and thieves, arose and put his knuckles to his forehead.

"Dropped in for a night," said Leary ; says he's only got a shilling."

"Oh ! well, we shall see about that. Come here, young green 'un."

"Why don't yer go forrard, Inkybust ? " said one of the boys, giving him a push.

Inky, with fear in his eye, and a faltering lip, arose and stood before the presence of the great man, who looked him up and down with a pretentious knitting of the brows.

"So your name is Inkybust ? " he said, when the inspection was over.

"Sech it are," replied Inky.

"Alias, I suppose ? "

"I've got another," said Inky, "but I can't use it yet."

"Been prigging your master's till ? "

"Oh, no, sir ! " returned Inky, speaking very rapidly, "I'm the heir and parent of the Booforth 'states, but owin' to my bein' stolen, and another chap taken out of the Covent Garden baskets and shoved on ter the Markis instead o' me, I was turned out o' Podley's, who prigged my five-poun' note."

"Go over that again—slowly," said Ripper Gooch.

"I'm the heir and parent of the Booforth 'states," rejoined Inky, "but owin' to Work-it-out havin' put away my gorging raiment, and the boys fallin' foul on and making a perfect picter on me, the reverend gent turned me orf ; but he was arterwards sorry, and comed down to the Row, when Jim's missis let him have it, and somebody run away with his gingham and hat. Jim sent two pounds to his missis, and sold the shop to a chap in a fur cap."

Well might Mr. Ripper Gooch look astonished as Inky poured forth the story of his career, and well might certain youths listening around go through a certain pantomime and cry "Gammon!"

"It ain't gammon," said Inky, weeping gently. "It's as true as I'm livin'."

The fact was, the events of the day and company of the night had so bewildered Inky, whose mind was not of the strongest at the best of times, that his ideas were hopelessly muddled, and ran out of his head as they came into it, like peas through a pipe.

"And yet you have the look of a liar," said Ripper Gooch; "anyhow, my lad, I'll not contradict you at present. Supper ready, Leary?"

"In a minute," replied the host, and in five it was put upon the table; a mess of Irish stew and bread, with a mug of tolerable good beer for each of the company.

Inky sat down with the rest, on the left side of Mr. Gooch, by that gentleman's particular desire; but even there he was not safe. While consuming his stew with the avidity of one whose appetite had grown fierce with hunger, his mug of beer disappeared, and an empty one was put in its place; and as Mr. Leary declined to furnish a second supply, he had to put up with water.

"Here," said Mr. Leary, "you must keep your eyes about you."

After supper, most of the boys fell to gambling for paltry sums, expressing their joy or anger, as the tables turned, in language, for the most part, happily strange to Inky, who, with all his faults and follies, had never been an associate of vice.

He was further interrogated by Ripper Gooch, who drew him apart, and questioned him closely upon his past life; finally eliciting from him the main facts connected with himself, Tom, and Sam, as set down here.

"What sort of a fellow is Tom?" asked Ripper, thoughtfully; "is he 'cute—knowing—does he know his way about?"

"He's as innocent as a lamb," replied Inky, "altho' he's spent all his life in the streets and down at the Garden."

"I suppose it would be an awkward thing for him if any of his old chums turned up?"

"It would rooin him," returned Inky. "Alas! when I went I got sech a cold shoulder as you never see—think on it—me! who's got ten times more right than he have——"

"Just so—just so," said the other; "and he's still staying in Belgrave Square?"

"No! I heerd he was goin' orf to school."

"Where?"

"Don't know where; but it's a crack place, you may bet your life upon it."

"And you can't give me the tip?"

"What do you want it for?"

"I don't mind telling you," said Ripper Gooch, confidentially. "I know this Tom, he's a sort of—kind of—'arf brother of mine, do you see—eh?"

"Well, I can't say I do, 'zactly."

"He is though, and I can show you the papers to-morrow; I thought it was, as soon as you mentioned him, and I want to look him up. Now he's among the nobs he ought to help me."

"So he ought," assented Inky.

"I see you've got some good sense and brotherly feeling about you," said Ripper, approvingly; "there's good stuff in you, Inkybust. I must find him; do you think this Sam—Sam—what's his name?"

"Sam Smarty."

"Yes! do you think he could help me?"

"Werry likely."

"Where can I find him?"

"At Kidem and Blowhard's, Shoe Lane. Ask anybody there, and they'll p'int him out."

"Thanks," returned Ripper, yawning, "I'll remember; of course, I'm not particular about seeing him, but if I can spare the time I'll run over and see him in a week or so."

He had, apparently, done with Inky for the time, and leaning back upon the settle, remained for some time in a meditative state. The silence between them was broken by Inky, who had been surveying him with an air of curiosity.

"You don't seem much like the rest o' these chaps," he said, glancing towards the boys.

"I have nothing in common with them," was the reply.

"You seem more delicate like—ain't so strong," hinted Inky.

"As for strength," rejoined Ripper, with a smile, "I could pitch any of them out of the window. Look at my wrists."

Inky looked at them—they were as sinewy as the legs of an ox.

"Feel my muscle—hard as steel. I'm strong enough; but look here, hadn't you better go to bed."

"I am rather tired."

"Then go up at once—first floor—with a figure three chalked on the door; don't trouble Leary, and take the bed furthest from the door."

Inky bade him good night, and slipping quietly past the others, hastened up-stairs, where a small rushlight burning on the landing revealed the number he sought.

The room was long and narrow, with a dozen beds, ranged side by side upon a board sloping slightly from the head.

The linen was rough and coarse, but

cleaner than Inky might have expected, and putting his bundle in the place of a pillow, he slipped off his garments, and getting under the wide counterpane, fell asleep.

Shortly after he left the room below, Ripper went into the private apartments of the house.

"Leary," he said, "I've got a new lay. A safe and a paying one, I think. Let me have two pounds?"

"I haven't 'arf the money in the world," grumbled Leary.

"Didn't I hand over the last," was the cool rejoinder. "You'll have good interest for the money."

After many vows and protestations from Leary, that he never was so poor as at the present time, and that he was thinking of hunting up a friend to help him, and so on—all of which met with contemptuous comments from the other—he brought out a canvass bag and paid over the money in silver, taking a receipt from his pupil and friend, which he inspected with much care, and placed in an old, well-worn greasy pocketbook.

"I shall be off early to-morrow," said Ripper, "and if I'm away a few days, don't fret and fume."

"And what about the freshman?"

"He'll do no good here," returned Ripper, coolly, "and may do harm—kick him out."

CHAPTER XXVII.

A PUBLIC BENEFACTOR COMES TO GRIEF.

WE left our particular friend, Sam Smarty, standing in the midst of a limited assemblage, listening to the outpourings of the latest champion of the people, Mr. Harris, *alias* old Work-it-out, late of Sceptre Court, but now of nowhere in particular.

"Here's a move," thought Sam, as the old man continued his rabid outpourings, "the loss of Inky has turned his brain. The idea of a-preaching to a lot o' young 'uns—*they* ain't perlitical."

But Work-it-out knew all he was doing better than Sam could tell him, smart as Sam generally was. Children only formed the substratum of his audience; they were the foundation stones upon which other materials were quickly piled. First, a man stopped, then a woman, then two men who were walking arm-in-arm, and evidently in the most charitable manner supporting each other after a day's enjoyment, then more men and more women, until a fairish crowd had gathered, and Work-it-out's point was gained.

"Men of Hengland," he cried, tossing his arms up wildly, "will yer stand by and see the Jugglenort cart of the landing purprieters crush the bones of posterity? Think of the thousands starvin', and the hundreds rollin' in a lapse of luxury, drinkin' wine by the butt, and turnin' up their noses at good meat. Will yer stand by and see a nation's tares, and not try to wipe 'em dry?"

"My handkercheve is at the wash," interposed a voice—it was Sam's. Work-it-out ignored the interruption, and went on.

"What air our rights—what air our doos? Them as werks ought to eat, and them as don't work oughtn't to eat, and the time is a commin' on when the rich as ride over us every day in their carriage will come down with a squash on to the stones, and where'll they be then?"

"All werry good, no doubt," thought Sam; "but how does old Work-it-out make a livin' at it."

The riddle was soon solved.

Diving deep into the tails of his old coat, Work-it-out brought forth a bundle of very small pamphlets, which he held aloft.

"Brother citizens, feller-contrimen," he continued, "I've got here a little pamflet written by a man who knows more than all the parlyments put together. He's only a contryman, one of Hengland's slaves, but he's got a mind s'perior to the nobs, like the rest of yer. The title of this 'ere pamflet is, 'The Hour and the Man; or, Five Hours Labour and Six Meals a Day, with a House in the Clear,' and the price on it is only a penny. There's a hoomerous Litany chucked in for them as likes to read it. Only a penny. What! nobody have one?"

Nobody ventured on the speculation, and Work-it-out descended from his stool in disgust.

"I weeps for my feller man; you ain't got a spark o' feelin' in yer," he said, suddenly abandoning the laudatory style of address, and verging on the abusive; "you're a low-bred lot; there you'll stand grinnin' round a man as turned up a good retail trade—in—in—leather for you—a man who comes out as bold as anything, and risks his life by a defying of the government, the queen, the r'yal family, and the bloated followers o' the court. Where's yer feelin's, where's yer manners, that's what I want to know?"

"Take it easy, old man," said a labourer who had been listening, and thoughtfully chewing a bit of straw.

"Go your ways," cried Work-it-out, "I've done with you. I turns you up. I lays down the cause."

So saying, he dashed his bundle on the ground, picked it up again, tucked it under his arm, and with the stool in his hand, walked off.

Sam followed, for he looked upon Work-it-out as an old friend, one in whose movements he ought to be interested. He anticipated the pleasure of hearing a little more of Mr. Harris's oratorical powers, but he was doomed

THE WANDERER'S RETURN.

7

to disappointment; the first place the friend of the people pulled up at was a marine store dealer's, where he disposed of his stool and several bundles of pamphlets, and received in return the sum of two shillings; the next place he halted at was a place duly licensed for the sale of malt and spirituous liquors.

"That's bad," thought Sam; "but Work-it-out allys had a deloosive weakness for liquors."

As the ex-cobbler had travelled his way, Sam kindly waited for him, and in a few minutes he came forth apparently much refreshed.

He kept on towards the city, and Sam followed, a few yards in the rear.

This he soon discovered to be troublesome work, for Work-it-out pulled up at every other house of refreshment, and partook of something, his eye growing brighter, and his legs unsteadier after each potation; at length he entered a house in one of the streets at the back of Shoe Lane, and there Sam left him.

"Nearly six," muttered Sam, looking at a clock in a baker's shop, "just about the time they expect me. But what a day it's been! who'd have thought o' meeting with old Work-it-out?"

The surprises of the day were not yet over. When the establishment of Messrs. Kidem and Blowhard hove in sight, there was Inky sitting upon the steps.

Ay! there was the "nobbly born," but in a most forlorn condition—no jacket, no hat, nothing but the check trousers, once his pride and glory, but now shorn of their splendour; front of the red waistcoat and a shirt much the worse for wear. There was an apology for a pair of boots upon his feet, but one could scarcely call them articles of apparel.

"Why, what in the name of His Royal Highness the Dook of Cork," exclaimed Sam, "is the meaning of this, Inky?"

Inky arose, and looked mournfully at his old friend—the very soul of dejection.

"Sam," he said, sorrowfully, "I'm brought down from my perk."

"Perch—that's the word," corrected Sam, upon the strength of his late training.

"It doesn't matter wot you calls it," returned Inky, "I'm down a rum un, and that's a fact."

"You ain't had a rise, that's certain," said Sam; "but I'm in a hurry now. Can you wait till I've been in and settled with the comps? They wants a lot o' lookin' arter."

"I'll wait as long as you like, Sam, but I'm starvin'."

"Get a penny buster," rejoined Sam, producing the coin. "Biffin in the court sells the biggest."

"Thanky, Sam. How long will yer be?"

"About an hour. I say, Inky, I seed—saw your old master just now."

"Work-it-out?"

"Yes; I left him in the Yellow Flag. He ain't been drinkin'—oh, dear, no! but ta, ta; when I'm away from Kidem's everything goes wrong. Come back in an hour."

The first thing Inky did was to purchase the article of refreshment denominated a "buster," with which he removed the edge of his appetite, then his thoughts reverted to Mr. Harris, *alias* Work-it-out, and a longing to see the old man took possession of him.

"I can jist peep in," he thought, "and get a glimpse of him. I needn't do any more. There's plenty of time before Sam comes out. I'll run over to the Yellow Flag."

But he never reached it, for he met his old master midway, in the hands of the police. The old sot was in a wretched state; his waistcoat was saturated with beer, which had either been spilled or thrown over him; his clothes were torn and wrenched awry, and from his nose flowed the stream of life.

But the spirit of the great orator was not entirely crushed. He called upon the people whom he had endeavoured to save, to save him.

"A rescoo! a rescoo!" he cried. "Men of England, will you stand by and see your champyan 'curserated in a dudgeon—a rescoo, a rescoo!"

"Come out of it, will you?" growled the officer, giving him a vicious wrench. "Stow your jaw."

"I'll lift up my voice to the land," roared Work-it-out. "Men of England, a rescoo, a rescoo!"

Base men and women of England! None stirred a hand to help the man who had done so much for them; on the contrary, they followed the officer and his prize with much enjoyment, and hailed each repetition of the great orator's appeal with shouts of laughter.

Inky followed and forgot his troubles, until his old master was hidden from view by the closed door of the police station, when he returned to Messrs. Kidem and Blowhard's to wait for Sam.

It was nearly half-past seven when he came out, and requested Inky to come with him to a quieter place.

"I'm not particklar ashamed of you," he said, "but a man in my position is obliged to be careful. People will talk—now here we are quiet enough, spin your yarn, Inky."

"It's werry 'ard for a chap o' werry nobble birth," began Inky, "and great 'spectations——"

"Suppose you leave 'em out," interrupted Sam, quietly, "put 'em aside, and go on straight. No road like a straight road for a short cut; beats all the turnings in the world."

Obeying this request, Inky gave a brief outline of his career from the time the Reverend Mr. Marall threw him upon the hands of Podley to the time when he sought and found a lodging in very questionable quarters in the east.

"I thought there was something wrong with the place," he said, "but I was so tired that I chucks my things on the floor, and goes to sleep. I never heerd nothin' throughout the night, and in the mornin' I gits up, and everything but my bundle were gone— my boots were changed—the rest of the things was prigged."

"Did you accuse 'em of it?"

"How could I?" returned Inky, rubbing his eyes, "when there wasn't a soul but myself in the room. I goes down to the landlord, a drunken, swearin' brute, and I ses to him, 'Who stole my clothes?' 'Hullo,' he ses, 'what does yer mean by that?' I ses, My clothes is stolen.' 'You lying urchin,' he ses, 'you've got 'em on.' 'I means the welveteens,' I ses. 'Jest you look 'ere,' he ses, feelin' in the corner for a stick, 'don't yer try to take the charackter of my house away—you never showed up in no welveteens. Get out, and come back if you durst, and I'll break every bone in your skin.' So I comes away," concluded Inky, bursting out with a copious supply of tears, "and as you're the only friend I know, I comes to you."

"Turn orf the tap," rejoined Sam, "and let us look at things coolly. If you piped away till you washed a house down, it wouldn't bring in a day's wittles."

"I can't help it, Sam, it is so werry hard."

"I wonder if the Markis would do anything for you, Inky."

"I've tried him, Sam, and he gave me a five-pun' note; and told me never to go anigh him no more."

"Where's the note?"

"Podley collared it."

"Then say adoo to it," returned Sam; "he's laid it out in porter long ago. Something must be done, I s'pose. I'll see Tom as soon as I can, but I can't go afore Sunday."

"That's three days to wait, Sam."

"So it is, but I'll send the hat round to my mates for you. We'll get you enough tommy to last till then; as for sleepin', I think I can get you a shake-down in a stable. Bevan's stableman is a kind-'arted chap. Will that soot?"

"I'm werry thankful to you, Sam."

"I don't want thanks," returned Sam; "but what I want to see is you pulling yourself together. Turn up that nobble bissness —you'll never make money at it—your proofs are werry wague, and no father could

be quite sartain of you—so turn it up, Inky, and come down to our level."

"I'll make a heffut for your sake, Sam," rejoined Inky; "but it'll be 'ard work, for 'tain't easy for a shepherd to change his skin, or a 'Thopian his spots."

* * * * * *

All things must have an end.

Philosophers say that the day will and must come when even our sun, whose vast flaming bulk out-measures this small earth a million times, will one day roll through the endless realms of space, a cold, black mass— its task performed—its fire extinct; but long ere then, this world and its broken planets, with their endless beauties, animate and inanimate, must expire, vanish—

> "Like the baseless fabric of a vision,
> Leaving not a wrack behind."

Thus much is surmised, this much we know—that all which is connected with our brief lives must end, be it a time of sorrow or of joy, and Tom's holiday, although so long as to appear another life to him, terminated at last.

He went back to Blackheath full of the memories of those happy times, his heart bursting with gratitude for the man who had shown the love and kindness of a father.

He went back with the memory of a thousand little acts of kindness from other and humbler hands, with an especial corner in his heart for Dick Rowley and his buxom wife, with the storehouse of his memory filled with the beauties of Hazeldean Hall, its hills and dales, its wooded valleys and sparkling streams.

Harry Stanley left a few days before him, his presence being solicited by his brothers for a short time prior to his return to school.

"Must spend some time with them, Tom," he said; "a fellow must show a little brotherly love, and that sort of thing—not that we do much of the milksop business—a few days together and we fight like Turks— but it's all over in a minute."

He did not return to the school until it had been open a week, and Tom, who had been secretly pining for his dearest associate, hailed him with joy.

"Thought you had left us," said Tom.

"Not until the end of this term," returned Harry. "You may open your eyes, but I'm going then—can't remain at school all the days of our lives. I stopped at home for a wedding."

"One of your brothers?"

"No, one of my sisters—Alice—tied up to such a brick of a fellow—tipped us of the male sex most handsomely, and I came out in a tail coat—such a sensation—two of the bridesmaids clean gone over me."

"In love with you, Harry?"

"Rather; just a little—melted like wax."

"I don't wonder at it," said Tom, looking at his chum's handsome face.

CHAPTER XXVIII.

A STRANGE INTERVIEW AT BLACKHEATH.

"It was a case of spoons, Tom—none of the Britannia metal, but the downright real thing. One is named Amelia, the other Clara. I had a glove and a rosebud from each—to wear next to my heart for ever and ever; but I have lost them somewhere. Confounded nuisance—a fellow can't write for a second supply."

"I suppose not; you will soon forget them."

"Never," returned Harry, looking sentimental.

Notwithstanding this bold assertion, he was, within half an hour, heart and soul in a game of football, shouting, pushing, and laughing with as little thought of the two fair ones as he had of the cannibals of the South Sea Islands—both being entirely absent from his mind.

Tom did not play that day, feeling more inclined for a walk, and strolled as far as the hill leading down to Deptford.

He sat down upon a large stone by the wayside to rest, looking down upon the smoke-covered cluster of houses at his feet. He fell a-thinking of the great town and his troubles therein; much as he wished to forget it, the sad past would recall itself whenever he was alone, standing out each time more heavily in contrast to his present bright life, like a huge blot upon a fair landscape.

"From cold and hunger to every luxury of life," he thought; "from wild, half-savage companions to such friends as these."

He looked back for a moment over the heath, where the coloured caps of the players moved about like agitated poppies, then turned again to the sombre city lying at his feet.

While engaged thus a young fellow about nineteen, wearing clothes flashily cut, passed him two or three times, as if seeking to confirm some half-formed recognition. He tried to arouse Tom's attention by scraping his feet upon the ground, and coughing. Failing in that, he addressed him with—

"Tom, old boy, don't you know me?"

Tom looked up startled, and surveyed the rakish intruder. There was nothing in him that he could call to mind having seen before.

"I don't know you," he said.

"Come, stow it," rejoined the other, with a leer; "don't cut an old friend when you get a rise among the nobs. Don't tell me you are going to turn up Ripper Gooch."

"I never heard of you, and don't know you," replied Tom, rising, and walking towards the heath.

Ripper Gooch followed.

"You may turn up your nose," he said, walking up to the side of Tom, "but you can't turn it clean out of the way. If you cuts old comrades I'll cooper you; I'll settle you among them high-born bully boys."

"Who are you, and what do you want?" demanded Tom, turning pale.

"I wants money, like most of us," returned the other. "You've lots, for you are taken up by a Marquis, and they've heaps to throw away. You must get me some."

"I cannot," returned Tom, "and if I could I would not."

"You won't?"

"Not a penny," replied Tom, firmly. "I don't know who you are, but I suppose you have got hold of the story of my life, and fancy I am ashamed of it. You are much mistaken. All that you can say is known to my friends."

"Is it?" returned Ripper, with a vicious smile. "We shall see. So you won't shell out?"

"I've said I won't—and I will not."

"A couple of pounds a-week will keep me quiet."

"If two farthings would do it I would not pay them."

"The worse for you—the worse for you," said Ripper Gooch, savagely. "You'll sing another song before I'm done with you."

Tom turned away and walked off, leaving the enterprising Mr. Gooch in a furious frame of mind.

He felt instinctively that Tom's fears were not to be played upon; and he must either abandon the attack or carry it out purely for revenge.

He resolved to adopt the latter course—and followed Tom, who had joined a group of exhausted players reclining on the turf; among them was Harry Stanley and others whom Tom numbered among his friends.

Unconscious of the close vicinity of the sneaking rascal, Tom threw himself beside his chum Harry, and inquired how the game had ended.

As Harry was about to reply, Ripper Gooch presented himself before them.

"Now, Tom," he said, "for the last time are you going to acknowledge an old chum?"

"I don't know you," rejoined Tom.

"Not know me?" said Gooch, appealing to the boys collectively, who wondered to see such a figure in their midst, "not know me? Where you ever on the streets?"

"I have been very poor," replied Tom, with trembling lips.

"Who is this fellow?" asked Harry. "Shall I kick him or punch his head?"

"Let him have his say out," returned Tom; "a bad interpretation would be put upon violence."

"You have been poor," pursued Ripper, "so poor that you had neither friends nor money. You lived upon the street as you could, didn't you?"

"I did," replied Tom, proudly; "and I lived honestly."

"Of course you did," returned Ripper, "that is, as honest as you could, as I do, and I'm a thief, and you were a thief."

"It's a lie!" cried Tom, springing to his feet.

"It's true," returned Ripper, "and I stand by it. How did you live—how could you live? It's bosh to talk of living honest without a friend in the world—and you know it. Don't tell me you were never at Leary's ken."

Tom did not answer, but he looked straightly and steadfastly at the face of his persecutor.

"If you'd been honest enough to give an old friend a hand," continued Ripper, "and not been a cur at the top of the hill when I first spoke to you, I wouldn't have exposed you, but you were too mean—and I don't like to see the gents round here with a sniggering thief in their midst—like you are. I'm straightforward, I am. I say I am a thief. I don't deny it. I'm proud of it."

"Get away, in heaven's name," cried Harry Stanley to Ripper, as Tom, overcome with contending emotions, sank insensible into his arms—"go, you have done your worst."

"He was warned," returned Ripper, smiling with evil satisfaction, "but he wouldn't take it."

"If you have a spark of humanity in you," cried Harry, "thief and rogue as you are, by your own confession, go away, I implore you."

"I'm going," replied Ripper; "I've tarred my bird and stopped his free flying among the nobs. Good day, gents all."

He raised his hat with an air as flash as his look, and was gone.

Harry Stanley, holding Tom in his arms, looked steadily around at the boys who were standing silent and grave.

"Do any of you believe that scoundrel's story?" he asked.

No answer. So much mud could not be thrown without a little sticking.

"Ay, I see," returned Harry, bitterly, "ever ready to believe evil in preference to good. Come, Tom—that's right, old fellow, rouse up. That fellow with his foul mouth is gone."

"It was all false," sobbed Tom.

"Every word," answered Harry. "Your every act here gave him the lie direct. Come, Tom, we will return together, and leave your judges there," pointing at the boys, "to their meditations."

CHAPTER XXIX.

WORK-IT-OUT IS PUT UPON HIS LEGS.

IT now becomes us to see how Inky and his master fared in their time of trouble.

It is a generally recognized fact that association has one of the strongest holds upon the affections.

Inhabitants of wild and desolate regions, of long extended plains, of heaths, moors, or busy cities, when transported even to the most distant parts of the globe, still think of the streets, moors, and plains, which awaken fond memories of their place of birth. These associations are very ardent, and it extends not only to places but to individuals with whom we have passed the spring-time of our existence.

It matters not if we lived at variance with them—even to the parting with ill-blood between us—time smooths down the rugged notches of the past; and if we have human hearts within us, we gladly greet old friends, be they men or places.

Thus it was with Inky. Our readers know full well that his life with Work-it-out was no flowery path—it was far from that. A daily dose of Stinger, however beneficial to a boy from a moral point of view, is scarcely entertaining in a physical sense; nor are pigs' feet the style of food calculated to awaken any particular sentiment of longing in the human breast. Nevertheless, Inky's thoughts turned kindly towards his old master. He had been the associate of his childhood—at one time his sole friend—and all but this, even Stinger and the extremities of swine, was forgotten when he saw Mr. Harris, *alias* Work-it-out, in the hands of the police.

Sam had promised to do something for Inky; but a few days must necessarily elapse ere he could offer him any substantial benefit.

Sam's idea was to get him into a printer's, where, with ordinary application and decent behaviour, he might eventually get on. But inexorable Fate decreed it otherwise.

Inky's lot lay in other places.

Having nothing to do on the morning following the arrest of Work-it-out, he went down to the police-court, where he saw the friend of the people in company with some score or so of other drunkards, each and all of whom had been sacrificing on the altar of

Drink everything good and noble in the nature of man.

Some had simply hooted, raved, and shouted, like Work-it-out ; some had broken windows, others had broken heads, one had stolen a cart-wheel from a greengrocer's yard, and urged on by his sodden reason, tried to pawn it. Another—a woman—had thrown herself from a first-floor window ; and one—hitherto a respectable, well-conducted man—had stabbed a wife he loved in his sober moments, and blasted her life and happiness, and his—for ever.

The light cases came on first—and Work-it-out having pleaded guilty, and promised amendment, was dismissed with a caution, the magistrate conjuring him to give up "madmen's politics, and return soberly to his work."

Having acknowledged the lecture, and given his word to profit by it, Work-it-out left the court, followed by Inky, who touched his old master on the arm as soon as they were outside.

Work-it-out looked at his *protégé*, and at first failed to recognize him. At last the familiar features brought back the long years they had spent together in Sceptre Court.

"Inky," he said, "is it thou ?"

"It ain't nobody else, Mr. Harris," returned Inky ; "I thowt you didn't know me."

"My thoughts," replied Work-it-out, "were fudder away."

"Are you goin' back to bisness ?" asked Inky.

"No—I ain't," said Mr. Harris, shortly ; "my tools is gone, my shop is let, and I haven't a brown. That's wot I was thinkin' on. What shall I do ? I've been a fren' to the people, and the people ain't been no fren' to me—so I drops the coolition from this time henceforth."

"I was in hopes," said Inky, timidly, "as we might come together agen."

"Well, 'taint unpossible," replied Work-it-out, "if you means straight. But, lor, wot's the use ?—I'm down on my back—and yet I thowt the game of the people's fren' would ha' paid. There's lots o' big chaps as was little once, and all out of the people. They chucks up work, and takes to mouthin' ; but I suppose I ain't ekal to it. What ha' you been doin'."

"Principally bird-fancyin'," returned Inky, as if he had been trifling with half-a-dozen trades ; "but owin' to a reverend gent and Mrs. Podley, Jim prigged my five-pun' note, and sold the shop to a man in a fur cap."

"Oh !" exclaimed Work-it-out, softly, not having followed the brief story with any particular attention. "Well, I suppose, Inky, somethin' must be done."

"I'm ready and willin' to work like winkin' "

"Well said, Inky. I respects you for them sentiments, for, arter all, you're like the child o' my buzzum—for didn't I," he added, with emotion, "as good as bring you up by hand ?"

"You did," answered Inky, with tears in his eyes.

"I might hev laid Stinger on pretty thick sometimes," pursued Work-it-out.

"I desarved it," murmured Inky.

"You desarved Stinger as a rool," rejoined Work-it-out, "but I were wrong to lay it on with wenom. Now, in the matter o' grub—"

"Pigs' feet," again murmured Inky.

"In the matter o' grub, Inky, I did as much as a father could hev done under the circumstantials. 'Ole j'ints it were hard to get, as it is a'most unpossible to work 'em out. I went in once for a j'int o' lamb, but some wicious party in the court prigged it while it were a-roastin' and I went for the beer ; and it tuk five weeks to clear it orf. Arter that I 'chewed j'ints for ever."

"And what do you think o' doin' ?" hinted Inky.

"I must ha' help," returned Work-it-out, "and there's only one man in the world that I can think on. It's fourteen year since I saw him—then we parted over the paying for a pot of 'arf and 'arf. Ah ! Inky, it were a sorrerful partin'. I had a cupple of black eyes, and Reuben lorst a front tooth."

"Who was Reuben ?" asked Inky.

"Him as fought with me," replied Work-it-out. "Reuben's my brother."

As he had not mentioned such an individual in Inky's hearing, the "nobbly" born could not help expressing a vast amount of surprise.

"When I left him," pursued Work-it-out, "he was in a thrivin' line. He did a deal o' wan lettin' and a tolerable coal trade. His place was down in Grubble Street, Old Kent Road."

"Is he there now !"

"That's wot I was calculatin' on, Inky. It ain't unpossible to say for sartin ; but we will go down and see. Got any money, my lad ?"

Inky struggled with his innate selfishness, but a better feeling conquered.

"I've got sixpence," he said, "given me by the boys at Kidem and Blowhard's."

"Hem ! sixpence—pint o' four 'arf and 'arf," mused Work-it-out, calculating on his fingers, "that's tuppence—fourpence for bread and cheese, that's enough for two. Come on."

This humble meal was soon disposed of at the nearest public-house, then Work-it-out and Inky went very lovingly together over Southwark Bridge to the Old Kent Road.

This thoroughfare is a lengthy one, and

Grubble Street lay far on the road to New Cross; the walk was, therefore, of considerable duration, and it was past noon when the wayfarers turned aside from the main road into the street they sought.

"He may be gone," said Work-it-out, "for fourteen years is a long time, but he used to live somewhere about here. Steady, Inky, give me time. I sees the old familiar board —steady, wot's the name on it, is it changed or not?"

As Work-it-out was too much overcome to read, Inky read aloud from a board, made dark and dingy by time and smoke—

"Reuben Harris, Coal Himporter, Light Wans every Munday to Hepping, from May to September. Furniture removed in a Spring Cart."

"'Tis him, 'tis him," murmured Work-it-out. "Anybody in the shop, Inky? I'm overcome with 'motion. Is there anybody in the shop, Inky?"

"Yes, a boy in a black slop."

"Anybody else, Inky?"

"A man with a pipe in his mouth, shovin' a sack of coals on to a boy's shoulder."

"That's Reuben," said Work-it-out, waking out from his overwhelming emotion. "Ruby was allers a smokin' and sendin' out coals. Hold orf, my lad, while I comoonicate a brother's return."

Inky discreetly retired to the other side of the street, and Work-it-out, with faltering steps, hastened towards the coal-vendor's. Having bounced against the boy as he came from the shop, with the sack upon his shoulder, and been requested to "come out of it," he stood before the brother, so long a stranger.

"Mornin', sir," said the coal-vendor.

"Ruby," cried Work-it-out, sinking back against a pile of coals, marked "Real Wallsend, one shilling the hundred, delivered," "don't you know me?"

"I can't say as I do," said the other; "it ain't old Buppers, who went with my party to Hepping, without a tanner to bless himself with, and runned away with the tarpaulin —it ain't old— ?"

"No, Ruby, it ain't," interposed Work-it-out; "it's none of them parties, whomsoever they may be. You had a brother," he added, struggling with his contending feelings.

"I had," returned Mr. Reuben Harris; "he knocked out my front tooth, and I keeps it in my puss. What o' him?"

"Ruby," again, "don't you know me?"

"Dashed, if I—and yet—why, it is Benjamin —now, what's your game?"

From a sentimental point of view this was scarcely the greeting one would have expected, but Reuben Harris was not a sentimental man. The coal trade, and dealing with van parties, had knocked all such nonsense out of him years before.

"Reuben," said old Work-it-out, "I hain't a friend."

"Well, then," said the other, heartily, "you comes to the right party; by-gones is allus by-gones with me, 'cept you takes a linchpin out of a wan wheel, and makes me spill a party inter a front garden, as happened last June, and cost me four pun' ten for stickin' plaister and loss of time. Wot's up, Benny?"

"I gave up business and went in for the cause of the people, that was my game."

"I thowt a brother o' mine would ha' knowed better," rejoined Mr. Reuben Harris, reproachfully; "the cause o' the people as put afore the public by spouters is gammon. No man can attend to pollyticks and his family at the same time. Well, wot can I do for you?"

"Anything to put me in the way o' gettin' a livin', Ruby."

"Come in, then, and talk it over."

"Shall I call in my boy, over there?"

"Son?"

"No, Ruby—left on my doorstep wrapped in a yaller hankercher."

"It must ha' been a tidy hankercher to inwelop him," said Reuben Harris; "but let him come in."

CHAPTER XXX.

THE ROAD TO FAME.

"There's heaps o' things for you to do," said Reuben Harris, sitting down in the little room at the back of his shop: "wan work, for instance. How should you like to drive a wan?"

"Lord help the wan if I did!" returned Work-it-out. "I've no more ideas of drivin' than I have of shipbuildin', Ruby."

"Well, I suppose you ain't," rejoined Reuben; "then there's carryin' coals—but you don't look strong enough; the muscle of hold seemith to have departed."

"It all went in the cobbling trade," said Work-it-out, sighing; "fourteen year in Scepter-court hev drawed me fine."

"Just so—just so, brother; and you've had this boy with you all the time?"

"Yes, 'cept a few months, when he runned away arter wissionary nobble fathers."

"And wot," demanded the coal-dealer, turning to Inky, and eyeing him with a searching look, "and wot did you do with yerself all that time?"

A ready reply did not escape Inky's lips; the question embraced so many points of his varied career. At length a luminous idea came to his assistance, and he answered—

"I bred game cocks and lops."

"Indeed!" said Reuben Harris, in nowise

astonished by the answer. "Well, you might ha' done wus ; for with care and fair dealin' a man ought to do well at it. Look here, Benny, I've got a thought inter my head about you ; you ain't werry well, judgin' by the looks of you."

"I'm sinkin' fast," answered Work-it-out, moodily."

"Then wot do you say to a bit o' travel ?"

"Travel, Ruby ?"

"Yes ! and make money at it too," said the coal-dealer, laying down his pipe, to enable him to speak with emphasis; "here's an offer for you. Some time ago, a mate o' mine—I picked up his 'quaintance at the Frizzly Boar—this mate o' mine gets well into my ribs, a pound, ten bob, and so on, at a time, until I pressed him to recooperate with me. Well, he couldn't do it ; but being a marynet man, and honorable and troo, he brings the figures and show ·here, with the drums and pipes, and says, ' Reuben, I can't pay you, but I'm going the round o' the fairs with Bob Smacker, to patter for him, and if I'm careful I can save enough to pay you when I comes back.' Well, I takes the figgers and the show, and away he goes ; but he never saves money, and he never comes back."

"Didn't he ?" put in Work-it-out, seeing his brother paused.

"He did not," returned Reuben, with a sigh, "contrari wise ; he goes altogether wrong, and arter drinkin' hisself blind, he gives Bob Smacker sech a tremenjous lickin', and so overcome hisself, that both went to the 'orspital, where Tootle—the man I speaks on—died."

"Ah ! he died," murmured Work-it-out.

"Yes, he went orf, playing marynets all the while, and finished with a howl about the public bein' mean and not chucking in their coppers. So the figgers, show, and drum, are with me now, and if you likes to have 'em you can."

"But what should I do with 'em ?"

"Work 'em, make money at 'em," cried Reuben, refilling his pipe, and waving it enthusiastically ; "as a yooth you were gifted that way—lor ! how you did play a penny whistle to be sure."

"But who's to play the moosic ?" inquired Work-it-out.

"There's your boy," returned Reuben Harris, impressively ; "let him do it, that don't want teaching. He's only got to blow inter the pipe, and run his mouth up and down and bang the drum to drown it. Come and see the show afore you refoose."

He took them into the back yard, where, in a rough description of out-house, the show and box were stowed away.

Perhaps many, or most of our readers have seen a marionette show, but for the benefit of those who have not been so favoured, we will briefly describe it.

The show itself is similar in size and construction to that of the immortal hero Punch; but the opening for the stage is lower, for the marionette performer is *above* the figures, whereas in Punch he is *below* them. The travelling marionettes are generally worked singly, and favour the audience with various specimens of dancing.

"Here's the figgers," said Reuben Harris, opening the box, "eight in all ; Tootle used orfen to talk about 'em, and I knows all their names ; I'll run e'm over : ' The Hold Henglish Gentleman,' ' The Forlorn Maiden,' ' Jack, the Rovin' Tar,' ' The Hemperor of Tartary,' ' The Lively Nigger,' ' Long John,' ' Tubby, the little Fat Un,' and ' The Skeletin',' with which you winds up the exhibition. I've worked 'em orfen to amoose myself and family on Sunday arternoon, and you can pick it up in no time. Here's the strings fixed to their arms, legs, and heads, with rings at 'tother end to fix on your fingers— and then you works 'em accordin' to the moosic or fancy."

He watched the glistening eyes of Work-it-out, and the eager curiosity of Inky with satisfaction. He saw that the job was done ; but, as a matter of form, he asked the question—"Well, Benny, what do you say ?"

"I ses this," said Work-it-out, seizing his brother by the hand—"that I'm on, and I'll make a name at it."

"And you, young 'un ?"

"I'd rather work the figures," said Inky ; "the drum's so big, and I ain't got no ear for moosic."

"Don't quarrel with your bread and butter," said Work-it-out, sternly, "but set to work at that drum at once."

On that very day and that very hour—the practice, under Reuben's tuition, began. Work-it-out took kindly to the figures, and Inky, perforce, took unto himself the drum and breast-pipes.

"I can give you house-room for a week," said the coal-dealer, "and then you must make tracks."

In a week Work-it-out declared himself to be ready for the public ; and Inky, whose progress in the musical department had not been very striking, declared himself to be prepared also.

"Half-a-sovereign a week you must pay to me," said Reuben, at parting, "and remember this :—whoever is outside must keep the public as far away as he can—for it ain't like Punch, and you musn't let them see the strings—never show 'em how you works 'em, or you won't draw a farden."

The liberal coal-dealer then pressed a sovereign into his brother's hand, and with , final good wish, went back to his business, and Inky and Work-it-out set out upon a strange road of life together.

Acting upon the advice of Reuben Harris, they crossed London early in the morning, and striking through the mazes of Hackney and the rustic beauties of Clapton, made straight for the country without a halt.

"We'll begin with small orgiances fust," said Work-it-out, as he put down the show in a quiet lane to rest, "and work up by degrees. Who knows but we may one day perform at the Crystal Pallis—we can't tell —and if that ever comes off our fortin's made."

"I want about ten years' practice on this blessed drum," groaned Inky; "I never did see such a drum—it's as big as two."

"I don't believe any drum would suit *you*," said Work-it-out; "from the herliest 'our when I found you in a yaller hankercher—"

"Gorging raiment," interposed Inky.

"Yaller hankercher," insisted Work-it-out, "up to the present time nothin' don't please you. What's the matter with the drum—don't it sound?"

"It ain't never quiet," moaned Inky; "the werry wind brings out a 'oller groan from it. It's as bad as carryin' a ghost about with yer."

"Can you work the figgers?" demanded Work-it-out in a fury.

"I should think I could," replied Inky; "workin' the figgers is wot I'm fit for—why don't you take the drum?"

"Acause I'm master here," returned Work-it-out, "and I'll do what I please. It's 'art-breaking to have such a miserable chap with me. 'Ere we are on the high road to fortin', wealth, and fame, and you're a-grumbling on account of the drum not bein' cut down to a size to suit yer. If you was so particular," continued Work-it-out, driven into impossibilities by the fractious nature of his adopted son, "why didn't you make your own drum?"

Inky furnishing no reply to this query, they slowly moved on, Work-it-out a little in advance, and Inky labouring in the rear, bearing the burden he was learning to hate. In this way, without exchanging a word, they kept on until a village appeared in sight. On the outskirts Work-it-out put the show down, and dropped the baize.

"Now, Inky," he said, "I'm goin' to show for the fust time—remember that the 'Hold Henglish Gentleman' comes fust—and then the 'Forlorn Maid.' Bang away quick for the gentleman; but make it slow and mournful-like for the maid—'tother characters I leaves it to your discreshing."

Inky growled something in reply, and fixing the pipes in his breast, gave a preliminary flourish, and banged the drum lustily until about a score of country bumpkins gathered around.

CHAPTER XXXI.
SAM SMARTY'S VOW.

TOM'S doom at Laurel House was sealed.

The principles of Christianity were forgotten there as much as if those boys had been grown members of society; it had been declared that Tom was, or had been, a thief, and they but too readily placed implicit faith in the story.

The boy was stricken sore, and, like the youthful Pharisees they were, they passed by on the other side.

In all that school but one good Samaritan could be found—Harry Stanley. He, conscious of poor Tom's true worth, rejected the imputations of Ripper Gooch, and despised those who believed them. No need for Tom to vow and protest to him, his instincts were too keen for him to mistake the ring of pure metal, and Tom was sterling gold.

He led his favourite friend and companion back to the school, where, in the seclusion of their private study, they considered what was best to be done.

"The fellow has shot his bolt," said Harry Stanley, "and it has struck home. The dolts here would rather believe evil than good."

"It is so hard to bear," rejoined Tom.

"Dear Tom, there are so many things in this life hard to bear, and that is why Heaven has given us strong arms and stout hearts."

"Perhaps they will soon think better of me."

"They may," returned Harry, shrugging his shoulders; "if so, the world's turned upside down. Nothing takes root so soon, or strikes so firmly, as prejudice. But we will give them a few days' trial."

The boys of Laurel House were weighed in the balance and found wanting. The prejudice which arose under the influence of the thief's words gathered strength every day.

In school, at the desks, or in class, they kept as far away as possible from the unhappy boy. If he asked for anything it was passed to him with silence and averted eyes; in the playground they left him and Harry together, passed them on the Heath without greeting, ignored their presence at the dining table, in the dormitory, and everywhere they met.

Tom and his friend was banished, as far as Laurel House was concerned, for evermore.

The masters could not fail to observe this,

bat as none informed them of the reason, they put it down as the result of some boyish offence, which would soon be forgotten and forgiven. It was their custom to be wisely blind upon such occasions.

The week passed, and Sunday came, and with it Sam Smarty, on one of his periodical visits. He met Tom in Greenwich Park, and the two sat down upon the hill overlooking the Hospital and the river.

For a little while, Sam rattled on in his usual way about matters of business and his private pleasures, until receiving only monosyllabic replies from his friend, he by degrees arrived at the conclusion that something was the matter.

"You look rather downy, Tom; what's up?" he paradoxically inquired.

"I'm ruined here, Sam."

"Eh! hallo—what—ruined—how—who did it?" said Sam, astonished; "ain't you good enough for 'em?"

"It's not that, Sam, but worse," said Tom; "I cannot do better than tell you all."

He quickly ran over what had passed, giving almost word for word the utterances of Ripper Gooch. The libels of the thief were graven on his memory.

As Tom proceeded with the story, a variety of changes passed our Sam's face, like a rapidly shifting kaleidoscope, first it flushed, then grew deadly white; his eyes shone with an angry light, his nostrils quivered, and his lips closed firmly together; finally, he sat like one upon whom some terrible misfortune has fallen.

When he had learned all, he sat for some moments in silence, plucking the grass nervously, and scattering the fragments about.

"Tom," he said, at length, "what sort of fellow is this Gooch?"

"Rather tall, and about twenty years old?"

"Rakish looking?"

"Yes."

"Wears a Champagne Charley hat and a blue necktie?"

"You are right."

"Talks quick, and has a general cheeky look?"

"A true picture, Sam; do you know him?"

Several moments' silence ensued. Sam seemed to have no reply ready.

"Surely this vagabond is no companion of yours, Sam?"

"Can you forgive me, Tom?" cried Sam, turning upon him suddenly with tears in his eyes.

"Forgive you, Sam?"

"Yes, Tom: I am the cause of your misforten."

"Oh! Sam, this from you?"

Tom bent his head upon his knees, and

Sam could see the hot tears falling from his face upon the grass.

"Don't think as how I went to go to do it purposely," continued Sam, growing frightfully ungrammatical as he became excited. "For I was took clean in, that I was. He comes to me—this wagabone—he comes and ses, 'You're a friend o' Tom's?' he ses; 'I am,' says I, proud as you like of the honour. 'Ah!' he ses, 'and a nice fellow is Tom, I wish he was a friend o' mine. 'You seem to know him,' I ses. 'Yes,' he ses, 'I do—but I'm not a friend. I'm one of the Markis's servants, and he's given me a parcel for Tom, and told me to take it at once. I've forgotten the address,' ses the wagabone, 'and it's as much as my place is worth to ax for it again, and I thought of you—can you oblige me—I ain't in livery,' he ses, 'acause it's my day out.' And then, Tom—as green as a young robin—I gives it to him."

"It can't be helped," returned Tom, quietly despairing, "I don't blame you, Sam."

"But who is the wagabone?" cried Sam, "are you sure you never knowed him—nowhere?"

"Certain, Sam. I never saw him before."

"It's quite a mystery," said Sam, "like a plot in a play—there comes in a chap who swears to find it out—and I swears now, that afore a month is out I'll know all about this Ripper Gooch, and why he's made a wictim o' you. I shan't kneel on one leg to swear it, 'acause the park-keeper's lookin', and he might think I was up to some game, but my intentions is good, and I'll carry 'em thro'."

"Thank you, Sam; I am sure that you will do all that a friend can or will."

"Yes, make your mind easy about it; afore the month is up, I'll have Mr. Ripper Gooch up here to 'pologise."

"I am afraid I can't stop here," said Tom, sorrowfully.

"Not stop here—why not!"

"I am miserable. The boys all shun me as if I were poison."

"Then write to the young Markis, and get him to take you away."

"I don't like to do that. It would seem as if I were dissatisfied."

"Tell him the trooth."

"He might believe as others do."

"It sartinly is a queerish fix," said Sam, scratching his head thoughtfully. "What will you do?"

"I don't know—I can't say," said Tom. "I am very miserable."

"But you must keep your pecker up," insisted Sam. "The meanest cove can lay on his back, and say it's all up—that's the easiest dodge out; but a true-born Brito stands up and fights agin it like winking. The werry lion and unicorn p'ints out that moral. So stand up, Tom; I got you in this hole and I'll have you out of it—or may I never start a printin' establishment, and shut up Kidem and Blowhard."

After the parting, Sam took a long solitary walk, musing deeply over what had transpired. Although not morally guilty of injury to his friend, he had been the involuntary cause of his distress, and he resolved to make amends if possible.

But how was it to be done?

He turned over a dozen schemes, but dismissed them as impracticable, and he was at his wits' end, on the point of giving up in despair, when a happy thought entered his head.

"I'll go and see Lord Holbrook, the young Markis," he thought, "and lay the whole straight forrard before him. It can't do any harm, and it may get Tom out of the mess."

He was so elated with this idea that he entirely recovered his wonted spirits; and it being still early in the day, he went by steamer to London Bridge, where he honoured the summit of an omnibus with his presence, and was finally deposited at the top of Constitution Hill.

A few minutes later he rang the visitors' bell at the great house in Belgrave Square, and the active Tummas opened the door.

Months had passed since he last saw Sam, and he had learned to look upon the visits of that youth as a half-forgotten, ugly dream, but here he was again, evidently in full life and vigour, ready for any amount of verbal combat, and Tummas visibly staggered—Sam was more to Tummas than Banquo to the murderous Macbeth.

"The young Markis in?" inquired Sam, with the easy air of an old acquaintance of the family.

"He—ah?—yes—no—I don't know," returned Tummas, despair lurking in his leaden eye; "p'raps I'd better inquire."

"I think you had," returned Sam, burnishing the soles of his boots upon the mat. "You know my name. It ain't likely as you've forgotten ME."

Tummas made no reply, but wandered away like a man rudely awakened from a dream of peace to a reality of turmoil, war, bloodshed, and ruin.

CHAPTER XXXII.

CONSOLATION FOR THE AFFLICTED TUMMAS.

HE was not long away; and returning with feeble steps, informed Sam, in a husky voice, that Lord Holbrook would see him, and would he step into the library?

"Sartainly," returned Sam, airily, "I thout he was at home to *me*. I say, my lad—you've wore well durin' the last three months—

Time don't seem to make much impreshn on you."

The outraged servitor of the house of Beauforth replied not, but he breathed deeply, and the vision of a dagger in company with a brace of pistols floated in the air before him.

Sam ought to have been grateful to the laws of the country which held the rage of Tummas in check.

"I suppose it's the life," pursued Sam, as they crossed the corridor, "with plenty of wittles and drink, and nothin' to do but to sit in the kitchen and oggle the housemaids—a man can't take any harm. The only wonder is that you don't get too fat—porpoising, like the fishmonger in Shoe Lane."

"That's the library door," said Tummas, in a voice of deep emotion, "his lordship will be with you directly. Oh! ah!"

"Ain't you well?" asked Sam.

"I—oh! yes, nothing but a pussing feeling," returned Tummas, as he hastened downstairs. He felt that if he stayed longer he might be tempted to strangle that demon in the bud.

Lord Holbrook did not keep Sam waiting. He came in a few minutes and gave the boy a cordial greeting, and asked Sam what service he required.

"Nothing for myself, my lord Markis," replied Sam, "but it's for Tom. He is very unhappy."

He then told all—from the time when Ripper Gooch "gammoned" him out of Tom's address to the interview in Greenwich Park.

"It stands to reason, my lord honourable Markis," concluded Sam, "that Tom is not an old friend of this wagabone's, for he comes to me and actually gets out of me what Tom is like, and as for his being a thief *we* know better than that."

"I am glad you came, Sam," said Lord Holbrook, after a pause, "there is something wrong here, and it shall be fathomed. Leave all to me, Tom will not be the sufferer."

"Thanky, my lord high Markis," said Sam, gratefully.

"Now is there anything I can do for you."

"Nothing my lord Markis, I'd rather not, thank you."

"But you will have some refreshment?"

"I think I will, my lord Markis, for I've had nothin' since dinner, when I partook of weal."

The bell was rung, and Tummas desired to place refreshment in the housekeeper's room, which he did, after breaking two tumblers in his agitation.

Sam, having taken leave of Lord Holbrook, devoted himself to the consumption of a pigeon pie and draught ale until he was fairly beaten. He then retired, only remarking to Tummas, as he went forth, that "he wondered how he stood such a life reg'lar, for a continivation of such feeds must amount to torter."

After he was gone Tummas retired to the kitchen, and for two mortal hours read the Sunday paper upside down.

On the following Tuesday Tom was removed from Laurel House, Blackheath, and taken back to Belgrave Square.

Sheltered by the mansion of the Beauforth family, one would think that Tom was pretty safe, but it was not so. Ripper Gooch had been aroused, and, like a wolf upon the track, he clung to his prey, resolved to hunt it down.

He had another quality of the wolf in him—he was not too ready to attack without the odds of success being many points in his favour; and, doubtful of his ground with the nobler part of the house, he resolved to strike the second blow with the servants.

He watched the house, and studied the inmates with the practised eye of one who had lived by area sneaking and other light burglary work, and in the course of a couple of days came to the conclusion that the best soil for planting the seed of venom was to be found in the long-suffering and much-enduring Tummas.

Had he exercised his abilities in any honourable calling, there is no doubt that Ripper Gooch would have made a creditable, thriving member of society, for he was the possessor of excellent abilities, which he had, to his shame, perverted to an evil use.

It was his shrewdness, his daring invention, and brute courage which gave him the power he held over the gang at Leary's.

He was the originator of a hundred daring schemes which had brought in profit to his associates, and the way he seized every opening to make money, was shown by the keen judgment with which he picked out from Inky's story a chance of making money.

In this, however, he failed; but like the victor of a hundred fights, defeat was the more galling to him. Revenge he wanted revenge he thirsted for with the inconsistency of an evil nature foiled in a base attempt, and revenge he was resolved to have.

Having selected Tummas to work upon, it was not long ere he made that gentleman's acquaintance.

In all fashionable neighbourhoods there are certain "houses," that is, public-houses, affected by gentlemen's gentlemen—places of resort where flunkies of every degree assemble for a glass and a little social chat about their masters' or mistresses' affairs.

Strangers are scarcely welcome in these lounging places of aristocratic plush; but Ripper Gooch knew how to work his way

with such men, and by dint of treating with marked respect those who assembled at the house Tummas patronized, he was speedily on a fair footing with them.

Choosing a time when Tummas was there, he one day worked the conversation round to the point of noblemen bestowing their patronage upon the poor.

"For my part," he said, "I think the low-lived beggars ought to starve. Why don't they think more of those around them?"

"'Ear, 'ear,' from Tummas.

"Pay 'em better."

"'Ear 'ear—brayvo," chorussed a dozen voices.

"Instead of that," resumed Ripper Gooch, what do they do but go pottering about and picking up a lot of ragged little wretches—"

"Good," from Tummas.

"A lot of ragged little wretches," repeated Ripper Gooch, warming with his subject, "and feeds them up, and pampers them, and sends them to school—and who suffers for it? That's what I want to know."

"Good again," cried Tummas; and the others sagely nodded their heads in approval.

"I know of a case," continued Ripper Gooch, "a case which is a disgrace to the country. Not far away from here there is a place which I believe is pretty well known as Belgrave Square."

This waggish allusion to the insignificance of Belgrave Square raised a general smile. The speaker was fast gaining ground.

"In that square, not far from two hundred and ninety-four, lives a certain Marquis."

"What's that?" cried Tummas, pricking his ears up like an ass sighting a thistle. Go on; I knowed somethin' would come of it."

"And in the house I speak of," Ripper Gooch went on, "there is a boy."

"There is," said Tummas, feverishly.

"A boy who has no known friends—no parents—no anything."

"Right, right—that's him."

"He's been fed up and togged up till he's that stuck up that nobody can look at him."

"He's the most huppish little hidiot as hever lived," emphatically assented Tummas.

"And the Marquis believes in him."

"He does."

"And his lordship, too."

"Both on 'em is as blind as bats, and they doats on the little willin. They believe he is honest, I know," continued Ripper Gooch, "but what would they do if it could be shown that he was born a thief, had lived a thief, and was a thief still?"

"They'd pitch him out, neck and crop," said Tummas. "But is there any one who can prove it?"

"There is."

INKY FIRED AWAY LUSTILY AT THE DRUM,

No. 8.

"Who is he—what is he?"

"That I shall not state here," returned Ripper, "or to more than one at a time when I do speak."

"Will you come out with me," cried Tummas, excited beyond control, "just for one turn up and down the street?"

"I don't mind; but I don't promise to say anything more."

"Come and walk," feverishly rejoined Tummas. "I thout we should get at the bottom of this organnysashin of printer's willins. Come along."

So eager was he that he pinched Ripper's arm as he pushed him into the street. Once there he urged his companion to let him know all. But the practised thief was a cool hand; the more Tummas implored, the more he held back; but in the end a compact was made, which amounted to this—that for the consideration of two pounds down Ripper Gooch was to ensure the utter ruin of Tom, and his disgrace with the house of Beauforth.

CHAPTER XXXIII.

THE FIRST EXHIBITION, AND WHAT FOLLOWED.

INKY, with the visage of a funky Buckingham going to execution, blew mournfully into the pipes and beat the drum for two or three minutes, with his eye upon the audience, who soon grew impatient at the non-appearance of the figures.

"Where be Poonch, measter?" roared one at last.

"It ain't Punch," replied Inky, "and p'raps you'll stand furder back. Now then!" he added in a whisper to Work-it-out, "ain't you ready?"

"Keep a-playin'," returned his master, in an agitated voice. "I shall have 'em right d'rectly—but I never was so narvous in my life—announce the 'Hold English Gentleman.'"

"The Hold English Gentleman!" roared out Inky, following out a style of address which he had learned from Reuben Harris —"The Hold English Gentleman will now appear, and go thro' warus evolutions of a 'ighly amoosing natur'. If you don't shuv him on," he added, addressing his master in an undertone, "you'll have some turnips chucked into the show! they're gettin' them ready."

"In a moment," answered Work-it-out, in a quavering tone, "bang away Inky— I'm ready."

Inky fired away lustily at the drum, and the "Old English Gentleman" appeared, not in the usual way, however, but all in a heap —body, strings, and rings—overcome by agitation, Work-it-out had let him drop.

The next moment the arm of the old man appeared before the astonished audience, groping about for the lost marionette. Inky knew, by the expression of their faces, that something was wrong, but what it was he could not see.

"I've got him," he heard Work-it-out mutter to himself, and fully satisfied that there was a hitch in the performance, again addressed his master.

"Wot's up now?" he growled.

"Go on with the moosic for the 'Forlorn Maid,'" groaned Work-it-out. "I've got the hold gentleman's strings mixed."

"So I thout," muttered Inky; "you'll get yerself mixed up directly."

"Go on with that show," bellowed a man in front.

Work-it-out, who had got the 'Forlorn Maid' ready for her slow dance, hastened to comply, and lowered the figure.

In his agitation he at first stood the fair one on her head, but, recovering his presence of mind, he righted her, and put the forlorn one through a series of contortions generally associated with an immoderate consumption of green gooseberries.

Several of the audience were much affected, and a weak youth, attached to the stable of the inn close by, retired completely overcome.

"How did that go?" whispered Work-it-out.

"They looks werry savage," returned Inky.

"I'll bring 'em round," replied Work it-out—"it was bein' disappointed with the Hold English Gentleman as riled 'em. Play up for the 'Hemperor of Tartary.'"

"The 'Rovin' Tar' comes next," said Inky, doggedly.

"You can't have the 'Rovin' Tar,'" replied Work-it-out, "for I've lost his 'ead."

Even Inky's perverseness could not withstand this—the Tar without his head must be no Tar at all, and he therefore played up for the "Emperor of Tartary."

His imperial highness, as represented by the present figure, was very much like a Chinaman without his pigtail, attired in the cast-off clothing of a Greek brigand. His performance was supposed to be one of the best features of the show, for his head and arms were detached and replaced by an arrangement of strings at the will of the performer, thereby enabling him to present to the public the wondrous phenomenon of an emperor dancing with his head and arms in the air.

Work-it-out did his best, but the effect was scarcely up to the mark—the head of his imperial highness was certainly removed from his shoulders, but after certain wild gyrations in the air, refused to re-attach itself, and having first rolled down his back, then over his stomach in a vague undecided manner, finally went aloft, where the body and one arm followed—the other limb being left upon the stage with the ring and cord hanging over the front.

"I don't know what to make of this 'ere show at all," said a true specimen of the genus bumpkin, scratching his shock head.

"It be summat new," suggested another.

"Then, dang un! let us keep to the old uns," was the rejoinder, to which most of the lookers-on cordially assented.

"The 'Lively Nigger!'" roared out Inky.

Here the legs of the "Lively Nigger" came down suddenly, followed by the whole of "Long John," and the different portions having swayed about a few moments, mixing themselves together in a frightful manner, went up again, pursued by a shout of execration from the spectators.

"It is well known," said Inky, pursuing his description as set down by Reuben Harris, "that the Hafrican, whether in his native state or in the fields of slavery, is a lively creetur, that he sings 'arf the day and dances all night. The one afore you now is——"

"Will you stop that nigger jaw?" said Work-it-out, poking his head out of the screen; "can't you see he ain't there?"

"Why ain't he there?" demanded Inky.

"Acause I've mixed him up with Long John," growled Work-it-out. "Play up for Tubby—he's all right."

"It don't matter much wot I plays up for," grumbled Inky; "if you go on in this way they'll have the show over: I see it in their hyes."

"Play up for Tubby—that's wot you've got to do," said Work-it-out as he disappeared.

Inky gave a few flourishes on the drum, flavoured with a few spasmodic breathings into the breast-pipes, and then, as usual, began to describe the character according to instructions received.

"Some people is thin and long," he said, "and some short and stout, the larse gentleman as comed afore you, and went orf werry sudden agen," he added, thinking of the slight disarrangements in the marionette affairs, "in consekens of hold Work-it-out bein' confoosed and mixin' him up with the nigger, were a long and thin un; and we now pursents you with a hopposite contrary figger, knowed to all his friends as Little Fat Tubby, the man as allers larfed and growed fat. Hi! here he is, gentlemen."

At this moment, Work-it-out's hat, being by some means detached from his head, tumbled upon the stage, and Tubby—the

party who always laughed and grew fat—fell bodily into it.

This sudden descent probably settled his laughing propensities for the day, for the arm of Work-it-out, now a familiar object to the public, dived down, bore him away in his improvised coffin, and Tubby was seen no more.

During this piece of pantomime, Inky kept the orchestra going, under the fond delusion that the antics of the jovial Tubby gave rise to the guffaws of the staring yokels, until a pair of stentorian lungs uttering these memorable words undeceived him—

"Danged if the old man beant in mops and brooms."

Peering cautiously round upon the stage, Inky beheld nothing but about six inches of a dirty red cotton handkerchief, with which Work-it-out had been wiping his heated brow, hanging from above; as for Tubby—we know his fate—he was nowhere to be seen.

"You ain't makin' no mess on it, are you?" he said, loud enough for all to hear; "come down with yer."

"I'll—I'll put 'em right," returned Work-it-out, nervously, "don't be afraid—I'll put 'em right with the Skeleting. Werry slow moosic, Inky."

"I'll wait for the Skeleting afore I pipe a note," rejoined Inky, doggedly.

"Don't be wicious," pleaded Work-it-out, "give me a chance to retriever my charackter. Werry slow moosic, Inky, and give 'em a bit o' mouth fust."

"The hend of our life is a skeleting," said Inky to the crowd, pursuing his description, "so is the hend of our show. The Skeleting will now appear and go through the celebrated Dance o' Death, as purformed afore the 'ole of the Crowned 'eds of Rurope."

The skeleton in question, a frail structure of pieces of tobacco pipes, strung on wire and string, with an earthenware skull, now appeared with its right leg doubled up behind, and one of its feet sticking through its ribs, a slight disarrangement which Work-it-out failed to perceive until it was too late. Confused and dismayed by this crowning disaster, he jerked the unhappy skeleton to and fro, banging it against the sides of the show, flinging it out to the front, and finally cracked its head upon the floor. Then he drew it up and leaned upon the resting board panting.

"The orgeal is over," he thought "I've broke the ice. I've showed afore the British public, but Lord! who'd ha' thout it were such hard work; talk of fixin' on heel pieces —its phantim work compared to it."

He let down the green baize in front of the stage, and dropped outside the show, prepared to meet the admiring gaze of the multitude. There was Inky sitting on the drum, with a visage of iron, but otherwise the road was clear.

"Why—where's the orgiance?" he inquired.

"The skeleting druv' em away," answered Inky, briefly.

"How's that?"

"It wasn't like a skeleting," rejoined Inky, "they all sed so—and then they went away."

"And what did yer collect?" asked Work-it-out.

"I didn't collect nothin'," replied Inky, with as much expression in his face as usually can be found in the figure-head of a ship.

"I—wot do you mean by that?" cried Work-it-out, drawing himself up.

"I means this," returned Inky, "that I'm not made o' brass, which a chap need be, to go round with sech a show as that."

"It ain't in me to deny the trooth," said Work-it-out, "some errors there was, which might be looked for at a fust pitch, but there was nothin' but wot a man o' Christian sperrit, and with the 'art of a man inside him, might ha' overlooked. P'raps you didn't try it on strong with 'em; you didn't touch 'em on the raw."

"I didn't touch 'em at all," said Inky, "when the skeleting come down and they began to go orf, I let 'em go. If I'd axed for anything it's ten to one that some on 'em would have kicked the drum—they looked that wicious."

"Well, we shan't make a fortin this way," said Work-it-out, after a pause.

"It won't be made while you works the figures," was Inky's rejoinder.

"The fust p'int is this," said Work-it-out; "we must take some time to repair, for I've got the figgers inter confusion—I'll put 'em inter the box and furl the baize, and then we'll go forward."

"Not through that village," said Inky, fiercely, "if the furus crowd were to fall on us—where wud be the show?"

"Troo," assented Work-it-out. "Then we'll turn down that lane yonder, and drop quietly into a field for a hour or so—but I feels as if I wanted a drop o' beer."

"Don't ax for it anigh here if you wally your precious life," advised Inky.

"Do you think they'll know me?" asked Work-it-out, undecided.

"Sure to—you look as if you'd been makin' a mess o' marynettes."

"Do I?" said Work-it-out, feebly—"well! I suppose I do—I feels like it—take up the drum and come on."

Shouldering the show, Work-it-out, with a heavy sigh, turned down the lane, and waited untii ne came to a field with a cluster of trees in one corner—this seemed to offer the needful seclusion, and under the shelter of the grove he pulled out the box of figures, and sat down to "repair."

CHAPTER XXXIV.
THE FURTHER PROGRESS OF THE MARIONETTES.

"I THINK this is more than I can manage," said Work-it-out, as he surveyed the cracked head of the skeleton, "gone right across in the most skewrious way."

"I heard it bounce down above the drum," rejoined Inky, "real chaney wouldn't stand it—let alone common airthenware."

"If the 'bacca-pipes had gone," mused Work-it-out, "it wouldn't ha' mattered so much—we could hev plenty on 'em at any time when we called for a pint o' beer—but a ed—'specially one like this—ain't to be picked up every day."

"I'm aware on it," grumbled Inky, "you needn't tell me *that*."

"I warn't a tellin' *you*," retorted Work-it-out, with some asperity, "I was in a sorri-roquery."

"In a what?"

"A sorriroquery—a thing that a chap talks to hisself, and people as knows what's troo and honourable don't listen to—that's wot I was in."

"Oh! that's wot it was — is it?" said Inky, sarcastically, "then I wish you wouldn't be in 'em where I am, for I don't like 'em."

To this Work-it-out made no reply, but busied himself with separating the strings of the marionettes, and arranging them in the box in something like order. When this was done he arose and proposed a move forward."

"For it is peckish, I am," he said, "and a bit of bread an' cheese with a mug o' beer will be welcome."

He spoke in a cheerful tone, for in the main he was a good-natured old man, but Inky did not in any way respond; he felt himself injured, how it would have puzzled him to say, but injured he was, and, in consequence, was very sulky.

With his drum upon his back, he crawled behind his master along the dusty lane, in a frame of mind bordering on the vicious; he would have given a trifle for the luxury of smiting Work-it-out once under the ear with a drumstick, but prudence and a healthy fear of the consequences, forbade it.

An hour's trudging brought them into the main road again, by a circuitous route, where they found a neat little village lying at the foot of the hill. It had an inn, just such a one as artists paint and poets write of, with a porch covered with honeysuckle, and an old-fashioned signboard swinging in the sunlight, by the side of a horse-trough.

The sign was the Three Fiddlers, three musical gentlemen portrayed, in a frenzy of musical excitement, by a wandering artist, who, like Work-it-out, took out his labour in food for the flesh.

"I don't think I'll ventur' on showin' agin to-day," said Work-it-out.

"I shouldn't," rejoined Inky, slowly.

"And I think here's jes' the place," pursued his master, ignoring the interruption, "to lay up for the night and recooperate my hideas."

"The best recooperation," said Inky, "you can make, is to turn over the figgers to me."

"It ain't unpossible but I may," amiably rejoined Work-it-out ; and Inky brightened up immediately.

"Arter all, Mr. 'Arris," he said, "you've a kind 'art."

"I'm full o' good feelin'," assented Work-it out ; "and here we are at the Three Fiddlers."

They were met at the door by the host, who matched the inn excellently, being a host from top to toe.

"Good arternoon," he said. "Wonderful weather."

"It's a biler," rejoined Work-it-out, tilting the show on its legs. "Let's have some beer—mildish to begin with."

The host hastened to supply a healthy-looking brown jug of beer — with a very enticing head upon it. Work-it-out fell upon it, and slowly tilted it in the air.

"There," he said, "I've done it—bring out another for the lad—he wants it, poor fellow."

This further kindness of Work-it-out touched Inky ; and when the beer came he drank the good health of Mr. Harris, "and many on 'em," — a sentiment which went down very well.

"Punch ?" said the host, alluding to the show.

"No ; marynets," said Work-it-out.

"Never seed marynets," rejoined the host, "but have heard on 'em. Going to stop the night ?"

"We thought on it."

"Then I'll give you the tip," said the host, "you show here about sunset or arter dark, and the sleepin' won't cost you a penny."

"Well, you see," said Work-it-out, slowly, "marynets is exhaustin', and we've had rather a heavy day on it, but if so be as I fee s ekal to it, I think we may show later in the day or airly to-morrer mornin'."

"Airly in the mornin' won't do," said the host ; "every man will be at work. It must be to-night or not at all."

"Then to-night it shall be," said Work-it-out.

He then ordered a little more beer and something to eat ; and while they discussed the meal he laid before Inky his reasons for accepting the invitation to perform.

"I must get used to it," he said, "for it is only practice as 'ill get my nerves right ; and until I've practised enough I must have something else to put 'em in condishing."

"Better give the figgers to me," rejoined Inky.

"Not afore I've made another wentur' or two," returned Work-it-out ; "and if so be as I don't himprove, then you shall hev' 'em, and I'll take the drum."

"Done," cried Inky.

"And now I'm goin' in for a steady preparashing for the evening."

Work-it-out forthwith began his preparation in the following manner :—Stretching himself at full length upon the seat he bade Inky remove the show and accessories to a place of safety, and order him half an ounce of shag tobacco and some rum cold.

"What's the time ?" he asked the host, who brought out the order.

"Half-arter five."

"And what will be the best time to show ?"

"About eight, I reckon."

"Eight ?" repeated Work-it-out, musingly.

"Yes. That be about the time when the keepers and sech loike come round."

"I understand," said Work-it-out. "Then send me out, every 'arf hour, a renooal of the licker—the last two hot—that," he added to himself, "will put me in condishing."

The host, a very respectable imbiber himself, was not by any means astonished at the order, but, nodding his head in assent, retired.

Inky returned directly, and learned from his master the arrangements which had been made—that is, as far as concerned the show ; the rest Work-it-out kept within his bosom.

Having two hours before him, the "nobbly" born expressed his determination to take a walk, and Work-it-out, who wished to be alone, said he could not do better.

Inky departed to a meadow close by, where he lay down, and concocted in his mind a variety of schemes to enable him to become exhibitor of the marionettes. He was not the sort of youth to work his way on the high road to fame. He preferred short cuts, forgetting the many obstacles which invariably obstructed those who choose irregular paths.

"Work-it-out is too old," he thought ; "he can do the drum and so on, but the figgers ought to come to me. If he fail agen I'll have 'em or strike against the 'ole consarn altogether.''

He lay thinking in this strain and arranging his future movements until the church clock struck seven. Then he slowly sauntered back, and found Work-it-out in the same position, with the tobacco all gone, and a steaming glass of rum before him.

"Don't you think you've had enough o' that?" said Inky, slowly, pointing to the glass.

"Inky," rejoined Work-it-out, as he struggled into a sitting position, with his hat very much over one eye, "the feelin' is a-comin' on. Them figgers will work to-night."

"Oh!" exclaimed Inky.

"Yes; to-night shall the people behole me in my glory. I'll put life into them figgers; they shan't be wooden dolls—they shall be flesh and blood."

"Oh!" again said Inky.

"I don't know as I shan't make 'em talk. Genus can do anything," continued Work-it-out, "and now I think on it, I'll go and have a look at 'em. Where are they?"

"In a hempty stable, at the back, close to the pump."

Work-it-out then made towards the door, but, miscalculating his distance, knocked himself against the wall, and staggered back against the horse-trough, in which, regardless of the water, he sat smiling.

"None o' your larks, Inky," he said waggishly shaking his head, "don't have no games with the man that's been more than a father to you—you as I found in a yaller handkercher——"

"Gorging raiment," said Inky.

"In a handkercher," cried Work-it-out, "wot's more, *I know where to put my hand on it any moment.* So don't rile me Inky, or I'll expose you. *That handkercher has got a name on it.*"

He arose from the horse-trough, and without waiting to see the effect of the visible pain he had given to Inky, retired within the house—his track marked by a watery trail, such as a leaking pail leaves behind it.

Inky was, indeed, terribly staggered. He had so long hugged to his heart the idea of his being highly born and connected, that to be undeceived would be equal to receiving a mortal wound. He instinctively felt that Work-it-out had spoken the truth, and dreading the revelation of a plebeian name, resolved to say no more about it.

"Better to *think* I'm nobble," he thought, "than to *know* I'm wulgar."

The news of the approaching performance of the marionettes had got about, and as the hour of eight drew near, a good many stragglers, for such a small place, assembled.

The performance was to take place in the high road, being a more suitable spot than the yard or garden in the rear; and when Inky came out and pitched the show on the opposite side, his arrival was hailed with a cheer.

In the meantime Work-it-out, accepting the advice of his assistant, had been indulging in copious ablutions at the pump to restore his somewhat scattered intellect, and when the figures were placed in the show he accepted Inky's assistance for support, and went forth to the eager spectators.

He crossed the road with tolerable steadiness, climbed into the framework of the show, and dropped the green baize.

"I'll give 'em a little moosic," said Inky, "to give you time to pull up a bit."

Fortunately for Inky he had not a very discriminating audience, or the "moosic" he favoured them with would have resulted in his very speedy departure, but as it was he blew wandering airs out of the pipes, and, keeping the drumsticks going, made melody which passed muster with the rustic blades.

The preliminary flourish over, he asked Work-it-out if he was ready.

No answer.

"Are you ready?" he asked in a louder tone.

Some reply came from the inside, but whether it was a word, a gasp, or a groan, he could not tell. Raising the baize with the drumstick he peeped in.

There was Work-it-out with his arms upon the resting-board—*fast asleep*—and snoring furiously.

"Come out of it!" growled Inky, smiting his master viciously in the small of the back.

"Eh? what?" exclaimed Work-it-out, waking up, "dash them boys in the coort—hallo—where am I?"

"Among the marynets," returned Inky, exasperated almost beyond control, "and the people a-waitin'."

"I remember now," said Work-it-out, feebly, "this place is enough to stifle a chap—with the hevening sun on it."

"Come out of it and take the drum," whispered Inky, "the fresh air will revive you."

Artful Inky, and foolish Work-it-out to fall into the trap. He seized the offer with avidity, and descended.

In a moment the drum was round his neck, the sticks in his hand, and the breast-pipes tucked in his waistcoat.

"Now for it," thought Inky, "I'll astonish 'em. I'll wake 'em up a bit."

He did so; in his eagerness he clambered too high, and leaned over too far—the show rocked—Inky's brain reeled, and the next instant he went head first through the stage

INKY WENT HEAD FIRST THROUGH THE STAGE, AND CAME A CROPPER TO THE GROUND.

opening in front, and came a cropper to the ground, with the show above him.

CHAPTER XXXV.

A WOMAN'S PROMISE.

"A WOMAN wishes to see you, my lord."

It was Tummas, the afflicted and oppressed who spoke, and he addressed himself to Lord Holbrook, who was seated at the breakfast table alone.

"A woman, Thomas?" said his lordship, with an angry flush upon his face, "what do you mean by such an announcement?"

"I—I meant nothink, my lord," stammered Tummas; "it is a woman—not—not a man—nor a lady."

"What sort of person is it?"

"A low, vulgar person, my lord," replied Tummas, after a few moments reflection, "much given to drinking, my lord."

"A beggar, I suppose?" said Lord Holbrook, contemptuously; "give her sixpence, and send her about her business."

"I hoffered her some broken wittles, my lord," rejoined Tummas, "but she said she wasn't a beggar—but your lordship would see her if I gave her name—she ses it is Mary Hann."

Lord Holbrook but indifferently succeeded in hiding a tell-tale spasm of pain as the name was mentioned. His face, often the involuntary index to his soul, flushed and paled in a moment.

"Mary Ann," he rejoined, breaking the shell of an egg with a trembling hand, "a common name, and one with which I have no remembrance—but show her into the library."

Tummas bowed and retired, completely disgusted with the affairs of Beauforth.

"The printer's himp," he thought, "were cheeky, but clean and 'olesome—but this creetur—dash it! I'll give notice to-morrow."

In a few moments Lord Holbrook, in his dressing-gown, sauntered into the library with an assumed air of indifference. He found there the besotted form of a woman, begrimed with dirt—her matted hair clinging to her head through neglect, a wretched, lost creature, a coin of humanity, with every image and ornament defaced—Mary Ann, Jim Podley's wife.

He looked keenly at her, but failed to recognize either form or feature; she, with folded arms, surveyed him with the brazen look of a lost, reckless woman.

"My lord," she said, "you do not know me."

"I have not the slightest remembrance of you, woman," he sternly rejoined; "the name you sent in bears some accidental resemblance to——"

"One who knew you well, years ago," she added. "Lord Holbrook, I am that woman. Few would recognise in me," she added, with a reckless laugh, "the servant, friend, and confidante of Miss Bella Pierson."

"Hush—for heaven's sake!" rejoined his lordship, looking hurriedly towards the door.

"That name may well make you start and colour like a detected rogue, my lord," continued the woman. "What has become of the pretty rosebud?"

"I would give up my wealth and name to know," replied Lord Holbrook, hanging his head.

He was cowed even by the ragged wretch of a woman before him.

"You do not know," returned the visitor. "I thought not. My lord, I came to tell you. It was but the other day that I heard you was back to your fine house; I heard through a babbling fool of a boy, and then I knew that you had forgotten her. But I am here to wake your memory on the subject."

"By what right, woman?"

"By the right of my determination, my lord. Miss Bella—poor thing—the sweetest, gentlest, prettiest flower that ever drooped beneath the ill-usage of man could die blessing you; but when she drew her last breath, I stood by her side, and cursed the house of Beauforth."

She paused for a moment, with a savage light in her eyes; he, awed, dumbfounded, horror-stricken, stood in silence before his ragged denouncer.

"I had left her before that, as you know," continued the angry woman, "to tie myself to another of creation's *brutes*, and here is his work—but never mind me. Although I left her, I kept watch over the pretty thing, and when I knew that she was alone I went to her side again; but it was too late—she was dying, and you, my lord, had *murdered* her."

"'Tis false! I never knew—suspected—"

"Hear me out, my lord, then make what excuse you can to yourself, they are thrown away upon me. For three months she lingered, with never a word against you, then she gave birth to a boy, and gave up her spirit at the same time, and died, my lord, as I have said, blessing you."

"Did the child die, too?" he asked, after a long pause.

"No," she answered; "he lived, and grew more like you day by day. I learned from that to hate him. I could not endure his presence, and almost as soon as he could crawl I turned him into the streets."

"Oh, Heaven!"

"Yes," continued the woman, who seemed to glory in her cruelty in a most unnatural manner, "I turned him adrift. He was of your sex, and education and fostering care would be thrown away upon him. I knew that—for all of you grow up heartless and vicious. He took kindly to a street life, for I saw him with several other waifs and strays of this dark city, living as they alone know how, gaining day by day more fitted for the hulks and prisons. I saw it, and rejoiced. He was so like you."

"And are you a woman?" demanded his lordship.

"I *was*," she replied, "now I have lost all sense of woman's nature. I have no kindness or love lying in my breast. Judge if I have, when I tell you that I deserted my own child long before I parted with yours."

"Oh, horrible!"

"I have nought left here," she added, striking her bosom, "but hate—for you and my tyrant, Jim Podley; let both of you look to it."

"You must have been mad to turn the child adrift," said Lord Holbrook, sternly. "Oh, Heaven! my son—my son!"

"You can feel for *his* blighted life, my lord, why did you not feel for hers?" inquired Mrs. Podley.

"Her blighted life?" cried his lordship, "what means this? I loved her fondly—truly."

"Why then ruin her?"

"'Tis false!" cried his lordship, "*she was my wife!*"

He neither saw nor heeded the startled look upon the wretched woman's face, but went on speaking rapidly—

"An outcast then, I left her to seek bread for us both—I found nothing. Weeks of weary tramping, with cold and hunger, brought on a fever. I was found in the roadway raving, and lay for months under the care of strangers. Youth and a good constitution triumphed, and I recovered. I at once hastened back to my love, to find the house in the hands of strangers; they knew nothing of my wife—she was gone, they said, with a gentleman they supposed, and I, Heaven forgive me for my base thoughts, judged her wrongly. I had been wild, careless, reckless before, but from that hour I became indifferent to all. I cursed mankind, myself, and all the world—I was utterly lost."

"What have I done—what have I done?" murmured the woman, hot tears falling down her face.

"That which you can never recall," replied his lordship, "as I and many others have done. Go—repent, and may Heaven pardon you. There is only one hope I have within me—that my boy is dead."

"If he lives," cried the wretched woman, "if he is above ground, I will find him, All my life—not that it is much to boast of—shall be devoted to this end. Oh! my lord, forgive me!"

"Go," he said, in a kinder tone, "and undo your wretched work if you can. I have little hope."

"And I have much," she cried, looking up with such a marvellous change upon her face that he started back. "No money, my lord I must do this unaided and alone."

She swept from the room like a shadow, and was gone, leaving Lord Holbrook dazed and overwhelmed by the result of the strange meeting with one associated with the unhappy past.

CHAPTER XXXVI.

A ROGUE'S VISIT.

THE memories of the past had been slumbering in Lord Holbrook's mind; the wounds of sin and sorrow are slow to heal, but they become less tender as time goes on, and the heir of the house of Beauforth had ceased to look back with very poignant regret, when the arrival of that wretched woman re-opened his wounds anew, and, what was worse, created others.

Lord Holbrook regretted the past, but he hitherto considered himself deserted and betrayed; now the bare truth was revealed, the curtain uplifted, and he saw how wretchedly he and the only woman he ever loved, misunderstood each other, and the hour for explanation was irretrievably lost. Death had stepped in and put his fatal barrier up, which the noble lord could not pass until the end should come.

Then he thought of his son, the child of whose existence he was up to the present unaware—left to a life of misery, dragging on, perhaps, a weary existence steeped in crime —a wretched outcast, with the seal of vice upon his brow, stamped by vicious courses— so that every man should know him.

His lordship's memory went back to the haunts *he* had known—the streets, the courts, where poverty and crime too often went hand in hand—and, bowed down by a thousand apprehensions, he wept and prayed for his lost boy.

He thought of calling in professional aid, but second thoughts told him that it would be of little use; nobody knew anything of the boy, none except the woman could provide a clue—and she gone—with a promise, it was true, to find the child and restore him; but would she ever return?

"A lost, degraded creature," he muttered; "what is her word worth? I was a fool to let her go—once among her companions, she will forget alike her promise and repentance. If

I wanted to learn how vice can change us, I have my lesson there. Who, in this wretched creature, would have recognised the pretty Mary, who attended upon poor Bella?"

Ay! who indeed? And yet the change was nothing rare; there are thousands such —the streets teem with them—they pass us daily by—and few, beyond a passing glance, note their weary, hopeless faces, stamped with the seal of the Evil One.

But enough of this. Let us turn to Tom and see how he fares.

Pending arrangements for his education, he remained in Belgrave Square, passing his time as he willed—mostly in reading, and an occasional stroll round the neighbourhood or into the parks. By slow degrees, the feeling of terror which Ripper Gooch had awakened died away, and he began to think he had seen and heard the last of that notable individual; but he was soon rudely awakened from that dream.

Returning from a stroll in Rotten Row, where he had been admiring the equestrians of both sexes, he rang the bell, and Tummas appeared, with a promptitude which laid him open to a suspicion of his being very near the door in waiting.

As Tom was about to enter, a voice from the pavement held him—

"Now Tom, old pal—this isn't right— don't turn your back on me—you ought to know better."

He knew the voice, and a chill ran through his frame. He lost all power to move, and Tummas, radiant with triumph, completed his confusion by blocking up the doorway.

"Look at him," again cried the voice— the property of Ripper Gooch—"that's the way some people get on—straight away from the thieves' kitchen to Belgrave Square."

"You lie!" cried Tom, recovering himself and turning upon his assailant. "You are an infamous villain!"

"Do I deny it?" returned the thief, with a grin; "ain't I proud of it? I'm not like you—ashamed of what I've done; why don't you own an old pal? Ask me to dinner once, and I'll never trouble you again—that's letting you off easy, I think."

"Let me pass, Thomas," cried Tom, trembling with passion; "Lord Holbrook shall know of this."

"He *shall*," returned Tummas, drawing aside a few inches; and then he winked at Ripper, and followed Tom indoors.

Lord Holbrook was absent at the time, but he presently returned, and was pounced upon by Tummas before Tom had a chance to see him.

"My lord," he said, "may I make so bold as to ask leave for a few words with you?"

"What is it?" demanded his lordship, frowning. Tummas did not stand very high in his favour.

"My lord," said the injured servitor, "I ham a respectable man, and I objects to wait upon thieves."

"Thieves?"

"Yes, my lord. The young *gentleman* as you have been kind enough to purtect hev got among some of his hold hassociates— which he brings 'ome here and quarrels with 'em on the doorstep; my lord, I can't bear it, and I wishes to say that I leave this day month."

"As for your leaving you may do as you please," said his lordship; "but I must first trouble you to be a little more explicit. Who has Master Talbot been quarrelling with?"

"A young man as said he was a thief, and was proud of it."

"What were they quarrelling about?"

"I think they had been playin' pitch-and-toss, my lord—but I am not certain."

Tummas considered this insinuation to be a master-stroke, little recking of the consequences to himself.

After pondering a moment, his lordship bade Tummas follow him to the library.

There he rang the bell, and James responding, he was desired to inform Master Talbot that his lordship wished to see him.

Tom came—his eyes and face showing the emotion he suffered—and stood before his benefactor to learn why he was sent for.

"Now, Thomas," said Lord Holbrook, "repeat your story."

Tummas was so much taken aback by this request, that he could only stammer out a few words and look foolish. He was willing to withdraw the tossing, he said, for after all, he might have been mistaken.

"I—I certainly heard money jink," he said, "but it may have been some other party, my lord."

"Now, Tom," said Lord Holbrook, "let me hear your story."

It was told in a few simple words, and carried conviction with it. His lordship heard him out, and patted him kindly on the shoulder when he concluded. Matters were going heavily against Tummas, and he saw it, but it was too late to retreat.

"Thomas," said Lord Holbrook, sternly, "you will quit this house at once, leaving that livery behind you; and I advise you not to apply to me for a character."

"My lord," returned Tummas, humbly, "I trusts you'll not be too severe on me."

"You have heard what I have to say," was the reply. "Go."

It was both folly and madness to stay with that angry look in his lordship's eyes, indicative of horse-whips, so Tummas departed, and sought out his comrade, James.

"Jeames," he said, patheticaliy, "I've done with the house o' Beauforth."

"Indeed," rejoined James, indifferently.

"Yes, I've got——that is, I've given notice, and I'm going at once. You'll go with me, of course?"

"Not if I knows it," returned James; "do you take me for a hass?"

"I wouldn't swear you wasn't one," retorted Tummas, bridling up. "It were a pitiful day when I fust stood behind a carriage by your side."

"You've got the sack—cut it," rejoined James, sententiously.

"What's that you say?"

"You've got the sack—cut it."

"Jeames, that's a hinsult."

"I meant it to be so."

"Oh!" exclaimed Tummas, "then p'raps you could spare a few minutes with me in the back kitchen?"

"With pleasure," returned James. "I wants a little hexercise."

This was not the reply Tummas expected, but he could not back out, so the two gladiators retired to the back kitchen, from whence shortly issued sounds of mortal combat.

The struggle was brief, and James was the first to emerge, without a scratch, leaving Tummas very much dishevelled, and ornamented with a fine black eye in the bud.

An hour later Tummas received his money from the housekeeper, and shouldering his box, went outside, where he hailed a cab. He gave the address of a cousin of his, with whom he intended to stay, and drew up the window to hide his contused optic from a too curious public.

"It's all through that young printer chap," he muttered, his thoughts turning upon Sam; "and if ever I comes across him in a quiet place I'll murder him."

CHAPTER XXXVII.

NEW FRIENDS AND FACES.

HALF the noise of Inky's fall was drowned by the drum which Work-it-out, with his eyes closed, was beating vigorously; and, totally unconscious of anything in the form of a disaster, he continued his musical performance until he received a blow in the chest, which sent him reeling into the opposite ditch.

Being in a frame of mind which takes everything as it comes, he quietly kept a sitting position, and saw Inky raised from the ground and carried within the house, without betraying any emotion or curiosity on the subject. Then he beheld the show being tilted in the air, and the figures, which had been scattered in the roadway, passed from hand to hand, and examined with much attention.

Vaguely conscious that this ought not to be, he staggered to his feet and advanced, beating impressively on the drum.

"Who struck me?" he demanded, waving a drum-stick in the air.

"Billy Stoat," replied one, "when he runned forrard to help the boy—it were an accident."

"Well for him it were," replied Work-it-out, with dignity; "he would find I'm not a man to be trifled with. Put them figgers down."

"Dang it, measter, keep yer temper," said one, "we on'y picked un up friendly loike."

"Then put 'em down friendly like," returned Work-it-out, "and leave me to surwey the rooins."

They saw that he was much affected, and kindly adjourned to the inn and left him; then Work-it-out sat down upon a bench by the door, and looked mournfully upon the wreck.

Putting down the drum, he, with much labour, collected the inanimate performers, and laid them in a row upon the little table by the porch; then he examined the show, and finding it but little damaged, put it against the wall, and resumed his seat.

"Here's a disapp'intment," he murmured, mournfully; "the Hold English Gentleman is bu'st, and the sawdust comin' out; and the Hemperor of Tartary have been trod upon. Here's a go—here's a wale o' grief."

"Don't be cut up, friend," said the host, emerging from the house.

"I can't help it, I'm broken 'arted," returned Work-it-out, in a frenzy; "a fortin' gone at one blow."

"I assure you," said the host, "that the boy is not serusly hurt; he drank a drop o' warm wine and water, and comed round straight."

"Dash the boy!" cried Work-it-out, "what's he?—there's plenty o' boys about; but look at Tubby, flat as a pancake—what's to cure him?"

"A few stitches and a little stuffin'," hinted the host of the Three Fiddlers.

"Stitches and stuffin'," repeated Work-it-out, contemptously, "to put a figger like that straight! Poor ole Tubby, cut short in yer prime. P'int out to me," he added, with a sudden fury, "the man as did it. Who upset my show?"

"Nobody didn't upset it," returned the host, stoutly.

"They must ha' done."

"When the boy climbed up it comed over."

"Don't tell me," persisted Work-it-out, "that a show like that could come over without bein' shoved ; I know better. I sees how it is—I've got among a bad lot."

"Draw it mild, my friend."

"Draw wot mild?" asked Work-it-out ; " don't think you can 'timidate me. I'm not the man to be put down in a minnit. I ain't been a degenerater of the people for nothin', let me tell you that !" he added, banging the table defiantly with his drum-stick.

By this time several of the men, hearing an altercation, had come forth from the house and gathered around.

Work-it-out rose with the occasion, multitudes, in his then frame of mind, could not have daunted him.

"When you try to git a rise out o' me," he added, "you gets hold o' the wrong man. Where's my doos as a man and a Briton, if a lot like you are allowed to shove my show over ?"

"We didn't shove the show over," rejoined several voices.

"Liars and knaves !" returned Work-it-out, "base minions of a bloated 'stocracy—downtrodden worms of a rampant, bloodthirsty olijarchy—can you look upon the figgers there—look at Tubby and the Hemperor alone—and tell me you didn't shove my show over ?"

"I don't orfen get wagabon' strollers here," put in the host, "which I'm glad on—and wot's more, they don't come agen if I can help it. You pack up that rubbish, and tramp."

"I'm not to be trodden on," returned Work-it-out, nevertheless putting the figures into the box with very commendable speed ; "there's nothing of the worm about me. I don't lick the boots of your squires and dames."

"Who do, then ?" demanded a sturdy gamekeeper. "Doo 'ee mean us ?"

"I mean nothin' but wot I say," returned Work-it-out, after a brief inspection of the querist with his eye. "I knows wot I am and wot I ain't, that's enough for me. Where's my boy ?"

Inky was summoned, and came forth pale, with signs of weeping on his countenance, but otherwise little the worse for the fall.

"Here, kitch hold o' this drum," said Work-it-out ; "we'll foot it from here, straight. I can't breathe any hair but the hair o' freedom. I'll take the box and the show."

"Afore you goes," said the host, checking him, "hand over four and fi'pence."

"And you're mean enough to take a score o' a man like me," replied Work-it-out, "and arter such an accident too ?"

"Arter your cheek," was the brief rejoinder, " I'm mean enough to do anything."

As the debt could not justly be disputed,

and a refusal to pay might result in the confiscation of the show, Work-it-out slowly and laboriously told out the required amount, and hoisting the show of the marionettes on his shoulders, metaphorically shook from his feet the dust of the Three Fiddlers, and departed, followed by the guffaws of the yokels.

"We must bear it, Inky," he said, "we must bear it. In time to come, when we've riz, we can be cheeky. The public will want us one day, and then it will be our turn."

"We have been trooly unfortunate," murmured Inky.

"We have—but sech is life—though how you got through the front o' the show, I don't know."

"Somehow," rejoined Inky, "I went clean over the restin' board, and, havin' nothin' to put my legs agen', went clean out."

"Better luck next time," said Work-it-out. "But we must be sharp about it, for Reuben's suvrin' melteth freely."

It was growing dark by this time, the sun having settled behind a heavy bank of clouds, which foreboded ill for the coming night. A few stars were glimmering in the sky, and an early owl was winging his flight across the sombre fields.

Pausing on the brow of a hill, Work-it-out surveyed the landscape. Behind them lay the village they had left—before them an apparently interminable range of fields and woods, with here and there a homestead on the summits of rising ground.

"It were bad policy," muttered Work-it-out, " to pitch inter the landlord chap, but the rum and water, and the confugion of Inky's comin' down were too much for me. Not a house where we can put up at in sight, Inky."

"That's like you," growled Inky ; "why couldn't you keep at the Fiddlers ?"

"I had my regions," replied Work-it-out; "and one on 'em was that the landlord might hev' pitched us out. But keep a stout 'art. We go on. It ain't dark yet."

Gloomy, impressed with forebodings of coming evil, Inky followed his master, turning occasionally to look at the bank of clouds, which was already sending dark patches across the sky—like skirmishers before the main army of battle.

"We shall hev' a pelter directly," he said, " and it's a growin' darker every minnit."

"Keep up, keep up," urged Work-it-out ; " if wust comes to wust we'll take refuse in a barn."

Another quarter of an hour's trudging, with the sky growing darker every moment, and then a few drops of rain—good solid drops, with no nonsense about them—came pattering down.

THEN THE BACK OF THE SHOW WAS CRASHED IN BY A VIOLENT BLOW.

"I told yer so," growled Inky; but Work-it-out made no reply, he reserved his breath for a better purpose, and increased his pace.

The few drops speedily became a shower, which increased in strength and power until the water swept like a torrent over the face of the land. To keep on was impossible, and, taking advantage of a hedge of more than ordinary dimensions, the two wayfarers crept under it, and, stowing the drum carefully away, drew up the show, in a horizontal position, in front.

They were just in time, for the storm, hitherto violent, now became furious, and, added to the rain, came lightning and deep, sonorous thunder, which seemed to shake the earth. Conversation for the time being was impossible, but they huddled together as if seeking mutual safety in contact with each other.

At their feet lay what had been a dry dyke, but this speedily filled, and the water went by them, a very respectable imitation of its larger brother the mountain-torrent. The road, too, appeared to be one sheet of water, with a million bubbles on its surface from the falling rain, lit up by the vivid lightning, which played continually in the stormy sky.

Inky had never seen anything like it before, and he cowered beside the ex-cobbler, his master, shivering, and muttering feeble prayers for safety. Work-it-out, too, was terrified, and the fumes of his late potations having departed, he was able to fully realize the terrors of the scene.

Once only was there any sign of life, and that only added to their alarm. A horse, with something trailing behind it, apparently part of a broken vehicle, came dashing furiously by, snorting and throwing up the mud and water from its heels; and Work-it-out thought he heard the cry of a man in the distance, but he was not quite sure, and being quite incapable of rendering any assistance, he remained under shelter.

The storm was brief, and its fury subsided. The rain ceased, the stars came out, and a rising moon threw her beautiful light o'er field and wood. Then the voice of a man was heard, and apparently not far away—shouting for help.

"Our fust dooty," said Work-it-out, as he crept from the hedge, "is to our feller-man. I hears a woice. Put a eye on the things while I run back to see wot it is."

But Inky would not be left alone on the lonely road; he flatly refused to do so, and Work-it-out, muttering something the reverse of a blessing upon his head, bade him follow.

"There's nobody about," he said, "and the things will be safe."

They ran back in company about two hundred yards, when they found a heavy, lumbering vehicle, half overturned, its back in the ditch, and resting almost on end against the thick fence.

"Hullo! hi, there!" shouted Work-it-out.

"Ahoy! bear a hand, will you?" shouted somebody from the interior. "Come to the window here."

There was a small sliding trap, about a foot square, in the side—dignified by the name of window—and to it Work-it-out went.

"What do you want?" he asked.

"How many are there of you?" asked the unseen.

"Two—a man and a boy."

"Not enough to lift us out. Take this hatchet, and cut away the hedge so we can get the door open."

Work-it-out then perceived that the vehicle was a travelling van, such as showmen use; and the door at the back could not be opened in consequence of the thick fence. Taking the hatchet, he stepped over the ditch, and went to work with a will. In a few minutes he had cut enough away to allow the door to be opened, and then two men came out.

They were sturdy fellows, clad in velveteen, with large caps, apparently of fur, upon their heads, and gaudy-coloured handkerchiefs round their necks.

"Thanky, mate," said the foremost; "you cummed in time, for we might ha' been fixed all night. Have you seen our horse anywhere?"

"One cut by us like winkin' a little while ago, with somethin' hanging behind him."

"That were the traces and shafts. I jist went in to my mate to get a tarpaulin, when the lightning, I s'pose, frightened him, and he back'd agen' the hedge, broke the shafts, and tore away."

"He won't go werry fur," growled the other; "we shall find him progging about in the morning."

"But that won't do," urged the first speaker; "we haven't much time to lose; but first let us get the wan out. You live hereabouts?"

He addressed Work-it-out, who replied that he did not.

"I'm a travellin'," he added, "bein', in fac', about with—a—sort of show."

"You don't speak like one of our people," said the other, eyeing him keenly. "What sort of show is it?"

"Marynets."

"And how long have you had 'em?"

"About three weeks," replied Work-it-out, throwing in the time he lived with his brother—and a trifle over.

"Ah!" said the man, drily, "I wishes you luck."

"He's a flytrap," interposed the other man.

"Don't be too hasty, Sawney."

"I can nose 'em anywheres," persisted the other.

This was double Dutch to Work-it-out, who had further cause for astonishment when the man who had spoken first took him by the collar, and led him into the moonlight—where he scanned his features, and giving him a gentle push, laughed aloud.

"There's as much of the flytrap about him," he said, "as there is about Johble's blind mare. I say, old man, where's your marrynettes?"

"Down the road; I left 'em to come to help you."

"Like a good fellow—now, what will you drink? Sawney, bring out the mops."

Sawney slowly crept back into the van, and reappeared with a couple of bottles and glasses.

"Gin or rum?" he asked.

"Rum," said Work-it-out, and a glass was filled for him. Inky was cold, and he took a little sip of gin.

The other men then tossed a glass a-piece down their capacious throats, and proceeded to take stock of the damage done. Nothing very serious they found, excepting the shafts and the loss of the horse; but the latter they both seemed very easy about.

After this, mutual confidences were exchanged. Work-it-out learned that his new friends were showmen—proprietors of a performing booth, and that their names were respectively, Bob Crossley and Sawney Tap.

"We are bound for Lincoln Fair," said Bob Crossley, "which I s'pose you are?"

"Well, I hadn't marked out a line," hesitated Work-it-out; "but I think Lincoln Fair will do—eh, Inky?"

"Anything is good enough for a poor unfortunate chap like me," replied Inky.

"It's plain to me," said Bob Crossley, "that you're a pair o' green uns."

"Werry green," growled Sawney Tap.

"Be quiet, Sawney. You're a pair o' green uns, I can see, by not havin' a course marked out, and not to know of Lincoln Fair; why, if you goes a-wandering about in a wague manner, it's unpossible for you to get a livin' in our line."

"Quite unpossible," assented Sawney Tap, in an undertone, which might have passed for distant thunder.

"Sich bein' the case," pursued Bob Crossley, "what do you say to goin' on with us—you've done us a good turn, and we'll do one with you."

"What do you say, Inky?" inquired Work-it-out.

"It don't matter to me—anybody will soot. I'm a forlorn child of destiny," replied Inky.

"We agrees," said Work-it-out, turning away from his adopted son; "and don't mind him—he's got the nobble tantrums on, I can see."

"Then fetch up your traps," was the rejoinder; "and you, Sawney, go and look arter the horse—we must hev the wan out afore daylight comes, or they'll drop on us for damaging the hedge."

Inky and Work-it-out speedily brought up the show, box, and drum, and a little later, Sawney, the broken shafts upon his shoulders, came up with the horse, now quiet as a lamb.

By means of a stout rope or two, brought from the van, the traces were re-attached, and the old horse, accustomed to the vicissitudes of travel, bent its neck, and with the assistance of the men and Inky, got the vehicle out of the ditch. Then it was slowly drawn down the road into a bye-lane, where Bob Crossley proposed to rest until morning.

"We can get up with the sun," he said, "and put the shafts right, and be away before a soul is stirring—until then, let us all turn in and have a pitch."

The show was then fastened to the top of the van, the box and drum taken inside, and Inky and Work-it-out, glad of anything like shelter, lay down beside their new friends, and were speedily sound asleep.

CHAPTER XXXVIII.

NEWS FOR WORK-IT-OUT.

THE silver light of the moon was yet struggling with the warmer beams of day, when the van, with its shafts carefully bound together, emerged from the lane upon the highway. By its side walked Bob Crossley and his mate. Inky and Work-it-out slumbered still.

"Curious pair," said Bob, pointing over his shoulder with his thumb.

Sawney Tap, whose great virtue was brevity, answered—

"Werry."

"Don't make 'em out, nohow," pursued Bob; "they've not runned away, and they don't belong to anything above common people, and they ain't in our line; and yet they've got as perfect a set of figures and show as ever I seed—not new, either."

"I think I knows 'em," said Sawney.

"The man and boy?"

"No—the marynetts."

"Oh! I don't."

"Do you remember Tootle?"

"Him as fell foul o' Bob Smasher, and died in the 'ospital?"

"That's the party—the marynetts were his."

"How do you know 'em?"

"By the box—name cut in the corner."

A lively discussion ensued as to how Work-it-out could become possessed of the property of the late Tootle; but nothing was made out of it. The affair was a mystery, and they resolved to leave it so for the present.

About nine o'clock they halted to give the horse a rest and to partake of the morning meal. Work-it-out and Inky were by this time entirely recovered from the fatigue of the preceding day, and joined them in the consumption of bread, cheese, and beer, at a wayside inn.

"We've got a long journey afore us," said Bob Crossley, to Work-it-out. "I suppose you will show a bit on the road."

"How long will it take us?" asked Work-it-out.

"About ten days; and you may as well make money on the road. It's easy to go forrard a mile or two in the morning, and let us pick you up."

"I want a little rest."

"Well, you can have it then," returned Bob, "for you can travel cheap with us; but I thought it a pity to waste time."

"Do you show?" asked Work-it-out.

"Parsonally, I never do," replied Bob; "but my people are gone on different ways, and I shall pick 'em up—some here, and some there—some on foot, and some with the other wans."

"They ain't a idle lot," put in Sawney Tap, as a hint to Work-it-out.

"I'll show the day arter to-morrer," said Work-it-out, and the subject dropped.

The truth was, that our friend was gradually awakening to a painful sense of the truth—that he and Inky wanted a deal more practice before they would be fit for the public eyes; he mistrusted himself a little, but he mistrusted Inky more.

"Whatsumever I did," he thought, "I kep' inside the show. I didn't shoot myself out like a narleyquin."

As for Inky, every hour he grew more and more depressed; after his first performance he could not lay claim to the figures, and Work-it-out, his heart told him, would not be able to carry the performance through—and if he did not, what then?

They must starve.

Grim Want would soon stare them in the face, unless they found a friend; and something told him that neither Bob Crossley nor Sawney would for a moment endure the presence of mouchers and idlers.

"Cuss the show," he thought. "If we hadn't that, somebody might take pity on us. I wonder whether I could gammon old Work-it-out to run away and leave it? But then

there's the drum, and when the worst comes we can sell it—it's worth money."

He drew a little consolation from this, and became more cheerful; and even entered into conversation with Sawney, to whom he imparted—Work-it-out being at a safe distance—an entirely new version of his birth and parentage, winding up with the hint that he was only travelling with Work-it-out, as his way lay on the road to the mansion of his "nobble" parents.

Sawney Tap was one of those men who never express astonishment; when the van ran back into the ditch during the thunderstorm, he lay quiet in the corner, and allowed his mate to do the shouting; it was nothing to him, for he was a philosopher who took things as they came.

A dragon suddenly appearing in the roadway might have given him a momentary shock, but it is doubtful if he would have considered it beyond the ordinary course of life, and, therefore, when Inky poured into his ears a long rigmarole, in which Jim Podley, Mr. Marall, lops, and a man in a fur cap, were hopelessly mixed, he swallowed the story with philosophic resignation.

"It is werry hard, ain't it?" pleaded Inky, "to be knocked over so young, and deprived of your five-poun' notes and mansions with a box o' lights growin' fat on the wittles, your mess of potash, which is yours by rights."

To which Sawney replied—

"I suppose so."

"But it will soon be all over," continued the veracious youth, "and when I come into my property I shan't forget you."

Sawney surveyed him with a thoughtful eye, and said—

"I hope you won't."

"But don't say anything to him," said Inky, pointing to Work-it-out, "or I shall allus hev' him hanging about me like a leech, and a man o' that sort I can't abear."

Again Sawney replied with commendable brevity—

"In course not."

"But there's another thing," pursued Inky, building another castle; "a man o' title can't hev' sech a name as Work-it-out about his place, and it sounds shoppy. Sawney Tap ain't bad, in fact, I rader likes it, so I do the name o' Crossley; and you would know how to behave like gentlemen—Work-it-out don't."

Sawney rejoined that "he knowed his way about," and grew reflective as he chowed a fragment of straw.

Shortly after, Bob Crossley joined his mate, and Inky went forward to the side of Work-it-out, and Bob Crossley imparted to

Sawney a little information he had been able to extract from the regenerator of the people.

"He's rather close," he said, "but from what I can make out, his brother lent some money on the marynettes, and, as Tootle never paid, he kept 'em."

"He'll hev' to prove that," said Sawney gruffly.

"At the proper time and place," returned Bob; "but until then not a word about it."

"Not from me," growled Sawney.

They halted that night on a common, where the old horse was turned out to feed, and Sawney lit a fire, gipsy fashion, although the night was warm enough to do without it. The object was soon explained.

He went away for an hour or so, and returned with a couple of fowls in his pockets, presenting an appearance of having had their necks twisted in a very scientific manner.

These fowls Bob and Sawney plucked, burning every feather as they worked, and put them into a pot with some onions, a cabbage, and a few other vegetables, which Sawney also produced from his capacious pockets; the result being a very relishable stew, of which the party freely partook, and asked no questions.

What was left they buried in a hole dug by Bob, much to the astonishment of Work-it-out and Inky.

"It's a waste, I know," said Bob, "but you can't tell who may call on you when they are missed in the morning. Some people have got cheek enough to swear to the bones."

From this Work-it-out gathered that Sawney had not come by the fowls in a manner creditable to a native of a commercial country; and Inky, with a sagacity beyond his years, concluded within his mind that they had been stolen, and both he and his master trembled as they thought of enraged farmers and the county prison.

They were very glad when, on the morrow, four or five miles of the road had been covered, without an armed force rushing upon them, and demanding justice in the name of the law, and even Bob Crossley breathed a little freer; but Sawney was as cool as usual, and the members of a complete force, armed with cutlasses and revolvers, would not have startled him.

"Four mile ahead," said Bob, "is Hitchen, and my advice is for you to go on for a pitch. We'll go round by the lanes and wait for you the other side of the town; good luck to ye."

The show was removed from the top of the van, and, with much reluctance, Work-it-out shouldered it; Inky took possession of the drum, and they went on as lively as two mourners at a funeral.

"Inky," said Work-it-out, hoarsely, when they were clear away, "what shall we do?"

"I don't know," returned Inky.

"The last wentur'," continued Work-it-out, "was almost too much for me. I'm afraid of the figgers."

"I ain't in love with 'em," said Inky.

"Then what shall we do; go thro' the town, and say they wouldn't let us pitch?"

"They knows better," said Inky, indicating Bob and Sawney with a toss of his head.

"Will you wentur'?" asked Work-it-out.

"I will not," emphatically returned Inky; "my adwice is—sell the lot."

"I can't sell Reuben," returned Work-it-out, pathetically. "I cannot deceive my brother."

"You knocked his front teeth out," insinuated Inky.

"When in liquor we does them things; but it's different to sellin' marynettes."

Hitchen hove in sight, and they had decided upon no particular course—both were afraid to attempt to exhibit, and when they entered the town they were still discussing what should be done.

"The hye of the public is on us," said Work-it-out, as two boys ran up and gave him a cheer. "I think I'll wenture."

Inky said nothing, but a gloomy foreboding settled in his eye.

"A pint o' mild and a bisket," said Work-it-out, "would give us a narve. Hold on, Inky, here's the King's Head. I'll have it here. You stop with the show and figgers outside. Do you want anything?"

"No," replied Inky, abruptly, "unless it's a dose of p'ison, for I've had enough o' this."

Work-it-out paid no heed to this outburst of grief, but disappeared in the inn, where his voice was presently heard calling for the refreshment he needed. A boy at this moment passed the doorway with a bundle of morning papers under his arm. He delivered one, and Inky, looking in, beheld the landlord offer it to Work-it-out, who was nibbling his biscuit in the bar.

A few stragglers were gathering up, but Inky regarded them with supreme indifference, until a bold urchin smote the drum with his fist. Inky spent a few moments in futile chase and then returned to the inn, where he found Work-it-out, pale and trembling in the doorway.

"Are you tuk ill?" he asked.

"Inky," humbly rejoined Work-it-out, "come here. I'm goin' to leave yer."

"Leave me—wot for?"

"Can you read?"

"I should think so."

"Read that."

He held the paper in a quivering hand, and pointed with a trembling finger to a paragraph in the "agony" column. Inky took the paper, and read the following startling announcement :—

"BENJAMIN HARRIS. — Return to town at once. By will of a distant relative you are entitled to FORTY THOUSAND POUNDS. Come at once, and all will be well. Don't delay.—R. H., Lincoln's Inn."

The head of Inky swam round. The intelligence was certainly overpowering. Forty thousand pounds, and he was Work-it-out's adopted son !

"I'm orf at once," said Work-it-out. "Here's three bob. The show and figgers are yourn—it's a good start in life for you."

"But you can't leave me," cried Inky, desperately.

"I will—I must," returned Work-it-out, wildly. "I can't be hampered with a half-daft kid as ain't no relation. I've my family to think on—my brother Reuben and his lot. Forty thousand pounds ! I'll build a big house, and buy a cask o' rum. Farewell, Inky."

"Look here," yelled Inky, clinging to his skirts, "I ain't goin' to be left behind."

"I'm not going to have you."

"You shall."

"Hands off."

"Shan't."

Work-it-out parleyed no more. Lifting up his hand he smote Inky heavily, and the "nobbly" born, reeling back, fell over the drum, and, knocking his head against the wall, lay there half stupefied. Work-it-out seized the opportunity and fled.

When Inky came round a bit his old master was no longer in sight, and he was alone in the world.

"Your mate's gone," said a bystander, offering a perfectly superfluous piece of information.

"Pick up your money, my lad," said another.

Inky looked moodily upon the ground, and there beheld three shillings—the offering of Work-it-out. He picked them up, and gloomily transferred them to his pocket. His eye then lighted on the show and its accessories. They were his property—that was something, and he brightened a little ; but how was he to get them outside the town ? Exhibiting was, of course, out of the question.

He looked around upon the gathering near him, and selected a man who appeared likely to want a job. Beckoning him with his finger, he asked him if he was at liberty to help him.

"What do you want me to do ?" gruffly asked the man.

"To carry some of these things across the town. I've friends there."

"What'll yer stand ?"

"Sixpence."

"Done with you."

The man shouldered the show, and Inky followed with the drum to keep an eye upon him, and in this order they went through the town, followed by a body of pertinacious boys, who lifted up their shrill voices, and demanded that the show be put down forthwith and the performance begin.

"Here's a good corner," shouted one. "Punch allus goes up here. Down with it."

"Hooray !" shouted the rest, "Let's have it."

But as the prospect of exhibition grew fainter, their jeers turned to groans, and presently, too, the more substantial form of cabbage stumps and other missiles ; but gloomily indifferent to all, Inky followed in the wake of his assistant, bent only upon getting clear of the town.

The streets ended at last, and once upon the road again his tormenters turned back by twos and threes. When all were gone, Inky bade the man put down the show, and paid him his sixpence.

"Good luck to yer," said the man.

Inky thanked him, and was once more alone.

He waited more than two hours undisturbed, save by an occasional foot-passenger or a vehicle passing, from which he received a stare of astonishment ; and then Bob Crossley's van came rumbling along the road.

"Hullo !—here we are !" cried Bob.

"Here we are," returned Inky ; "at least, one on us."

"Where's the old man ?"

"Gone."

"Gone where ?"

"Somebody's left him forty thousand pounds."

Bob Crossley staggered back against the wheel of the van. Sawney Tap looked up to the sky, and whistled " My Mary Anne " in a quiet, impressive manner.

CHAPTER XXXIX.
LINCOLN FAIR.

"FORTY thousand pounds !" repeated Bob Crossley, drawing a deep breath ; " so he warn't wulgar ?"

"Wulgar ?" rejoined Inky, curling his lips in contempt, "no more than I am. He's a markis in disguise ; and it's all thro' his brother, who lost me, that I'm in the state I am."

"I hurd summat about it as we came through the town," said Bob Crossley, "but I didn't listen much to it, for I'd no idea it was our friend as had come into the luck— had you, Sawney ?"

"I had not," returned Sawney, with great emphasis.

"Well, I envy no man," continued Bob; "but I think he might ha' stayed a little while—an hour or two—and told us all about it."

"I don't think he's gone for good," said Inky, who saw an opportunity to better his position; "it's agin his natur', and he's fond of a stroller's life He'll come back, and may be, spend a year or two with yer."

"He'll be welcome," rejoined Sawney Tap: "give us a hand with the show, Bob."

The Royal Temple of Marionettes was then hoisted upon the roof of the van—the box and drum put inside, where Inky went also, as he was fatigued with the exertion and excitement of the day.

"Sawney," whispered Bob Crossley, as the van moved on, and they trudged by the horse's head, "what's your candid opinion of this story?"

"There air some rummy starts in life," replied Sawney, cautiously.

"A'ter all, these two may be s'perior to what they look."

"They may," replied Sawney.

"You remember that I said it was curus their having the marynettes at all?"

"You did."

"And here's another fac', Sawney. This Work-it-out—evidently a nummy de ploom—this Work-it-out, or his brother, *lent* money on the show—perhaps bought it outright—people can't lend or buy without money, Sawney."

"They can't."

"And so I says, Sawney, that we had better stick to the boy and treat him well; if the old 'un turns up it will be the better for us; if he don't, why, there's no harm done."

"He'll eat a lot," suggested Sawney.

"So he will, for he's a growin' lad; but there's the figgers and drum, Sawney—they'll cover a heap o' wittles."

"Then, wot I ses is, stick to him," rejoined Sawney, with a burst of eloquence; "for lookin' at the bearin's of the case, it's a speckerlative wentur' as is open to recooperation—and wot have you got to say agin' it?"

"Me?—nothin'," returned Bob Crossley; "ain't I been sticking up for it all along?"

"Perhaps you have," said Sawney, who avoided every possible chance of committing himself.

"I wonder how he parted with the hold man," mused Bob.

"Ax him," said Sawney, which Bob, who had great reverence for Sawney, decided to do.

Inky slept soundly for two hours, until the sense of an increasing appetite aroused him; then he came forth and asked Bob Crossley how long it would be before they stopped.

"Hungry, my lad?" said Bob.

"Yes; I could eat anything a'most."

"We shall put up in a hour or so; but if you can't wait, there's a biscuit in the pocket of my jacket hanging behind the door. Have that to nibble."

Inky fetched the biscuit out, and rejoined his companions. Bob soon led up to the subject of Work-it-out and his fortune.

"I wonder," he said, "how a man feels when he suddenly comes into a lump like that?"

"All depends if he's had such a lump afore," returned Inky; "*I've* lost two fortins."

"Lor'!"

"It's troo; one on 'em I've told you of—the Markis's; t'other was Miss Pierson—a sort o' cousin to the Markis like; she lived in a big house, up north, with a private reverend gent to pray for her; *he* put the pot on me, and arter tearin' the werry clothes orf my back, fetched up Jim Podley, who took me home, and made up my bed on the game-cock box."

"How did you part with your fren'?" asked Bob, who had not listened very keenly to the story.

"Miss Pierson?"

"No—Mr. Work-it-out, Eskvire," replied Bob, wishing to be respectful to the great man.

"I don't know what you mean."

"Did you part fren'ly like?—did he shake hands?—did he wish you well?"

"He wep' on my shoulder," replied Inky, "and said he'd come arter me as soon as he could."

Bob exchanged a gratified look with Sawney. So far, so well; they might reasonably expect the recipient of fortune back.

Everything being amicably settled, Inky had a very happy time of it; during the rest of the journey exhibiting was out of the question, for there was nobody to work the figures; but Sawney said he "knowed a chap who could work 'em—a chap as would be sure to be at Lincoln." So until then our friend had a time of ease, and, we might add, of feasting, for both the showmen plied him with victuals and drink to an incredible extent.

Furthermore, a rivalry sprang up between them, each having a private hankering after the wealth of Work-it-out, which they hoped to obtain through Inky, and each resolved, if possible, to obtain the larger share.

"He is sure to shell out something for the

care of the boy," thought Bob, "and I don't see why I shouldn't have it. It was my idea to be friends with him."

Sawney thought something after the same fashion ; but, as became him, his thoughts were briefer, and took the form of—"If there's anything to be got, I'll have it."

And in this frame of mind they jogged on, amiable and kind to Inky in public, devoted to him in private.

Two days' journey from Lincoln they began to pick up portions of the troupe.

First they came across a short, sturdy man, with a barrel-organ and a troupe of performing dogs. Bob shook hands with him, and hailed him as Fourfoot Riley—a name which might have been associated either with his stature or calling. Bob asked him how trade was.

"Well," he said, "it ain't bad and it ain't good—there's jist enough for you and nothin' over ; and I had the bad luck to foller some one with a Happy Family."

"Who was it ?"

"That's wot I can't make out. I didn't know, Bob, there was one on the road."

"I haven't heard of one for years, Fourfoot—do you know who it is, Sawney ?"

"No, I don't," replied Sawney.

The subject seemed to puzzle them all, for they continued to speak of it after Fourfoot Riley had put his organ in the van, and was trudging on the road beside them.

The dog performer could not describe the personal appearance of the stranger, beyond that he was a thin man, a little over thirty.

"I don't want to know," he said, sulkily ; "he's no right to go afore me, taking the bread out o' my mouth."

The next party they fell in with was a tumbling troupe, three in number, and a fourth with a drum ; they had a van with them, upon which Inky read the names of Messrs. Crossley and Tap, which led him to conclude that the tumblers were part of the company belonging to those gentlemen.

He was right ; and on the morrow a party of three girls on stilts, a woman with a tambourine, and a man with pipes and drum were overtaken, with whom they at once fraternized, and Inky learned that they were all friends, and had met by appointment.

They all went on merrily together, until Lincoln appeared in sight, on the outskirts of which they fell in with half-a-dozen vans and a number of men and women, all associated with Bob and Sawney, and then, forming a sort of procession, they made an impressive entry into the town.

The fair was to begin on the morrow with a cattle market, and to last several days. At present there was nothing more than a chaotic mass of vans, carts, poles, men, donkeys, and the excitable boys, who had mustered from the town in force.

Inky could not help expressing his doubts on the point of their being ready, at which Bob Crossley laughed, and Sawney smiled kindly ; under any other circumstances than a reasonable expectancy of reaping a benefit from the wealth of Work-it-out, they might have told Inky that he was a fool, and didn't know better ; as it was, they received his remarks kindly and smiled.

Ten minutes after their arrival all were busy. Fourfoot Riley disposed of his dogs somehow, the tumblers put off their fleshings, and turned out in velveteen ; the ground was marked out, and the erection of the booth began. The women remained in the vans attending to the cooking.

All night long the sound of the hammer never ceased ; old and young had something to do. Inky was kept hard at it, handing cord and nails to the workers until far into the night, when Bob Crossley, in consideration of his wealthy connections, dismissed him to rest.

He lay in a corner of the van until the sun had been up some hours, and going out, he found his friends still at it, and apparently but little the worse for their labours during the dark hours. It was a bright morning, promising well for the fair, and they were all very merry ; and a number of pewter pots scattered about showed that the inward man had not been entirely neglected.

"Mornin', my lad," cried out Bob Crossley.

Inky returned his salute ; and the people around, who had heard of the story of Work-it-out's fortune, surveyed the "nobbly" born with much curiosity.

"I'se been thinking," returned Bob, "that you can't do much with us, and the marynets wouldn't soot the fair ; it'll be too crowded, and it would be better for you to show round town."

"I'd rather not try it alone," faltered Inky.

"Alone ? my lad, I should think not. Sawney's found a man who knows how to handle the strings. Hullo, there, Sawney !"

"Here," replied the voice of Mr. Tap from the roof of the almost completed booth.

"Where's Shy Kailer ?"

"Up with me. What do you want with him ?"

"To go round with Inky."

"He can't come," returned Sawney.

"It's all right," said Bob Crossley to Inky, in a matter-of-fact manner, as if he had received a most cordial assent, "they'll be down directly."

And sure enough, Mr. Tap was seen a few minutes later descending the ladder, followed by a thin, melancholy man of about fifty, who appeared very silent and reserved ; eyes that looked anywhere but straight before him, from which he probably obtained the sobriquet of " Shy."

"There's your man," said Bob Crossley ; " Kailer, here's your boy."

This introduction effected, Shy Kailer declared in a hollow voice that he was ready.

"You plays the pipes, I suppose ?" he said.

"He plays 'em well enough," interposed Bob Crossley.

"Anything will do for me, as long as it soots the public," rejoined Shy Kailer, in a most dismal tone. " I ain't got a moosical ear."

"Have yer breakfast first," said Bob, "then start."

The morning meal of coffee, bread and butter, and a herring or two, was quickly prepared and served by the wife of one of the tumblers ; and the show, figures, and drum were brought forth, and Inky and his new associate went forth to work the town.

* * * * *

Either Inky was marvellously unfortunate or he was constitutionally at variance with all mankind. Barely had he walked a hundred yards with Shy Kailer when they came to loggerheads.

"I think," said Kailer, "that we'll pitch fust in the market place."

" Will you ?" returned Inky ; " I know you won't."

The showman's visage lengthened, and he cast a look of strong dislike upon his companion.

"Why not ? " he asked.

"Acause," replied Inky, " the show's mine, and I'll pitch where I like."

"Oh !" returned Shy Kailer, and retired into his show like a snail into its shell.

Presently he came forth again.

"Perhaps," he said, " you'll tell me where to pitch ; I can't carry this thing about all day."

" Here's the place," returned Inky, halting before a big red house ; " I likes to show afore the rich and aflooent."

" I don't think you'll get much there," rejoined Shy Kailer ; " it don't look as if there were any kids in that house."

"Put down the show," said Inky, impressively, " and begin."

Shy Kailer said no more, but put down the structure, dropped the baize, and disappeared. Inky brought a melodious howl from the pipes, and smote the drum.

The effect of this was astonishing, but not entirely what Inky expected.

The door of the big red house opened, and an old gentleman, without a hat, rushed out.

" Where's the police ? " he roared. " Can't I have five minutes' peace without being annoyed by these accursed tramps ? Police, there !—police !"

"I told you so," said the voice of Shy Kailer from the top of the show.

"Come down, can't you ? "returned Inky ; "do you want to stop there until we are locked up ?"

CHAPTER XL.

THE FATE OF THE SHOW.

As the old gentleman was still bellowing for the police, the showman rapidly descended, and in five seconds was hastening down the street, followed by Inky and some half-score of the public, whom the stentorian lungs of the proprietor of the big red house had brought together.

The strangers were evidently tickled by the event, especially one man, in the garb of a dustman, with a shovel upon his shoulder, who had undoubtedly drank something stronger than tea that morning.

He followed close upon the heels of Inky with a swagger of authority as if armed with a magisterial order to see him out of the town.

As soon as possible, Inky gained his comrade, and a whispered conversation took place.

" Do you know the place ? " asked Inky.

" I've been here afore," replied Kailer.

" I think I had better leave the pitch to you."

" I think you had better ha' done it afore,' was the reply.

He soon found a spot which promised to prove suitable, where several children were seen at a window. Kailer put down the show, and was about to enter when the dustman advanced.

"You get on," he said, "you don't show here."

"Who are you ? " asked Kailer.

"A citizen of Lincoln," replied the dustman, gravely. " I pays rates and taxes, parokal and r'yal ; you get on or I calls the perlice."

"Brayvo," shouted several of the crowd, keenly enjoying the scene. The dustman received additional confidence from approbation.

"You'll find I'm right," he said ; " we don't want no beggars or tramps here—so get out of it."

"What shall we do ? " whispered Kailer to Inky.

"Oh ! go away," replied Inky, who was very pale and trembling.

" But he ain't got no authority."

" I couldn't stop here," said Inky ; " I shouldn't be able to play a bit."

"All right then ; on we goes."

And once more he trudged forward, with Inky by his side—the dustman and his supporters following, the former proclaiming in a loud voice that he would put all beggars and tramps down in Lincoln. After a time his voice died away, and Inky, looking round, found that he was no longer to be seen. The crowd had, however, increased, and kept well with them. Here was a chance to exhibit without interruption, and he resolved to avail himself of it.

"Down with it," he whispered.

"Where's the dustman ? "

"Gone."

Shy Kailer wanted no more. He made ready immediately, and disappeared. Inky settled the drum, moistened his lips, and blew a preliminary flourish.

There was a commotion in the crowd, and the dustman, forcing his way through, again appeared.

"Wot's all this ? " he demanded, with drunken dignity. "Am I to warn you twice ? You ain't no right here, and you shan't be here. Get out of it."

Inky was unable to reply, but Shy Kailer shouted through the stage opening—

"If you don't like it you needn't stop."

"I don't like it," returned the dustman ; "and you ain't goin' to stop. Come down, and cut it."

"Why don't you leave us alone ?" asked Inky, shaking all over.

"Yes—why don't you leave them alone ?" cried a voice in the crowd ; and the tide turning against the dustman, a score of others took up the cry.

"Who ses I'm to leave 'em alone," asked he, surveying the crowd solemnly.

"All of us," replied one of the foremost.

"Then I'll leave 'em alone," rejoined the dustman ; "but I maintains my point—there's no law for a man as pays rates and taxes when wagabones like them rools the streets. Let 'em play up if they like ; I've done with them and done with you."

The crowd laughed, and the indignant dustman retired—but not far away, for in his breast a sense of injustice rankled, considerably augmented by his morning potations.

"All's clear," said Inky. "Down with the Hold English Genelman."

Shy Kailer lost no time, but out with the marionette, fixed the rings up his fingers, and lowered it.

He heard Inky "doing the patter" descriptive of the toy performer, and finish with a flourish of the drum.

Then came a frightful yell.

He recognized the voice, and knew that it proceeded from the throat of the dustman. Then the back of the show was crushed in by a violent blow, Shy Kailer was heavily smitten, and the Royal Marionette Theatre went over.

Nor was this all. The infuriated dustman screamed horribly, and jumped upon the show, and, of course, upon Kailer, as he lay beneath the baize. Then the maddened destroyer proceeded to kick at the exhibition indiscriminately, bent upon its total destruction.

"Tramps and wagabones," he cried, "have no right to defy a ratepayer. You were told to move on, and you wouldn't, so I'll move you—with a wengeance."

All this Inky beheld aghast, unable by word or movement to check the work of destruction. As for the crowd of spectators, one exhibition was as good as another, and they looked on with the enjoyment which is a peculiarity of most people, when they see the property of others—brittle property, such as windows and earthenware, especially—being destroyed.

The petrified Inky saw the dustman leap upon his comrade, heard his cry of agony as the heavy boots of the assailant drove the breath from Kailer's body, and beheld the wretched exhibitor, after a frantic struggle, rise to his feet, with the broken frame-work hanging about him, and rush to and fro like a dishevelled Jack-in-the-Green, pursued by the dustman, who, shovel in hand, smote him with might and main.

"Oh ! stop him, please, do, genelmen !" pleaded Inky ; and a few of the best-natured stepped forward to the rescue of Shy Kailer.

It was no easy matter to save him, for a shovel, wielded by a pair of strong arms, is a very effective and dangerous weapon ; but, exhaustion setting in, the dustman relaxed his efforts, and Kailer, falling on the pavement, was speedily surrounded by a sympathizing crowd.

"Hurt much, mate ? " said one.

"I'm pounded all over," groaned Kailer. "I don't think I've got a 'ole bone in my body."

"Here's the boy," cried another. "Let him come to his father."

"Don't let him come a-nigh me," said the showman, fiercely. "He's no son o' mine—I wouldn't own him if he was—and he's no mate, or he wouldn't have stood by to see me murdered."

"What could I do ? " urged Inky, who was now in the front near the injured Kailer. "I'd the drum and the pipes—what could I do ? "

"Hit him in the hye," returned Kailer scornfully ; "a blow anywhere would have stopped him."

"Oh, do look at the show !" cried Inky,

the tears streaming down his face. "It's smashed to little bits."

' I'm glad on it," returned Kailer, rising, and shaking the fragments from him; "it were a cussed hour I ever saw you or your show."

"And the figgers, too," cried Inky, looking about him in a vague, purposeless manner; "I don't see none of 'em."

It was true—they were all gone—stolen by some members of the crowd. The Old English Gentleman, the Emperor of Tartary, the Forlorn Maid, and so on, down to the Skeleton, had disappeared for ever, and when Inky had fully realised this fact, the dustman and Shy Kailer had disappeared too.

"Oh! here's a loss," he thought. "I'm rooined in the flavour o' my yooth. The Child o' Destiny was nothing to this. And to think that I've never been able to show, an' arter all the practice, and tryin' to cut out old Work-it-out! The show and the figgers were worth a couple o' pound, and I might ha' sold 'em. Here's a loss, genelmen," he added aloud, addressing the crowd. "This was all my property, the little I had left of a large fortin, and now I've lorst it. I'm nobbly born, and the fust unfortunet thing I did was to get lorst from my nuss, when she was a talking to a sodger; and then Jim Podley sold the bisness, and prigged my five-pun' note. Help a Child o' Destiny, genelmen, if you please."

This touching appeal melted the crowd away—for it was one thing to sympathize and another to give—all but one, a thin and tall man, in seedy habiliments, with a very inflammatory nose, which looked like a red light on the top of a black lighthouse. He sighed, and gave Inky—a tract about the naughty boy who bought black-jack with his money instead of saving it, and afterwards died in the workhouse. Inky accepted it—slung his drum upon his back, and with slow, measured footsteps turned towards the fair.

CHAPTER XLI.

SAM SETTLES AN ITEM OF AN ACCOUNT.

It was not long before Sam heard of Ripper Gooch's second attempt to ruin Tom—our hero wrote a letter to his friend giving an account of the meeting, and winding up with a warm eulogy on Lord Holbrook, who was unchanged to him.

The wrong wrankled in the memory of Sam Smarty; he was always reasoning with himself that his want of caution —"gumption" he called it—had been the cause of Tom's suffering, and a burning desire took possession of him to make amends in some way—to remove, if possible, the scoundrel Gooch from the field.

Easier thought of than done, for he knew nothing of the usual haunts of the thief; nothing of Leary's, or of his meeting with Inky, and was, in short, completely in the dark as to the origin of the movements of Gooch, although he had long perceived his object to be extortion.

How he longed, thirsted—boy as he was—to meet the thief and bring him to book! Sam had no thought of the difference between them; of the little chance he would stand in a personal encounter; he only wanted to see the scoundrel and do——, what he would not say—he only wanted to meet him.

Whenever he was about the streets he kept a sharp look-out for Tom's enemy—for a long time without success, but at last he met him.

Mr. Ripper Gooch was out on a professional tour, and showed a devotion to elderly ladies which must have appeared remarkable to an intelligent observer, halting when they halted, and clinging to their skirts when they moved on, with the fidelity of a dog.

"Oh!" thought Sam, "there you are, are you—on the pocket-picking lay."

Sam was out copy-hunting, and knew he could very well take an hour for himself, which he resolved to do, and devote it to watch the movements of the unconscious Ripper Gooch.

The efforts of the pick-pocket were not apparently crowned with success, for he followed several ladies, hovering about them like a bee over flowers, from one end of the Strand to the other; then he turned back, and Sam thought it time to put the police upon his track.

He accordingly spoke to one of the blue-coated fraternity, and in company they kept upon the track of the thief.

A lady emerged from a confectioner's shop, purse in hand, which she carelessly thrust into her pocket, the next moment Ripper Gooch dived for it.

The policeman was a young hand, or he would have allowed him to complete his work. As it was he seized the thief as soon as the attempt was made.

Ripper, accustomed to all sorts of surprises, turned upon him with a—

"Now then, what do you want?"

"You know what I want you for," was the answer. "Have you lost anything, madam?"

"No," replied the lady; "not that I know of."

"This fellow tried to pick your pocket."

"I!" exclaimed Ripper Gooch, feigning surprise admirably. "Well, that's a good thing. I haven't been in London two days—came up for a holiday."

"No doubt," grinned the policeman.

"I have lost nothing," said the lady, who had made a hasty examination of her pockets.

"I told you so," said Ripper; "it's absurd for you to go on in this way. Let me go."

"Not yet," replied the officer.

"You can't stop me?"

"Can't I?—come on."

He jerked Ripper across the road, and looking round occasionally to see if Sam was following, made a short cut through the quiet streets to the station-house.

The charge of attempted larceny was entered, and then, and not until then, Ripper Gooch perceived and recognized Sam Smarty.

"What do you want?" he growled.

"I saw you attempt to pick several pockets," replied Sam, "and I intend to appear against you."

"Do you!—mind you don't get into trouble —you are an old prig yourself."

Sam laughed. Such a shaft fell upon him harmless—he would have no difficulty in proving his character.

"I work at Kidem and Blowhard's," he said, "and have been there a long time; it's no use your lying against *me*."

Ripper Gooch felt this was true, and went upon another tack.

"You'd better not appear against me," he said, with a ferocious frown, "it will go wrong with you if you do."

Sam smiled; he was not afraid of Ripper Gooch personally, and he intended to carry out his purpose. Having stated what he had seen to the inspector, he was requested to be at the police-court by ten on the morrow; and Ripper Gooch was taken below to the cells, breathing a host of threats against his persecutors.

The police were used to such outpourings, and they so far affected Sam, that he ate a rather heartier dinner that day, and treated himself to sixpenn'orth at the Drury to celebrate the vagabond's capture.

On the morrow he obtained leave for a couple of hours, and appeared at the court punctual to the time.

After the usual night charges, Mr. Gooch was put into the dock, where he stood with furtive eyes wandering slowly over the faces of those present.

The officer got into the witness-box and related what he had seen. Ripper Gooch had nothing to say to him; but when Sam appeared to confirm the evidence of the previous witness, he attempted a little cross-examination.

"You say you work at Kidem and Blowhard's?"

"I does," replied Sam.

"And you've always been honest?"

"I defies any man to prove contrarywise."

"Do you know Tom?"

"I know lots of Toms."

"You know the one I mean—he is now in Belgrave Square."

"Oh, yes!—I know him well enough."

"You are great friends?"

"Tolerable."

"And hasn't he been a thief?"

"No."

"Wasn't he an old pal o' mine?"

"Never," returned Sam, warmly, "could he have sat in the same room with a thief."

"Ah! very virtuous, no doubt," sneered Ripper; "but there, what's the good of my questioning you? You would, like him, lie to any extent. I've nothing more to say to you—stand down."

This Sam did not do until the magistrate said he was no longer required.

After Sam, several detectives appeared in the box, all of whom knew Ripper Gooch as a skilled, practised thief, who had hitherto managed to evade the law.

"He's connected with a bad lot, Bethnal Green way," said one—"Leary's lot, who have given us a deal of trouble."

All this was against the prisoner; but he had been detected too soon—the crime was not committed—and all the magistrate could do was to commit him as a rogue and vagabond.

This he did, and made out an order which empowered certain gaolers to have and to hold the vicious body of Mr. Ripper Gooch for two calendar months.

"Which I can sleep away," said he, impudently, as he left the dock; "and, I think, when the time's up, it will go very hard with Master Sam Smarty. If blows can bruise, I'll blacken him from head to heel. I'll tear his flesh. I'll pound—I'll murder him!"

And thus it fell out that two individuals— Tummas and Ripper Gooch—thirsted for the blood of the printer's devil.

CHAPTER XLII.

A FOUL BLOW.

ONE morning Sam received a letter from Tom. There was nothing new in this, for Tom often wrote, and Sam, on the receipt of the letter made much thereof, flaunting the coron upon the envelope in the eyes of the cou to the amusement of some, but to the dir exasperation of many, whose connections were very humble, and seldom, if ever, troubled them with an epistle.

The particular letter above alluded to, Sam did not read in the court; its contents troubled him so much that he forgot his usual line of proceeding. Tom was going abroad—to be educated—so the letter in-

THE FATE OF SAM SMARTY.

formed him, and his benefactor was going with him for a few months at least.

"I may stay for years," Tom's letter ran on, "for Lord Holbrook thinks it advisable that I should be forgotten by all my old associates, excepting you. I could not forgive myself if I were to forget you, dear Sam."

"And yet you will," thought Sam, with a sigh; "four or five years abroad will do a great deal to wipe out Sam Smarty. Well! let it be so, I can't help it; life's made up o' meetings and partings—to-day we lose a friend, to-morrow we gain one. I suppose I must grin and bear it."

Nevertheless, his mind was troubled, and it seemed as if the parting with Tom was a severing of the dearest tie of his life; he was gloomy at his work, short and snappish with his comrades, and it was not until his abruptness had brought upon him two combats with his youthful brethren, that he at all recovered his usual equanimity.

In the evening he obtained leave of absence, dressed himself, and went over to Belgrave Square. He knew that Tom would not be sorry to see him, and that his lordship would pardon what he meant to be his last intrusion.

The door was opened by a strange footman, rather a quiet, civil fellow, who showed Sam into a side room, and sent his name up to Tom. Sam would fain have asked the footman what had become of Tummas, but prudence forbade it; but when Tom came down he put the question to him.

"He was sent away," replied Tom, "for falsehood, without a character."

"Whew!" whistled Sam, "then I pities him, for a footman without a character is like an engine without steam—he can't go anywhere."

"I believe he deserved it," said Tom.

The interview between the boys was a long one, for they had much to tell—Sam dilating upon his adventure with Mr. Ripper Gooch, whom he had successfully placed in durance vile.

"And now I think of it," exclaimed Sam, "his time is up to-day."

"I should avoid him," said Tom; "he seems to me to be a very cruel fellow."

"I'm not afeard—ahem!—afraid of him," returned Sam; "if he touches me in a public place, all the worse for him; if he shows up in our lane, we will small-gang him—you know what that is."

"I have not forgotten everything of the past," returned Tom, with a shrewd smile.

A little later Sam took his leave.

The parting was a sorrowful, but a hopeful, one; both had good prospects before them—

Tom's was brilliant, and Sam's all that he desired.

Their hands lingered together, and something fresh cropped up to talk about, until the streets were growing dark, and the lamplighter going his rounds; then Sam tore himself away.

As he emerged from the house, a familiar form flitted by—the form of Ripper Gooch, the thief.

A minute's hesitation on the part of Sam, and then he followed in his wake. At the corner the thief halted, and Sam came up with him.

"So you will hang about here," he said; "you've not done showing your venom."

Ripper looked around; there were a good many people passing to and fro; it was, therefore, no time to attack Sam; otherwise he would have strangled him there and then.

"I've warned you," he replied, with a snake-like gleam in his eyes; "why do you come near me?"

"You have no right hanging about here," returned Sam, slowly, "you are a well-known thief. I give you one minute, and if you don't clear out I'll hand you over to a peeler, as sure as I'm named arter my father."

"You had better hand yourself over," hissed the thief, "it will be the safest course."

"Half a minnit gone," said Sam, quietly, "and a peeler comin' round the corner—racing pace for a peeler—half a mile an hour."

"You must be mad, you whelp," continued Ripper Gooch; "you are playing with an edged tool when you touch me—you are sporting with a barrel of gunpowder."

"The peeler don't see nobody down his favourite hairy," said Sam, "and he's comin' on."

"If you had ten lives multiplied by ten," said the thief, "I'd have your heart's blood one day for this. Look to it, you whelp—look to it!"

"The peeler's here," said Sam, turning towards the official.

Mr. Gooch, so lately released, could not stand against another incarceration quite so soon, and he ignominiously turned and fled.

"You saw that young fellow?" said Sam, addressing the official.

"I saw somebody *like* a young man," replied the man guardedly.

"Would you know him again?"

"P'raps I should."

"Then if you see him hanging about here, lock him up—he's a thief."

"I couldn't lock up a man on your recommendation," said the officer, shaking his head—"what's your name?"

"Dear me!—hum!—ha!" murmured Sam,

feeling in his various pockets ; " I left my card-case at home ; but you can hear of me at the club."

He saw that the policeman was not in the humour to accept this information seriously, and could not refrain from having a joke.

"It ain't often," he added, "that I comes out without my card-case, but it's all the fault of my wally—I'll give him notice when I get home."

The official, at first overwhelmed with amazement, now made a dive at Sam with the object of inflicting personal chastisement on his body, but Sam was too quick for him, and dodged into the middle of the roadway.

"Give me your number," he said, in a loud voice, "and I'll call upon your inspector. Give me your number, you owdacious wagabone."

"If I get a-nigh you," said the man, "it'll go hard and 'eavy with you, I can tell you."

"Let me have your number," cried Sam, making a great pretence of feeling for a pocket-book.

"I knowed you was a warmint," said the policeman, making ineffectual efforts to lay hands upon his tormentor, "let me only come a-nigh you."

Having danced the policeman into a state of heat and exhaustion, Sam dived dexterously under his very arm, and scampered away towards Pimlico ; and from thence, by a circuitous route, home.

On the following morning he was due at a very early hour at Messrs. Kidem and Blowhard's, and it was barely light when he footed his way through Shoe Lane.

The thoroughfare was silent, the shops closed, and his shrill whistle echoed among the housetops as he went cheerily on his way.

He was thinking of Tom in a hopeful manner, of him in a happy one ; he looked up at the pale sky, clearer then than at any other part of the day, and thought how beautiful it was, and how he should like to live where there were more trees and less smoke then generally could be found in London, when suddenly the sky grew blood-red, and a mighty crash, as if the houses had suddenly collapsed, and then he fell into a vast black gulf, and knew no more.

Ripper Gooch, with a demoniacal smile, stooped over him for a moment, and put a hand upon his heart. The thief held in his other hand a narrow canvas bag filled with sand—a fearful weapon in the hands of one expert in its use.

"Dumb as a dormouse," muttered the villain. "I've stopped your pulses, my lad, and the day is a long way off when you'll be able to stand up and speak once more against me."

Then, with soft, cat-like steps, he stole down a narrow passage into Farringdon Street, and hurried towards the east.

CHAPTER XLIII.

MORE CHANGE FOR THE UNFORTUNATE INKY.

WHEN Inky returned to the fair the shows were in full swing.

Bob Crossley, dressed in a most extraordinary manner—something between an Italian peasant and Charles the Second—was haranguing an open-mouthed crowd of spectators on the ground below him.

"Now," he said, "now's the time, my lads, to walk up and see the only real hentertainment in the fair. Rumbustybos, the fire-eater, who will swallow burnin' pitch, knives and forks, a sweet of furniture, and even hisself if anybody wish to see it done ; also Signur Turnerovero, the great gymnastic performer, who will leap from one hend of the booth to the other, and arterwards stand on his 'ed on a single wire ; also the Man Fish, the performin' pony, and a hundred other wonders, and the price of admission is only one penny. Hi! there, hi! walk up and be in time."

Sawney Tap, in the dress of an English tar, hammered away lustily at a gong, and the public walked up in a mass.

Inky went round to the private entrance with his drum, which he put under the frail stage, and then went in search of his friends.

He met Bob Crossley in the side-wings, and saw in his face that Shy Kailer had returned before him.

"Was there ever such an unfortunet job?" whined Inky.

"If wot Kailer ses is troo," returned Bob Crossley, "you ain't much fit to show in the streets ; but I can't talk to you now, I've got to go on in the drama."

Several of the company now hurried in ; most of them looked at Inky and laughed, but none spoke to him. With a heavy heart he waited until the conclusion of the performance, which, with the fire-eater, the wonderful gymnast, the drama, and its other marvels, occupied something under a quarter of an hour.

When it was over, and the company again out upon the parade, Bob Crossley came to him again, and bade him come into the travelling van.

Then he sat down and contemplated our unfortunate friend for a few minutes, with a solemnity which made him very uneasy.

"Upon my word," he said, at last, "I don't know wot to do with you."

"It wouldn't matter much if I were poisoned or drownded," returned Inky, tearfully ; "it's allus so ; why couldn't the dustman pitch into another chap's show ?"

"Well, the show's gone," said Bob Crossley, thoughtfully scraping his chin ; "and the figgers is gone ; and Shy Kailer is laid up for a good two days, for laid it heavy on him that dustman did—right away from his calves uppards he's a mask 'o bruises. You've got the drum ?"

"It's under the stage," said Inky.

"Good ! there's summat saved from the wreck, but it ain't much when you've got *one* drum in the company. Howsomever, my lad, I'm goin' to be plain with you. We don't want idle hands here."

"I'm willin' to work," said Inky.

"No doubt, if you could ; but howsomever wallyable you may be in a gineral way, you ain't no use here. You can't even turn a wheel."

"I can't," replied Inky, shortly, "and if I could I wouldn't."

"That's all right, my lad, but don't you take me up so uncommon sharp, for I've a stiffish hand, and when I lays it on I undertakes to draw an howl out of a tougher boy than you. But to resoom ; as you ain't no good here I can't keep yer, but if a friendly hact can be done for you it shall. I'll get you summat to do if I can, and I'll keep the drum as the price of the wittles you've had and your keep until you've got summat to do. In the meantime, you can go inside and help to make the boys sit close, for every penny's a penny, and we are drawing scrowdging houses."

With a melancholy face Inky went to his new employment, and Bob Crossley joined his company on the platform.

We will pass over what Inky suffered that day among the wild youths who patronized the show. To say that they defied his authority, is to say little ; some pelted him, others pushed him, and all resisted him. Twice was he precipitated through the frail woodwork of the seats into a dark, cavernous hollow beneath, and when the day's work was done, he had been so mauled, hustled, and maltreated in every possible way, that he walked about like a boy in a dream ; but he did not complain for fear he should get an immediate notice to quit.

All the company supped at an inn hard by, where he had the pleasure of beholding Shy Kailer seated in a chair upon an unlimited number of cushions. Mr. Kailer for the time was evidently a great invalid.

Inky took a seat opposite him, but neither said a word. Inky was too much confused after his day's exertions to speak, and Shy Kailer looked, breathed, and snorted at the wretched boy unlimited hatred and contempt.

As Inky recovered his senses, he became more and more uncomfortable under the sick man's stare ; it was like being haunted by the spectre of a murdered man, and he burst out suddenly with a remonstrance.

"Don't, Mr. Kailer," he said, "I can't abear it ; *I* couldn't help it, you know."

"Where was your hyes," asked Mr. Kailer, in a hollow tone, "not to see that 'ere dustman a comin' ?"

"I didn't see him," was all Inky could say.

"That 'ere dustman," continued Shy Kailer, addressing the room generally, "came on me like an evvylaunch of bricks. The first blow on my —— back sent me and the show over ; then he jumped on me, then he guv me another with the shovel, then another jump, then the shovel; and so on, shovel and jump, shovel and jump, ontil I thowt he'd jellied me, and all acause that hidiot there ain't got hyes in his 'ed."

"Don't, Mr. Kailer," remonstrated Inky ; "I didn't mean to do it, and I can't be sorrier than I am."

"That's the song of all on 'em," said Mr. Kailer, "arter a man is pounded to pieces ; what does they care ? While I was a wrigglin' about in my hagony like a eel, I heard him asking arter his marynets. He never thowt of me, and I'm werry glad they're all prigged and busted."

"Don't be 'ard on the young un," put in Bob Crossley.

"If you had my bones," said Shy Kailer, with a groan, "you'd be hard on anything."

"There's summat in that," returned Bob. "Jimmy, is my chop ready ?"

Jimmy was the landlord—an old stroller, who, having spent forty years on the road, now sought in a public-house the repose he had so fairly earned.

He said that it would be ready directly.

Each of the strollers, except those who had families, supped independently, and Inky, clinging to the remnant of Work-it-out's gift, had some beer and bread and cheese at Bob Crossley's expense.

While he was eating it, a strong-built man in a tiger-skin waistcoat, and a whip in his hand, entered the room. He stepped over to Bob Crossley and shook hands with him. Bob hailed him as Busby.

"Where's Sawney ?" he asked.

"Rollin' the canwasses," replied Bob ; "he'll be here directly."

"I saw him on parade," continued Busby, "and judging by the look of the people, you've had a good day."

"So we have—a buster—never had the booth fuller."

"I don't complain," said Busby, "but th public with us are sech a trouble—they ain't never satisfied. I tied the boa constrictor round my neck to-day, but that didn't please 'em. Ses one man, 'He don't wriggle,' as if a mortal throat could stand the wrigglin' of the constrictor."

"It ought to be enough for 'em to see 'em in the cases," said Bob.

"So it ought," replied Busby, "but it ain't; and then everybody as pays thruppence wants to see the pelican gorge hisself with five bob's worth o' fish, and the helephant too—there ain't a better one than mine on the road—he can ring a bell, put money—when he can get any—into a box, turn a barrel-organ, and dance the polka; but, lor! that ain't enough. One warmint, arter that interlecterril feast to-day, says, 'Make him stand on his head, master;' I couldn't stand that, so I up and tells him that the helephant warn't up to it, but I'd teach him the trick to show by the next time I came to Lincoln, when I hoped to see the gent—that shut him up."

"So it ought," said Bob.

"I sometimes feel that savage," pursued Busby, giving his waistcoat an angry tug, "that I feel inclined to let a tiger or two out among 'em, or a pol-cat, or a hyena; and if there warn't a law agin it, I'd do it. What's the matter with Kailer?"

"Had a turn-up with a dustman."

"Bein' inweloped with the show," groaned Kailer, "and havin' a hidiot outside, the dustman 'ad it all his own way."

"Dustmen is musculuer in gineral," said Busby, philosophically. "What, Sawney! how goes it, my hearty?"

Sawney, who entered the room at that moment, shook hands with his friend, and with his usual brevity, replied—

"Bobbish."

"You wears well, Sawney," continued the wild beast proprietor; "you've got a good forty year more on the road for you."

Sawney replied, "I hope so."

"He won't be no forty years on the road," cried a little excitable man in the corner; "no, nor any of us; before 'arf that time is over we shan't have no roads, and not a bit o' ground to plant a booth on."

"You takes a dark view o' the matter, Skitter."

"I takes the right one," replied Skitter; "look how fast they're closin' in. Where's Bartlemy Fair?—as used to bring in a little pile—and Greenwich is to be shut up this year, I hear; that's another nail in our coffin. I tell you that ten year hence we shall be starvin'."

"It'll be a bad day when they stop the amoosement o' the people," said Bob Crossley; "when they does, the men will turn to politics, and there'll be strikes and risin's without end."

"True for you," said Jimmy, the landlord; "when I was fust on the road fairs were plentiful, and you never heard of no strikes then; down goes a fair, and up comes a strike—a strike for hevery fair."

"What's come of Muntle?" asked Bob Crossley of Busby, to change the conversation.

"Gone to 'Meriky, with the performing monkeys," was the reply.

"Ah," said Bob, reflectively, "he knowed how to train monkeys."

"So he did; but he took his boy with him," said Busby, "and I'm in want o' one now."

"For what?"

"To clean 'em out."

"The monkeys?"

"Yes."

"Not to show or do anything of that sort?"

"Certainly not—I does all that myself."

"Then here's a boy as will soot you," cried Bob, pointing to Inky; "he ain't got no friends, and he's jolly 'ard up. Now, Inky, you could look arter monkeys, couldn't you?"

"I never tried," returned Inky, dubiously.

"Then have a shy now. What do you think of him, Busby?"

"Well, I don't know," said Busby, after running his eye over Inky; "I don't think he'll run away with the helephant or a camill-leopard; but we don't want genuses for the cleaning out, and I'll give him a trial."

"Thanks, Busby."

"When can he come?"

"At once."

"Then let him drop in about nine to-morrer."

CHAPTER XLIV.

THE MENAGERIE.

THE travelling menagerie owned by Mr. Busby was very extensive; it consisted of sixteen vans besides his own little house on wheels, and the huge affair wherein Jack, the performing elephant, resided.

The collection consisted of lions, tigers, a pair of hyenas, a cage of monkeys, a polar bear (supposed to be the only one travelling), a pelican, a pair of giraffes, and numerous other specimens of the wild and tame beasts of foreign lands.

Inky packed up the few things he owned in a cotton handkerchief, and took a temporary adieu of Mr. Bob Crossley and Sawney Tap.

"We are likely to meet often," said the former, "and I shall be allus glad to hear you are gettin' on. Busby ain't a bad chap, he lets out now and then, but he don't mean anything—do your dooty by him and he'll do his dooty by you."

"And don't you," added Sawney Tap, putting spice to the dish of advice, "try on any 'nobbly' gammon with *him*."

"If people don't believe me," said Inky, "I would rather not tell them of it."

"There ain't a born man," returned Sawney Tap, "as is such a fool as to do so."

"Well, get along, my lad," said Bob Crossley, "and remember that dooty is the loadstar of life, and him as is perwerted against it goes to the contrairy, and nothin' can put the skid on a man as is too far down hill."

This piece of sage advice did not impress Inky much, and having shaken hands with his friends, and taken a general adieu of the company, he went to his new home.

The last exhibition of the evening was then on, and Mr. Busby, with a boa constrictor round his neck like a comforter, was haranguing a crowded audience.

"The boa constrictor," he said, "is the most powerful of the reptile tribe. It can envelope an ox in its folds and crush him to a jelly; but the moral power of man is greater than the strength of reptile or beast, and in the hands of man the boa constrictor is as tame as a mounting kid."

He then, by a few dexterous moves, gave the almost inanimate reptile the appearance of life; a few women screamed a little, the boa constrictor was restored to its case, and the show was over.

The people slowly filed out, and when the last were gone, Mr. Busby became aware of the addition to his establishment.

"Ha! Inky, here you are," he said.

"Yes, sir."

"Had your supper?"

"I've had somethin' to eat with Crossley," replied Inky; thereby gently insinuating that he was still open to a slight relish.

Busby took the hint, and said that supper would be ready in half an hour.

"Until then," he added, "make yourself useful—give the man with the happy family a lift. He's fresh here, and my men and he don't get on together."

Inky knew what a happy family was, and looking round the menagerie espied a cage apart from the rest—close to the performing elephant.

A man was stooping over it, groping about in search of the amiable pets.

The form seemed familiar to him, so familiar, that his breath came quickly as he advanced and touched him on the shoulder.

The man turned.

Inky uttered a scream worthy of a paroquet.

It was Jim Podley.

These two acquaintances, separated so strangely, and brought together so strangely, stood stock still, until a raven, part of the happy family, hopped out and restored Jim Podley to his senses.

Capturing the bird, he put it back for the moment, and closed the cage door.

"Ham I dreamin', or is it you, Inky?" he asked.

"It is Inky," replied our friend; "and more unfortunet than ever."

"And yet you can waste your money in menageries," said Jim, slowly.

"There you go," whimpered Inky, "down on a poor boy straight. I ain't wasted no money here. I've come for good, to look arter the monkeys."

This announcement quite overpowered the bird-fancier, he rolled his eyes about the place and gasped in a most feeble, helpless manner.

Presently he aroused himself, and as if to direct his thoughts from an overwhelming subject, he resumed his occupation of parcelling out his happy family into a series of smaller cages.

"Don't tell me no more," he said, at length, "until I've had some supper; but it are most astounding."

"Can I help you?" asked Inky, remembering the instructions he had received.

"No, thank you," replied Jim, "they are gettin' off their dose and growing wicious."

"But I thought a happy family never quarrelled," said Inky, innocently.

"No more they don't—real ones," replied Jim, pausing for a moment; "but a real one takes years to put together. You have to bring 'em all up young, in a bunch—cats, sparrers, squirrels, rats, mice, and so on; but I had to put mine together all in a hurry; and all growed up; so I does what others do, I gives a dose o' laudenum every morning to all but them as is naturally tame; by night it wears orf, and I parts 'em then."

"Then all happy families ain't real?"

"Very few are," replied Jim, shaking his head. "The only real un as ever I knowed used to stand in the Blackfriars Road, but it cost a sight o' money. The man as owned it spent years over gettin' it up, and he then scarcely made enough of it to buy bread. He died broken-'arted; but here comes the supper."

A man appeared with several plates of savoury stew upon a tray, one of which he served out to Inky, with some bread, and distributed the rest to the keepers, who were scattered about the different parts of the arena.

IKY FINDS NO FAVOUR WITH THE DENIZENS OF THE MENAGERIE.

Beer was supplied by a potman, who brought a couple of large cans from a neighbouring public-house, and each man bought and paid for what he required.

The first cravings of appetite appeased, Jim Podley bade Inky tell his story, which Inky did with several embellishments of an entirely novel nature, in which moreover he endeavoured to make Podley believe that the fortune Work-it-out had left to claim was in reality his, the long-expected riches which were his by right of birth.

"He looked as guilty as anybody could," he concluded, "and knocked me down such a cropper, that I ain't got over it yet; but we shall meet agen, and I'll have my rights."

"Perhaps if you had your rights," said Podley, with a meaning look, "you wouldn't care so much about 'em."

"What have you been doin'?" hastily inquired Inky, to change the theme.

"When I sold the business in Bunhill Row," replied Jim, "I had some thought of settlin' down in a odd corner in London, but that were a mistake. A man in my line can't open a shop anywheres; in some neighbourhoods they won't have us, and in others, if we opened forty shops we shouldn't sell a sparrer or a rat in a month. We have our regular cribs, and if we wish to do a trade we must stick to 'em.

"Now, Inky, I'm a man for trooth, and I don't mind tellin' you that I'm afraid of that ere wife o' mine. She'd have found me out in any of my old haunts, and you've seen enough to know what would foller. Now you wouldn't hardly think it, that I once loved her and she loved me, but we warn't suited to each other. When we were married I was a rough and ready man, werry rough at times, for I've had a 'ard training, and I lived among rough people. She had been a lady's maid, and naturally picked up, while with high folks, a lot o' fal-lal notions, that didn't suit *me* nor our ways o' livin'. The house warn't good enough, the furniter warn't good enough; she wouldn't mix with the wives o' my mates, and at last she fell foul o' me.

"The first quarrel, my lad, was the father of a good many more, each one more vigorous than the last, and then came blows. I don't know who struck first, but it ended in the ruin of us both. You've seen what she is—Heaven help her!—and you see me."

Jim Podley was undoubtedly much affected, but he tried to conceal his emotion by coughing, blowing his nose violently, and other stratagems of our weak nature used upon such occasions. Having mastered his emotion, he proceeded—

"I dursn't let her find me agen, so I gives up all idea of settlin' in town, and buys that

big cage and the smaller ones. 'I'll have a happy family,' I ses, 'and travel about with it all over the country, and then I shall be free of her.' So I starts off and works my way down here, when Busby sees me and offers me reasonable terms, which I closed with, and here I am."

"It's better than nothin'," said Inky; "but I never thought I should have come down to keep monkeys."

"You've had a rise or two, to be sure," said Podley, with a grin; "but you must take the thick with the thin. Time for bed, I see."

"Where do we sleep?" asked Inky.

"Here."

"In the wan?"

"No, that's Busby's, we sleep round the fire."

"With all the animals?" exclaimed Inky, horrified.

"Just so."

It was true; the floor of the menagerie was the sleeping-place of the keepers, and Inky had to share their lot; already some of the men were pulling out a quantity of rough bedding materials from various nooks and corners, and arranging them around the fire, which was always kept burning, with irons ready heated, to use upon any of the beasts who might turn fractious.

Inky and Podley obtained for their use a couple of large sacks filled with hay, and a rug a-piece; with these they made up the best beds they could, and lay down to rest.

CHAPTER XLV.
MONKEY-KEEPING.

"If I was you, Inky," said Podley, as they were putting away their beds in the morning, "I should write to old Work-it-out."

"I don't know where to write to," returned Inky.

"At his brother's, I should say."

"He ain't likely to be there," said Inky, contemptuously, "with all the money he's got."

"If that's your idea o' human natur'," rejoined Jim Podley, "the sooner you gets rid of it the better."

"It's my idea o' Work-it-out," said Inky. "But I'll write on the chance. I don't want him to forget me."

"And afore you write," suggested Jim, "ascertain where we are goin' to next, or a letter from him won't reach you."

Inky took the first opportunity to inquire of Busby which way they were going—urging as an excuse for the query the necessity of keeping some of his highly-born relations acquainted with his movements.

"I'm going to London, taking a few places

on the way," replied the proprietor of the menagerie. "I've taken a bit o' waste ground in Camberwell, and I means to show there for a time."

It was yet early in the day when Inky received this information, and as the exhibition did not open until noon, he had most of the intervening time on his hands, which he devoted to an epistle of a most affectionate nature, addressed to Work-it-out, and acquainting him with the probable early arrival of his adopted son in town.

The letter written and posted, Inky, in obedience to certain instructions he had received the evening previous, held himself in readiness for his initiation into his duties, which was done by Mr. Busby in person.

"Monkeys," he explained, "are naturally untidy. You may put their straw straight for one moment and the next it's all over the shop; so we doesn't do anything to 'em until it's near time to show, and then every 'arf hour or so you gives 'em a look up, and with this iron put the straw to rights a bit. You can do it through the bottom bars, like this —easy—but don't go for to open the door, or there will be the deuce to pay."

Inky promised obedience—he always did that—and Mr. Busby left him.

The iron alluded to by Inky's new master was a species of rake used to put the straw in order; and Inky set to work, wielding it with immense satisfaction, and stirring up the monkeys—about twenty in number—to his heart's content.

Inky, not over learned in monkey ways, raked about, and kicked up such a dust, that the ire of the occupants of the cage was aroused.

By their looks they had shown a strong dislike to Inky from the first; and one very old stager, who had been many years on the road, put his hairy arm through the bars, and shook his fist at the strange attendant with all the animosity of a Christian, while several others hissed at him in a very disparaging manner.

Not to be behind-hand in expressing feeling, Inky, when he rested a moment from his labours, indulged in a variety of faces calculated to raise the ire of any monkey not exactly dead to what is due to his race; and the comical little wretches, fully appreciating their attendant's signs of derision, clutched the bars, and shook the van in their rage.

Inky, alarmed, took a look round. He was alone. Podley was gone to the chemist's for some landanum. Busby and the keepers were outside unfurling the painted canvas.

Rejoicing over his solitude, Inky took advantage of it, and gave the old stager—a blue-faced monkey of a venomous breed—a very painful prod in the stomach. Blue-face

seized the rake, and all his brethren came to his assistance.

In a moment it was drawn out of Inky's hand, and jerked into the interior of the van, and every monkey, apparently satisfied, retired hurriedly to the seclusion of the sleeping-house, out of sight.

"More misfortunes," muttered Inky; "here's a go agen. If Busby comes and finds I've lost the rake, there's the sack for me, and I can't reach it. Confound 'em for wicious brutes. If I was to open the door a little way I could get it. But he said I warn't to."

Still, something must be done; the rake must be regained if he wished to stay at the menagerie. The door went with a bolt and chain outside, very easily worked, apparently; and all that was needed could be done in a moment.

"I must risk it," murmured Inky, as he heard Busby bawling outside for the men to look sharp; "all the beggars are in the house. I'll do it."

He had sense enough to be very stealthy, and gently raising the bolt, he pushed open the door a few inches; then, like a flash of light, Blue-face dashed out and laid his strong hands upon it.

Inky, half-maddened with fear, clung to it manfully, but the whole troupe descending in a state of excitement, he was overpowered, and fell back.

What followed he never could precisely tell, but he dimly remembered running about the show at a furious pace, followed by the chattering brutes, armed with any weapon they could lay their hands upon. He believed that he leaped over the fire twice, and he *knew* that he climbed up the woodwork of one of the vans, for he carried about him for many a day a proof impression of the fore paw of the polar bear, and that he was beaten and maltreated by his impish pursuers was a fact established by a number of cuts and contusions on every assailable part of his body.

He had fallen upon the ground, hopeless of escaping with life, when Busby and the keepers, hearing an unwonted disturbance, rushed down.

They took the scene in at a glance, and closed the outlet of the place. Then with cart-whips they brought the refractory brutes to their senses, and drove them back to the cage.

"I thought he was a cursed fool," muttered Busby, as he barred the door. "Is he much hurt, Jack?"

"He's got a bit taken out on him by the Polar," was the reply, "and they've whopped him pretty well over the head and nyes; likewise they've chopped his knuckles a bit."

"I'm a dyin'," groaned Inky.

"I'll bring you round with some vinegar and brown paper," said Busby; "they ain't none of 'em bit him, Jack?"

"No, he's had clean cuts with sticks and so on; nothin' more."

"I'm glad o' that," said Busby, "for a monkey bite is wenom."

Though terribly angry, Busby was a good-hearted fellow, and he resolved to keep Inky, trusting that his first experience would be a warning for the future; and his wounds and bruises being attended to, Inky was desired to resume his duties at various intervals during the day.

A feud, however, was established between the "nobbly born" and his charges; the arranging of the straw was one long fight between him and the brutes; but as it amused the public and did not hurt the animals, Busby took no notice of it—in fact, it soon became one of the features of the exhibition.

The keepers found a variety of names for Inky, all of a more or less offensive nature; but we will not name them here, we only record the fact to show that our friend was far from popular.

The men did not like him, especially after being regaled with a few of his visionary ideas, and a distinct intimation from Inky himself that they ought to be proud and glad of his company.

With Podley, however, he remained tolerably intimate, and what leisure time they had was passed in each other's company.

Sometimes they looked in upon Bob Crossley and his mates, but the first question from Bob was invariably.—

"Any news of the old 'un?"

"No."

"Not a line?"

"Not a word."

"And I don't think you will," Bob would say, "as Sawney's is the same."

To which that soul of brevity, Sawney, would reply with emphasis—

"It is."

When the fair ended the other shows went in a northerly direction, the menagerie alone turned towards London. Inky made one last effort to recover his drum, but Bob refused to give it up.

"A drum," he said, "is no use to you, and you'd lose it in a week; besides, you owe me something for taking your size and looks; you are the heaviest grumbler I ever clapped eyes on.

Which Sawney confirmed with the simple declaration,—

"He is so."

Of the journey towards town we have little to record; they stopped here and there for a day as a rule, but occasionally two, and at Bishop's Stortford three, and in this way three weeks passed on.

When they neared London the autumn was nearly spent, and the cold mists and fogs were gathering fast upon the river.

They went through the great city at early dawn to avoid the traffic, and crossing London Bridge passed through the Borough on their way to Camberwell.

Inky was walking with one of the horses; Podley was dozing in the carriage belonging to the band, his head just visible among a heap of canvas and other "properties."

The thoroughfare devoted to the sale of hops was not so quiet as the streets on the opposite side of the bridge, for a number of waggons were lumbering along, and men and women hastening towards the markets.

There was one woman who looked curiously at the passing vans of the menagerie. She caught sight of Podley's face—started, and hurried on. At the same moment Inky caught sight of hers, and a cold feeling came over him.

He looked back many times apprehensively on their way, but she came near them no more, and when Camberwell Green was reached, he breathed freely again.

Jim Podley was aroused to take part in the unloading, and during that process Inky said not a word to him, but after breakfast he spoke.

"As we were comin' through the Borough," he said, "I saw somebody."

"Not—a woman?" said Podley, turning pale.

"Yes; a woman."

"Not—my wife?"

"Yes, your wife, Mr. Podley—and she saw you."

"I must cut this, then," said Jim Podley, rising hastily; "my life isn't safe with her now."

"I don't think you need run away from her now," said Inky, detaining him; "she seemed to be changed—how, I can't tell you; but I'm sure if you were to meet her now she would neither abuse nor kill you."

CHAPTER XLVI.

WORK-IT-OUT'S RETURN.

THE dismayed bird-fancier shook his head; he had very little faith in Inky's discernment, and his remembrance of his wife and her ways was very keen.

"You don't know her, lad," he said; "you haven't seen so much of her as I have."

"But she is so much changed," persisted Inky; "and although the clothes were the same and the face the same, she didn't look like the same woman that she was."

"Can't you give me a idea of the change?" asked Jim.

"She looked cleaner and quieter," replied Inky, "and she walked quickly, as if she had somewhere pertikler to go."

"And she saw me?"

"Looked up at you and changed colour in a moment. She knew you right enough."

Jim Podley was troubled, very much so, for he held his wife in keen remembrance; but he resolved to stay with the menagerie, and make the best of whatever might transpire.

"She can only rout me out," he thought; "if she comes here I can go then—it's no use meeting trouble half way. I'll stay."

He was nervous and apprehensive throughout the day, and his worst fears were confirmed in the evening when one of the men came in and told him that a woman wanted to see him.

"She's behind the elephant van," the man said; "and she wished me to say that her business was werry pertikler."

"I know—I know," groaned the bird-fancier, to himself; "her business is my ruin—and she'll carry it through."

He dared not refuse to obey, and he went round to the place named, and there he found his wife. She was, as Inky had said, dressed in the same clothes, but she was changed, and she received him quietly.

"Jim," she said, "I am sorry to trouble you, but I want you to give me a little help."

This form of address was so unexpected that Podley was unable to reply.

His wife mistook his silence for hesitation, and continued—

"I have no claim upon any one in this world, least of all upon you; but you are my husband, and I want a little help—a few shillings is all I ask, just to keep me from starving for a time. I have set myself a task, and it is almost done."

"Bless you, old gal," said Podley, heartily, "you're welcome to a pound or two, let alone shillings. I ain't one of the wenomous sort; I can forget and forgive, just as I hope to have many little things o' mine overlooked."

"Give me two pounds," she said, quickly, "and I will never trouble you again."

"As for troubling me," replied Jim, "I don't think nothin' of it, unless you come down on the violent——"

"I shall never be violent again," interposed his wife.

"You sartainly don't look and speak like the same woman," said Podley, doubtfully.

"I have had my eyes opened in a terrible manner," she returned, "to one terrible mistake in my lifetime—or more—but one I must put right before I die."

"Dont' talk of dyin'," said Jim, uncomforably; "you're young yet, and if you was to get into a small house and do a little needlework, washing, or mangling, or something of that sort, I could help you, and you might be all right, you know."

"I have no such thoughts," she answered, sadly; "the work I have in hand once done, I care not how soon I die; and yet I should like to find our child, Jim."

"You left it on a doorstep, didn't you?" asked Jim, without exhibiting much emotion.

"I did. I went the other night to enquire after it, but the house was closed, and the man gone. I learned this much, however, that he had taken care of our child to the best of his ability; but our little one went to the bad."

"I don't like that," said Jim, fetching a sigh from under his waistcoat.

"It is such wretches as I am," said his wife, knitting her brows, "who fill the prisons. Bad mothers make bad children."

"I don't know as you was a bad mother," returned Podley, venturing on a little piece of consolation.

"You know better, Jim," she said; "I was a brute to him—and you; but I will waste no more of your time. Give me the money and let me go."

"Can't I bring you to think of the cottage business?" asked Jim, as he told the money into her hand; "mangles can be hired, and there's heaps of work for anybody as is decently civil."

"Thank you, Jim," she replied; "but it can never be. Good bye."

She held out her hand, and he took it. Forgetful of the past, he bent down, and would have kissed her, but she repulsed him, gently but firmly.

"No, Jim," she said, "not now. When I see you again, if you will."

She glided away, and left him in a state of incredulity as to the evidence of his senses.

Was this the wife he had so lately feared? This the woman who made his home in Bunhill Row a house of terror—the drunken, vile harridan, apparently lost to all sense of shame and feeling?

He could scarcely believe it; and yet it was true, for there was the moonlit sky above him, the menagerie near him, with its roaring, sullen beasts, and an inspection of his purse showed that it was two pounds short of what it had contained in the morning.

"It's all true," he murmured, as he slowly retraced his steps; "she's a changed woman—her heart is touched at last. If it had only happened a few years sooner, anyhow!

but what's the good of thinkin' o' that? It's all past and done. *I* don't bear no animalosity agin' her—not **I**; but I don't think that I really durst live with her agin."

Jim Podley belonged to a very rough school; he had not that delicate sense of feeling so prominent in the upper walks of life; but his heart bled for his unhappy wife, for himself, and for his lost child, and it was with a heavy heart that he resumed his exhibition of amiable pets inside the booth.

The menagerie was planted on a good spot, its manager and owner were walking in pleasant ways—the public rushed up and the money rolled in.

Inky had a dreadful time of it; his mischievous charges held him in supreme contempt, and his appearance with the rake to put the den in order was the signal for a general monkey scream, and a variety of acts expressive of derision.

This was capital fun to the public, and rather amusing to Busby and the keepers; but Inky regarded it very seriously, and entered into the contest with Spartan-like resolution and Roman fortitude.

As before remarked, Inky was not a great favourite with the keepers, who trained the animals under their charge to hate and detest the unfortunate boy.

The pelican of the wilderness, as it was described to the public, was wont to pursue him, and when he went near the den of the performing elephant, an unmistakable snort warned him away.

"I don't think I can bear much more of this life," he said one night to Podley; "everything nigh me grows wiciouser every day. The elephant threw a pail at me this morning with as true a aim as a man could, and the pelican got one o' my boots in his mouth, and tried to swaller it."

"Whatsumever life you may be thrown into," returned Podley, "it will have its wississitudes—its trials and its troubles. Suppose you runs away from here, what would you do?"

"Starve, I suppose," replied Inky, tearfully, "*I* don't expect nothin' better. Why was I ever born? Why didn't Work-it-out strangle me when he found me on his doorstep? Or he might have throwed me into the road under a cart-wheel."

"You wouldn't ax for a cart-wheel twice if you ever had one over your little toe," said Jim Podley, drily, "which I had once and rolled it out flat. But talk o' Work-it-out, have you heard from him?"

"Not a word."

"You are sure he knows where we are?"

"I put it down plain at the bottom of the letter, and told him not to forget."

"Ah! Inky, it's all the world over when a man gets a rise it's like goin' upstairs to another floor—you can't see your friends you left in the kitchen; it's natur', all the world over."

"But he was so fond o' me," murmured Inky.

"Was he?" rejoined the bird-fancier; "well I'm dashed if I should have thought so, arter your stories of how he let into you that 'eavy with Stinger that you was numb like,"

"He let inter me at times," said Inky, "but as a rool he dewoted on me."

"And now he shows his dewotion by slippin' out of your way. Ah! my boy, you and Work-it-out are sivered for ever."

Their conversation was interrupted by an altercation on the outside of the show. Busby was speaking in a loud, angry tone.

"I tell you we've closed for the night, you can't come."

"And I tell you," returned a voice very familiar to Inky, "that I WILL come in. I've footed it from the Kent Road to see him, and I will."

"What do you mean by *him*?"

"My boy, my orfspring—my adopted son, Inky."

"'Tis him! 'tis him!" cried Inky, rising, with exultation in his countenance; "he's come at last."

"Whose voice is that?" demanded Jim.

"Mr. Work-it-out's," replied Inky.

"Oh! him," said Jim, with a sneer.

"Yes, and don't you be rude to him, or it'll be the worse for you."

At that moment Work-it-out appeared, heated by his altercation with Busby, who followed behind.

But how did he appear?

In gorgeous raiment, chain, watch, seals, and shiny hat, as depicted in Inky's mind?

No!

Was he followed by abject servants in plush, with gold-headed canes, as Inky had fully arranged in his mind as a matter of course?

Again—no!

"He returned humbly, in the same old seedy clothing, a little the worse for his pilgrimage; boots a little more leaky than of yore, and a hat in the last stage of mouldiness and decay.

There was evidently no pride about him; he did not come to flaunt his riches in the face of others, but his object—Inky saw it at once—was to appear before them with meekness and humility.

There was a horrible thought in Inky's mind for a moment.

THE ELEPHANT SEIZED INKY, AND TWISTED HIM INTO THE AIR.

Had Work-it-out carried out his Radical principles and handed his wealth over to the people? But he dismissed the thought instanter, and received his old master with what he considered to be a very appropriate form of address—

"All 'ail, thou receiver of good fortin'!"

Work-it-out folded his arms, and gloomily surveyed his adopted son.

The joy in Inky's eyes met with no response in his.

"Hold orf a moment, Inky," he said, "you spoke of a fortin'."

"I did," murmured Inky; "forty thousand pounds."

"Then don't name it no more."

"Why not?"

"Acause that fortin' wasn't mine," cried Work-it-out, waving his arms; "acause it wasn't me they advertised for, but another party as had the cheek to hev the same name. It hadn't anything to do with me, and I couldn't get a farden. But don't talk about it—don't speak of it. *I've* buried it for ever. Where's my marynets?"

CHAPTER XLVII.

SAM SMARTY.

A STRANGER was the first to discover Sam Smarty.

He was a labouring man, bound for the Fleet Market in search of a job, and his first thought when he saw Sam lying on the pathway was that it was a bundle of clothes lost by some passer-by. The next, when he raised the boy in his arms, that he had fallen down in a fit, for there was no blood to show the evil deed which had been done.

His cries brought a few people to his assistance, one of whom, being a workman at Kidem and Blowhard's, recognized Sam, and they bore him to the nearest open house —a public-house—and then tried to force some cordial down his throat.

This had no effect upon him whatever; then they rubbed the palms of his hands and chafed his limbs, but all through Sam betrayed no sign of life beyond the faint pulses of his heart.

"It's a purpuletic fit," said one of the men.

"At his age?" returned another contemptuously. "It ain't the likes o' him or us as gets them, it's the heavy feeders—the nobs and swells and such like."

"Whatever it is," said a third, "jawing won't bring him round. Where's the nearest doctor?"

One was named and a willing messenger went in search of him.

He came in a few minutes, looking very sleepy about the eyes and hastily donning his attire.

After the first glance at the boy his drowsiness departed, and he looked very grave.

"Where was this lad found?" he asked.

"In the lane."

"Who found him?"

"This man."

The labourer stood forward, and the doctor measured him up and down with his eyes.

"What is your name?"

"Richard Stammers."

"You found this boy in the lane?"

"I did, sir."

"Have you any objection to remain here while I send for an officer?"

"None at all, sir," replied Richard Stammers, looking nevertheless very uneasily about him.

A second messenger went to the police station, and one of the reserve promptly appeared.

"Officer," said the doctor, "there has been attempted murder here."

The policeman nodded.

"This boy has been struck at the base of his skull in a very scientific manner. This man found him. This boy must be got home at once. I leave the rest to you. Where does he live?"

"In Cradle-court," replied the policeman. "I know him very well; he's been a regular imp for all his being so quiet now."

"He won't play the imp again for many a long day, I fear," said the doctor, shaking his head, "but let us have a shutter, a hurdle, or anything to get him home; and if any of you know his friends, go forward with the men, but don't say too much about it; don't flurry, say he's had a fall, anything for the present, so as not to disturb them more than we can help."

The printer from Kidem and Blowhard's volunteered for this little service, and did it very well; but he could not hide all the truth, and when half a dozen men appeared carrying poor Sam on a shutter between them, the whole of the little household went into commotion.

But the doctor put an end to it by declaring that if there were any disturbance, he would send the boy to the hospital. This threat made Mrs. Smarty and the little ones quieter, for they had an instinctive dread of such places, founded upon the mass of suffering always accumulated there.

Sam's father was away at the time, and was not expected till the evening.

Stretched upon his little bed, Sam lay while the doctor examined him carefully, and the court, now alive from one end to the other, discussed the mysterious occurrence.

The examination was a short one, and

when it was over the doctor dismissed all but the weeping mother from the room.

His first question took a pecuniary turn.

"I must ask you at once," he said, "if you have any money to spare?"

"We have saved a few pounds," replied Mrs. Smarty, "and I'm sure you can have anything in the house if it is wanted to save him."

"*I* do not want it," replied the doctor; "it is not for myself I speak. The fact is, I must have professional help, and of a class that costs money; if you are not in a position to pay it, he had better go into the hospital. He could not go to a better place."

"I am sure of that," replied Mrs. Smarty, "but I am certain his father would feel as I do, and wish to have him here. We can nurse him, I am sure."

"He will want a great many things."

"All that we can get, sir, he is welcome to."

"His illness will be a long one."

"Poor boy; I am sorry for his sake. How did it happen, sir?"

"I cannot tell you at present," was the reply; "keep him quiet till my return. Don't allow the idle and curious to crowd about the room—and bathe his forehead constantly with cold water; and if he shows restlessness, moisten his lips with a little wine and water."

The mother passed three anxious hours before the doctor's return; and then he came with a tall gentleman, with iron-grey hair, and a face tanned by a sun warmer than England can boast of.

The latter advanced to the bedside, felt Sam's pulse, turned back the eyelids, and placed a hand for a few moments upon the back of his head.

He then desired Mrs. Smarty to retire, and the two professional gentlemen were left with the unfortunate boy.

"You are right, Mr. Peyton," said the sunburnt gentleman, "he has been struck behind—with some soft but powerful substance—a sand-bag probably—a favourite weapon in India, and one which only leaves a trace for experienced eyes to discern."

"I have read of such things, and thought I recognized the symptoms," replied the doctor. "I am glad to find I was not mistaken."

"For your own sake, of course?"

"For my own sake."

"With regard to the boy, Mr. Peyton, I can say very little at present; recovery in these cases is always doubtful, and not at all times desirable. A recovery is too often followed by helpless idiotcy."

"Good heaven!"

"It is the painful truth; but skill and vigil-ance may do much. I will visit him daily until the symptoms change. He is quiet now, but before twenty-four hours he will be raving."

"Will it be necessary to confine his arms?"

"No, that would be dangerous; only take care that he does not touch his head."

These and many other instructions were given, and the learned stranger—who had risen to the summit of his profession by pure ability and hard work—left to attend upon his other patients.

Mr. Peyton, who was in a smaller way, and had few patients, and many of those of the poorest, did not leave Sam for long throughout the day; and towards night a change took place in the patient.

CHAPTER XLVIII.
WORK-IT-OUT'S WRONGS.

THE lethargy appeared to be breaking off, and occasionally a word, half-formed, escaped the boy's lips; then half a sentence, and by sunset he was raving of a thousand boyish pranks, friendships, and hatreds he had been associated with.

But it was all a jumble—Tom, Inky, Tummas, Work-it-out, his companions in the workroom, appeared to be rushing through his mind in a confused mass; sometimes he laughed, at other times he cried, and now and then a deep groan escaped him, as if wrung from him by more than natural pain.

Throughout the night he was watched—his father having returned—by one or the other of his parents.

Some of the neighbours had volunteered to take part of the duty upon themselves; but for the present those nearest and dearest to poor Sam refused to leave him for a moment.

On the morrow the grey-headed surgeon came back, and his brow darkened as he examined the raving boy.

He bade the mother be of good cheer; but when he left the house with Mr. Peyton he confided to him the truth.

"The boy," he said, "is in a highly dangerous state."

"I feared it."

"And if he remains where he is, he cannot live a week. Change, even that, might not be able to restore him, but it is his only chance."

"What change?"

"The country or seaside for the present—that might recruit his body; his mind—well, that must of necessity be an after consideration."

"What can this poor family do? It is as much as they can do to meet your fees."

"My fees," replied the surgeon, quickly,

"can stand over. These people are very honest, I can see. The boy must be removed—it is his only chance, again I say. I am interested in the case. Remove him at once, and apply to me for the expenses."

"This is too generous of you, Sir Charles," replied Mr. Peyton.

"Remove the boy at once," was the surgeon's rejoinder, as he stepped into his handsomely appointed carriage, which had been awaiting him in Fleet Street.

* * * * *

The inquiry of Mr. Benjamin Harris, *alias* Work-it-out, at first met with no response.

The few keepers and Mr. Busby, who gathered around, although they knew the story, wisely refrained from saying anything about it.

Podley was a man who meddled with his own affairs only, and Inky, staggered by disappointment respecting his old master's fortune, was unable to reply.

"I ax again," cried Work-it-out, smiting his hands together, "where's my marynets?"

Continued silence on the part of Jim Podley and the menagerie men; but Inky recovered himself a little, and screwing up his courage, framed an effective answer in one word,—

"Bust."

The eyes of Work-it-out gleamed with anger; he seized the wretched Inky by the throat and shook him as a dog would a rat.

"What do you mean by 'bust'?" he cried; "hout with the truth, you himp."

"I mean this," replied Inky, shaking himself free; "that if Kailer had stood up agen the dustman like a man, and not been afeared of the shovel, then we might hev had the 'ole of the figgers now, and Bob Crossley wouldn't have collared the drum."

"Is that an answer, you hidiot?" cried Work-it-out, in a frenzy; "what ham I to make of it—who's Kailer, who's the dustman, and what's the meanin' of the shovel?"

"That kid o' yourn," said Busby, pointing to Inky; "went out with Shy Kailer to show the marynets—but a dustman, as was beery, fell on 'em and spiled the show—the figgers was lost, and Bob Crossley kept the drum for the kid's keep."

"He ain't no right to take my drum for the keep of another chap," returned Work-it-out, violently. "There ain't no law as allows him to do it—I'll hev my drum."

"It warn't yours," said Inky; "you gev the lot to me—show, figgers, and drum."

"I guv 'em to *you!*" cried Work-it-out.

"Yes, you," said Inky, "when you came inter that fortin'."

"I ain't the man to go from my word," rejoined Work-it-out; and don't mind admittin' that I told you to keep that show *in case of the fortin' bein' fair and square.* Those were my words, Inky, and I stands by 'em. The fortin' wasn't fair and square, it was gammon, and I wants my marynets."

"Which you can't hev," said Inky, stoutly.

Work-it-out was about to rush again upon his adopted son, when Busby interfered.

"Hold orf," he said; "it's no use you wolloping the boy right and left. He did'nt lose the show on purpus, and you can't blame him; if you wants to drop onto the right party, go down to Lincoln and have it out with the dustman."

"Hear, 'ear," chorussed the rest, Inky's shrill voice above them all.

"As far as I can learn," pursued Busby, "the 'ole job were unfortenet. Here's a boy with a show and drum, and nobody to work with him; he gets introduced to Shy Kailer, and they goes out together. Now mark what follers—they pitches, and a crowd comes round—then all of a sudden this dustman shows up, and down goes Kailer; which there was no gammon about, for I seen him settin' on cushions, with his hed tied up. So it ain't no fault 'o the young un's."

"Well, I suppose it ain't." groaned Work-it-out; "but when I found the fortin' was gammon, I reckoned on the marynets."

"It's the way o' the world," said Busby, philosophically. "What you reckons on you don't orfen get. I allus sympathises with a man as loses a thing, and sympathises with you. I suppose, not to be rude, that you are hard up?"

"I ain't had a copper these three days," replied Work-it-out.

"In that case," returned Busby, "you can make free o' the fire to-night, and I'll send you out a bit of supper with the rest. You ain't got no objection to knuckle o' mutton stew, I suppose."

"It were allus a relish to me," replied Work-it-out, smacking his lips.

"Then sit down and make yourself at home."

Work-it-out needed no further invitation, but sat down on the sawdust and warmed his pinched hands before the coke fire.

By-and-bye the stew appeared, and Podley stood treat for a pot of porter.

Under the combined influence of these stimulants, Work-it-out gradually mellowed, until he became affectionate to all, and tenderly forgiving to Inky.

"The misfortin' is yourn as well as mine," he said, "so we'll say no more about it. But if I'd only got the fortin', what a night we'd make of it now."

He appeared to forget that had he been the fortunate recipient of wealth, he would never have troubled any of his old friends again ; this his audience knew, but they did not remind him of it.

"Forty thousand pounds," mused Work-it-out, as he toyed with the pewter pot containing the porter ; "it's a pile."

"So it is—so it is," said Jim Podley ; "but may I be so free as to ax how it was you didn't get it."

"You may," replied Work-it-out ; "and if all the genelmen is agreeable, I'll spin the yarn."

All were agreeable, and filling their pipes, they settled themselves comfortably to hear how it was that Work-it-out had come to grief.

"When I left this young un—Inky here," Work-it-out began, "I thowt the money was as good as in my pocket ; for you see the advertisement seemed plain enough—Benjamin Harris, as lately left London ; and I'm Benjamin Harris, and I hadn't left the great merrytropolis many days, so that's what deluded me, and as I said, I went.

"In the 'eat of comin' inter so much property, I chucked three bob at Inky there, which redooced my ready cash to about six shillings, and this I laid out in a railway ticket at the nearest station I could get at, which warn't above four miles away. At sech times man is heager, and shillin's get thrown away like fardens ; but a time for repentance comes, and comes pretty soon, I tell you—mine came about four hours arter I reached London.

"The fust thing I did when I got clear of the confuging railway—which bein' the fust time I'd rid on it, I thought every moment we was goin' to be bust or crushed—I rushes down to my brother Reuben, for I wanted company to help me through with it, you see.

"Reuben was much surprised to see me, and looked a little black ; but he clears up when I tells him the news, and says, like the Reuben of old,—

"'I'm glad on it, Benny, my boy.'

"Then I axes him,—

"'Will you come with me to the office ?'

"'Won't I,' he ses, 'and wot's more—we'll make a party on it, and go in a wan. Piper is out o' work, and will be glad to give us a tootle on the cornet for a considerashing, and go up to take your money in style.'

"In my 'art," pursued Work-it-out, "I thowt we might ha' gone quieter, but Reuben had been kind to me, and I couldn't refoose him, so the wan was got out, and Reuben puts the story about and offers the seats to the neighbours free—resarving half the vehicle for the wimming, without which no wan party can be complete.

"We gave 'em 'arf an hour to dress, and they comed out as only wimming can—green and blue dresses, red and yaller shawls, and

bonnets so full o' flowers, that the thin 'uns looked quite top-heavy ; but so it is, no matter how shabby the husbands is, the wimming gen'rally get enough flowers in their bonnets to fill a fruit garding—but I resoom,—

"Orf we started, Reuben drivin', and the boys, as come out stronger than ever I seed afore—cheerin' us like mad—runnin' under the horses' 'eds and wheels, and comin' out untouched wonderfully.

"We was werry merry goin', and pulled up at several houses, where Reuben put the story about, and stood a lot o' drink on the strength on it—which we all drank free, without leavin' the wimming out, and didn't show none the worse for it—although it all comed out arterwards, as I shall tell you.

"We crossed Southwark Bridge—for toll warn't nothin' to Reuben, he was that free—and so on by the main streets up to Droory Lane, and so on to Lincoln's Inn Fields, and all that way the people turned out to see us, runnin' out to their shop doors, and out of courts, and so on ; and Reuben kept hollerin' to 'em—'We are goin' to take a fortin'—forty thousand pounds,'—which made a lot keep up with us, as wasn't in no way either hornamental or useful.

"We was obliged to leave the wan in the Fields, and walk the rest. I wanted to go alone with Reuben, but our party havin' got—to put it as mild as I can—werry frisky, they all insisted on goin'—the wimming especially ; and so leavin' a man in charge of the 'orses, we sets orf two and two, arm-and-arm.

"The orfice," continued Work-it-out, looking solemnly around at his spell-bound audience, "was half up a little house squeedged in the corner of the Inn, and our party choked it up quite : when Reuben and I got inter the room, the hend of the party was arf way down the staircase. There was a little man sittin' on a stool, a'most as tall as hisself—who turned werry pale when we bust in—which we did, for the licker, as I said afore, had made us frisky, and the wimming's tongues were goin' like clappers.

"'What does you want?' he axes, werry pale.

"'My fortin',' I says, in a loud woice lookin' at him furusly, for there is nothin' to get your back up like the prospec' of forty thousand pounds.

"'This must be some mistake,' he says, 'you've come to the wrong room.'

"'No I ain't,' I says, 'here it is':—R. H., Lincoln's Inn ; and the man in the gold-lace hat, as is lookin' arter the sparrers, told us this is the place."

"'My name,' I says, louder than hever, 'is Benjamin Harris.'

Then a change comes over him, and he bolts through a little door into another room.

"We couldn't make nothin' of that movement, and Reuben was for follerin' him up, for he thowt the chap might be stuffin' the fortin' in his pockets, ready to run away; but he comed back in company with a old gentleman, with a powdered head, who looked at us over the gold rims of his spectacles in a way which made us all—even the wimming—quiet.

"'Now, ladies and gentlemen,' he says, 'who do you want?'

"I tell him, as I told the tother, that I wanted my fortin'.

"He says, 'Go away.'

"I says, 'I shan't; for you can't rob me with compunity,' for I thowt I seed in his eye that he meant to swindle me.

"'You're not the man,' he says.

"'Who ain't?' I axes.

"'You ain't,' he says. 'Mr. Benjamin Harris is a gentleman—you're a low fellow—get out of my office.'

"'Don't you go,' says Reuben, bold like, 'ontil he pays it all over, to the larst brass farden.'

"All our party says the same, and one of the wimming—which her name is Purkis—wanted to thump the powder out of the old gentleman's head.

"But the old gentleman was firm; he wasn't at all frightened, and he says again, 'You are not the Benjamin Harris advertised for—if you are Benjamin Harris at all; the right man is in my office now.'

"'Bring him out,' we says; and the old gentleman beckons out a fine-looking young chap, about five-and-twenty, who was laughing like winking.

"'This is Mr. Harris,' says the old gentleman, 'and the money is left to him by his aunt—Mrs. Sarah Harris, of Clapham Rise—are you any relation to her?'

"We seed our mistake then," said Work-it-out, mournfully, "and Reuben and me were quite 'bashed—we hadn't nothin' to say, and we wanted to go, but our party behind began to let the old genelmen have it; they called him a swindler, a thief, and a willin, and when the little clerk came forrard and tried to push us out, the wimming got hold of him. The warious drops we'd had on the road began to show up, and they smit him heavily.

"They smit him on the 'ed, they smit him on the face, they smit him all over; they tore his coat, and rumpled him so, that when they let go he fell all of a heap inter the fender.

"Reuben and I worked hard, and we got 'em out at larst; but they went downstairs screechin' and made Reuben stand another round afore they got into the wan again.

"We went home noisy, but the mirth warn't real—it were the 'oller 'art that wears a mask to break your own to see; and when we got nigh home, there was at least five hundred people waitin' for us at the bottom o' the street.

"They 'ollered so that we couldn't explain nothin'; they called on me and Reuben to chuck out a handful of shiners, and when we wouldn't, they pelted us frightful, but we got 'ome at last, and the troo story is told.

"The next mornin' Reuben got a summons from the clerk for assault, and had to square the damage, and there warn't no chaff about it, certainly; but it went down a bit afore I left, which I did as soon as I got your letter, Inky, and Reuben gave me another 'arf suvrin to start in life, which I spent too free like, and now I haven't got a brown."

CHAPTER XLIX.

SHIMLEOH, THE WILD SON OF THE DESERT.

INKY had suffered much himself; he had demanded sympathy at all times, but he gave none to his old master in the hour of trouble.

Busby and the men going away, Inky and Work-it-out were left together.

The cobbler shifted restlessly upon his feet, and occasionally looked at Inky, who was silently gloating.

At last he asked—

"Inky, how do I look?"

"You looks more like a guy than any I ever seed," was the satisfactory reply.

"Don't you think they'll take me for a Arab?" said Work-it-out, uneasily.

"A Arab," returned Inky contemptuously; "a babby in arms will see through you with his eyes shut. Everybody will find you out, and it's my belief they won't stand it."

"Who?—won't stand what?"

"This sort o' gammon," returned Inky "they'll have you down and jump on you, they'll tear orf your costoom, and give you worse than Shy Kailer got at Lincoln, that's what they'll do."

"Oh, Inky," cried Work-it-out, trembling. "I wish I'd never come here."

"But you can't run away now," said Inky, "you must stop. Busby's got your other clothes, and if you turns out into the street in that soot, you know wot would become of you."

"They'll tear me to scragments," said Work-it-out. "Who's that coming downstairs?"

"Wisitors," replied Inky, briefly, and taking up his rake, stirred up his old enemies the monkeys in a frenzy of joy.

The Wild Son of the Desert endeavoured to compose himself into a fitting attitude, but he was not so successful as he might have been. The light of agony was in his eyes when an elderly gentleman and two ladies, apparently his wife and daughter, followed by Busby in person, appeared.

Busby had come down to see how Shimlech acquitted himself.

With his eyes fixed ahead, Work-it-out endeavoured to shut out the palpable truth that there were visitors now staring at him with intense curiosity, and that Busby was calculating the effect his new Arab made upon their minds.

"The camel, my dears," remarked the old gentleman, "is a wonderful animal, much used in sandy, sterile countries. It can bear fatigue to an extraordinary degree; outlives its hardy attendants, of whom we have a specimen here—stuffed, I presume," here he gave the Wild Son of the Desert a very painful poke in the ribs, which made him rock again.

Work-it-out was about to deny that he was at all approaching a stuffed condition, when Busby advanced to the rescue and explained.

"This sir," he said, "is Shimlech, a wild son of the desert, whom I have just imported at an enormous cost. At present he does not speak our language. The camels are werry sensitive about their attendants, and won't have any but the real thing."

"Remarkable instinct," exclaimed the gentleman, holding up his hands, and both the ladies said so too.

"We are obliged to put a little sand in the camel's grub, or food," pursued Busby, looking fixedly at Work-it-out, "so as they still has the flavour of the desert with it; otherwise, they would refoose to eat and perish o' want, starve and die."

"Wonderful!" exclaimed the listeners.

Busby, refreshed and encouraged, went on.

"This Arab," he said, pointing to the quivering Shimlech, "sacrificed his feelings to his dooty, and left behind him a wife and family. As long as the camels are here, he will stop; he never leaves 'em, night or day; eatin', drinkin', or sleepin', he is perpetivally with 'em."

A cold perspiration broke out upon our friend—was his duty to be thus defined, or was Busby only joking with his auditors?

He was left musing, and Busby accompanied the visitors round the entire show, confining himself, with regard to the other animals, more strictly to the truth than he had with the camels.

He dismissed them with a profound bow, and hoped he should see them again.

"I have been highly gratified," said the old gentleman as he ascended the steps, "especially with my Arab friend there, whom I intend to visit again with some friends of mine learned in the tribes and nations of the earth."

"Only keep that mouth on yer," cried Busby when they were gone, "and you'll be worth pounds to the booth; you're more real than a real Arab, you shows up the camels wonderful."

"But about stopping with 'em night and day?" inquired Work-it-out, "you didn't mean that?"

"You mustn't leave 'em in the day time *now*," returned Busby; "for I've committed myself with that gent. He's a great man about here—head westry-man, and so on—he's sure to be poppin' in and out with friends, and it wouldn't do for him to find you away."

"It'll be a 'orrid life," moaned Work-it-out.

"Only for a few days at a time," said Busby, soothingly; "you'll have plenty of rest at nights, and when we are on the road. You will get used to it."

"I've my 'pinion on that p'int," groaned Work-it-out, as he settled himself to receive a further supply of visitors now popping in.

It was a long, long, wretched day to the wretched Work-it-out; but the more he suffered, and the worse he felt, the more Arab-like he became.

The public, as a body, admired him intensely, but a few of the jocular sort insulted him profusely when they heard that the English tongue was strange to him.

"If I had them legs," said one, "I'd make pipe-tubes o' 'em; and look at his 'ed, it's shaped all ways. I'd make a better one out of a kidney pertater."

"He can't take kindly to his wittles," said another, "or he'd be fatter."

But this imputation was virtually denied by Work-it-out when Busby sent him out his dinner, which he consumed with avidity, as he sat in the straw between the camels, surveyed by a curious multitude.

Inky, too, behaved very unhandsomely, frequently shoving himself in front of the throng with a mighty grin upon his face; once he ventured to rake him up like the monkeys, but Shimlech, the wild son of the desert, exhibited a bit of his latent ferocity by seizing that implement and smiting the daring Inky over the nose with the handle.

Inky retired precipitately, and for an hour the Arab was left in comparative peace.

But the night was the worst time.

Then the booth was crowded mostly by working people, who crowded round the camels and their attendant, until the latter was half dead with heat and fatigue. Tongue-tied, he endured the comments of the crowd with Spartan fortitude, keeping his eyes, for the most part, surlily on the ground.

This did not detract from his merits as a foreigner, and he became more popular every hour, and Busby, proud of the success, announced him outside as he would an additional kangaroo in any other portion of the managerie.

The booth was at its fullest, the crowd so dense that it could scarcely move about.

Work-it-out felt himself going, when he was aroused by the voice of a man speaking in a tone of merriment.

"What do you say?—a real live Harab—here, let me have a look at him."

"There he is," said another.

"How are you, old cock?"

"He doesn't speak English."

"Then I'll give him a dose of Harab," returned the first speaker. "I say old boy,—"High cockery, ohingo bungalore tooral bung."

Shimlech shuddered, he fully recognized the voice now. Screwing up his courage, he slowly raised his eyes, and beheld,—

His brother, Reuben Harris.

CHAPTER L.

MORE EXHIBITIONS THAN ONE.

"He knows his *native* tongue," said Reuben, looking round upon the crowd for approval. "I'll give him another dose—Rum tum, tiddy iddy, tum tal tay."

The recognition Work-it-out dreaded was not in Reuben's eyes, and yet, as their looks met, he started and seemed puzzled.

The disguise was effective, but not entirely effectual.

"Hullo," exclaimed Reuben, "there's something about you I've seen afore—I knows that look well enough, but where?"

Shimlech steeled his heart against his brother, and never said a word.

"I know I've put eyes on this Gimcrack, this Wild Beast of the Desert afore," said Reuben, addressing the crowd; "but I can't say where. I'm blest if it aint a staggerer."

Busby, who happened to arrive as these words were uttered, saw his Arab was giving way, so he roared at the top of his voice,—

"Jack, the performing helephant, will now go through his waried tricks; the other end of the booth for Jack, the helephant."

A rush was made for the opposite side, and Reuben followed, in company with two or three ladies and gentlemen, who appeared to be his friends.

Work-it-out gave a sigh of relief, and leaned wearily against one of his charges.

"Keep up your pecker," whispered Busby

hoarsely; "you'll get used to it. There's allus a lot o' bother with the night people."

"It ain't the bother," returned the Wild Son, "but that chap who chaffed me just now—is—my brother."

"Phew!" whistled Busby; "did he know you?"

"He swears he's seen somethin' like me afore."

"He must be looked to," said Busby, hastily. "It's that fat jolly-looking chap standing a tip-toe, ain't it?"

"That's him," replied Shimlech, wearily.

Busby crossed the arena, and posted himself beside the unsuspecting Reuben, who being somewhat of the shortest, had no little difficulty in getting a view of what was going on.

The voice of the keeper was now heard.

"Ladies and gentlemen,—this wonderful 'ighly-trained animal will go through his performance. Fust he will let you know he is hungry, and ring the bell for his wittles. Are you hungry, Jack?"

"Ooh!" bellowed the elephant.

"Call the waiter, then."

The monstrous brute elevated his pliable trunk, and rang a bell suspended above his head, which brought down a round of applause.

"The hanimal will now show his strength in warious ways," continued the gratified keeper; "this trunk of his will fust pick up a weight weighing one hundred and twelve pounds, and then take up a straw. Jack!"

"Ooh!" bellowed the elephant.

"Are you strong?"

"Ooh!"

"Then show the ladies and gentlemen how easy you can lift up that weight."

Now it so happened that Inky had been forced into a front position by the rush of people, and once there he made no effort to retire.

Secure in the presence of the keepers, he forgot the elephant's animosity towards him; but the elephant remembered the object of his hatred, and having debated in his mind the most appropriate object to raise, settled upon Inky.

Seizing that unfortunate youth with his trunk, he twisted him in the air, amidst the shrieks of his victim and the cries of the crowd, who having seen our friend with the monkeys, naturally looked upon it as a part of the regular performance.

But the keeper rushing to the rescue, whip in hand, undeceived them, but not before Inky had been seen and recognized by an old friend in the rear.

"It's the boy Inky," said Mr. Reuben Harris, aloud, "and the Harab is my brother Benjamin."

Further exposure was prevented by a hand being placed over his mouth, and the horrified Busby whispered in his ear,—

"Hush! don't holler so loud; if you exposes him afore the crowd, his life ain't worth a feather."

Stunned and confused by the discovery and the strange warning, Reuben Harris allowed himself to be pushed through the crowd, and hustled with more haste than ceremony into the interior of Busby's little house upon wheels.

CHAPTER LI.

DEEPER AND DEEPER STILL.

"Now sit down," said Busby, pushing Reuben Harris into a chair; "you've got a bit excited, and must cool yourself a little."

"I wants my brother," answered Reuben doggedly; "I wants to know wot he means by disgracing his family in this way?"

"May I ax what your family have got to be proud on?" asked Busby, with stern politeness.

"My fam'ly is 'ard-working and honest," returned Work-it-out's brother in a loud tone; "we never had a mounterbank in it afore."

"The one you're got now, is a mounterbank by ch'ice," said Busby, "so don't mouth it too loud here; we reckons ourselves quite ekal to you."

"I want my brother," cried Ruben, violently.

Busby rang a small hand-bell, and a keeper came.

"How about that boy?" he asked.

"He's all right. Jack tried to get him inter his money-box," was the reply, "and when he found he couldn't, he shoved him inter the manger; he aint hurt a bit."

"That's all right—send him and Shimlech here, and tell 'em to look sharp."

While waiting for Work-it-out and the "nobbly born," neither Busby nor Reuben exchanged a word. Both were out of temper, but neither cared to vent his spite upon the other.

Shimlech, the Wild Son of the Desert, was the first to appear, looking rather tame on the whole, and his angry brother fell upon him at once.

"What's put it into your head, Benjamin, to disgrace the family like this?"

Work-it-out hung his head, and muttered, "any living is better than none."

"Do you call *this* a livin'?" demanded his brother; "mixed up with tramps and wagabones—"

"Draw it mild," interposed Busby.

"Tramps and wagabones, I say," repeated Reuben, firmly; "the offsprings—I mean the

houtcasts of society—men as don't know Christian manners, and lives all their days in wans instead o' goin' down to Hepping Forest in 'em when the season's on, like respectable people."

"What could I do, Reuben?" pleaded Work-it-out; "bein' hard-up, I naterally fell into low company."

Busby made a mental note of this observation, but he did not openly comment on it.

"I never thort," said Reuben, weeping copiously, "that a brother of mine would ha' come to this."

At this moment Inky, with a rumpled head of hair and a face ghastly pale, entered the van. He recognized Mr. Reuben, and held out his hand.

"Like your imperance," said Reuben, "I had enough on yer the fortnight you lived with me. Wot's he brought here for?"

"I thort you seemed inclined to take 'em both away," said Busby, quietly.

"Not I," rejoined Reuben; "I've got a wife and kids at home. I've enough to bother me."

"Then why do you make a fuss about their bein' in low company?"

"Because it breaks my heart to see one o' my flesh and blood dressed up like a Crimean Tartar on the war trail," replied Reuben, mixing up the dress and habits of two distinct races. "I've no right when I pays my tanner for admission, to be insulted with seeing my brother stuck atween two camels, like a Chinese junkman who ain't had no wittles for a fortnight."

"He was fed to-day," said Busby, "and he made a tidy peck of it."

"It's the wittles of shame," replied Reuben, rising, "and I tells him now, that I've done with him. Don't let him darken my doors agen—either on 'em—him or that brat; or, if they do—I'll—I'll chuck some water over 'em."

With this rather lame conclusion to his denunciatory address, Reuben Harris stalked from the van, tumbled down the steps in his haste, picked himself up in a towering rage, and disappeared.

"Now then you two," said Busby, "sit down there."

Work-it-out and Inky exchanged mournful glances, and sat down upon a short form. Busby eyed them sternly for a few seconds, then he spoke.

"It seems to me," he said, "that wheresumever you two go, you carries summat wrong with you."

Work-it-out groaned; Inky heaved a deep sigh.

"It seems to me," pursued Busby, "that everything in natur' is ag'in you—the werry animals objects to you (to Inky), and the camels (to Work-it-out) seem to be pining like ever since you stood atween them."

"Then turn me away," said Work-it-out, slowly, "they can't feel wus than I do over the job."

"Gently," returned Busby, "there's reason in everythink; you're announced here, and I can't let you go for a week. Then our time's up, aud we can move on without you —which I mean to do, and at the same time act the handsome with you. I shall give you both a week's pay over, to give you a start upon the road."

"It's werry hard for me," murmured Inky, "it wasn't my brother as kicked up the row."

"You're bad enough without a brother. Look at your time with Bob Crossley," replied Busby, in an argumentative manner; "wasn't it the rooin o' Shy Kailer's constitootion? Do you think that he'd have got such a series of busters if he'd been out with any other chap? Did you ever hear on a crowd falling foul of a show afore?"

"No, never," said Inky, tearfully; "it's jest my luck."

"It's the woice of natur' raised ag'in you," replied Busby, impressively; "it's the hinstinct of man and woman pitchin' into somethin' they don't like. You're full of nobbly ideas—you puts yourself up above the men, and butter bacon, as one may say, by turnin' up your nose twice as much as natur' turned it up for you."

"I didn't make my nose," said Inky.

"No, but you elevate it, which is offensive in the eyes of your fellow-man. Howsumever, far be it from me to put matters too strong upon you. You leaves when this week is up, and there's an end on it."

The two unfortunates went out together, and separated to their respective duties without a word.

Work-it-out's visage would have done credit to a Chinese malefactor under sentence of death.

Inky was simply woe personified—the concentrated essence of all that is miserable and forlorn.

All other woes paled before this great fact, they would shortly be upon the world again, friendless and helpless, with the stern smiter fast drawing nigh.

The prospect was black indeed, without one ray from the beautiful star of hope.

What were the antics of the monkeys— the gibes of the public—now? Even Reuben, he who had been their friend, had deserted them, and to whom should they turn? One thing Work-it-out wondered much about— his brother had not even alluded to the marionettes with which he had entrusted him; but the truth was that Reuben, excited

by the degrading position in which he found his elder brother, forgot them entirely, nor did they cross his thoughts until many days after Work-it-out had left the menagerie.

Of the rest of the time spent there by the forlorn ones a few words will suffice.

Jim Podley was sorry to hear of their dismissal, but he was not surprised; he had seen enough of Inky, and divined sufficient of the character of Work-it-out, to understand that they were liable to any disaster, however great or small.

"I can't keep you," he said to Inky, "or I would for a time; my pay ain't very much, and some of the family, such as the howl and the raven, are heavy grubbers; but I can spring you five bob to give you a lift, and I'll do it."

Inky thanked him, but in so mournful a tone, that a listener might have imagined he was acknowledging an injury instead of a benefit; but Jim Podley, knowing his young friend better than most people, paid no heed to it.

On the Saturday, the day of their departure, Inky, who had of late encouraged a spirit of animosity against his old master, resolved upon the perpetration of a trick, which, if successfully carried out, would thoroughly humiliate the ex-cobbler, and place him entirely under his thumb for a time at least.

We will now proceed to ascertain how far his diabolical scheme succeeded.

After the booth was closed for the night, Busby brought out the drum and paid his company.

First the band was disposed of, then the keepers and Jim Podley, and, lastly, Work-it-out and the forlorn Inky.

"Now," he said, "I didn't make a reg'lar agreement with either of you, but I put down your pay, Shimlech," he could not forget the name, being his own choice he felt rather proud of it, "I put down your pay at ten bob a week over and above your grub and bed, so here's a pound. Now for you, my lad, what do you think your work is worth?"

"I could have done better work if you had set me to it," replied Inky sulkily.

"That ain't no answer, my lad; you must put a price upon your work."

"If Work-it-out is worth ten bob a week," said Inky, "I'm worth a pound. He'd nothing to do but to stand still and be stared at. I had to rake up the monkeys like smoke."

"Ah!" exclaimed Busby, drily; "I knew you would make a mistake the right way— for yourself; but if you're worth a pound a week what ought my head keeper to get?"

"All he can," replied Inky, after a moment's reflection.

The answer was not a bad one, and Busby seemed struck by it.

He laughed and put some silver upon the drum.

"There's your money," he said ; "it is a little more than I intended to give you, but you were smart just now, and I like smart people."

Inky counted the money put before him, and found it amounted to ten shillings.

It was a very handsome sum in his eyes, and for the moment he felt grateful.

But he thought of Work-it-out's sovereign, and his face darkened.

"You might ha' given me as much as him," he said.

"I know I might," replied Busby ; "and I might have given you more. I might have made you a present of a silver watch, a cocked hat and a pair of Wellington boots, but I don't choose to do it. You be thankful for what you can get, and remember this— it's all charity, come from where it may, for if you are worth a tanner a week to anyone, I'll go up to the top of St. Paul's and pitch head-first down the nearest chimbley."

Having thus expressed his opinion of Inky's qualifications, he rolled up his money-bag and arose.

"To morrer's Sunday," he remarked by way of adieu. "We strike the poles in the evening ; if you like to stay until then you can, if not, you can cut it."

The other men had gone out for a time, and when Busby had departed, Work-it-out and Inky were left alone.

The forlorn condition of both touched them simultaneously, and, actuated by a common impulse, they grasped each other's hands.

"Oh, Mr. Work-it-out !"

"Oh, Inky !"

Was all they could say ; the sorrow of that one moment was too deep for words, and Work-it-out, in his character of Shimlech, looked more lean, lank and miserable than any real Arab who ever subsisted for a month upon sand, simooms, sand-pillars, and other engaging trifles of desert life.

But grief, however much it plays the part of a vent-peg in our life, can neither make nor mend the disasters of life, and Work-it-out went to change his things.

Since he had taken up the character of Shimlech, the Wild Son of the Desert, his well-worn suit had been kept in an old corn-bin, with certain banners and other properties of travelling life.

Opening this place of stowage, he felt for his bundle, which ought to have been on the top.

It was not there.

Alarmed by a thought that sprang into his brain he rapidly tossed everything out of the bin, until the square, bare bottom was under his eyes.

Then his doubts were confirmed and he knew the horrible truth.

His clothes were gone.

CHAPTER LII.

A TURKISH PHYSICIAN.—THE EXCITEMENT OF THE GINGERBREAD TRADE.

THE first impulse of Work-it-out was to shriek for help, not that he required it in a physical sense, but a feeling of being utterly wretched came over him when he found his usual habiliments gone.

The vision of a life in the street in the garb of Shimlech, arose before him ; hooting boys, howling mobs, stern police, and a general sense of being chevied and moved on.

Stifling his desire to cry aloud, he tottered towards the private van, and knocked at the door.

Busby opened it with ill-concealed impatience, for he was in the midst of his supper, and was little disposed to be troubled with business.

"Oh, it's you, is it !" he said, with a look of strong disfavour, "what now ? "

"My clothes," gasped Work-it-out, feebly.

"Well, I ain't got 'em."

"No, but they're gone—prigged from the cornbin."

"I don't understand nobody prigging things like them," said Busby, "except for a lark."

"I don't know who'd lark with me," said Work-it-out ; "but if so be as you'll be kind enough to ax 'em, I'd thank you."

"Wait till I've done my supper," growled Busby as he shut the door.

With a terrible foreboding at his heart, Work-it-out waited till Busby had finished his evening meal.

By that time most of the men, among whom was Jim Podley, had returned.

They all denied any participation in the removal of the missing apparel, some expressing very strong opinions on it, such as— "Wouldn't touch 'em nohow, and at no price ; " and one man more excited than the rest, expressed a desire to have a "turn up" with Work-it-out.

"You ain't no right to suspect us," he said, "so stand up like a man, and let us have a turn-up together."

This Work-it-out declined to do, on the plea that he was not possessed of "turn-upping" propensities or powers ; but if any gentleman would assist him to find his clothes, "he'd be werry much obliged to him."

They cheerfully gave him a hand, down to Jim Podley and Inky.

Every nook and corner of the menagerie was subjected to a strict investigation, but not a vestige of the clothes could be found—from the dilapidated boots to the battered hat, all had disappeared.

"There's nothin' for you but to keep up the character of Shimlech," said Jim Podley.

"But I can't do it in the street," returned Work-it-out, despairingly; "I ain't got no ramels."

"Try the distressed foreigner dodge," advised Podley, "it orfen pays. There was Noker Marley, a chap with a face like a model cut out of a turnip—eyes anywheres —a mouth like a post-office, and no nose to speak of. He got into trouble through fallin' in love with a old lady's dawg, and takin' it home with him. Arter he come out, he didn't know what to do; it warn't safe for us to mix with him, wheresumever he went the perlice knowed him; but he didn't like the idea of starvin'—so what do you think we did with him?"

"Don't know," said Work-it-out, moodily.

"We bought a pigtail!" rejoined Jim Podley, triumphantly; "and we made a distressed Chinyman on him. Lor! how he did take as long as he held his tongue; grocers hired him to give away bills at the doors, and wheresumever he went they did a roarin' trade; but he took to drink, and that rooined him.

"It warn't the drink itself," pursued Podley, after a pause, "so much as wot he said when he was in licker. Any old woman could have told that no Chinyman could swear as he did—and when he pulled off his pigtail to wop the grocers, who wanted to pay him all in coppers, that shut him up. In the fight which ensooed that pigtail was lost, and nobody never got him another, so he went to the bad, and now hangs about starvin' —a sight to see."

Silence followed this affecting story— Inky gazing into the fire in a meditative manner.

He was the first to resume conversation.

"Foreigners, Mr. Podley," he said, "is ginerally poplar."

"They air," replied the bird-fancier.

"Then I've an idea for Mr. Work-it-out."

The discharged Shimlech turned a pair of mournful eyes upon his adopted son, and asked him what he meant.

"Turkey roobub," repeated Inky, with a triumphant air.

"WHAT!" almost shrieked Work-it-out.

"Turkey roobub," repeated Inky, "on a tray—a penny a piece—cure everything. I've seen a chap selling it on Saturday night like winking."

"There's somefin' in that hidea," said Jim Podley, "and it does you credit. It's a payin' game."

"But I aint got no tray and no roobub," urged Work-it-out.

"The tray's easy made," returned Podley; "as for the roobub, you can get a ton of it of any Jew dealer in Houndsditch for about five bob; they make it out of all sorts o' things—cabbage stumps, horseradish, and other wegetable producks. You won't go fur without getting what you want down there."

"But is it safe to sell it," asked Work-it-out; "mightn't I p'ison somebody?"

"No, it don't do no good, and it don't do no harm; but people, when they takes it, believes in it, and gets better 'mediately."

"I think I'll wentur on it," said Work-it-out; "it's better than nothing."

"And you must do something, too, Inky," continued Podley. "I think a tray o' some sort would suit you."

"I don't think it would," returned Inky, savagely.

"Well, for the matter o' that," said Podley, "nothin' don't suit you—for you ain't easily suited; but never mind that, you must do something—have a tray—try gingerbread."

There was something very toothsome in this idea, and it pleased Inky—completely revolutionized his ideas, in fact, and he jumped at the notion with joy. A tray of gingerbread! If trade was slack, why—there was the stock, and if he had nothing better to do, he might pass the time by a personal consumption thereof.

It certainly was a capital idea.

"I promised you five shillings," said Podley, "but instead of it, I'll set you up in business. To-morrow I'll go down to Houndsditch and buy the stock for both of you—Sunday's a busy day down there."

This was agreed upon, and on the morrow Podley and Inky went over to Houndsditch, Work-it-out preferring to remain at home, as the garb of Shimlech was not exactly a regular Sunday attire.

They returned in time for dinner, and spread out before the people of the menagerie the stock provided—a large tin of the most diabolical looking gingerbread, sundry pieces of stuff which looked like the roots of trees, and two trays.

With these, the ex-cobbler and his *protégé* were to begin the world anew.

The parting on the morrow was not particularly affecting; Busby and his men wished them well, and Jim Podley gave them a few parting words of advice and friendship.

RIPPER GOOCH DENOUNCING TOM.

"I don't know as I've any particular reason to love you," he said ; "at the same time I've no cause to hate you ; we've met on what I may call the tideway of the world without running against each other."

"'Cept in the matter of a five pun' note," put in Inky.

"That note," returned Podley, "was allus a puzzle to me. You deceived me on it, and therefore I stuck to it ; but I gives you my word that *it ain't changed!*"

"Then why not hand it over ?"

"No," said Podley, decidedly, " not until my mind is clear on it. We shall meet agen —and if we don't, I'll put it into the sinking funds in your name."

"What are the sinkin' fun's ?" demanded Inky.

"The sinking funds," replied Podley, rather vaguely, "are a sort of kind of place in the bank where one chap puts money in for another to call for."

"But do they allus get it ?"

"I can't go so far as to say that, but I believes as a rool the chaps who've got charge of the place act pretty straight ; if you don't hear on me in a year or two, you look 'em up."

Inky was not particularly delighted with this notion, he would have preferred an immediate handling of the flimsy bit of paper, which rustles so musically ; but Jim Podley was evidently very firm on the point, and he pressed him no further.

"Now, afore you goes," continued Podley, "take a bit of advice about a place for a pitch. You, Work-it-out, can't do better than take the Blackfriars Road—just over the bridge ; and you, Inky, on the other side, by Stamford Street ; there's a large population about there, and as far as I can see they're good for any quantity o' sweet-stuff nd physic."

"There's no end o' sarsparilly shops about ere," remarked Busby ; "they draws it out a tap like beer."

"I thout it *was* beer one Sunday mornin'," id Work-it-out, "until I saw the faces me on 'em made when they were gettin' it down—a'most as bad as some o' the old ladies over their gin."

"Well, adoo," said Jim, holding out his hand ; "and don't forget this—when you do the patter for the roobub give it a furrin mossoo accent. If that don't go down turn the trade up."

"I will," returned Work-it-out.

Then the final adieus were said, and they parted.

From the moment that Work-it-out's clothes were missing, Busby had made up his mind to sacrifice the attire of Shimlech.

Neither he nor his men were troubled with superfluous clothing.

When they bought a thing they wore it until it was beyond cure ; then they threw it away.

Such being the case, it was necessary either to purchase some clothing or to let Work-it-out depart as he was, which, being by far the cheapest course, was accordingly done.

Busby had certainly reflected upon the consequences of sending the old man out in a state bordering on nature ; but apart from the cruelty of the act, he had a fear that he might be breaking the law ; and none have so great a terror of the law as your stroller.

Accustomed to a wandering life, to pure air, liberty, and change, a day's confinement in a prison is to him an age of suffering ; so all things combined to set Work-it-out up in the Turkey rhubarb trade.

It was about eleven o'clock as they footed it down Waterloo Road ; and Work-it-out's first appearance as Shimlech in public was not exactly encouraging.

His tray and stock were strapped upon his back, pedlar fashion ; Inky's the same ; and the pair presented a nondescript appearance, exceedingly bewildering to a curious public.

The boys were especially put out ; it was a mystery to them ; and to leave a mystery unravelled is contrary to the nature of boys in general.

"I think he's a musical glasses," said one.

"No, he ain't," remarked another, " his stand ain't got no legs. I say, darkey, down with it, and begin."

This allusion to his walnut-stained countenance Work-it-out wisely ignored.

Finding him impregnable, the boys naturally fell upon Inky.

"What have yer got, young 'un ?" asked a butcher's boy, who carried a leg of mutton in a tray.

"What's that to you ?" asked Inky, savagely.

"I'll let you know," rejoined the other ; "who'll hold my j'int ?"

A dozen volunteers came forward, but Inky, sidling up to his master, kept the enemy in check, until a street where the joint was required compelled the pugilistic butcher to depart.

By the way, why are butchers' boys invariably pugilistic ? Is it the smell of blood which makes them ferocious ? One would imagine so. Our experience of butcher life tends to confirm this idea.

Not far from our humble home a butcher resides, who had suffered much with his boys ; he keeps them, and is perpetually going through a mad struggle with one or the other on account of a youthful misdemeanour all day long Driven nearly to distraction, he resolved to have the mildest specimen of youthful humanity he could get.

He obtained one—a mild boy, who was a star in the Band of Hope ; a boy who was a pet at all the tea-fights he honoured with his presence. On him prizes for good conduct showered like rain ; nothing could be more lamblike ; he was the pride and delight of a host of street preachers, the beloved of neighbours, and a joy to his mother.

He came to that butcher's on a Tuesday at 11 a.m., and before 2 p.m. the same day he suddenly, and with but little provocation, kicked that butcher's shins.

Since then he has unmercifully beaten the street preacher, broken half the neighhours' windows, and cost his mother a little fortune for vinegar and brown paper to heal his bruises.

He is hated by all, the terror of many, and the parish outcast. The butcher has given him notice, but he won't go, and the butcher being afraid of him, he stays on.

There must be something brutalizing in the atmosphere of the slaughterhouse.

But to resume.

The progress of our friends was like invading a savage country ; everybody came out, and without inquiring their business fell foul of them.

'Bus drivers chaffed them, boys hooted them, and respectable foot-passengers, who ought to have known better, shouldered them off the pathway.

Facetious youngsters treated Inky's gingerbread tin like a drum, and smote it with sticks and stones ; they whipped Work-it-out's calves with knotted string, and called out "Spindles," and when Inky came a cropper over a loose paving stone, they howled in triumph.

It was the march of ignominy—an advance, and yet a miniature retreat from the contact with hordes of remorseless savages around.

How thankful they were when Blackfriars Bridge hove in sight at last ; the usual mass of life was throbbing at its foot, but to the gladdened eyes of the wanderers it seemed a haven of rest.

They did then what they ought to have done before—they divided and took opposite sides of the roadway, and their attendants, partly distracted by this movement, and partly tired of their pursuit, gradually melted away.

CHAPTER LIII.

WORK-IT-OUT AND INKY COME TO GRIEF AGAIN.

THE foot of Blackfriars Bridge is like a broad part of a stream where the water flows swift and strong, for there the stream of life ebbs and flows from morn till night, from north to south.

Throughout the day and night it is never free from one or the other class of little tradesmen.

The early dawn sees the coffee-stall, where for a sum too ridiculous to mention, the homeless, houseless wretch, the prowler, the night cabby, and sometimes the stern official sufficiently human to relax for a moment, may obtain an *al fresco* breakfast.

Later come others of the enterprising class ; the artist who scrawls on the pavement the orthodox mackerel, mouse, and lighthouse ahead ; the man with the "save-alls," curious bits of tin and wire-work to help the due consumption of candle ends ; a seller of old books, with a stock worth about fivepence, who boldly marks a thumb-worn shilling novel at ninepence, and a mixture of old Bradshaw's tourist guide-books, Dr. Pill's essay on the cold water cure, pamphlets on the effect of drink, and a hundred other varieties of strange indiges tible literature, at a penny each.

The man with a barrow of fried fish, the fruit and flower seller, and many others, find standing room near the foot of the bridge, where the stream of life unceasingly ebbs and flows.

This was the point chosen by Work-it-out and the sapient Inky, and here they took their stand ; Work-it-out on the east and Inky on the west side of the road.

Just let us see how Work-it-out fared.

With trembling hands he unbuckled his stall and fixed it on the ground.

Then spreading out his wares very much like pieces of old walking-stick, he prepared to astound the public ear in a fashion he had acquired under the teaching of the astute Busby.

"Ladies and gentlemen," he said, "it may not be known to you that the warious hills which flesh is heir to need not be endoored when they can at all be cured. Some persons——"

Here a small boy came up, and standing with his legs very wide apart, stared the vendor of Turkey rhubarb completely out of countenance.

"Some persons," he repeated, then stopped again, and coughed gently behind his hand, and another boy pulled up.

Work-it-out felt that he could not go on, and the extraordinary contortions of his face, combined with his attire, were sufficient attraction for the public, and a little knot quickly gathered round.

They gave him time, most of them being members of the lounging class, the idlers of the street, who were always glad of anything or anybody to help them through the day.

"Ladies and gentlemen," continud Work-it-out, nerving himself a little, "it may not be known to you——"

"You said that afore," said the first boy.

"And if so be I have, wot then?" sternly demanded Work-it-out.

"You ain't no right to keep the public a waitin'," replied the boy, with an injured air; "I'm on a arrand, and I'm rather in a hurry."

"You ain't called on to wait," said Work-it-out, loftily; "I don't know as I've got anything that could do you any good. Get out of it."

"When you've done sparrin' with that boy," put in a man with a strongly-marked countenance about the eyes, which were ornamented with two black rims, "p'raps you'll tell us wot you're making yourself a himage for."

"Wheresumever you may be," explained Work-it-out, "and whatsumever your game, the boys are sure to put a foot in it, and spile it. Boys are the cuss of man, the inkybus of natur', and the rooin of the constitootion of the country. Feller workin' men—be up and doin', for the destroyer is afoot, and he will soon inwade your hearths and 'omes. Down with the tyrants of a bloated stockeracey, and raise the elewated sons of soil and toil!"

"Here, cut it, will you!" said the man with the black eyes, with an expression of strong disgust. "Tell us wot you're here for, and wot you've got to sell."

"That's what I axed him," put in the injured boy.

"*You* ax him," said Work-it-out.

"Yes, I axed you."

"Like you imperence."

"Look here," said the man, elbowing his way to the front, "you let the boy alone; he's done nothin' to you. Get on with you, or I'll have it out of yer—like a tooth I'll draw it."

His threatening air, his brawny frame, the ferocity of his expressive countenance, awed Work-it-out, and put him in a tremble.

"Give me time," he asked, "and I'll come out. If so be as any of you ain't exackly right——"

"Hallo!" demanded his self-elected guardian, "so you're goin' to insult us."

"So far be it from me," said Work-it-out, emphatically, "that I axes your pardon, as it is, and did not derloode to in mentallic sense, but to the waried sufferers of mankind in general."

Greatly refreshed by this lucid beginning, he lifted up his voice a little higher, and proceeded,—

"If, on risin' airly in the mornin', you feel a 'eaviness about the 'ed and a lightness about the legs, it shows that the bootiful machinery

o' natur' is out o' gear, and that onless attended to your works will soon stop."

"That's good," said a man who looked like a gasfitter.

"But no matter how you feels or wot you feels," continued Work-it-out, "this root of life—dug from the deep deserts of Hafrica, and brought over fresh every mornin' on camels' humps, will put you as right as ninepence. I ham the sole importer of this extraordinary reviver, and I sells it in lumps at a penny each."

"Let's taste it," said the man with the illuminated optics, taking up a lump, and biting off a quarter of an inch.

He chewed it thoughtfully, turning it over like a connoisseur, while the crowd, on the tiptoe of expectation, awaited the result of his investigation.

He was in no hurry. It was evident that he was a man who never moved quicker than circumstances compelled him, and he slowly and laboriously rolled the piece of stuff about in his mouth, until an impatient movement in the crowd showed the people were getting tired.

Then he spat it out.

Looking slowly around, he said—

"I knows the stuff well. It is——no it ain't."

He bit another piece, and masticated it with a little—very little—additional vigour; but he got his clue this time.

With a triumphant look upon his face, he cried out—

"I've got it!"

As he offered no further information, one of the lookers-on asked him what it was.

"You'd like to know?"

"Yes, I should."

"Then don't worry. I'll tell you directly. Do you know what it is?" addressing Work-it-out.

"The root o' life," replied Work-it-out, shaking all over, "brought on camels' humps from the deep depths of the Hafrican desert."

"Oh! that's where they comes from. And who brings 'em?"

This was a question for which Work-it-out was not prepared; but his late life had brightened him up a bit, and he managed to reply—

"Shimlech, the wild son o' the desert."

"And who's Shimlech?"

"Shimlech—oh—he—o—a—a—Shim lech."

"Now look here," said the questioner, holding up a warning forefinger, "do you mean to tell me you ain't a liar—a downright old villainous perwerter of truth?"

"I ain't no call to say anything to you. I want to sell the root o' life."

"No doubt you do. So you shall, if anybody's foolish enough to try it arter I've exposed you. Now, friends and feller-countrymen, what do yer think this stuff is ? "

He paused a moment to give due effect to his revelation—then he cried—

" It's dried cabbage stalk."

Murmurs of indignation arose, and one man, who had got his penny ready, put it back, and turned up his coat-cuff.

Work-it-out shook so that his stock rolled about the tray.

"Cabbage stalk," repeated the analytical one, "that's what it is ; and he comes here calling it the root o' life. I'll root him. Look here."

A swift blow, and the contents of the tray were scattered about. Then the tray was torn from his shoulders, and Work-it-out saw the man with the contused optics deliberately put his foot through it.

Then he walked off, and the crowd admiringly followed him, leaving Work-it-out standing like a man in a dream.

In good earnest truth he could scarcely believe the evidence of his senses, and leaned against the wall to think it out.

He looked at the street, so busy, so full of people—all so utterly indifferent to him. He found no consolation there.

He looked upon the ground for some fragment of his tray and stock, but both had as completely disappeared as if a wave of the sea had passed over and swept all away. Nothing was left, not even the smallest boy of his audience. All were gone their different ways, and at the corner of a street lower down he perceived his exposer standing, thoughtfully and as easily chewing a piece of straw as if he and Work-it-out had never met.

"The life of a man is warious," mused Work-it-out thoughtfully, wiping his face ; "from cobbling and degenerating the workin' man—from want to marynets—a fortin' —camels and roobub, and all swep' away by the remorseless hand of fate. I wonder how Inky's gettin' on—roobub's a failure, we must rely on gingerbread now."

He looked across the road in search of his adopted son, but the crowd of vehicles and passers-by was too great ; the precious youth was invisible.

"I'll go over and give him a look," he thought ; " but I'll say I've left the stall in the hands of a man at present. If I tells him the trooth, he'll be for cuttin' me—Inky's awfully selfish."

He crossed the road by Stamford Street, and advanced by degrees towards the spot where he hoped to find his young friend, and presently he saw him.

Selling gingerbread ?

Not a bit of it.

Standing idly on the pavement ?

Certainly not.

But this is how he found him—

Grasped by the hair of the head, in the hands of a furious old woman, in a bent bonnet, who was punching his head against the wall, encouraged by a lot of idlers, among whom were several of those who had assisted at the downfall of Work-it-out.

" Have I sat here for years," screamed the old woman, " by lave of the gintlemen of the parish, and is the bread to be taken from my mouth and the mouth of my childer by a little spalpeen like you ? Be jabers !—it's a bad day you tried you luck at cutting me out. Take that, you measly, herring-boned bogtrotter."

She was old, but she was vigorous, and Inky was truly a child in her hands.

She knocked his head against the wall until she was tired, and then she let him go.

The first thing Inky did was to sink to the ground in a sitting position, and stare at a lamp-post near him, which, to his disordered imagination, appeared to be bent like a horseshoe.

Shimlech, fearing to encounter any of his old assailants, held aloof, but kept his eyes upon his adopted son.

The lamp-post having returned to its original shape, Inky managed to rise to his feet, and came staggering down the road.

Work-it-out kept up with him until they came to a quiet street, into which Inky turned, and became aware of the presence of his old master.

The two ruined tradesmen paused, and looked at each other.

Work-it-out looked sentimental ; Inky, very much ruffled and ferocious.

" Well ! " said the nobbly born.

" *Is* it well ? " asked Work-it-out, deferentially.

" Where's your stuff ? "

" It's in the hands o' different people," replied Work-it-out.

" You ain't sold it ? " cried Inky, brightening for a moment.

" I speak as the 'art of man ought," returned Work-it-out. " I can't say as I've 'zactly sold it, but *it's gone*, and wot could you expec' when a man with two black hyes comes a chawing it, and swears it's cabbage stalk ; but he didn't taste the tray, and he'd no right to spill *that*."

" One moment," said Inky, holding up his hand ; " you've lost the roobub ? "

" I don't know," replied Work-it-out, anxious to make the best of circumstances, " *some on it* may turn up ; but still, I shouldn't wish you to be too hopeful on that ere p'int."

" *I* hopeful ! " rejoined Inky, scornfully ; " wot have I to be hopeful for ? Ain't I been persecuted from my birth ?—ain't I been robbed o' my rights, and had my five-pun' notes prigged 'olesale ? And now, when I turns out to make a honest livin', wasn't there a old woman kept ready by fate to come up behind and let me have it with my head ag'in a wall, while a lot o' himps pegs inter my gingerbread ? *I* 'opeful ! it ain't you, Mr. Work-it-out, as ought to insult me so, and I don't like it."

"Inky," said Work-it-out, his voice broken with emotion, " it don't seem as if things went right with us ; the woice of the scorner is down upon us wheresumever we may be."

"It is," said Inky.

"We've tried two or three things together," pursued the old man, " and if you're willing we'll try some more."

"I don't mind—it don't make no difference to me—I'm squashed."

"Come, Inky, we'll go to the country, it's better than town—we ain't so likely to starve ; there's turnips there."

"And young nobbles comin' of hage," added Inky, with gleaming eyes, " with beef and beer for every chap as turns up—and the wine a flowin' and the bugles blowin', and, all is 'appiness and peace. We'll do a round o' them festivities, and p'raps some young nobble may take a fancy to both on us, and make me a page and you a old man with a long thin stick to stand ag'in the door."

"Is the country anywheres like that ? " asked Work-it-out.

"Not the part we have been to before," said Inky ; " but somewhere the other way, and we'll go to find it, Mr. Work-it-out."

"We will, Inky."

And then the two unfortunates shook hands upon it, and went away in search of that land of coming of age and feasting, which only existed in the poetical brain of the " nobbly born."

CHAPTER LIV.

TWO YEARS AFTER.

TIME has rolled on since the fearful failures of the two enterprising tradesmen who endeavoured to establish a connection in the Blackfriars Road.

Thousands have since then come into the world, and thousands have left it.

The intelligent work of nature has been going forward, the seasons have come and gone, friendships have been formed and severed, love and hate engendered, houses established and broken up, the ties of long years severed.

These two years have been a long and weary time to one, and now he lies upon a couch by the window of a small cottage in the heart of Kent.

It is Sam Smarty.

Grown, in spite of his illness, but sadly pale and weak ; his hand resting on the cover of a book is very thin and transparent, like the hand of one in consumption, and his hollow eyes and cheeks tell of the long suffering he has borne.

He is alone in the cottage, but the window looks out upon a green meadow, where a number of young lads are playing at cricket, with a good sprinkling of spectators scattered around.

It is a grand day in this quiet place, for Turnlake had ventured to challenge Beechgrove, and the result is now apparent in the careful play of the two elevens, and the eager, criticising cries and shouts of laughter or approval as the game goes on.

The match is nearly over, for the sun is sinking behind an old larch tree, and the night is fast approaching.

Sam is keenly interested in the game, for one young batsman, who has brought down approving shouts during the past hour, and is still holding his own, is his old friend Tom ; the ragged urchin transformed into a well-dressed, handsome, high-spirited youth.

Hark to the shouts ! what music can equal it ?

The match is a close one.

Beechgrove relies upon their two last batsmen, and Tom has just given a splendid cut for a four.

Sam rises and puts his elbow upon the window-sill.

All pain—the giddiness now being familiar to him—is forgotten in the excitement of the game, and when Tom hits for three with the very next ball, he shouts with the shouters of Beechgrove, whose lungs are stentorian and spirits high.

Beechgrove wants but five to win.

Turnlake growing desperate changes the bowling, and puts on a man who is celebrated for his " grubs."

He has a trial ball, then steps back with venom in his eye.

Now, Tom, be careful ; woe betide you if hand or vision fails now.

The ball comes, a regular sneaker ; but Tom is prepared for it, and away it goes for a good four but for that confounded fellow who picks it up neatly, and gets a ringing cheer from the Turnlakes.

But Tom gets one run, and Beechgrove is confident.

His *vis-à-vis* is a good hand at breaking the bowling, a regular sticker at the wicket, but seldom scores many ; he simply blocks the grub, and the next over Tom gets the ball again.

Beechgrove cheers and Turnlake groans.

A swift ball, straight for the wicket, and Tom blocks it.

The next is a little wild, and away it goes far over the field for another four, and the match is over.

CHAPTER LV.

THE CHANGES WROUGHT BY TIME.

THE match ended, the usual jubilee took place, the best batsmen were cheered, their deeds commented upon, and all the features of the match discussed.

Tom did not wait for his ovation, but slipping quietly away, returned to the cottage where Sam lay.

As he entered, the invalid boy's face brightened, and he made an effort to rise, but Tom put him back.

"No, not yet, Sam," he said; "the doctor's orders are that you are to be kept quiet, and doctors must be obeyed."

"But it is such weary work," said Sam, with a sigh; "only think, that for two years I've been a cripple, and——"

"Now you are going on famously," added Tom; "I don't want to preach to you, Sam, but just think how many would never have recovered from such an attack."

"I know I've kind friends, Tom."

"I don't mean that exactly, but still, you have been fortunate that way. Your physician took a deal of trouble with you, and when he found that you were not entirely unknown to Lord Holbrook, he looked us up like a jolly good fellow."

"When is his lordship coming down, Tom?"

"I don't know, Sam; he has been very much unsettled for a long time; and from what he says, I gather he is waiting for the return of some woman who has promised to find some relation of his from whom he has been separated a long time."

"Did he give her any money?"

"I don't know."

"If he did she wouldn't turn up," replied Sam. "You've only to lose a relation to find fifty people to volunteer to look for them."

"It would puzzle them to find mine," said Tom, with a laugh.

"And yet it seems to me that I've seen some of 'em somewhere," replied Sam; "often lately, when I look at you there is something familiar in your face. Only to-day I was thinking that I'd seen somebody as much like you as two peas, but how or where I can't tell any more than the Dutchman who lost his way in the Seven Dials."

"Perhaps it is as well," sighed Tom; "I fear my relations are not very creditable, and yet I should like to have known my mother."

"That's where you differ from Inky," said Sam. "He always wanted to know his father, who he insisted was 'nobbly born.' By the way, what's become of Inky, I wonder?"

"I should like to know," rejoined Tom, "for after all, I have reason to be grateful to him."

"He was rather selfish, Tom."

"No doubt, but I've found out this, Sam, that every fellow has more or less good in him. It's very rarely you come across a fellow wholly bad."

"And that is why you wish to see Inky?"

"Certainly."

"I shouldn't be sorry to see him myself, but I'm afraid he's gone to the bad. I did hear that he was on the tramp with old Work-it-out, but the news came from Nick Mawley, and since he ran away from the works and took to the card trick at races, I don't think he can be relied on."

"Nick was an old friend of yours?"

"We worked together for two years—at Kidem and Blowhard's—ah! I wonder whether I shall ever be able to work there again?"

"To be sure you will," said Tom; "doesn't everybody say so? The doctor says you've got over the turning point, and will go on like a house a-fire, but you are not to go back to Kidem and Blowhard's."

"I shall as soon as I'm strong enough," rejoined Sam, firmly. "I don't like to be always sponging on people's kindness."

"Oh, Sam!"

"It's all very well, Tom, but I stick to my point. You were regularly took up and made one of the family; I wasn't, and if I was I shouldn't be fit for it—my sphere is a working one. I may make a good tradesman, there's a chance of that, but I should make a precious bad gent. I should be quite out of place in drawing-rooms and Rotten Row. As for getting on horseback or playing the piano, I should just as soon think of dancing a Highland fling on the weather-cock of St. Bride's steeple. No, Tom, as soon as my pecker is properly pulled up I go back to business, and neither you nor anybody will be really kind to me if you try to make me act otherwise."

"I suppose we must let you have your own way, Sam. There goes the bell for the cricket dinner, I wish you could make one of the party."

"You will go, of course?"

"No, I prefer to remain with you, Sam. There are plenty to eat it down to the last scrap, for I never saw so many tramps and beggars down here before. Two especially—an old and a young one—appeared to me as if they had been starved for months."

"Poor fellows."

"I felt vexed that I had nothing to give them," said Tom; "but no fellow carries money in his cricketing flannels. I am sure they were starving, and by jingo!" he added, looking out at the window, "here they come."

He raised Sam up to enable him to obtain a view of the strangers, who seemed fully deserving of sympathy and assistance.

One was old and grey, with such a combination of tatters hanging about his emaciated frame, that he seemed to be a veritable puzzle for a tailor, a problem for him to work out as to which article of attire each scrap of clothing originally belonged.

The other was apparently very young, but his lean, lank frame was so worn with travel and want, that he at a distance looked to be forty years old at the least, and it was only when he came close that anything like his real age could be guessed.

"Strangers to roast beef for a long time, I'll warrant," said Sam; "we must let them have something to eat."

"Certainly. I say, hallo there!"

The two wayfarers who were strolling past looked up with a weary, hopeless expression, and the old man feebly touched his hat.

"Come here," said Tom.

They looked at each other as if doubtful of his meaning, and it was only when Tom shouted again his urgent request that they crawled slowly up the garden and halted at the porch.

"Are you hungry?" asked Tom.

The question was barely asked; their quick, eager looks answered it; and Tom, disappearing for a few moments, quickly returned with some bread and beef, and a large jug of beer.

These he placed on the table near Sam's couch, and then he asked the strangers in.

He had some little difficulty to induce them to enter, both declaring that the open air was good enough for them, and that they "weren't fit for a decent house or decent people;" but Tom would hear none of this, and accordingly they took their seats, and after a hasty recognition of Sam's presence —a short and sharp piece of politeness—they fell upon the bread and beef.

We say "fell upon" advisedly; for surely, never since the days of Adam, did two human creatures more vigorously assault cold meat and bread; it seemed as if they were eating for a wager, or were compelled by Act of Parliament under certain pains and penalties to get through a maximum of provisions in a minimum of time.

While they ate and drank, Sam lay and watched them with a puzzled face, which gradually expanded into one of intense astonishment, mingled with amazement.

But he said nothing until repletion set in, and then, as the younger of the two took a concluding draught of beer, putting down the jug with a sigh of relief, he said—

"Hope you enjoyed it, Inky?"

The long jaw of the individual addressed fell a couple of inches, at least, as he stared at our sick friend, but recognition dawned upon him as it had dawned upon the other.

"Why, it's Sam Smarty!" he said.

"What is left of him," replied Tom.

"Now ain't this a go," said the "nobbly born;" "here's a old friend as I've been thinking about for days turnin' up right sudden—here's a strange go, Work-it-out."

The elder wanderer not having known Sam intimately, was not so particularly interested, but he looked up and muttered something about "allus bein' glad to see an old friend."

"And who may this genelman be?" pursued Inky; "not—not—"

"Yes it is, Inky—it is no other than Tom."

"Here's news, old man," said Inky, enthusiastically, addressing his old master; "two old friends, and both on 'em in clover, I'll be bound, with plenty o' money—and to spare."

"Don't make too sure o' that, Inky," said Sam, drily.

"I don't, Sam—for I never make sure o' nothing since Work-it-out and I was driven by the perwerseness of fate to go on the perpetuil tramp——But there, I ain't a goin' to spin a yarn about it; I'd better congraterlate you upon your risen fortins."

"My fortune," said Sam, "has been two years on a sick bed. What has yours been?"

"Kicks, thumps, snarls, hoots, 'arf bricks and no coppers," replied Work-it-out, surlily.

"Our life," added Inky, "have been a long journey of persecootion, willifying, and houtrage."

"We have been the footballs o' willans," groaned Work-it-out.

"Suppose you tell us the story?" suggested Sam.

"I ain't ekal to it," said Work-it-out.

"Will you do it, Inky?" asked Tom.

"If you can make up your mind to listen to me," replied Inky, gloomily. "I've laid hold of lots of people and tried to tell 'em, but they've allus cut me short or runned away."

"That I will promise you not to do," said Sam.

"Then, as I feels pretty comfortable," returned Inky, "I'll give you it now. Perhaps you wouldn't mind Work-it-out's pipe?"

"Not a bit."

"I ain't got no 'bacca," growled Work-it-out, "and you knows it."

"You ain't never got anythin, you ain't,"

returned Inky, angrily; "there never was sech a old man as you."

"Don't quarrel," said Tom, "I can get you a pipe from the cottager here—he is a great smoker."

Work-it-out expressed his gratitude, and the tobacco being procured, he filled a pipe, composed himself into a listening attitude, and bade Inky "fire away."

The long-suffering and much-enduring Inky occupied two moments in reflection, and then began.

CHAPTER LVI.
INKY'S STORY.

"I'VE allus found," Inky said, "that the more a chap's trodden on the more the people puts a foot on him; and if a man gets a kick promiskus he can allus reckon on havin' a few more afore he's out on a clear road agen. Arter Work-it-out and I happeared with Busby——"

"Who's Busby?" asked Sam.

"Oh, I forgot," said Inky, "you didn't know him. I must begin at the beginning;" and he then told the history of his career down to the memorable morning when he and Work-it-out made such a miserable failure in their respective lines of trade.

"Deprived of a means o' livin'," he went on, "we turned our backs on the world in London, and made up our minds to foot it for the country. 'You can allus do somethin' there,' said Work-it-out. I said we couldn't, but Work-it-out were obstinate, and to the country we went."

"If my mind don't deceive me," said Work-it-out, removing his pipe from his mouth. "the country spec were litterely your own."

"If we arger," rejoined Inky, "there'll be a row; let me tell my own story my own way, or tell it yerself."

Work-it-out, thus rebuked, retired to the consumption of his tobacco, and Inky threaded the mazes of his story as he willed.

"We thought that the south o' London was the best way for workin'," he continued, "and 'cordingly we went straight on through Sydenham, and Norwood, and reached Croydon during the fust day. We weren't entirely destitoot when we turned up then, but the perwerseness of Work-it-out brought down poverty on us.

"He wanted to make more of his capital, by a swindle, or t'otherwise—which is the trooth, and it's no use his groaning—and the wickedness of his 'art led him into a skittle-ground, which game he used to play when he were young and strong—at least, so he says, and if he don't speak the trooth it ain't no fault o' mine.

"There was two men in the skittle-ground; both on 'em with faces like bits o' beef, and one had a squint, which gave him a hinnercent appearance, and completely took Work-it-out in.

"He was knockin' down the pins one by one, and throwin' the ball all over the ground, which Work-it-out laid to his hinnercence and I to his squint.

"'I never could play this game,' he ses, 'never; somehows I don't see the pins like other people, the 'ole thing is a mystery to me.'

"'You shouldn't throw so wild,' ses Work-it-out.

"'How, then, should I throw?' axes the man.

"'This way,' ses Work-it-out, and taking up the ball he makes a 'spectable effort, and knocks down five pins.

"'I can beat that, I think,' ses the man.

"'No you can't,' ses Work-it-out; and after a werbal row over it they made up a game, the tother man and myself agreeing to set up the pins, and help 'em to drink the beer, which no help is ever wanted in a skittle-ground for that.

"Well, the game began, and never did I see sech a game in all my born days. Work-it-out wasn't in it from the beginning; if he got five pins, t'other chap got six, if he got six, t'other chap got seven; and they went on in this way until Work-it-out were cleaned out of every copper, and that wild you couldn't hold him in.

"He calls the fellow a swindler then, and him with the squint takes off his coat, and they has one round, which ended in Work-it-out lying insensible among the pins, with a hole in his right boot showin' quite plain.

"Now all this time Work-it-out was in costoom, which he had worn as Shimlech, and when I hollered for help as soon as the others runned away, some of the ostlers came in and finds him 'elpless, with the turban off his shaved head, and lookin' awful.

"They goes and tells the landlord and his wife—which both on 'em, luckily, was romantic—that a foreign gent has been skittle, sharped and knocked silly; so they takes pity on him and puts him to bed, while I gets a good meal and some beer, on the strength of bein' a interpreter, which idea came inter my 'ed as soon as I finds they took him for foreign.

"'Whatsomever you do,' I whispers, as they carried him upstairs, 'don't know a word of Henglish.'

"He winks, and bein' nearly round, talks some nonsense, which I said was axin' for rum and water.

"They brings him some as soon as he were laid on the bed, and while he drinks it all the servants, boots, chambermaids, and a b'iling of ostlers stands round hawe-stricken with hadmiration.

"The landlord took kindly to me, and as soon as Work-it-out was composed a bit axes me down inter the private parlour, where a cold round o' beef was laid out ready for supper,

"I didn't want much axin', and when the beer was put on I did my share on it, and growin' bold like, must admit that I did sartinly spin some whoppers to the landlord and his wife.

"'Now, what nation,' axes he, 'is our fren' upstairs?'

"'Harab,' ses I.

"'What's Harab?' axes he.

"'A Harab,' I replies at a venture, for know the trooth I didn't, 'is a Circasshin of the Nile, a hocean of the Southern Seas.'

"I sees the landlord look puzzled and nod in a cur'us way to his wife, but I takes a little more beer and makes up my mind for the wust.

"'I'm fond of furrin countries,' says the landlord, 'altho' I've never been to 'em; but I've got a son somewhere out there. We ain't heard on him for some years, but I hope to hear of him some day.'

"And then the landlady begins to cry a little, but when I said that most people who were long away ginnerally came back, she gets a little calmer.

"'I thort somehow,' said the landlord, 'that your friend bein' a Harab——not long from his country, is he?'

"'Not long,' I ses.

"'Your friend bein' a Harab, and not long from his country,' ses the landlord, 'that he might ha' seen or heard o' my son.'

"'I don't think it likely,' I ses, shakin' my head to look knowin', 'but as soon as he comes round I'll ax him. But I must do it private, or we sha'n't get a word out of him.'

"All this wickedness cummed inter my hed, has a chap as is as 'ard up as we was do go in for desprit things sometimes; and I goes upstairs to talk it over quietly with Work-it-out, fust sending out all the servants, who'd got more skewrious every minnit, and didn't seem inclined to leave him nohow. But I gets 'em out at last, and locks the door.

"Then I tells Work-it-out what the landlord wanted to know, and axed him what we should do.

"Work-it-out speaks up to gammon him, but I says No—for I had a simplethy for a man as had lost a son, for I had lost a father, and a nobble one to boot, let Work-it-out say what he may, or be as perwerse as he will for havin' lost that hankerchif, and forgotten the name. It beats him to put a wulgar father on me."

This piece of elocution, particularly de-signed for Work-it-out, had no further effect upon him than a few extra whiffs of his pipe expressive of a deep conviction respecting Inky which he did not care to express—and the unfortunate one continued:—

"The fust thing I hinterpreted for Work-it-out were, that he must have some more rum and water, which was brought to him by a fat waiter, on a silver tray, while he wouldn't have stirred a step had he known who Work-it-out was, and that he warn't no Harab.

"Work-it-out drinks that glass, and axes for more.

"I tells the waiter to bring some more, and he brings it.

"This went down like the last, and then I ses I won't hinterpret no more, when up fires Work-it-out, and vows he'll split upon the 'ole affair.

"So I orders more, and Work-it-out drinks it, until he gets so meller that you couldn't get anything out of him but, 'More rum and water.'

"Arter a time he goes into a sound sleep, and I goes down to the landlord agen.

"'Well,' he ses, 'is that Harab ready?'

"'No, he ain't,' I ses. 'I've told him what you want, and he's thinkin' it over.'

"So we sits quiet for 'arf an hour, and then I goes up agen.

"Work-it-out was a-snoring like a young whale.

"Down I goes agen, and ses he warn't ready yet, and as it was nigh eleven, and the house about to close, we agreed to put it orf till to-morrow, which I wasn't sorry to do; for I wanted to get to bed.

"Howsumever, I didn't go just then, but I sits with the landlord and his wife, who treated me to negus ontil I was right orf my hed, and I tells such lies about Work-it-out as I turns pale over to this day.

"And so we went on until the clock struck twelve, and the head waiter brings in the plate afore goin' to bed—for it was a decent-sized hotel which we'd got into, and the skittle-ground belonged to the tap.

"Just as the waiter brings in the plate, we hears somebody bawlin' upstairs.

"Nobody 'cept myself didn't know the woice, but I knowed it was Work-it-out, and I trembled as if I'd just got the ager.

"'Who's that?' axes the landlord.

"'I don't know,' says the waiter.

"And then one and all goes out to look—I cold as a icy pole of the north, and with a wague idea that I should come in for somethin' hot directly.

"Once in the passage, we looks up the staircase, which was broad and straight, and there at the top stood Work-it-out, with his dress of Shimlech flowin' free and his turban on the wrong way.

"He looks down at us for a moment with a meller smile, and then he hollers out—

"'Three o' rum hot, with a bit of leming.'

"If he had chucked hisself and a chest o' drawers right on the top of 'em, they couldn't ha' been more hovercome.

"The landlord looks at the waiter, the waiter looks at the landlord, and then they both collars me, and, as a prelimingary, they shakes me until I couldn't see nothin' that wasn't mixed up with something else.

"Then they rushes upstairs, and I sees 'em lay wiolent hands upon Work-it-out, and he comes down with a wiolent squash, right on to the mat below, where he lays a minute, and then busts out with—

"'Brittanniar rools the waves!'

"I don't want to give no more partiklers of that night," pursued Inky, "acause it ain't a pleasant subject; but we got it so warm that Work-it-out was all rags, and I hadn't a sound bit o' skin anywhere on my body—and in that state we went out to find a bed wheresumever we could, and without a copper or a friend in the world.

"Croydon's a pretty place when the sun is shining and the birds a singing, but at midnight 'tis rather lonely.

"But we makes up our mind not to be cast down, and so works our way to what I now know to be the race-course, and passed the night by the side of the grand stand—just out o' the miler—where Work-it-out slept his rum off, and took in a stock o' rheumatism sech as he won't get rid of in an hurry.

"In the morning we rises, and gets away pretty well, considerin' that Work-it-out was as stiff as a wall and groaned so that he frightened half the crows out of their nests."

CHAPTER LVII

THE FURTHER DOINGS OF WORK-IT-OUT AND INKY.

"I SUPPOSE," said Tom, with a smile, as Inky concluded the Croydon narrative, "that you gave up the interpreter business then?"

"I was willin'," replied Inky, mournfully, "but Work-it-out, in his skewrious way, stuck to it."

"'Inky,' he ses, 'one failure ain't nothin', we shall make a hit on it yet. I sees a life of wictorious gammon afore me.'

"'How?' I axes.

"'Never you mind,' he ses, with his usual perwersness; 'from this hour I don't speak my native tongue no more, and you must be the middleum atween me and my feller man.'

"I didn't say nothin' to his proplesition," pursued Inky, "altho' an' eavy 'art told me wot would come of it.

"All that night we kep' to the high road, and as soon as it was light we lay down ag'in a haystack to get a little sleep.

"I must hev slept some hours, when I was woke up with what I thought was the sting of a wopse, but I found it were a cart-whip, which a red-headed and beef-faced farmer was layin' into me like winkin'.

"'Come out of it,' he ses; 'I'm not going to have tramps and wagabones sp'ilin' my hay.'

"I jumps up and axes his pardon—anything is better than a cart-whip—and then I sees that Work-it-out wos already upon his legs, trying the gammonin' game, and makin' signs to show he was foreign all over.

"I arterwards learned that he was awake when the farmer come up, and acause he couldn't speak English the farmer laid into me.

"'I ain't no tramp or wagabone,' I roars; 'you let me alone.'

"'What are you?' axes the farmer.

"'Inkterpreter to him,' I ses, 'which he is a Harab prince come over on a wisit to the Queen.'

"The farmer stops and looks doubtful.

"'A Harab prince,' he ses.

"'Yes,' ses I, growin' bold as brass, 'a Harab as left his country in South Ameriky on a wisit to the Queen.'

"'Where's his traps?' axes the farmer.

"In a moment I was doubled up, I admit, but my genus," said Inky, modestly, "come to the reskoo.

"'He was wrecked off the Isle of Tight,' I ses, 'and all on board drowned 'cept himself; he swum ashore on a hencooper, and was picked up by me, as was on my way to Brompton. You'll be sorry you've laid into me, and into him.'

"'I don't know about bein' sorry for you,' ses the farmer, 'but as I hain't touched the tother I've nothin' to be sorry for. Howsomever, if you likes to take a bit o' breakfast with me you can. I don't care about furriners, but my missus is a gummer for skewriosities, and allus goes thro' the lot when she goes to the fair, so p'raps she won't mind you.'

"The farmer's wife didn't mind us; contrary like, she quite took to Work-it-out, and axed him so many questions for me to inkterpret that I'd little or no time to peck my food; but I got through a fair share at last, and we was about movin' off when one of the farm men rushes up and ses there's a lot o' wans goin' by the high road, which bein' a sight there everybody rushes down to see.

"Work-it-out and I went with 'em, and at

the bottom of the lane who should we see but two old friends of ourn, on their way to the south with their company, and these friends was Bob Crossley and Sawney Tap, which p'raps you've heerd on."

"No, indeed," replied Tom, and Sam said the same.

"We knew 'em well enough," rejoined Inky, "but as we stood behind a lot of farm people they didn't know us; but as soon as they passes I whispers to Work-it-out, 'Here's a chance for us, let's cut, and we can soon overtake the wans.'

"As Work-it-out was ready for anything, we shakes off the agricultooral lot and pegs along the high road until Bob's wans heaves in sight, and then I goes forrard and makes myself known to him.

"I can't say," pursued Inky, "that his welcome was all that the 'art of man nobbly born could wish, for he looked askewer at me, and Sawney Tap, who never was over perlite, axes me plainly where I got the cheek from to turn up again. But I soon squares 'em, and when I ses that Work-it-out was a little way behind in Harab costoom, they pulls up and waits for him.

"'Oh!' ses Bob, 'so you're my old fren' with the marynets.'

"'Don't speak on 'em,' ses Work-it-out, weepin' like, 'unless you've found 'em somewhere.'

"'Not I,' ses Bob, gruff like, 'and Shy Kailer ain't been the same man since. He can't go up a ladder, and all his woice is gone. As for the penny whistle he used to be strong on, I'm blessed if he can get a note from it.'

"We were sorry for Kailer, but as I was mixed up in it I didn't say much.

"We jogs along for a time, while Bob was thinking over what to do with us.

"Fust he axes us exactly what we'd been up to, and we tells him; then he meddletates agen, and arter goin' to sleep twice, and fallin' once off the shafts o' the wan, he up and ses that he thinks he can do somethin' for us.

"'I can't pay you much,' he ses, 'but it's better than common trampin'. I've added a circus to my booth, and you, Inky, can put the sawdust in order, and Work-it-out can take the money, which a real Arab, I think, will be a draw.'

"It weren't a bad hidea, as the next place we pitched at proved.

"I found that Bob Crossley had got a much bigger concern than when we fust knew him, and not only was there a stage, but a big circus with the clowns, which one on 'em, who was long and thin, thowt I were a rival, and showed his wenom as soon as we met by

wanting me to go behind the booth and 'ave it out like a man.

"I did not go behind the booth, and when he knowed what I'd really come for, we was great friends, and he drove me nearly wild by perpetually asking me to have something to drink."

"He made you top-heavy more nor once,' put in Work-it-out, parenthetically.

"Which may you be forgiven for a downright lie," returned Inky, fervently; "although I did once rake the sawdust the wrong way, you ain't no call to throw it in my teeth."

"Don't quarrel," said Sam.

"We ain't," replied Inky, and resumed—

"The fust night Work-it-out took the money he was a great draw, and he paid in more ways than one; for when they gave him too much money he allus gave 'em short change, and as he couldn't speak English they couldn't quarrel with 'im, especially as Bob put up the follerin' notice."

Inky then drew a placard from his breast and held it up before the eyes of his old friends.

It ran thus :—

NOTICE !

ANY DISPUTE respecting change CANNOT be rectified, as our MONEY TAKER,

SHIMLECH,

THE WILD SON OF THE DESERT,

Speaks no language but that of his

NATIVE WILDS.

The public are respectfully requested not to TORTURE or ANNOY HIM in any way as he belongs to a

WILD AND PASSIONATE RACE.

ADMISSION, ONE SHILLING. CHILDREN HALF-PRICE.

BABIES IN ARMS NOT ADMITTED, and if brought in in baskets or under shawls will be TURNED OUT.

"That," said Inky, "was the notige posted up above Work-it-out's head, and while people read it he took the money and give 'em a ticket, which when he guv a man six feet high and weighin' twenty stone a babby's ticket, and he was refused admittance, there was a free fight, in which our coropean, who was in the way, got a black eye, and lorse a front tooth.

"The fust night I raked, the ring wasn't pleasant, for a man as had been haymaking, and drunk a heap o' beer, got over the fence round, and layin' hold o' the rake, insisted on showin' me how to do it.

"He fust shoved the rake in a boy's eye, then he hit me on the head and broke it, and when Sawney Tap comes in to the reskoo he

"CAN'T YOU FIND ANYWHERE ELSE TO SIT DOWN ?"

struggled all over the ring, and throwed him such a buster that Sawney broke the glass of his watch and lost fourpence in coppers."

"He was that shook," put in Work-it-out, with a growl, "that he winked for five hours arterwards, and it took eight pots o' porter to put him fairly on his legs."

"The dooty of rakin'," pursued Inky, "wasn't the sort o' work for one born in a spear o' wealth and influence, altho' chucked out of it while a hinfant, and lost in the parks by a nuss as never did her honest duty by him; but I puts up with it, and rakes away day and night, for it was bread and meat and lodging, which we can't look over at no time, nobbly born or otherwise.

"The fust three nights the circus did well, and Work-it-out took so much money that it was more than I could lift in the bag, and Bob Crossley, as soon as the house was full, put it in the strong box, which he or Sawney Tap didn't never leave night or day.

"We then shifted quarters, and went down to Tunbridge Wells, where a great conjuror, engaged for the purpus, was to make his fust appearance. His tricks was somethin' novel, and one on 'em was to cut off a boy's head and show his trunks to the public.

"As the trick was gammon, we couldn't have a boy from the orgiance, altho' they was invited to walk up, which several did, with allus one belonging to the company, which in course the purfessor selected.

"I was the one app'inted to have his 'ed cut off at Tunbridge Wells.

"Now, I put it to you or to any one," said Inky, "if I was a figger likely to get on to the stage without bein' known, 'specially arter raking round the ring for a hour or more in a set of tights, which bein' red, were, to put it nicely, conspicuous.

"Howsomever, to come to the p'int. The purfessor, which his name was Sandyson, and a great duffer, showed up the fust night, and standing on the platform, goes through a lot o' tricks which any one ought to have seen with 'arf a eye, and then he comes to the cuttin'-off trick, and showin' a big knife to frighten the little boys, axes some of the little ones to walk up.

"Boys ain't frightened with a knife, and about a dozen on 'em rushes up, all little chaps; and when I, as inkstructed by Bob Crossley, goes up with 'em, the contrash was so great that the orgiance wouldn't stand it.

"'Don't hev the long un,' roars one.

"'Send old scaffol pole back,' ses another, and the purfessor smiles, to make 'em amiable like.

"'I was thinkin' of havin' the long un,' he ses, 'for there can't be no mistake about him, and he can't be packed so easy away like these little uns if there is any trick about

it, which there ain't, and so, ladies and genelmen, if you be advised by me you'll let me have the long un.'

"This smooths 'em wonderful, and they makes up their mind to have the long un, 'on condishing,' as a old fellow with a wenomous face said, 'that his head wos handed round on a plate,' which the purfessor promised to do, 'if time permitted.'

"The fust part of the trick is to lay a chap on a table like a pig goin' to be killed, and he stretches me out and proceeds with his palaver.

"'Ladies and genelmen,' he said, 'this operation is on the werry climax of surgery, and altho' some are very clever and can cut a 'ed orf neatly, I am the only one as can cut it orf and put it on again.'

"He then lays the cold knife on my neck, and I, being frightened a bit, hollers like winkin'. Then the orgiance laughs, and a old man in front bellors, 'Cut him up, mister, he ain't no loss to nobody; you won't find no mother cryin' for him.'

"The purfessor smiles, and ses he'll go to work at once.

"Now the 'ole trick is, that they'd got a wax model o' my head and a bit of my neck separate, which was ready on a dish in a holler of the table, which was a long one with a big holler at the back, and a trap door for me to slip through as soon as I got notice from him.

"This table the purfessor had brought with him, and had been in use many years, consequentially it was rotten rather; and as I, though thin, ain't sech a light weight, he didn't ought to have put me into it.

"When cutting my neck, he touched a spring, and up come a piece of looking-glass, which hid me, and down I goes and up comes the wax head, which the purfessor cuts off, of course, and puts on the plate, where there was some fresh red ochre gore.

"Then he begins his speech.

"'Ladies and gentlemen, behold! there is no deception; the head is removed from the body, and the boy have ceased to exist.'

"Just then the box fixed under the table creaked a little, and I felt it giving way. Lord, how I hoped that he hadn't much to say, and the trick would soon be over! But it warn't to be, it warn't to be.

"He went on yarning and yarning, and the table went on creaking and creaking, until just as he offered A HUNDRED POUNDS for anybody as could bowl him out in a trick, the box under the table gave way, and down I came between the legs, right in full view of the orgiance.

"The purfessor looked round, saw me, and dropped his plate, and that kantankrus ole man wot made a parsonal allusion to me afore, lays hold on it, and holds it up in triump.

"The howls was frightful, but it warn't agin the purfessor; no, my ill-luck, which hath iver follered this Child o' Destiny, comed up then stronger than ever, and they fell foul o' me.

"'Bring that boy here,' shouted the wenomous ole man, 'and I'll take his 'ed off, and no gammon.'

"The purfessor bolted at once, and so would I ha' done, but I couldn't get away—a lot o' people jumped on the stage, and they carried me orf—screamin' and yellin' like mad creeturs.

"I shouts for help, but nobody came, and as it wasn't lawful to cut orf a fellow's head, they lays me down and larrups me so that I was a bag o' bruises for a week afterwards.

"Then they lets me go, and Bob comin' forrard to say he'd been deceived in the man who'd that night volunteered to do the trick, peace was restored.

"Restored," continued Inky, mournfully, "for him, but not for me.

"No; the werry next night he sends me in to rake the ring, and then a lot as had been there the night afore knows me, and the fust thing they calls out, when they sees me, is—'Have his 'ed off, have his 'ed off,' and they makes such a row that Bob Crossley puts me into a soldier's soot, and blacks my face to make a Sepoy of me; but it wasn't no use—they knowed me; and long afore the performance was over I was turned out by Bob; and Sawney Tap let me have the length of his tongue for a hour or more, as if I could help it.

"Still they didn't pack us off, for Work-it-out as money-taker drawed well, and did a world o' good going out in the daytime with the handbills; but as for me, I dusn't show my face out of doors, for everybody runned arter me with knives, to have my 'ed, until I was tortered into a state of madness, and broke the winder of a baker as larfed at me with a brick.

"The next day, when I got a summons for it, the booth moved on, and we made for the coast, where Bob intended to visit Dover and a few other sea places.

"It was at Dover that Work-it-out and I parted with him—as I believe, for ever.

The solemnity with which Inky uttered these words led his hearers to believe that a most momentous event was about to be recorded, and they settled themselves down to hear it told.

"I suppose," said Work-it-out, "that you haven't such a thing as a drop of brandy in the house?"

"I think not," replied Tom; "but you can have some more beer."

"Beer must do then," rejoined Work-it-out; "but I must have something, for I ain't so strong as I was, and the memory of hold times is a little too much for me."

The beer having been obtained, Work-it-out poured out a glass, held it up to the light, drank it, heaved a deep sigh, and bade Inky proceed.

"We all has our weaknesses," continued Inky, "and Work-it-out's is wittles and drink, specially drink, and he *will* mix, say what you will.

"When we got to Dover we pitched on a bit of waste ground, and Work-it-out went out as usual with the bills.

"He was gone nearly all day, and from what I afterwards heerd he got mixed up with sodgers, who took to his furrin look, and he drank so much with 'em that he lost all the bills, which Bob arterwards found at a marine store dealer's, where they'd been sold by somebody as the man didn't know for fippence.

"Howsomever, to go on to the night, when Work-it-out was found rather earlier than usual sitting in his box, ready to take the money.

"Bob didn't notice the state he was in, I didn't, and nobody didn't; but we found it out when too late.

"When the time came for the people to come in, they crowded in so quickly that Sawney Tap, who was mending a 'elmet, said—

"'Work-it-out gets brisker every day; he's a inwallyable man to take money.'

"And Bob Crossley said so too.

"It *was* a crowded night.

"I never saw the booth so full.

"Gallery, boxes, pit—up to the very roof; and as soon as the fust act was on—a lady on horseback—Bob ses to me—

"'Come on, Inky; as we can't make no better use of you, you shall help me to bring in the bags o' coppers'—of which we took a sight of the people in the gallery.

"I tells him I was willin' to do anything for my money—which I was—and that I should only be too glad to carry bags o' gold for him.

"He answers, gruff-like—

"'Don't jaw, but do it then.'

"Then I follers him to the pay place, where we expects to find Work-it-out tying up the money in the usual bags.

"As we got ag'in the box, I looked in, and so did Bob.

"I felt a cold chill, and Bob swore awful.

"*Work-it-out was sound asleep.*

"I felt bad, acause I knew that he ran a good chance o' being robbed, and Bob thought so too, for he seizes him by the collar, and knocks his head ag'in the wooden wall, until he comed out of his nap, and stared at us like a frozen Christian.

"'This is a pretty way to look after my hinterest,' bawled Bob; 'where's your money? It'll go bad with you if you've lost any of it.'

"Work-it-out stares at him harder, then round the box, then at Bob agen, and axes—

"'Are the people in?'

"Bob and I was both so overcome that we tumbled ag'in each other, and both of us began to suspect the trooth.

"'Ain't you taken the money?' axes Bob, hoarsely.

"'I think I took some,' stammers Work-it-out.

"And so he had—fourteen and fourpence—then somehow he dropped off to sleep, *and all the rest had gone in free.*

"It were pitiful to hear how Bob went on; he tore out of his 'ed more hair than he could grow in a twelvemonth; he shook Work-it-out; he shook me; he kicked down the pay place, and wolloped a boy as he caught tryin' to have a syrnptetious peep under the bottom of the booth; he rushed into the ring, intending to stop the performance, but couldn't, as he lost his voice, and at last he fainted in the arms of Sawney Tap, who was doing ring-master, and was carried out.

"It was long before they brought him round, and when they did he couldn't speak for a long time, but looks wildly round, and slaps his pockets, and axes for his money-box to put sixpence in, like a little boy—and all the company thought he was demelted; but he comed round at last, and axes Sawney Tap to go into a corner with him for a minute, when I sees him whisper to Sawney Tap, and Sawney's werry cap was lifted up by the 'air of his 'ed, although his face didn't move a muscle.

"Then they both goes out, and comes back biting their lips, and I knowed they'd been out for a stimulate, to stand ag'in the blow.

"I was near 'em, and I could hear what they said.

"'We can't turn 'em all out,' ses Bob.

"'We cant,' ses Sawney.

"'They're too many and too strong,' ses Bob.

"'They are,' scs Sawney.

"'But we can cut the performance short,' ses Bob.

"'We can,' ses Sawney.

"'And arter that we'll settle with our money-taker,' ses Bob.

"'We will,' says Sawney.

"I didn't know what the settlement meant," said Inky; "but I saw that in Bob's eye which I'd never seen afore, and I trembles all over with a aspen's quiver, and thought I'd better steal away, and warn Work-it-out

what was in store for him; but just as if Bob had read my innard thoughts, he turns to me, and ses—

"'You stop here, Inky; and move a peg for your life, if you durst;' and, in course, I natterally stops."

CHAPTER LVIII.

INKY'S NARRATIVE CONTINUED.

INKY paused for a little rest, and the interest of his hearers being now fully aroused, they awaited with silent impatience the resumption of his story.

Our old friend, fully conscious of his importance, was, like many other great characters, in no hurry to proceed, but, on the contrary, tantalized those around him, by indulging in a few minutes' reflection, which Work-it-out alone bore with philosophic resignation.

At length, Sam restlessly shifting on his couch, and Tom coughing, brought Inky back to a reasonable state, and he resumed:—

"It turned out that Bob Crossley had put a man over Work-it-out—Jack Soper, one of the hackerybats who did the somersalts over the 'osses, a werry strong party, with legs and arms like thick ropes; so it warn't no use for Work-it-out tryin' to get away from *him.*

"The performance was over a little arter ten, and havin' got rid of the audience, Bob closed the tent, and summoned the company into the ring, and then Jack Soper brought Work-it-out forrard like a pris'ner at the bar, and Bob sat upon the drum, to be the judge.

"P'raps he didn't ought to be the judge, for he was witness too, and he laid it on thick ag'in Work-it-out; and although the company was silent I could see their looks was wenom, for Bob told 'em that they'd all hev to bear a part o' the loss, each man accordin' to his pay and his persition in the company.

"What was due to me he stopped altogether, which was just my luck, wheresumever I may be.

"But the wind up was the greatest p'int, when Bob stood up, and puttin' his hand forrard like a norator, said—

"'It's a fortenet thing for that old ijiot that he's a hold man, otherwise it would have been my dooty to have had it out with him as man to man, and the best wictorius; but it can't be. It wouldn't be right for me to lift up my 'ands ag'in him, and so I has him another way. Bring pen and hink.'

"It wasn't often that they used it; but they found a bottle and a rusty pen at last, and then Bob draws up a dockyment, which all the company signs, and he gives Work-it-out a copy, which he's got now, tied up in a bit o' leather."

Work-it-out admitted the truth of this, and produced the document in question, which was read with much interest by Tom and Sam Smarty. We give it to our readers entire :—

"Dover—December 9 18—

"HI HOWE YOU bob crossly and sawney Tap and the rest of the compinny

FORTI SIX PUNS

for sleepin' in the box and hadmiting the publick free which shud I ever cum into another

FORTIN

i undertaikes to pay

"b. harris
"halias workitout"

"This dockyment," pursued Inky, "Work-it-out signed, for he considered that he never could cum into a fortin ekal to the last, and when that were done Bob stood up, and gave us wot he called a partin' lectur'.

" ' Look here, you two,' he ses, 'far as it be from me to lay it on thick on two people as is down in the world, circumstantials compels me for to say sumfin, ere we parts for hever. You've got somethin' wrong in your complexition,' he ses ; 'for from the fust hour we got together, summat allus went wrong with you and me.'

" 'It did,' ses Sawney Tap, backing up his partner.

" 'If hever you comes anigh me again,' goes on Bob, 'you take the fust turnin', and keep clear o' me ; don't you let me even see so much as the tip of either of your noses, or I shall probably forget our differs, and fall foul on you. Go now, with the best wishes of myself and the company, and don't never come anigh me no more.'

"We went on then, the company makin' way for us, with never a word for good or bad, and it was nigh midnight when we got clear o' Dover, and struck out on the road to London.

"We was both on us down ; I was suppressed—Work-it-out sulky——

"I warn't," put in Work-it-out.

"You was," returned Inky, positively.

"And so we went on together, hatin' our feller man, and a long way from bein' in love with each other ; for, put it as you will, Work-it-out, when in his tantrums, is very tryin'."

"And you," growled Work-it-out, "ain't always a subjec' of joy."

"We goes on," pursued Inky, ignoring the last remark, "through the darkness, with the wind rushing down upon us from all p'ints, and making our faces tingle and our fingers smart, until I was fit to lie down and die ; and Work-it-out sat on a mile-stone, and cried like a child ; and then, when I found that he gev way, I cried too.

"I knows I've been a bit of a fool," Inky went on ; "but I never did nothin' downright wrong, and I felt that I suffered a little too much ; and when you are out on a lonely road, at midnight, you gets little marcy from the wind ; and the rain, when it falls, seems to take pleasure in fallin' a little harder upon you than it does on other people.

"We walked all that night, and in the mornin' lay down to sleep behind a shed.

"It was werry cold, but warmer than it was in the night, and we were worn out, and so we slep' on till late in the afternoon.

"When we woke up we both felt hungry, but neither hadn't no money, and we—we—were forced to beg."

A flush passed over Inky's face, which Tom and Sam were glad to see ; it showed that he had not taken to the life of a mendicant without a struggle, and that he was still averse to it.

"What could we do ?" pleaded Inky ; "it warn't no use axing for work, and if we had, and got it to do, we must have had some food fust, and so we made up our minds to beg, and I bein' the youngest, made up my mind to have the first try.

"Close to where we slep' was a park with a big house in it, and then we knew there was plenty of food, so I went through the gate and walked up the path as led to the big house, and gets there without moluskation ; but then the big door frightened me, and I daren't knock, so I looks about until I sees a smaller one with a brass plate on it marked ' Servants,' and then I goes and rings.

"I waited a long time and nobody came, then I rang again, and a man opens the door with a bounce and hollers out—

" ' You are in a hurry, ain't you ? Now, then, wot do you want ? '

" ' A crust o' bread,' I ses, 'for I'm starvin'.'

" ' You get out of it,' ses the man, and was about to close the door in my face, when a woman's woice ses—

" ' Give the boy a bit o' bread. Heaven forbid that anybody should starve about here.'

"I looked in and seed a old woman like a housekeeper leaning on a stick, and I thanks her for her kindness, and she sends out a 'ole bag full of bread and meat and a jug o' beer.

"Work-it-out and I sat down under a tree and made sech a meal as I never dreamt of afore.

"We didn't find everybody like this, for at most places they wouldn't hear us, and more than one put the dogs at us ; but we got used to the life, and tramped about until one day we was took up."

Inky shuddered and buried his face in his

hands, but he speedily recovered, and continued his story.

"We'd done nothing worse than beg for a bit of bread, but the gentry, as was magistrates too, sent us both to prison for seven days.

"We warn't separated, but it was a 'orrible time, and we mixed with a lot o' men as turns me cold now to think on.

"Arter this we was broke; Work-it-out's costoom had got so seedy and ragged that you couldn't tell whether it were the dress of Shimlech or wot it was, and I hadn't a bit o' shoe to my feet, and in that state we tramped the winter through, sleeping for the most part in the wurkusses, with a barn for a wariety, but allus cold and nearly allus in a starvin' state.

"We tried for work lots o' times, but it warn't no use; people looked at us in a way that told us it warn't no go. They either laughed at us or abused us; mostly the last, but we didn't care much for that, for we'd got hardened like, and in that state that we didn't care whether we lived or died.

"Years ago," continued Inky, "when I was in Scepter Court, I've heerd boys talk o' the pleasures of a roamin' life; all I've got to say is, let 'em try it, and if they don't sing another tune I'm a conger heel.

"It wouldn't be so bad if it were allus sunshine, and no such things ar rain, frost, and snow, but anyway, it ain't pleasant, for you gets tired of walking, walking, walking on and on, without any purtickler place as you can stop at and call 'Home.'

"But to resoom.

"Arter a time the summer came, and we was still down the south side of London; then I saw a lot o' things growing up poles, which people said was hops, and that they would soon want to be picked, and that anybody that wanted work there could have it, and we kep' about the neighbourhood until the time came; but we found out our mistake.

"The reg'lar pickers came over together all in a bunch, and they wouldn't have us with 'em, but dropped in on the first Sunday mornin' and stoned us out of the place; then we went to begging ag'in, and we've been at it ever since, tramp here, tramp there, sometimes with somethin' to eat, sometimes with nothin', but never so much as a Christian-like meal until this werry night—and that's my story."

"And a very sad one," said Tom, "although it has made me smile; you must have had a dreadful time of it."

"We shall come out of it," returned Work-it-out, elated by the beer, "we've—at least *I* have got the stuff to 'stonish the world yet; give me the chance, and the woice o' Work-it-out will be heerd in the nation."

"No doubt," returned Inky, contemptuously, "and much good it'll do the nation when they do hear it."

"I've got a hinspiration comin' on me," said Work-it-out, "a feeling that my hour is come, and it was time I was up and doin'."

"Take away that beer jug," said Inky; "don't let him touch another drop unless you want to see all the furnitoor topsy tivvy."

CHAPTER LIX.
NEW WAYS AND MEANS.

"WHAT you have gone through within two years, Inky," said Sam Smarty, "has been more varied than mine; but we have both seen very great changes."

"My changes is all wrong," returned Inky, sorrowfully; "I'm a goin' down, down, every day."

"And so you *will* go down," put in Work-it-out, "until you get them nobble ideas out of your head. Hain't I told you a dozen times that your real name is as common as common can be."

"And hain't I axed you a score o' times to tell me what it is?" demanded Inky.

"And don't I tell you again and again," rejoined Work-it-out, "that I've lost the hankercher, and forgotten the name?"

"Then how do you know it's common?"

"Acause I remembers well bein' struck with it at the time when I found you, as flabby a babby as any man wished to get upon him."

"Could I help bein' flabby?" asked Inky.

"You could not," replied Work-it-out; "and if you could, it wouldn't ha' mended matters; all I've to say about it is, that flabby you was, and it didn't make you the better."

"You have no intention of putting up anywhere to-night?" put in Tom, to ward off the rising quarrel.

"Our intentions was," returned Work-it-out, "to have a pitch nigh the first lime-kilns we came across, for it's better to be warm at nights, whatsumever the time of year may be."

"For the night, I can find you a place to rest," said Tom. "It is a very humble lodging—a mattress and a rug or two. Wil' that do?"

"Which we takes it with gratitood," returned Work-it-out, fervently; "and what I ses is, three cheers for your honour, with a hip—hip—hoo-ra-a-y!"

"A little quieter, if you please," said Tom, smiling; "and now, if you will come with me, I'll see if I can get you stowed away."

"Good night, Inky," said Sam.

Inky hesitated a moment, and then went up and held out his hand.

"Will you take it?" he asked.

"Won't I!" said Sam, and took it accordingly.

"I've never done anything that's wrong," continued the "nobbly born," with tears in his eyes. "I know I'm a bit of a fool, Sam, but don't think no worse of me, for unfortunet I am, and shall, I think, be so allus."

"Let us hope not, Inky."

"Are you coming?" cried Work-it-out, putting his head in at the door.

"Yes, yes," replied Inky. "Good night, Sam."

There was something in poor Inky's throat as he uttered these words, and he went out with his knuckles in his eyes.

Sam, too, was a bit affected, and there was an unusual brightness in his eyes as he turned towards the moon, which was now shining in the sky.

Who knows but a tear or two might be rising there?

Tom came back in about half an hour, and said he had found a resting-place for the wanderers at the village inn.

"It's in the loft," he said; "but it won't do to be too particular just at present. To-morrow we will see if we can make them more presentable."

"Poor fellows!" sighed Sam. "By the way, Tom, have you heard from his lordship?"

"You have asked that question before," replied Tom; "but I don't mind saying again that he is still abroad, and so far as I know, likely to continue there."

"Strange tale about that son of his," mused Sam.

"Yes—and strange that the woman never turned up again."

"Who was she?"

"The servant of the wife of Lord Holbrook. She married some man in Whitechapel, I believe."

"What was his name?"

"I don't know."

"Now just listen to me for a moment," said Sam. "You have heard Inky's story about Jim Podley and his wife, in Bunhill Row—does that strike you as being at all familiar?"

"Not a bit."

"Do you not think that Jim Podley's wife and this woman may be the same? Come, Tom, put all we have heard together, and think it over."

"Well, now you name it, Sam," said Tom, "it is possible that you have hit the right nail on the head. But before we go further into it ourselves, we will have a little more talk with Inky."

This they resolved upon, and as it was near midnight, they retired to their respective rooms—Tom giving Sam, who was still very weak, a helping hand.

During his illness Sam had not been entirely idle.

It was true he could do but little, but what was possible to be done under the circumstances he readily performed.

He improved his education, read useful works, and formed certain resolutions destined to have great influence in his future career.

The expenses of his long inactivity had been defrayed by Lord Holbrook with a delicacy which took away the sting attached to ostentatious charity, his lordship insisting that Sam's companionship was beneficial to his *protégé*, Tom; and Sam, insensibly allured by the kindness of his noble friend, fell into his new way of life without thinking much of the origin of the means for his easy life.

In the morning Tom was up betimes, and out in search of some clothing suitable for his new-found friends.

But this, in such a place, was no easy matter to procure; but he had the satisfaction of obtaining for Work-it-out a coat and trousers of velveteen, and a waistcoat with a very striking charity pattern, which positively glistened in the sun.

Inky, with his usual luck, was not so fortunate, for him Tom could only procure a pair of leather smalls and a smock about eight sizes too big for him, in which he looked like the waist of a shrimping yawl wrapped up in the main-sail of a man-of-war.

But it was better than his rags, and Inky was tolerably reconciled.

"I've found out," he said, "that you can't have everythin' your own way, so I'm not goin' to grumble."

This much had travel and suffering taught Inky.

At length he was profiting by the horrors of the life he had been inundated with.

He and Work-it-out breakfasted at the cottage with Sam and Tom, and put away so much fried ham and eggs, that the old lady who fulfilled the office of cook stopped the supplies on medicinal grounds.

"Not another rasher or another hegg," she said. "If they was took ill, there ain't a doctor within a mile—and one inwallid is enough at a time."

Thus curtailed in their gormandizing performances, Work-it-out and Inky topped up with a few slices of bread and butter and all the dry toast, and then declared that they could rest until dinner time.

"It ain't manners to swoller everything round you like a canibril, I know," said Work-it-out, apologetically; "but when you've lived principally on skilly and turnips for a year or so, you've got a good heart to go in for good wittles, and you do it."

With this idea Inky cordially agreed, adding, that for his part, "he knowed the time when a pair o' boots wouldn't have been amiss—but when it came to good rashers, then he was bound to do his dooty."

As soon as the four were left alone, Tom opened the subject of Jim Podley's wife, and asked Inky to describe her fully.

This Inky did, leaving no doubt as to the identity of the two.

Tom, then, under a cross-examination from Inky, revealed why he was so anxious to learn more about the woman, and, as usual, Inky's hankering after a noble birth led him on another tack.

"What age did you say the boy would be?" he asked.

"About fifteen," replied Tom, "more or less. I am not exactly certain."

"More or less," thought Inky. "I'm gettin' on for seventeen—why shouldn't it be me? Some time ago," he added, aloud, "when his lordship was advertised for, I went down to see if it's me that was wanted, but it warn't. Perhaps I'm wanted now."

"I think not," said Sam.

"You can't tell," returned Inky; "she was a strange woman, and often looked at me in Bunhill Row, as if she'd seen me afore. I'll look her up; she's hanging about Covent Garden, you say?"

"Yes."

"Hain't you had enough o' them tant-rams?" asked Work-it-out, indignantly.

"No," cried Inky, enthusiastically; "never will I desert my course until I've got my rights, and the nobble hair is full o' triump in the heart of his nobble fathers; until that time comes I don't give up the pussoot."

"Better go into the newspaper line and earn a honest living," said Sam.

"I'll do both," said Inky; "who'll set me up with enough to get a quire o' Daily Mellowchaffs?"

"I will, with pleasure," said Tom, "and a little to help you to London with."

"You show up in that soot," said Work-it-out, "and the reg'lar boys will have your life."

"I don't care about the reg'lar boys," said Inky, defiantly; "let me have the money and I'm off to London to find the woman to lead me to my nobble father's."

CHAPTER LX.
A WOMAN'S WILL.

NIGHT dark as Hades.

A dense fog and a moonless sky to add to the usual nightly gloom of crowded Wapping.

Night dark and cheerless, with the air full of damp mist, which blinded the eyes and penetrated to the very marrow of the bones of the wretched woman who skulked beside the houses and slunk against friendless blank walls, shaking from the fever engendered by want and suffering.

It was late, and not a night for those who had a home to be wandering about, and the woman had the streets almost entirely herself.

See objects around, she could not the very lamps of the streets were hidden, and she only knew of the vicinity of houses by the touch and the discordant howls from the adjacent taverns where hapless Jack ashore was finding some wild relief from many months of monotonous life at sea.

This woman moved on, guiding herself with a trembling hand, and ever and anon wiping away the mist from her tangled hair.

Whither was she wending her way, and what was she seeking?

Her course lay towards the river, and the end was to be death.

Coming to a flight of stone steps attached to a church or chapel—it was impossible in the gloom to say which—she sank down to rest.

"And this is the end of all," she murmured; "have I toiled for atonement, and toiled in vain? Oh! what a miserable life has mine been. Wrong every way, from first to last—wrong in the beginning, wrong in the end. Heaven forgive my sins, for I am indeed wretched!"

She cowered down sobbing bitterly, heedless of the approach of several men who came cautiously on through the fog, talking aloud to warn others of their approach; one of the foremost stumbled over the woman's lap.

"Hallo!" he cried, "I've tumbled over a bundle o' something. Why, it's a woman!"

"Go your way, man," cried the woman, "you will find fitter company than me where those fools are howling yonder."

"As for that company," said the man, "it ain't none for me, and you don't speak as if it were any for you either. What's the matter, missus, hard up—can I help?"

"Go your way, go your way, and let me be," muttered the woman.

"Not if I knows it," cried the other; "what say you, Sawney?"

"Stick by," was the reply.

"I've got a wife o' my own," continued the previous speaker, "and several gals, in fact, all my family is gals, and as they've got to grow up into the world, the Lord forbid as I should let any woman die in the street on such a night as this. What say you, Sawney?"

"My sentlements 'zactly," said the other.

"Now, missus, we ain't fur from our lodging; will you trust yourself with us? my missus will put you right."

"Heaven bless you for saving angels!" ejaculated the woman.

"There ain't much o' the angel about us," returned the man; "angels don't wear corduroys. Now, Sawney, bear a hand, will you; this poor crittur is weak; and, Busby, just step forrard and give 'em warnin', will you?"

The voices of the men were very gruff, and came, apparently, from behind thick woollen wraps about their mouths; but there was a friendly ring in their utterances which gave encouragement to the wretched woman who had laid down to die.

"Heaven bless you!" she murmured, again and again, as they led her onward.

And so they went forward in the gloom, until the noise of the taverns died slowly away.

Suddenly the men stopped.

"What place is this?" she asked.

"A bit o' waste ground," replied one of the men; "we've got our booths here; we are going to show to-morrow."

"Show people?" murmured the woman.

"Yes, missus," said the man; "there ain't much harm in us; we're rough and ready, but we does our best to stand by each other, and rob no man."

A shouting ahead, and a faint glare, which somebody said was torches, put an end to the conversation: and the woman, reassured, allowed herself to be led on, and soon she slowly ascended one flight of steps and descended another, when she found herself in a large canvas arena, where several fires were burning, and the atmosphere tolerably clear, in comparison to that outside, of course.

Around the fires were scattered a number of men and women, many of them cooking herrings, small bits of steak, and other light relishes for supper.

As the new-comers appeared, they were hailed with a general welcome, and he who had shown such kindness to the woman—no other than our old friend Bob Crossley—did the office of introduction for her.

"Here's a poor homeless, 'ouseless crittur," he said, "sittin' on the steps 'ere, so I axed her in for a bit o' shelter. I don't ax you if you've any objection, for I know you've none."

They made way for the woman at once, and as she sat down before the fire, holding out her pinched, frozen hands, it became apparent how poor and miserable she was.

One or two of the women, who shrank back a little when the stranger was introduced, readily changed their minds, and came forward to offer her food and comfort.

Bob Crossley, after conversing apart with some of the company, turned to look after his *protégée*, who was sitting with her eyes bent upon the fire in deep, serious meditation.

"Come, missus," he said, "it's no time for the dumps; the fog's outside, and there's good company in. See if you can't find a smile somewheres; look at my old lady, handsome as a harvest moon."

"I don't want none of your perlaver," replied his spouse; "don't patter soft to me, if you please."

"I never pattered rough," said Bob, "and I don't mean to begin now."

"That's what they all say," said the stranger, looking up; "but time takes the goodness out o' em, as it does out o' fruit. They soon find other words for the tip o' their tongues."

"Some on 'em," put in Sawney Tap, who had joined the group.

"All," said the woman.

"Some on 'em," insisted Sawney.

"I speak as I have found," said the woman; "my life began with honey, and ended with vinegar. The sun shone very bright at first, but the clouds came quickly. *My* husband soon changed."

"What changed him?" asked the voice of a man as he joined the party.

The woman turned, saw who it was, and shrieking out, "Jim!" sank into a huddled heap before the fire.

CHAPTER LXI.

A WOMAN'S LAST WILL AND TESTAMENT.

THE recognition was mutual.

Podley started back with the old look of affright, but he had little cause for fear.

His wife smiled sadly, and said—

"I'm sorry to have troubled you again, Jim—I didn't mean to. It's quite an accident."

"We met her in the street," said Busby, in a stage whisper which might have been heard fifty feet round.

"Starvin'," added Sawney Tap, in a sepulchral tone.

"Yes," said the woman, "they found me, Jim, as they say, starving. I don't think I shall trouble you long. I've something here," she put her hand upon her bosom, "which tells me I shall soon be at rest."

"I don't know that I am sorry to see you," said Podley, seating himself, "'cept that I don't like to see you so weak and wan-like. She were a buxom lass," he added to the assembled company, in sorrowful tones, "when fust I married her."

"I'm glad you are not ashamed to own you married me," said the woman. "God knows you might have been, and still been just."

"We *was* married," returned Jim emphatically, "and what I've got to say is, that so far as it lies in a man, let him uphold the laws o' the country, and stick to the marriage knot when he's put his foot in it, and bring every man to think so."

Shortly after this, supper was served, but wretched Mary Ann could eat none of it.

In vain they tempted her with the choicest morsels; she loathed it all, so they made her up a bed in the corner of the women's tent, and persuaded her to lie down and rest.

She slept through the night, and awoke in the morning very quiet, and evidently much feebler.

She asked for her husband, and they brought him in.

"Jim," she said, "I've a strange fancy to see Lord Holbrook before I die."

"But you are not going to die," interposed Jim.

"I am," she replied, in that tone of quiet conviction which leaves no doubt. "Will you try to find him? He'd come if you ask him. I want to tell him that I tried to do my duty by him, and gave in only with my life. He lives in Belgrave Square. I don't know the number, anybody will tell you—lose no time."

Jim, full of vague repentance for the past and sorrow for the present, hastened away; first despatching Bob Crossley for a doctor.

While Jim was away the doctor came; he examined the dying woman, looked at her tongue, felt her pulse, and put his ear to her heart.

"I don't know what rest and good food may do," he said; "I can do nothing."

"Why not tell the truth?" said Mary Ann; "you know there is no help for me."

"There is none," said the doctor, gravely. "I will stay by you if you think there is."

"There is not," she said; "you may go."

And being a man with a very large practice demanding his attention, he wisely went.

The day slowly crawled on, the dying woman asked again and again for her absent husband, but it was not until late in the evening he returned.

He entered alone, and a shade of disappointment crossed his wife's face.

"He will not come," she said.

"He will," replied Jim. "I waited all day, as he was not at home, but he was expected every hour from abroad, and I hung about until his travelling carriage arrived, then I fought my way through the flunkies and begged him to come. He'll be here directly, in half-an-hour or so."

"'Tis well," muttered his wife, "I can wait. Half-an-hour is a short time after this weary day."

Jim Podley was alone with his wife, and he sat down by the side of her bed.

There was an anxious look in his face, as if he wanted to ask her something, but was doubtful about the advisability of so doing.

At length he seemed to have summed up courage, and touched her upon the hand.

"Mary."

"What is it, Jim?"

"We had a child—what became of him?"

"Would you care to know?"

"I think I ought, Mary. If I can find him I'd try and do justice by him. I'm rough, but I ain't stony-'arted."

"You are not that, Jim. Well, I will tell you all I know."

Jim settled himself to hear the story of his lost child, which he finally reduced to writing, forming a document of some half-dozen lines, which he called in Bob Crossley and Sawney Tap to sign.

As this document will appear in a future column, we will leave it for the present, and come to the time when a commotion outside announced the arrival of his lordship.

He first sent in one of the women to announce his coming, and followed immediately.

He was not alone, Tom was with him, and the boy approached the bed of death with a pallid face.

"I'm sorry for this," said his lordship, approaching the dying woman. "I fear you have suffered much."

"My lord," she replied, "I did not send to you to tell of my sufferings. I only want to assure you that I've tried to keep my word. I've looked day and night for that boy."

"It was a hopeless search from the first, you could scarcely have known him."

"I could not have forgotten him, he had poor Miss Bella's eyes. Merciful Heaven! Ah! here at last."

She had half risen from her couch, and was staring straight at Tom, who was shrinking back in the shadow of the curtains.

"No, no," returned Lord Holbrook, soothingly; "that is only a *protégé* of mine. He came with me at my request."

"I tell you it is he," persisted the dying woman; "let him come here."

With a strange, palpitating heart, Tom advanced, and Podley's wife put her worn hand upon his wrist.

"What of your early life," she asked, "do you remember it?"

"I remember it but too well," replied Tom.

"Where was it passed?"

"Mostly in the cold streets by Covent Garden."

"Had you no home?"

"Not since I can remember; but I often saw a woman who came to taunt me when I was hungry, and tell me to starve."

"Heaven forgive me!" cried the poor wretch in a passionate tone; "that was me.

My lord, he is your son ; look at his face, any of you assembled here, and tell me if I lie. If you want any further proof than the word of a dying woman, I have none to give. Look at him, all of you."

It was indeed true ; there was a strong likeness between the pair as they stared at each other in bewilderment. Lord Holbrook was the first to speak.

"I have been blind," he said, "absorbed in my selfish sorrow. I must have seen my Bella's look in the eyes—of this—my son."

"You acknowledge him, then ?" cried the dying woman.

"Truly, he is already my son, and can be no more except in name. Tom, my dear boy, come to me."

He folded the lad to his breast, while Podley's wife looked on with a triumphant smile, strangely out of place on her worn, wan face.

"My task is done," she murmured, and sank back insensible.

At first they thought she was dead ; but the end was not yet come. She slowly opened her eyes, and put out her hand.

"Jim," she murmured.

Poor Podley, who had been sniffing vigorously, and wiping his eyes with the corner of a red cotton handkerchief which he wore round his neck, took the thin hand in his strong brown hand.

"Mary," he murmured, and broke fairly down.

"Why, Jim," said his wife, with the dawn of a smile upon her face, "who would have thought that you could shed a tear for me."

"I didn't think it once," replied Jim, "but I never thought to see you so broken down as this. I never thought to hear you say that you were sorry for what passed atween us."

"But I am sorry, Jim, and I want you to forgive me."

"I am not the man to hold it back," replied Podley, "when I want the same thing myself over and over again. My poor lass, if wishes could save your life, you shouldn't die now."

"It is better that I should," she replied, softly. "Jim, I would not let you kiss me when last we met, will you kiss me now ?"

Brushing away his tears, he bent over her, and touched her lips with his.

She feebly returned it, and sinking back, left this world, and the sorrow and agony she had known, behind.

Tread softly, ye who leave the couch of that poor woman, for she is gone, and Death is master there.

Look back upon her life, if you will ; but who shall dare to say that, outcast as she was in this world, that she is outcast in the next ?

"I don't know as things could have turned out better," sobbed Podley, as he stood surrounded by sympathizing friends, "seeing we were so opposite in our ways ; but I do wish that I'd let her go on as she liked, and ruined me a hundred times over, afore I'd raised a hand against her."

CHAPTER LXII.
REST AT LAST.

"Morning pipper ! Daily Mellerchaff !" roared Inky at the top of his voice, as he rushed out of the office with a quire of that gushing and all-powerful medium of the arts, sciences, and general news.

In a moment he was, in street boys' parlance, "spotted." It was impossible for the countryman's slop and leathern leggings to long escape observation, and a dozen rival vendors of intelligence fell upon him.

"Here's a move !" roared one, "a cove comin' the aggerycultural dodge—hi, there ! —spot his leggings."

"You let me alone," muttered Inky, "I hain't done nothin' to you."

"You've no right here," sternly replied a small boy, with a bundle of papers on his shoulder ; "come out of them leggin's, will yer ?"

"Why can't I sell papers as well as you ?"

"Because you can't," was the satisfactory reply.

"I will."

"You won't."

The next moment a charge was made upon him.

Inky fought valiantly, and battered one end of his quire of Daily Mellerchaffs to rags, dealing some nasty knocks among his assailants.

But multitudes too often prevail, and the numerous foe was triumphant.

Inky's little stock-in-trade was scattered to the four winds, and then the marauders, thirsting for further fame, fell upon Inky.

Inky's weight told among the smaller fry, and many a gallant youthful assailant bit the dust ; but this only roused the rest to increased exertions, and they at length got the "nobbly born" down upon his back.

What would have been Inky's fate then we are unable to say ; but fortunately, a policeman appeared and bore down upon the scene of action.

The host, daunted by the voice of the officer, fled, and Inky arose from the ground, ragged, bloody, but comparatively safe.

"Now, what are you doing here ?" demanded the officer, sternly.

"Nothin'," replied Inky, adding, after a pause, "'cept bein' wolloped."

"Cheek, that is," said the officer. "Come

on—a fine of two bob and a bender will do you good."

Without any further ceremony he hauled Inky towards the station, but changing his mind, dismissed his prisoner with what he called "a clout of the head."

"The next time you hang about here," he said, as a final warning, "I'll have you up before Sir Robert: he knows how to deal with your sort."

Inky was too broken-hearted to reply—his usual luck clung to him still, and with a vague idea in his mind of knocking down a man, robbing him of his watch and living on the proceeds, he staggered into the main thoroughfare.

"I've been honest long enough," he muttered, "nothin' goes right with me ; I'll turn wenomous and break a winder."

At that moment, a hand was laid upon his shoulder, and looking up, he beheld the companion of his travels—Work-it-out.

"I've had a stiffish run about this street arter you," said the old man ; "where ha' ye been ?"

"What do you want ?" asked Inky.

"Inky," exclaimed Work-it-out, his voice broken by emotion, "there have allus been one sore point atween us."

"There's been a heap," said Inky.

"But the greatest point of all have been your parients, Inky ; I've found 'em."

The "nobbly born" changed instantly, and seized Work-it-out by the hand.

"What is that I hears ?" he cried ; "where are they, old un ?"

"Come with me," said Work-it-out, briefly, and Inky, with a hopeful face, followed him, leaving all his troubles behind.

Found at last ! No more trouble, no more starvation—nothing but "gorging raiment" and unlimited feasts.

But the way chosen by Work-it-out did not lead to lordly mansions.

He kept on in silence through the City, down by the Minories, and so on to the Commercial Road, to a piece of waste ground, where a menagerie and circus stood.

Inky's heart had been sinking for the last half-hour ; it now fell far below zero.

"Work-it-out," he cried, "is my father a menagerie man ?"

"He ain't," replied Work-it-out.

A little re-assured, Inky mounted the steps of the circus and entered.

In the ring a little group of men and women stood, apparently awaiting some *dénouement* ; in the midst—Jim Podley.

Work-it-out leaped into the ring, struck a dramatic attitude, and pointed to him.

"Inky," he cried, "behold your parient !"

"There ain't no doubt about it, Inky," said Podley, coming forward ; "your poor mother died four days ago, and afore left this walley o' grief she told me to pu in writing. Read it."

He then put into the hands of Inky following interesting document :—

"i, maryan Podley dyinge du declair th lef my child on a doorstep in Septir co fleet street which was kep I think b cobler name Arris, in a yaller hankchif.

"sign for Maryan, jim Podley
"witness bob crossley and Sawney tap th mark +"

"I wrote it out myself," said Jim, mou fully, "almost word for word."

"Podley were the name in the han kercher," added Work-it-out, "but I forg it, and so couldn't put the lorse chile into father's arms afore."

To all this Inky said nothing, but simp stood stock still, staring on the ground li one who had gone in search of gold and fou nought but the dull, cold earth.

Podley looked at him sternly for a f moments, and then inquired—

"What ! ain't I good enough for you ?"

"Anything's good enough for *me*, I su pose," replied Inky ; "but I do think th arter waiting all this time for a father, ar goin' into all sorts o' messes in search him, I ought to have something more nobble

"You take what you can get," advise Sawney Tap, who, as we acknowledge, occa sionally came out in the style of the bird wisdom, and uttered wonderful things, " father's a father, be he ro—bed in hermin an fine gold, or togged out in fustian."

"Hear, hear," cried Work-it-out.

"What have you got to do with it ?" de manded Inky.

"Nothin', but this," replied Work-it-out impressively : "that if I was your father I' inwest a couple o' shillings in a stinger, anc bring you round a bit. You shouldn't b ashamed o' *me*, unless I had somethin' for it.'

"Who's ashamed on him ?" asked Inky. "Can't I wish him better off without bein' howled at ? Is it wrong to wish your father well, and see him a reg'lar gentleman ?"

"It certainly ain't," replied Podley. "Come into my arms, Inky."

And father and son were folded in a touching embrace, which met the entire approval of the assembled company.

*   *   *   *   *   *

The shifting scenes of life we have endea voured to portray are drawing to a close.

The inevitable of all things—the end—is near.

Sam Smarty, Tom the street arab, Inky, Work-it-out, Crossley, and Sawney Tap, will soon—to the author—be things of the past.

THE END.

www.ingramcontent.com/pod-product-compliance
Lightning Source LLC
Chambersburg PA
CBHW080832250626
47160CB00008B/2905